STILLIARDS) Hansa, Gothica dictio, conuentum, vel congregationem sonans, multarum ciuitatum est confœderata Societas, tum, ob præstita Regibus, ac Ducib. beneficia: tum, ob securam terra, mariquæ, mercaturæ tractationem, tum denique, ad tranquillam Rerumpub. pacem, & ad modestam adolescentium institutionem conseruandam, instituta: plurimor. Regum, ac Principum, maximè Angliæ, Galliæ, Daniæ, ac Magnæ Moscouiæ, nec non Flandriæ, ac Brabantiæ Ducum priuilegijs, ac immunitatib. exornata fuit. Habet ea quatuor Emporia, (untores quidam vocant, in quibus ciuitatum negotiatores resident, suosque mercatus exercent. Hor. alterum hîc Londini, domestica œconoma nitet, habens domum Gildehalla Teutonicâ quâ vulgo Stilhard, nuncupat.

FIREDRAKE'S EYE

FIREDRAKE'S EYE

Patricia Finney

St. Martin's Press
New York

Library of Congress Cataloging-in-Publication Data

Finney, Patricia.
    Firedrake's eye / Patricia Finney.
        p.   cm.
    ISBN 0-312-07749-1
    I. Title.
PR6056.I519F57   1992
823'.914—dc20

92-3293
CIP

First published in Great Britain by Sinclair-Stevenson Limited.

First U.S. Edition: June 1992
10 9 8 7 6 5 4 3 2 1

To Christopher,
with love

Author's Note

This is an historical novel, a thing of the imagination built around the partial skeleton of historical fact. It is not a history book and wherever it has suited me to throw out evidence or alter what is known of the Elizabethans, I have done so. Similarly, the language it is written in is not intended as a true imitation or pastiche of their splendid rhythmic tongue, because frankly I find such attempts either accurate and difficult to read, or inaccurate and irritating. However, it seemed to me that the way Sixteenth-century people thought and felt was reflected in their language and so, although this is modern English with a modern vocabulary, I have tried to give it a flavour of the Elizabethan.

Footnotes, unless humorous, are silly in a novel, but all the same I like to know where the borderline between fact and fiction lies and so there is a historical note at the end, as well as a glossary of the more specialised words and a list of characters, stating whether they are historical or invented.

In many ways the Elizabethans were not very nice people. They were sexually and racially prejudiced, often bigoted, often unashamedly cruel to animals and each other. It is as daft to give nice liberal opinions on homosexuality or feminism or even democracy (a dirty word to an Elizabethan) to the people of 400 years ago as it would be to dress them in top hats and frock coats instead of ruffs and doublets and give them Colt 45s to shoot. I have tried to avoid this hideous and infuriating crime of psychological anachronism. However, it would be very depressing if people thought that I agree with some of my characters' opinions on politics or religion, race or sexual orientation.

It has taken me years to research and write this book, and I have benefited from so many people's kindness it would be impossible to include them all. My husband has helped enormously, both with the plotting and with the military history about which his knowledge is encyclopaedic. My parents have, as always, helped and encouraged me and I have pillaged my father's library and knowledge for information on the history of London and the use of herbs. I have had the privilege and irreplaceable assistance of taking part in Historical ReCreations of the Elizabethan period at Kentwell Hall, Suffolk. I have had extremely useful criticism of earlier drafts of the book from my agent Jennifer Kavanagh, and from Melanie Raymond and Yvonne Kalms. Through Yvonne I was able to spend a happy day at Jews' College in North London getting answers to questions that had annoyed me for years – there is no computer search as fast, thorough and effective as a truly erudite scholar.

All mistakes, inaccuracies, gaffes and anachronisms are, of course, mine.

Tom O'Bedlam's Song

From the hag and hungry goblin
    That into rags would rend ye,
And the spirit that stands by the naked man
    In the book of moons, defend ye.
That of your five sound senses
    You never be forsaken
Nor wander from yourselves with Tom
    Abroad to beg your bacon.

While I do sing, 'Any food, any feeding,
    Feeding, drink or clothing?
Come dame or maid
    Be not afraid
Poor Tom will injure nothing.'

Of thirty bare years have I
    Twice twenty been enraged
And of forty been three times fifteen
    In durance sadly caged.
In the lordly lofts of Bedlam
    With stubble soft and dainty
Brave bracelets strong, sweet whips, ding dong,
    With wholesome hunger plenty.

A thought I took for Maudlin
   And a cruse of cockle pottage,
With a thing thus tall, sky bless you all!
   I befell into this dotage.
I slept not since the Conquest,
   Till then I never waked,
Till the roguish boy of love where I lay
   Me found and stripped me naked.

When I short have shorn my sow's face
   And snigged my horny barrel
In an oaken inn I pawn my skin
   As a suit of gilt apparel.
The moon's my constant mistress
   And the lovely owl my marrow;
The flaming drake and the nightcrow make
   Me music to my sorrow.

The palsy plagues my pulse
   When I prig your pigs or pullen,
Your culvers take or mateless make
   Your Chanticleer, or sullen –
When I want provant with Humphrey
   I sup, and when benighted,
I repose in Paul's with waking souls
   Yet never am affrighted.

I know more than Apollo
   For oft when he lies sleeping
I behold the stars at bloody wars
   And the wounded welkin weeping.
The moon embraces her shepherd
   · And the Queen of Love her warrior,
While the first doth horn the star of morn
   And the next the heavenly farrier.

The Gypsy Snap, and Pedro
   Are none of Tom's comradoes;

The punk I scorn and the cutpurse sworn
  And the roaring-boys' bravadoes;
The meek, the white, the gentle,
  Me handle, touch and spare not,
But those that cross Tom Rhinoceros
  Do what the panther dare not.

With a heart of furious fancies
  Whereof I am commander,
With a burning spear and a horse of air
  To the wilderness I wander.
By a knight of ghosts and shadows
  I summoned am to tourney
Ten leagues beyond the wide world's end
  — Methinks it is no journey.

I

It was I that saw most and have said least in the matter of the firedrake and the nightcrow, the soldier of God and the hunting of that fair white hind, the Queen of England. There has been a plague of silence upon it, made by Sir Francis Walsingham, the Queen's Moor, darker than the blackest flurry of wings over a dunghill. But Tom of Bedlam is mad and unaccountable, being a Bedlam beggar, and since I wear his poor scratched hide and stare out of his poor mazed eyes which make my prison windows, so I will tell the tale. And all of it will be the truth.

First must I ask forgiveness, that this has somewhat of madness colouring it. For my poor skullmate Tom was always at my side, and would often elbow past me and the Courtier to bow to the Queen Moon, and dance and discourse with angels and cower from his devils which were suddenly both his and mine. Let the Queen Moon judge between us.

And yet Poor Tom had his uses, for his angels made him windows in men's heads to see their souls. So I beg you, forgive his yammerings and do not put all of them aside. Perhaps it is only the weight of the infinite that made him rave. So here also is Tom's madness, woven like gold thread into a good cloth of sense, though who would put gold into a winding cloth unless it were for a prince?

Which it is not, it is a Turkey rug of windings and divergings and turnings and foldings, all in a dance of spiral upon counter-spiral, star upon star, swirl upon movement upon unquietness, all woven by the Queen Moon that sits above us in a silver damask petticoat and smiles. And puts her silver finger with its nail of scarlet upon this knot and that: here was the tale's genesis, here . . . and there, and there . . . .

5

II
Autumn 1583

One beginning took place in a London alley, in the old liberty of White-friars, lit only by a rushlight in a paned window – which window was surely a waste of time and money since the sun never shines on Noon Alley, save on midsummer day, though the rain falls there in plenty.

Which beginning was in itself begun in the bubbling marshes of Good-wife Alys Flick's brewing vats.

There are women who can draw sweet nectar from base malted barley and water and there are women who can turn the makings of Jove's own ambrosia into horse piss and pig dung. The Gatehouse Inn's lady, Goodwife Alys, had magic of the second kind: give her wine from the grapes of Dionysus himself and she would stretch it out with sloe berries and vinegar and sugar, because the times were bad and she must have her return on the outlay.

Which makes it all the stranger that David Becket had drunk enough to cause him to fall out of the doorway of the Gatehouse and trip over the foothills of the midden that blocks Fleet Street there. He belched, waited in suspense to see if anything might follow the belch, and when it did not, picked up his hat and lurched with his bellyful of muddy beer down towards his lodgings on Fetter Lane. He had unbuttoned the front of his doublet to give his gut room to breathe; no need for peascod padding in his clothes, he grew his own and saved a fortune in bombast.

For a moment he stopped under a dripping overhang on the corner of Crocker's Lane, one hand on the wall, and wished the alehouses nearer home would still give him credit so he would have less far to walk, seeing how the curvature of his direction gave him two miles where there was less than one in truth. Furthermore the ways were muddy and dark and infested with vermin, small and large.

Meanwhile, as Dr Nuñez says, beer cannot be transformed into blood as can meat, so must it be turned to piss and removed from the body's economy. Hiccupping faintly, Becket fumbled at his codpiece and pissed into the gutter, watering the sad shape of a dead dog. Tears pricked at his eyes: poor dog, cast out to roam and never know his old home again, foraging for what he could, better a life in the Bear Gardens than that . . . . He would go back. They still needed fighting men in the Netherlands, by Christ, and if the pay was bad, at least they mainly did not hang you for stealing . . . .

As he made a third attempt to refasten his points, muttering that a man was in a pretty state when his own codpiece defeated him, at last the sounds of scuffling, of soft thumps and gasps, battled their way past the fumes stopping his ears.

He straightened and blinked. The noise of a fight was coming from Noon Alley, off Crocker's Lane. For a moment he swayed: some fights were better left alone . . . .

Out of pure-hearted and disinterested curiosity, and a vague flickering optimism that some fights were like rainbows in that gold was at the bottom of them, Becket slid crabwise along the wall of the corner house, buttoning up his doublet and old buff coat as he went. He peered round the corner into the murk and shadow-devils clustering about the whore's brave pale rushlight.

A hand shoved a sagging bundle up against the wall, the other hand busy inside its clothes. Blindly the bundle swung at the footpad and got its head rammed against the stones for his trouble; thus brought into the glimmer of light, Becket could recognise the face despite its mask of blood.

Which was all he needed as excuse for the pleasure of a fight to round off his evening. While the man fell heavily sideways and the footpad cursed and prodded the soupy blackness with his knife, Becket drew his own dagger and slipped towards the tangle of men, left hand outstretched until it closed on a coarse jerkin. He found the neck, lifted it up to the green glimmer to be sure it was the footpad and not his victim and then, as Bonecrack Smith shrieked and waved his arms, Becket did the hangman out of a fee and split his backbone.

Too slow. Booze is not so easily conquered. Someone charged into him low from the side and he felt, rather than saw, the cudgel swinging down on his head. He roared in anger that there should turn out to be more of them, took the blow on the thick muscles of his back and bellowed like a bull in spring when he felt someone try to get a grip round his neck from behind.

He lurched upright, the footpad clinging like a monkey, and slammed backwards two steps into the opposite wall of Noon Alley where it is

7

still stone from the old abbey, and scraped the man from his perch. He turned, catching a little flash of light upon metal, and stabbed at venture, feeling a warm spurt of blood on his hand, but not knowing what he had hit, though it screamed. Then there was the sound of scurrying and sliding, and in the new silence came the rhythmic thumping of the whore's truckle bed against her wall.

He wiped his dagger blade and sticky hand on his back, under the leather of his coat where it would not show, sweeping up the packet that had fallen from Smith's hand and putting it away absent-mindedly. The melancholic black velvet of his doublet and paned trunk hose was browned and spattered with grease and mud and gravy, but still it had the effect hoped for but never approached upon its original owner, who lost it at primero. It made a fat man look taller. Becket is two yards high and at least a yard broad, a square man run to lard with black ringlets and a square face thatched with a badly trimmed black beard, and an ugly thing to meet in an alley on a dark night.

Having caught his breath and cleaned his dagger, Becket remembered the man he had rescued. He found him by touch, lying on his face in a pile of slimy onion peelings. He picked him up under the arms and carried him out of the alley, into the Gatehouse's lantern light.

The smaller man's head lolled, draped and shiny with blood and snot: Becket tutted sympathetically at the glazed eyes, patted a bruised cheek.

The man began to wake up, muttered and essayed a punch at Becket. Becket caught the fist in his great hand and pushed his own face very close, speaking very clearly and distinctly.

'I am Master David Becket, Provost of Swordplay,' he said. 'We were arguing earlier. About the divine essence of man and its nature. Remember?'

The other man frowned cross-eyed, bent forward and puked on Becket's boots. Becket sighed. 'Christ, who would play the Samaritan,' he said, but charitably did not dump the man's face in it. Scraping the worst off his feet, he hoisted up the footpads' leavings with one unresisting arm over his shoulder, and carried him on towards Fetter Lane. Though in strict truth this was less for the teachings of our Lord God and more for the beckonings of our Lady Silver, whose shade and image peeked shyly between the thick velvet folds of the man's gown and the supple Spanish leather of the man's boots.

III
Autumn 1582

And there was the firedrake also, coming slowly to full growth behind secure walls of brick and lies. It was an egg laid a year before, the progeny of a solemn and light-hearted allegory that marked the Queen's Accession Day Tilts of 17th November 1582 Anno Domini. The young bucks and hinds of the Court had arrayed themselves sumptuously in gilded armour and embroidered silk, presenting themselves as the Children of Desire, beseeching entrance at the Castle of Virginity. Which rare and prized thing is as much sought for at Court as a unicorn, and as seldom found (save in the Queen's Grace Herself).

Within the glamour of the Tilts, sweating under his layers of armour and leather padding and linen and in desperate fear of rain, Philip Sidney had made a punning sermon to the Queen in which he, the Child of Desire, and all his fellows, were beaten back and owned themselves laid low by the exceeding purity and power of Her Majesty's Virginity. Which is to say that she should not marry the foul frogling Duc d'Alençon, the least of the whelps of the she-wolf Catherine de Medici, she who massacred the Protestants upon St Bartholomew's Day.

There was daring in so preaching, no matter how scented the means, for the Queen had borne herself most sweetly towards the French prince, in despite of his face scoured like a siegeworks with pockmarks, his nose a rotten testament to his pillicock and his stature a head shorter than the Queen's, who hath a very proper size for a woman. The Prince's envoy Simier, that she termed her Monkey, was a fairer sight and a prettier gentleman who made her laugh, but it was not him she would have bedded, and no better if she had for he killed his first wife.

None of which was Her Majesty willing to hear of anyone. A printer by name Stubbs exhorted her in print to have no truck with Papistical Frenchmen, and had his hand chopped off by the common hangman. Being His Honour, Sir Francis Walsingham's prospective son-in-law,

9

Philip Sidney was not like to lose his hand nor any other member, but there is always the Tower and the tedium of disfavour.

So there was impudence in this speech of symbols, and also danger. Sir Francis agreed with the sentiment and supported it though silently. In the end, the Queen heard and saw the parable and smiled and was gracious. Who knows if it was Sidney's elegant argument of coursers and canvas scenery that defeated the onrush of her intention. Or was it the Queen Moon that put her finger in the pie? Was it perhaps that the courses of women which had been stuttering in the earthly Queen for the years when she had been so pressed with strange haste to marry, so contrary to her earlier ways, was it that her monthly courses stopped at last? Did she see then that all she had she would lose and gain not even a child in payment, and so she drew back from the brink. Alençon was paid off at last in fish barrels of gold in a quantity that spoke loudly of the Queen's embarrassment.

Who would dare ask her? The Courtier laughs and turns the ring in his ear, but I know that Sidney was much pleased by his pretty conceit at the tilting, to speak of policy in a poetry of silk and armour and speeches. He wrote to his friend Henri Estienne in Vienna, a letter that lies within Walsingham's fine oak chest, and likewise a copy turned to Spanish in one of the many chests of papers belonging to the King of Spain. So harmless, so kindly, and yet was this the letter that laid the serpent's egg, this bore the thought that caused a dragon to be born in London, even in the Queen's own capital, the dragon that breathed fire and fear and sorrow upon me.

IV
Autumn 1583

Up five flights of stairs that Becket must climb sideways for their narrowness, and through a low door at the top, and into a cold and musty darkness, smelling of foul linen and fouler hose, ancient rushes, rats and damp. As always, Becket ducked his head too late and rammed his head on the ceiling. Cursing mechanically, he dropped his burden in a heap on the rushes while he searched for the tinderbox. Once he had a stub of tallow dip grudgingly lit and giving off clouds of black rancid smoke, he remembered there was no wood since he had not the money to pay for it.

A movement behind him made him turn to see the man he had rescued, now on his knees, fists planted, head hanging down and bleeding a steady drip drip from his nose. No doubt the fleas were delighted, being more used to having to jump in search of their meal than have it drop like manna from the sky. Behind the plaster came the familiar rustling of rats. One large black brute trotted out onto the chest and looked up expectantly at Becket.

'Here now,' he said, smiling and reaching inside his shirt for the hambone he had filched. 'When have I ever failed you, eh?' The rat's family came out to share the largesse while Becket picked up the bowl of water on the chest and dug out the ragged remnants of a shirt.

'Ndo, I need do help . . . .'

'Shut your mouth,' said Becket, hoisted the man onto the edge of the bed and began cleaning blood and vomit off the bony pale face. 'I have forgot your name, sir, though I recall you are a friend of Mr Ellerton. Is it Arnes?'

'Abes.' came the answer after a pause for thought, 'Sibod Abes, hodoured to dow you, sir.'

'Then hold still Mr Ames.'

By the time the man's particoloured face could be seen clear in the rushlight, the water was darkened to a soup not even the rat would touch, so Becket opened the shutter and tossed it into the distant street. Then he waved the rat off the lid of his chest and dug in the depths to find the last of his aqua vitae. Mr Ames' earth-coloured velvet gown with its murrey silk piping might never recover from the blood and the onion peelings, but Becket did it honour nevertheless. 'Put the bottle neck into your mouth,' he advised kindly, 'else the spirits will sting you.' Simon Ames coughed and gagged but held the drink down.

'I rebeber you, Mr Becket,' he said. 'You would have bed brute beasts leavened by a divide spark, and I say they are corrupted by dividity misunderstood . . . Pox od this blood, is by dose broked?'

'No doubt,' said Becket, 'I can recommend you a good barber surgeon for its setting, if you wish.'

'Do, thanking you. By uncle will see to it.' Ames was feeling for his purse and Becket flourished out the packet he had found by Bonecrack

Smith. Ames frowned at it. 'But this is dot my . . . Hm. I thank you, sir. Did you see ady of the bed who attacked me?'

'Other than Bonecrack who is dead now, God rot his soul, no,' said Becket. 'Have you lost much?'

'Ah. You saw dode of the others.'

Becket spread his hands. 'It was dark. I marked one of them, though. How much were you carrying?'

'Some shillings and a gold half crown . . . .'

'Christ, what possessed you to carry so much in Whitefriars?'

'I was . . . playing cards earlier.'

'Cards?' Light dawned on Becket's face. 'Oh, Tyrrel's game?'

Ames nodded once, uncertainly. Becket made a sour face and spat into the corner, missing the misshapen target carved on the rotten plaster.

'Jesu, you are a lamb without his dam, how came you ever to full growth? Do you not know the only game is Pickering's? And having won a full purse from Tyrrel, you came and argued philosophy at the Gatehouse in a nest full of wasps that could smell your honey gold at three miles distance, and addled your brains. Christ's bowels, if I had known that . . . .' He let the sentence dangle and turned back to his nearly empty chest to hide his disgust. Better not to offend one so rich and stupid. While he dug in the festering depths for his remaining spare blanket, his brain spun glittering plans for separating a particular fool and his money. 'There's no returning to the City at this hour with the gates shut and no boats for Christians neither with the watermen all going home, so you may have this and sleep on the . . . .'

He stopped. Ames had toppled onto his side, dumped his mud-caked pattens on the bed, hunched his narrow shoulders deeper into his gown, and passed out of this world into the continent of dreams.

For a moment, Becket wondered would he play the part of the two old Greeks in the story who gave Apollo their bed and themselves slept on the floor.

'My arse,' he muttered, went over, lifted Ames' light body up by a fistful of ruined velvet and deposited him on the floor where the rushes were thickest. The blanket he dropped on top, doused the light and got into bed as he was, bar his own boots. The rat came to whisker him goodnight, and settled down companionably to sleep on his chest.

V
December 1582

The coming of a firedrake to his full strength and baneful beauty is a complex matter and in his beginning is only a breath of thought, as with all the works of man. Sir Philip Sidney has a sunny nature and all are agreed he is a most pleasant fellow, a most perfectly complected gentleman. Even his handwriting shows the glimmer of sunlight, reason and charm in every bend and curve. Mine own hand, I know, is a galloping farrago, swooping from Secretary to Italic to its own device, curling and running before itself as if my pen were a runagate beetle. It was near a miracle I could write at all with the angels bothering me, but Mr Sidney (as he then was) wrote easily, copiously and freely, smiling at his own wit as he shook sand in punctuation upon the turning of pages.

Now the Queen Moon hath ever delighted in little things, the better to show her power, and it was a small thing that the Huguenot M. Estienne had asked his friend Sidney to write in English, that he gain practice in reading this our little-known, half-barbarian tongue. Mr Sidney had laughed, protested that the French was better apt to a civilised pen, and given way with his usual grace.

Thus he wrote his letter and it being signed and folded and sealed, he stood and stretched and thought he would prefer to use his legs than shout for a man to take it for him.

And so he walked down the back stairs and through the passage leading behind the kitchen of Sir Francis Walsingham's house in Seething Lane, that gives onto the stable yard. There he saluted his favourite horse, paused for a grave conference with a groom upon the subject of a dog, and then peered into the little office by the tackroom, piled high with canvas bags.

'Mr Hunnicutt?' bellowed Sidney, his head poked between the two large canvas sacks on either side of the door, that held the incoming harvest of letters and reports. 'Are you there, Mr Hunni . . . Oh, good day to you, Mr Hunnicutt.'

Beside neat rows of dispatch bags, each one marked with its destination and date of sending and the rider that was to take it, stood Hunnicutt like a monk in a scriptorium. His rotund smile answered Sidney's great beam, two dimples pecked into his two pink cheeks, and he sheathed his pen in an inkwell.

'Mr Sidney, how may I serve you, sir?'

'No great urgency,' smiled Sidney, as if he were not Sir Francis' prospective son-in-law, could the Queen be got to agree which she would eventually. 'If you have a man bound for Vienna with not too full a bag . . .' and he waved his letter vaguely.

Mr Hunnicutt blinked and turned to a list of names pricked and marked with destination, load, horse and expenses.

'Pellew will be going to the Empire this day, if that will serve.'

'Excellent,' said Sidney, his hand in his purse, 'Give him a little drink-money in recompense for his trouble, if you will, Mr Hunnicutt . . . .'

Two bright sixpences peeked over the top of the scrivener's desk beside Mr Hunnicutt and rolled downhill into his own purse. Hunnicutt, though a man of the cloth in addition to his talents at despatching, bowed and smiled and brushed self-deprecatingly at the buttons of his new doublet, fluttering untruths about his willingness to serve to which Sidney replied with a cheerful wag of his finger. While Hunnicutt bustled the letter into its particular canvas bag, Sidney went on his way to see a hunting dog with a septic paw, stepping gravely over the game of jacks Hunnicutt's silent page was playing by the door.

What good is paper if it move not? In written words hideth a great magic, bearing gold or death or lust as meetly as a laundry list or a receipt for comfits, all pinned upon paper and no one word weighing more than another its own length, if it could be prised from the paper and its scratching of ink weighed. Being static and preserved as rose petals in sugar, then the words may be carried. Like water in a millrace, the power of the World of Paper, the *Mundus Papyri*, to move our own Globe cometh purely of its motion.

Pellew was a long leathery man in worn hose and a buff coat, hard to tell from all the other lean weary men that gather about the stable blocks and kitchens of Whitehall and Theobalds and Barn Elms. They fill the air with talk of horses and their many ailments and a vast range of proven remedies, complaints of foul roads to Dover and fouler Channel packet-boats, the corruption of salt-tax gatherers in France and the miserable lack of good inns in Germany, all interspersed with stirring tedious tales of how they crossed the Alps last winter, sick of the flux, on a horse with three legs lame and beset by robbers on the way.

Pellow rode out of the Seething Lane stable yard at a pace that brought him to the river for the turn of the tide, whence he took a horse-ferry down to Tilbury to find his berth upon the Swan of London. Behind him a lesser messenger trotted from the house to give a piece of paper to the ballad singer doing fine trade by the gate.

A courier that knows his business will take a steady pace in preference to a hectic one and needs a stoic's resignation to bear him company while he waits for the right weather to cross England's moat.

With the water once behind him the roads and foul ways of Europe stretch before him. It is work for a philosopher, a great jogging tedium upon ways Roman or clerical or purely theoretical, upon barges and ferries, here fording unbridged rivers, there paying toll to some petty nobleman's steward with no legality in it save the swords of his men-at-arms.

Pellew passed quietly behind armies and Spanish agents, a mere one of many upon the roads, keeping company with common carriers wherever he could. Once in Catholic parts, he was marked as an Englishman and caused to cool his heels at the gate whilst his bags were inspected for any contraband of English Protestant polemic or unLatined Bibles. Strange how long the searching of a mere dispatch bag might take: it was dawn before he could continue to Vienna and the house of an English merchant. He had slept upon a bench at the guardhouse trusting that anything in need of secrecy would be double-locked behind walls of cipher and if it was not, to be sure, he could do nothing about it.

Those letters seeming to be of import had been copied by hollow-eyed clerks and in a little while, an accumulation of them set forth across Christendom once again, behind the saddle of another lean weary man that might have been Pellew's twin save for the trifling distinction of language, before fetching up in the Netherlands, in the office of the Spanish Governor's secretary.

This clerk had a tame Englishman to help him riddle out his work, a Catholic, a long thin man with a fair freckled skin and ginger hair, and his mother's pale grey eyes hardened by certainty. Also he had a little scar at the corner of his mouth that I myself made with my fist when I was twelve and he was eight, in a desperate rivalry for a box of sugared plums. It is not given to all of us to boast a brother working for the Spaniards.

To the Spanish secretary, Sidney's letter to Henri Estienne was a minor matter, of interest only in that it was in a new hand and unciphered nor with any hidden writing upon it (as reported by the clerks). My brother

Adam translated it faithfully to Spanish and as he did so, his face became faraway and his eyes smeared with memory. When it came to finding a man who would carry the packet to Spain in the dangerous waters of March Biscay, he raised his voice to the task when all about him were silent. The Secretary entrusted the journey to him, being short of couriers as always, and not requiring to know why he had a fancy to visit Spain at last.

Through which complexity came this following part of the letter under the eyes of His Majesty, King Philip II of Spain.

'. . . And now with the poor Dutch Protestants backed to the wall again, Fulke Greville and I have purposed that our poetical jousting next year shall touch upon the danger of Spain and the wise use of all of us who hold to the pure religion. We have hit upon the figure of a Red Dragon that was Her Majesty's grandfather's badge when he threw down the foul usurper Richard Plantagenet. It is also a Dragon of Discord, that none but Her Majesty's brilliant eye and beauty can tame. Then once being submitted to his rightful Queen, the Dragon shall turn upon the Beast of the Apocalypse (I mean, Rome) and fight in her behalf as her most loyal champion and utterly overthrow the Beast and its rider, Philip of Spain. Greville and I drew straws for which should be Philip and which should ride the Dragon Discord, and he took the short straw. Poor man, he cannot tell whether to be delighted that the expense will be less for a Beast, or disgusted that the mob will hiss and clamour against him, but he is making a hymn even now in cod Latin for his attending monks and nuns to sing . . . .'

To make soldiers to grow from a ploughed field, the Greeks will have it that you must first sow dragon's teeth. To gain dragons, must you sow soldiers' teeth?

VI
October 1583

Having fought his Provost's Prize in a brief time of ill-gotten wealth the year before, David Becket was now allowed by the Four Ancient Masters of Defence to teach the use of arms. This included the longsword, the two-hand and bastard swords, backsword, sword-and-buckler, sword-and-dagger, dagger alone, and the right wielding of polearms, namely pike, half-pike, halberd, quarterstaff and battleaxe.

The school he began had foundered in unpaid debts, quarrelling and drink, but still with a couple of veney sticks and a pupil he could begin again, be the pupil never so small, spindly of limb and unhandy. So Becket laid his plans for Simon Ames, full of hopes. First, he thought, a visit to an apothecary, then to wherever he lived and on in gentle sequence to the payment of 40 shillings, being half the fee for a set of lessons in swordplay.

Ames, when he woke, was deep sunk in misery and should have been easy meat. Evil humours from Goodwife Alys' brewing infected his brain with headaches and sickness, his body was covered with bruises and grazes and fleabites from Becket's noisome rushes, his face was too stiff to move, his eyes blackened and his nose swollen up like a man with the French pox.

Becket had woken before him and moved him back onto the bed, which was a better resting place than the floor, though narrower and lumpier. The noise that had woken him was Becket coming up the stairs; he blinked his bruised eyes away from the window-shutter where winter sunlight was squeezing through knot holes and cracks, and wondered blearily at the small round leather buckler armed with a nine-inch point at its centre and a large dent, that hung in state upon the wall.

Becket opened the door and came in more quietly than seemed possible for a man of his size. Simon sat up recklessly and had to clutch his head like a man with the first onset of the plague. Becket ducked under the beams and brought over a chipped earthenware bowl full of wine and water with an egg in it and a few meagre shavings of cinnamon and nutmeg floating on the top.

'I do dot . . . .'

'An infallible cure for that sour beer at the Gatehouse, sir,' said Becket, full of sympathy, and then a cunning stroke, 'I pawned my old breastplate to get it.'

Simon swallowed greenly and of pure politeness took the bowl and drank half. Becket's lodging at that time was at the top of Mrs Carfax's house in Fetter Lane, crammed up under the rafters with the pigeons whose squabs Becket stole on occasion to make a pie. There was in it a battered chest, a bed, the buckler, a rushlight holder with an inch of tallow dip in its jaws and a dish-of-coals for frying eggs and collops sitting by the fireplace, empty, its handle bent and the fireplace empty as well. There were nails hammered into the walls where other things had hung and marks in the foot-deep rushes where once had stood a table and a stool. It would have taken a braver woman than Mrs Carfax to sweep out the rushes and find the floorboards, but at least the roof only leaked in one place, under which Becket set the now empty bowl. His dirty shirt and hose had been kicked under the bed.

'Shall I open the shutter, Mr Ames?' Becket asked.

Ames nodded bravely. 'What time is it?'

'About eight of the clock. The sun is coming up.'

'Oh Lord,' moaned Ames, defending his eyes from the watery light, 'Oh. Let me see. I cannot attend on Mr Phelippes today, not in this state. Ah . . . Mr . . . um . . . Becket, I already owe you great gratitude – will you do me a further favour?'

'Name it, sir.' said Becket, full of eagerness.

'Will you hire me a horse and then go a message for me to the Court?'

'I would Mr Ames, but . . . I have not the money for it.' Ames raised his eyebrows. The pawning of the breastplate had been necessary anyway, for the rescue of Becket's sword on the argument that a swordmaster without a sword on his hip inspired no confidence. Also Becket was aware that he would have no black bruise griping his back had he been wearing it the night before. But that had left enough for the wine and egg and no more.

'Are we still near Fleet Street?' Becket nodded. Ames swallowed at the thought of motion, 'Then if you will take me to a pawnbroker's I think we may make shift.'

Assuming he meant to pawn the impressive court gown he wore, Becket helped Ames up off the bed and made an attempt at dusting alley mud, onion skins and dried blood from it.

'There are two pawnbrokers in Fleet Street,' Becket said confidingly. 'One is a good Christian man, a Mr Barnet, that charges two pennies in the shilling and the other is a foreigner that *says* he is no Spaniard, and I have heard he charges as much as a sixpence in the shilling and more and so . . . .'

Ames half-smiled, winced.

'Will you take me to the foreigner, Mr Becket?'

Tom of Bedlam saw the two of them that morning, and marked them despite our continuing argument with the devil that lives in the waterbutt by Sergeant's Inn. To Tom's Moon-struck sight, the angel that guards

18

Becket and the angel that guards Ames were deep in converse, while the two themselves walked leisurely but in silence along Fleet Street to Fleet Bridge where the foreigner had set him up to lend money at usury.

They walked in by the little barred window under the sign of three brass balls and waited while a trollop redeemed her cooking pot. Becket was angry at his friendly advice being ignored and also at losing his commission for bringing Mr Barnet a new customer, so he stood back with his arms folded, not prepared to advise.

The old man in his skullcap and good clean robe turned from his strongbox and blinked through the bars at Simon Ames' carnival face.

'Umhm?'

'*Bom dia*, Senhor Gomes.' said Ames, and continued in a babble of language that made the hairs on the back of Becket's neck prickle until he realised that whatever kind of filthy foreign it was, Spanish, at least, it was not. He took his hand off his swordhilt and tried to look calm as the pawnbroker unlocked his gates and ushered them within, and gave Simon an embrace as if he were a long lost kinsman. Ames neither looked nor sounded foreign, but it was a sad blow to Becket to think that he might have helped some manner of Spaniard. Still, he decided to reserve judgment until he knew for certain. There were always dark alleys and a quick knife in the ribs.

By the time they were out of the shop with five shillings in Simon's new purse and his gown still on his back, Becket was disposed to be friendly for a little while longer.

As they passed over the bridge and up Ludgate Hill he said, 'You speak excellent fine English for a foreigner, sir.'

Simon smiled nervously, winced again. Delicately feeling his swollen mouth with the flat of his fingers where it had been trodden on, he said, 'I was born in this country, sir, though my family are Marranos, which is a type of Portuguese that have taken refuge here by the Queen's kindly grace.'

'Oh.' said Becket, lightening a little. 'Then you are no follower of King Philip?'

'If I were, I should hardly speak Spanish where I could be heard.'

'That was not Spanish, Mr Ames.'

'*Habla vuestra merced castelane?*'

'*Comprendo solo.* And have no wish to speak it, by your leave, sir.' Becket spat as if to take the taste of the words from his tongue.

Ames has little pale brown eyes that seem weak and squinting, and yet still colder than Thames water.

'It was Portuguese. Will you still go unto Whitehall for me, Mr Becket, though I have no English blood.'

Becket's long lashes shaded his eyes and he smiled. 'I have taken orders even from Spaniards, Mr Ames, when I must. And I have no other business this day.'

'Then here are two groats and a message for you to carry to Mr Phelippes in the Secretary's office.'

For a man of common birth this might have been the end of the matter, but Becket was gently born and carried a sword of right.

He gave back one of the groats. 'You know as I do that the fare to Westminster is tuppence there and tuppence back.'

'The other was towards the redemption of your breastplate,' said Ames quickly. 'But I had not finished telling you of my family. First you may know that a year ago the King's Majesty of Spain burned my mother's two brothers at the stake for that they were Jews. And second, I would like to beg the favour of your company at dinner this afternoon at mine Uncle Hector Nuñez's house in Poor Jewry. Ask the Watch at Aldgate and they will direct you. Perhaps we shall finish our argument.'

Becket was none of those fools who think Jews bear horns on their heads for the killing of our Saviour, and further he knew that Dr Nuñez was physician to my lord the Earl of Leicester, which explained the gown and the gold of his nephew. Hopes no longer entirely dashed, he made his bow, accepted the invitation and headed down to the river.

VII

Now I will not give in detail this argument and that argument over the well-laden dinner table of Dr Nuñez: this lambasting of Hermes Trismegistus by Simon Ames, that defence of the Seven Angel Governors of the Planets by David Becket. The candlesticks and nutshells went journeys about the empty chargers and trenchers on the table to demonstrate the truth of Aristotle, with Becket as his advocate. And then Simon made a counterblasting rearrangement of them to show the gospel of Copernicus according to Thomas Digges which rejoiced his heart as Catullus or Horace might rejoice another man. Both were ignorant and well-read enough to have loud and fixed opinions, oiled by wine.

When the heat of the argument rose too high, Dr Nuñez and his wife Leonora discoursed on the humours and the origins of the French pox and the strange fact that dairymaids rarely suffer from the smallpox and whether this means that, being as it were protected by the sign of Taurus, which is that of earth, their humours are more soundly rooted and less subject to overheating. And after Simon Ames had described his notable fight with the footpads for the third time, Becket said, 'I wish you had not fought in a way, Mr Ames.'

'Why sir? Will you have my honour lost with my purse,' Simon asked jokingly.

'No, indeed not. Only I would say you are not a man used to dagger-fighting.'

Here Dr Nuñez barked with laughter and his wife smiled.

'I have never studied the art,' said Simon, a little cross. 'But surely it means only to stab first and not be stabbed.'

'Cleanly put,' agreed Becket, 'but still there is an art in it. You are exceedingly fortunate to be alive and unwounded. It is my belief that a man foolish enough to fight without knowing how it is done deserves the beating he invariably gets, though not perhaps to lose his life. In which case justice was done to you.'

Ames's nose was throbbing, his jaw aching at the hinges, his eyes ached, the wine had stung his lips, his body was covered with bruises, and his left arm hurt where Dr Nuñez had let him eight ounces of blood to guard against infection. He frowned. 'Why? Should I give my purse to any man who asks for it, meekly, without a struggle?'

'It might have been less painful.'

'Why not to the first beggar I meet on the street?'

'Only if he have a knife in his hand and a dark alley to use it in. The alternative to such dishonour, as you put it, is learning to fight.'

'And you can teach my nephew to fight, Mr Becket? Is that what this is preface to?' Dr Nuñez was smiling in his black beard, his voice lightly tinged with the Portuguese and vastly amused.

'Ay it is, sir,' said Becket, thrusting out his jaw and looking like a bulldog in the ring. 'I am a Provost of Arms, licensed to teach the use of arms, and I am the best sword-and-buckler man in London, properly proved at my prize last year at the Belle Sauvage Inn on Ludgate. Further, I have fought the Spaniards in the Netherlands and know more of fighting

21

than all of the drunken brawlers and Italian catamites in London put together.'

Dr Nuñez eyed Becket quizzically. 'And what would you teach my nephew? Sword-and-buckler play?'

Becket coughed. 'Er . . . no. Nor would I expect him to take his prizes or graduate from Scholar to Free Scholar. But I can at least teach him the proper use of a dagger and the avoiding of blows . . . .'

'Why not sword-and-buckler play?' asked Simon, bristling, 'I am stronger than I look.'

'But sword-and-buckler is suited to a man of a choleric or sanguine complection,' said Dr Nuñez smoothly, 'and you, as you know, incline more to the phlegmatic.'

'He has endless colds,' confided Leonora Nuñez while Simon flushed and finished his wine. 'It is the dampness of England, will always have such an effect. Since we came I have never been warm once. I too am phlegmatic of nature.'

'In addition, he ignores my advice.' Dr Nuñez was smiling still and wagging his finger at Simon whose ears had gone red. 'The least a courtier must pay me is a gold crown each time that I should attend on him for his piles, costiveness, attacks of the stone, et cetera. Mine own brother's child, who pays nothing for my words, heeds not a single one of them. When I tell him to drink tobacco for the calming of his brain and to lessen his making of phlegm, he pays no attention.'

'Tobacco?' asked Becket.

'Henbane of Peru. Strickly speaking, one drinks the smoke.'

'So I have heard, but I have never tried it.'

'Why you should. Come with me to my study and we shall share a pipe. It is a most valuable herb, lenitive, soothing, reduces phlegm as I have said, and it is sovereign against pains in the head or stomach. Some say it should be taken in the morning only, fasting, but to my mind it is best taken on a full stomach and in the evening so as to procure an easeful night. The savages of the New World are said to . . . .'

VIII

Leonora Nuñez would not hear of her nephew's saviour traversing London after sunset when she had beds in plenty in her house, the Almighty be thanked. When Becket had gone, still coughing and his head spinning, to the fair clean linen and broidered curtains of his bed, Dr Nuñez went into his study and sat down in his chair, lacing his fingers across the straining brocade over his belly. Without being asked, Simon Ames shut the door, and took out of his penner the small leather packet that had been rescued from Bonecrack Smith. He laid it down among the account books, empty piss bottles, clyster thread, papers and lancets on Dr Nuñez's desk.

'It is not sealed,' he said, in Portuguese, and wandered across the rushmat to examine the rows of sealed bottles in one of the book-cases. Dr Nuñez opened the packet with the ends of his fingers and the tip of a lancet, as if anatomising an organ, and spread the papers before him. He grunted several times as he read.

'Have you broken the code?' he asked.

Simon nodded, left his examination of a docket marking one small bottle as the urine of a child, and put another piece of paper before the doctor.

'Ah. Simple enough. Where did this come from?'

Simon went quietly to the door, opened it, shut it again.

'From one of the footpads.'

Dr Nuñez raised his eyebrows. There was a short silence.

'There is a tale here I have not been told, I think, Simon.'

Simon fiddled with the Cordovan leather flap of his penner, where it was worn with his fingers, paced once across the room to examine a tapestry of Joshua at the walls of Jericho, and then returned to take the child's piss bottle in his hands.

Hector Nuñez sighed. 'It is a most valuable sample,' he said. 'Seldom have I tasted urine so sweet.'

Simon blinked down at the bottle.

'The child died, of course. They always do with the sugar sickness, though by starving they may be made parodixically to live a little longer. It is an empirical treatment and I like it not, for it has no right justification in astrology nor in balancing of humours. I hold it but a palliative, based upon superstition, which causes suffering of hunger but cannot prevent the end. And she was a gentle child and died in much pain and fever. So I pray you Simon, if you must break a thing before you answer me, break the bottle next to it, which is only your master's piss, and of which I may harvest more whenever I will, seeing he lives yet.'

'Mr Phelippes?' asked Simon, putting the one bottle back and taking the other.

'No, Sir Francis Walsingham. He has the stone, as you surely know.'

'I knew he was ill.'

'He has gravel in his bladder again and must pass it before he may be easy.' Nuñez smiled. 'If you choose not to tell me of your tale, shall we drink another pipe?'

Simon put back the piss bottle sharply, almost knocking down the two on either side, and came to sit down by his uncle.

'Somewhere in Whitehall, or somewhere in Walsingham's household is one who belongs to Spain. There is too much that goes astray, too pat, too much known in San Lorenzo that should not be . . . .'

'A recusant?'

'One that goes not to Mass and takes gold in no way that I can trace, which is the reason for my letter to Cousin Isaac in Rouen.'

Nuñez nodded, examining his fingers.

'You are certain now?'

'There was a dispatch sent by my action, speaking of supplies for the relief of a certain fort. I had men placed . . . . In short, the Spaniards were bringing up troops to the place within a week.'

'Hm. And Sir Francis?'

'Sick of the stone this past week as you said. And with this matter of the Mouse and the Guisan plot . . . .'

'But surely then he is French.'

'I think not. Thanks to Mr. Fagot we have the French ambassador stopped up so tight in his earth he cannot fart without we know what he ate for his dinner that day.' Nuñez grinned and began filling his pipe again.

Simon began to pace, knocking over a small table bearing a pestle and mortar and some teeth. He bent to pick them up, carefully piling the teeth in the mortar.

24

'And now this. They know there was no relief for the fort . . . .'

'Is it still holding out?'

Simon blinked at him, began to stir the teeth about with the pestle. 'Why no, of course not. And it seems the Spaniards have understood why I coneycatched them.'

Nuñez took the mortar and pestle from Simon before he should begin to grind the teeth to powder, which was not in fact to be their fate, but rather to be dissolved in aqua fortis in pursuit of a little alchemy, being Nuñez's hobby. He offered Simon the pipe.

'And with such a packet found upon your dead body, then any other man's suspicions would fall upon you, that you were the conduit, discovered only by chance, and the inquest wound up quickly.'

Simon was coughing again, but he nodded.

Nuñez half-hooded his eyes, sucked at the smoke. 'Which being prevented by Mr Becket, thereby poses a further question, alas.'

'Indeed,' said Simon, sitting down at last, to Nuñez's relief. 'Is he as he seems a simple man of the sword there by chance, or is he a chimaera with a Spaniard heart in an English body.'

'I cannot anatomise him for you, Simon, nor do I carry windows that the Queen will not use to see into men's hearts.'

'What shall I do though?'

'That depends upon how much of the sanguine humour you have within you. To be utterly safe from any such betrayal, why, dismiss him now. To take a chance on the throw of dice to find out more, keep him by you and learn his nature fully. You may even learn a little knife play which is never amiss.'

'Would that not make it easier for him to kill me?'

Nuñez took back the pipe and patted its bowl carefully.

'You have let it go out,' he said, searching for the tinderbox, and forgetting the candles at his shoulder. 'So it would indeed make it easier to kill you, if that were his purpose, but even if he is a Spanish chimaera, logic will teach you that it was not. Better unknown footpads killing the man than a known swordmaster, and if he rescued you in order to impose on your confidence, well, why should he want you dead?'

Simon nodded slowly. 'I would like to learn swordplay,' he said unexpectedly.

'I pity the man.'

'Worse fools than I have learned fighting.'

'Your own brother William told me this: fighting is like singing: it is natural to men but may be transformed by training: most can learn it,

25

some have a genius for it, and some are blind and deaf to it and so must content themselves.'

Simon sniffed and made a move to go to his bed. Nuñez stopped him by reaching for another packet.

'Speaking of Cousin Isaac . . . .' This packet of papers had a little spatter of blood and a lancet lying by it. 'I have decoded most of it, but there are parts in your own private cipher.'

'May Isaac be mentioned to Sir Francis?'

'I leave that to your judgment, Simon.'

IX

Becket got his forty shillings Scholar fee of Simon from which he paid five shillings to the Italian swordmaster Rocco Bonnetti for the use of a corner of his swordschool hall at Blackfriars. The Boys of the Chapel had used it for their plays but were embroiled in a dispute with the landlord who had let it in the interim to Rocco. It was once the refectory to the monastery and still smelled a little in hot weather of cabbage soup. Rocco Bonnetti and Jerome, his boy of the moment, slept in the wine-fragrant rooms of the convent butler hard by.

This made Rocco and Becket both near neighbours to Tom and I and our band of angels, for in the old stone lace of the monastery cloister are many little holes and shelters and cubbyholes that once were writing carrels. Stranger creatures than I live there. Once in a corner under a loose stone I found some pretty things, a piece of parchment written in Latin which was jewelled along its edge with a P that breaks into snakes and dogs and devils and sometimes invades my dreams. There was also a little plate of gold with a fish on it, rimmed with enamel and garnets that I cherish to pay for my burial, and because the angels love it too.

Once there was a monk in his black robes came in and sat down and began to write while I half-slept, though the little cell was lightless. One of Tom's angels rose up and debated with him. I was afraid but Tom my skullfellow was not. At length the monk smiled in surprise at the angel and the angel took him by the hand and they flew through the roof

26

where the painted gold stars and moon are covered by fungus. In the morning there was an old man dead of cold and hunger by the cloister and we buried him in the garden among the shanties, since the parish would have nothing to do with a pauper.

I saw them, Becket and Ames, at the daggerplay with wooden weapons in the little cloister courtyard. It is full of garbage and a sick old walnut tree, a tiny weed-smothered pond, a cat and her kittens, near full grown, hencoops and a neatly tended raised bed full of winter-sleeping herbs that Simple Neddy grows to sell to housewives.

'Why here?' protested Simon Ames as he tripped on an old boot. 'We can scarcely move for all this.'

'For a demonstration and so that Rocco sees not the tricks I will show you. Do you think that a footpad will come upon you in a good open place, cleared of rubbish? Or that he will abide by the laws of a sword-school?'

Tom and I peeped out of our door and then scurried across the covered path to hide behind the stone fretwork and peep through a cross to see the lesson. Tom's usual angel sat on a pillar where a saint had been once, but none save Tom and I could see her.

Now David Becket is so big a man it seems near a miracle how fast and lightly he can move if he wants. He skips like a doe in spring and by the time the blow arrives he has shifted away. It is true what Dr Nuñez said, and Becket was near to genius at swordplay: once I knew something of Defence, though dancing was more the Courtier's mark, and it was wonderful how unhandy Simon Ames was and how patient was Becket.

First Ames played the footpad's part, coming at Becket from behind or before and being put aside gently, one way or another. Then Becket took the part of the footpad to test if Ames had learnt his lesson. Once and once only Simon managed to land the blow as he had been taught, which was the one time he should not have let it land and Becket, who is only flesh and blood, sat down on a hencoop and cradled his cods tenderly while he caught his breath and uncrossed his eyes.

'Very good,' he whispered. 'Argghhum. Do it that way and you may keep your purse next time.'

'Lord,' said Ames, quite upset, 'I am sorry. I slipped. I never can seem to time things right, or else my arms and legs do a different thing from the ordering of my brain. I see it perfectly in my head yet do all except what is needed. It was the same in archery.'

'Archery?'

'My father tried to teach it to me when I was young. He said as the Almighty had made me small and puny, blessed be He, I must kill from a distance, but alas my sight is too bad for anything but a near shot.'

'Christ preserve me from ever being within a mile of your archery practice.'

'I gave it up after I shot a man by the windmill in Finsbury Field. It was an expensive lawsuit and my father brake my bow.'

'Never say he did.'

'Oh he did and he told me . . . . It was far from funny at the time, be sure of that. I nearly died of shame.'

'The man. Did he live?'

'In the end, yes. Uncle Hector attended him. He recovered and did not need his arm amputated.'

Becket nodded, pulled himself to his feet and walked with only a slight limp to the rail where I was hiding.

'Now then Tom,' he said. 'Have you learnt anything?'

I stood up. 'This is the Clever One,' I told him, 'not Tom.' Indeed David knows my right name of old, but has kindly forgot it as I have, to keep it safe from devils.

'Well then, did you learn anything from your spying?'

'I was not spying neither,' said I. 'I have no need for it. Only I thought you would prefer not to be disturbed.'

Ames was hovering behind him with that eyebrows lifted, expectant look men have when they are waiting to be introduced. I made a Court bow, which raised his eyebrows a notch higher, and told him who and what I was, viz., Tom the zany, Tom of Bedlam, who talks with angels.

And now his face was turned to a polite mask, and Tom could see behind it all the questions, so he smiled in answer and nodded at the angel on the pillar.

'How do you know him?' Simon asked, while Tom stood on the rail, the better to converse with his angel.

Becket smiled and scratched behind his ear. 'Once we failed to study law together at Gray's Inn . . . .'

'No, no,' shouted Tom, waving his arms. 'That was before, I was never there then.'

'True enough. He was no less sane than any of us then, unless drink and women and overmuch philosophising at two in the morning were signs of lunacy.'

'Nor was the Courtier,' added Tom.

'And it may be the Court did send him mad, or maybe the seeds of it

28

were already sown in him. I recall his poetry was always strange.'

Tom was singing and so I could not say what I wanted, which was that now I was myself a poem like unto the one I sent my brother to show I was not dead of the plague in Bedlam where he put me.

'Later I broke him out of Bedlam Hospital for old times' sake and later still he saved my life.'

'How?' asked Ames, fascinated.

Becket shrugged, cracking the louse he had caught absent-mindedly between his thumb and forefinger. I smiled at him, recalling his face beyond the bars when he paid his penny with the other sightseers to see me caper, how it was impassive, with neither dreadful pity nor ugly merriment nor even unease upon it, to save my feelings.

'I essayed to kill myself and he prevented me,' he said, making of it a joke, 'and then tempted me to it again by haranguing me about his angels.'

'Why not?' shouted Tom again, for all I tried to stop him. 'The angels did it, all I do is what the angels tell me, and Gabriel saw the fiend on your shoulder sucking your blood.'

Simon Ames stepped back a pace, paling. Becket stopped him with a hand on his arm.

'I hoped you would meet him, first because he is an old friend and has more sanity in him than you would suppose now, and second because he is in a way an illustration to my argument. You say that men are in fact not much better than beasts . . . .'

'No indeed, sir, I do not.' said Simon. 'I have expressed myself very ill if you think that. It is that there is a kind of phlegmatic rage in men, very much worse than that of beasts which is choleric, for it may twist and warp all that is best in them, yea, even their Faith in the Almighty, and turn to evil all that they would do for good . . . .'

Becket blinked at him as anyone would. He blew through his teeth. 'And where have you seen such men?'

Simon shook his head, as if he had not meant to speak so brutally, as if the words had been unknown to him before he heard his mouth speaking them. Becket plowed on, less sure himself of what he wanted to say.

'What I wished to show you was a man that has been treated by . . . others as they would scorn to treat a beast, brought as low as Saul when he walked on all fours and ate grass in his madness . . . .'

'Never,' said Tom, 'I never did. I do not like grass.' Becket was think-ing of my sorry state when he brought me out of Bedlam Hospital in a cart full of plague corpses, and myself free of plague but near enough to a corpse, with sorrow and hunger rotting my insides and shackle galls my arms and legs.

'. . . – yet catch him in his soberer mood and he can talk to you as sanely as any man of the Court, which he once was.'

'That says little enough.'

'As any man then. And even the lunatic frenzy which he calls Tom, even he has a strange sense in him. I have questioned him and there are personalities among his angels and devils which he talks to, and none sorts so ill with what others have spoken about angels and devils. Perhaps his brainsickness has stripped a film from his eyes which we have and know not. Perhaps in very truth he sees angels and speaks with them, and for that we call him mad and lock him up.'

> 'On the lordly lofts of Bedlam
>   With stubble soft and dainty
> Brave bracelets strong, sweet whips, ding dong
>   And wholesome hunger plenty,'·

sang Tom, dancing on the carved railing, words from that last poem I made.

'Surely you cannot mean that the mad may teach the sane of the world of spirits?' said Ames.

'Perhaps he sees in the glass more clearly than we do.'

'Pfft.' said Simon. 'You will have the Archbishop's men on our heels with talk like that.'

'Lord, I am no damned Puritan to preach a sermon on it, only curious. Have you never dreamed you were awake and not realised the truth until you woke?'

'I never dream.' said Ames sadly, which caused Tom to look sidelong at him. In Tom's sight, of a sudden, it seemed that there was a man held in a block of ice which showed through the flesh only at his eyes, and yet in its centre beat his heart and struggled to make heat to warm him and melt the ice also. And the ice itself was in the nature of a desperate defence, that sundered him from himself, as if he were at Civil War and could not bear to acknowledge his division, but rather lost himself in a glacier of untruth. And yet, as men who have traversed the Alps attest, in all glaciers there are lumps of rock and mud and whole trees, as the land beneath is murdered by their weight.

30

Tom wrapped his arms about himself, clasping his sharp elbows, and shivered.

'Hm.' said Becket, watching Ames with his eyes narrowed down to long-lashed slits. 'Would you deny that men have souls?'

'No, never!' Simon's voice was sharp. 'Only that they are not so simply known as through the ravings of a . . . .'

I caught at Becket's sleeve. 'If you are my friend, David Becket,' I said, 'buy me food and drink with the money in your purse.'

At that he laughed, although it was not meant as a jest, and turned to Simon and said, 'You see? This madness is not so simple as all that neither, Ames. Where will they still have you, Tom? The Silver Fish?'

'No.' I said. 'Tom fought a devil in there that was climbing in the cooking pot and upset it all over the fire and so they beat me and threw me out the door and Goodwife Lily said if I came back she would let my devils out herself with her butcher's knife. Even though it was a very evil flux devil, full of poison, green and purple like a bramble jelly . . . .'

'So the Gatehouse is the only place?'

I nodded. 'Goodwife Alys likes me to put a good word on her brewing.'

'My God, are you the one to blame for her beer?'

'Not at all,' I told him with dignity, coming down off the cloister wall. 'When I have blessed it, both the beer and the ale are much better.'

Which I had not done for a while, but no matter – the worst booze in the world is better than Thames river water.

Goodwife Alys let Ames and Becket sit in a booth by the back door and in lordly fashion, I left them to call for drink and food while I followed the Goodwife into her yard sheds where her bucks bubbled to themselves under their covers. That day's mash was into its third strain-ing to make very small beer indeed, and her poor drudge of a daughter was bending at the fire with her eyes streaming, building it up to boil the wort with hops. I jabbered nonsense in the midst of the room and waved my arms, while she stood by with her thick arms folded and her lips pressed firm together like a mousetrap for words.

We ate the ordinary, which was a mutton pottage with dumplings, and I kept Tom tight-reined. Becket who knows my fits sometimes better than I do called for a board and for chessmen and set him to play me, while Simon watched. After I mated, Ames took the board himself and we played three in succession and each time I beat him, though the third time I gave him a pawn. Becket sat back drinking steadily, playing bearmaster.

At last Ames took his green velvet hat off and straightened the feather with his thumb.

'Are you a counterfeit?' he asked directly. 'One of those who coneycatch by feigning lunacy?'

Becket smiled. 'Touched your pride, has he, with his artfulness at chess?'

'I cannot conceive that a man could be mad and play so well . . . .'

'Ah but sir,' I said, 'you are ignorant of madness having never suffered it. Besides, I am not mad, it is the world and men like you that are mad and blind both, being unable to see Tom's angels.'

'Who is Tom?'

'That is what he calls his skullmate, as it were another man locked in his brain,' explained Becket. 'It is not his true name.'

'Just so,' I said and smiling patted my belly full of stew and penny loaf. 'Some of him hides here, and some in here,' – I rapped my pate – 'and when the angels come he speaks to them and is instructed by the Queen Moon.'

'Is Tom a devil?' asked Simon disbelievingly. 'Is this an occasion of possession?'

'There are devils truly that possess,' I told him. 'I have fought with them on occasion, to save the unangeled from them, for which no thanks, but Tom is a poor mad lunatic who cannot help what he does. And when he captures this my body and makes me caper I must suffer it meekly . . . .'

Ames was looking questioningly at David Becket.

'As to his trueness,' Becket said judiciously, 'I think a counterfeit Tom of Bedlam would get more by begging, and carry soap to chew, and live better than Tom does who has forgot the use of soap and lives in a little hole in the Blackfriars cloister which is empty because no one will pay for such a den. As to whether a devil has a hold on him, our Saviour told us to judge a tree by its fruit. I think a devil would rather have encouraged me to murder myself, not saved me.'

Ames nodded. 'How did it happen?' he asked in a quiet neutral tone of voice.

'Why, I jumped in the Thames,' Becket said lightly, 'well weighted with beer and aqua vitae and breastplate full of stones, and Tom jumped in after me.'

Tom must be heard. 'Angels,' he said, 'it was angels.'

'Whatever.'

'And what brought you to such a pass?' asked Ames.

'Ah.' Becket smiled, shifting his bulk and drinking. 'No doubt it was the fighting against Spain in the Low Countries, a thing which I thought would be very fine and glorious when I went and found to be far different when I got there, though I think I was none so ill a soldier. I little knew myself when I returned but now am cured I think. Perhaps I shall go back to Holland again.'

'Was it angels with you also?'

Becket laughed. 'No,' he said, 'though Tom often tries to make me see his spirit friends. Only the world seemed so far distant from me that it was as if I stood upon a tiny island with water all about but could see the smoke from friendly fires on either shore, and knew I could never come there; that my doom was to stand upon an invisible island in the midst of a cold grey river.' He stopped and finished his drink, clearly not tasting it which was the better for him. 'So it seemed to me in such melancholia that the true river could cure me of the river in my mind, and in some sense it did. And there was a woman who spurned me to marry another, and a friend that was no friend . . . . But the Spanish are a melancholy breed, they carry it on them like the plague.'

Now Tom and I have been with Becket while he fights in his drunkenness with many enemies, bearded and fiendish and speaking Spanish, and so I knew this was not all the truth, though more of it than he usually tells.

A ballad singer came in by the back door, his broadsheets pinned to his jerkin and spilling out of his basket. Simon Ames stared in silence at his own pierced and defeated bone soldiers and then nodded.

'An invisible island in a cold broad river,' he murmured to himself and smiled briefly at Becket. 'A good figure for melancholy.'

'You speak as one that knows the river?' said Becket.

'No, I know it by report only,' said Ames to Becket too hastily. 'At least not in such a way as to desire death. No. And so it was this man Tom that restored your hope?'

And now the ballad singer was tuning the house lute, which needed it sorely. He would have been a handsome man if he had been taller and less pockmarked, and his hair and old velvet cap cleaner and less gypsy black. I knew him for he pulled the crowds on Fleet Street having a better voice and more memory than most ballad sellers. He never minded if I begged among the listeners.

Becket smiled at Ames again, marking the change from near honesty to dissimulation. 'In the tale of Pandora and her box, some say that a single blessing was left after all the evils and fiends and miseries had made their escape from the box she opened, and some say there was yet a last and most insidious curse. But they call it by the one name of Hope, and I think so must I . . . .'

One of Tom's angels was singing and darting about the room. I could see no danger there, though there were two cutpurses drinking in a corner and some weighted dice skinning a poor coney of a farmer under the stairs. The ballad singer strummed the lute a little and began to sing the newest song, hot come from the printing press, he said, and the tale of Tom O'Bedlam.

'From the hag and hungry goblin
   That into rags would rend ye,
And the spirit that stands by the naked man
   In the book of moons, defend ye.
That of your five sound senses
   You never be forsaken
Nor wander from yourselves with Tom
   Abroad to beg your bacon.

'Alas, the sorrow of that bastard child
   Which soweth love will make me wild,
And if I must die so on I moan
   'Till her Moon's face become mine own
And sorrow has ceased for her silver feast,
   Hey diddle, sing diddle, hi diddle I drone.

'Of thirty bare years have I
   Twice twenty been enraged
And of forty been three times fifteen
   In durance sadle caged.
In the lordly lofts of Bedlam
   With stubble soft and dainty . . . .'

No more could I bear to hold Tom upon the leash, so let it slip and Tom jumped up on the table and kicked away the treacherous chessmen with their twin faces of black and white, and shouting of Lucifer who is my kin, and all his works. In a minute Becket had caught my arms in a grip of bronze, while Simon Ames chased the rolled men about the sticky few rushes and the ballad singer smiled and nodded at my drumming up of his trade and pitched his fine bell-voice louder.

'A thought I took for Maudlin
  And a cruse of cockle pottage,
With a thing thus tall, sky bless you all!
  I befell into this dotage.
I slept not since the Conquest,
  Till then I never waked,
Till the roguish boy of love where I lay
  Me found and stripped me naked.'

I howled that I was betrayed and that they should pay me the fee for it, but none understood me and Tom was flailing at Becket who gripped and shook me and now came Goodwife Alys's eldest son towards us with a stout veney stick in his great fist, and Becket tripped my legs from under me, lifted me up and carried me like a maiden to the back door.

'. . . The moon's my constant mistress
  And the lovely owl my marrow;
The flaming drake and the night crow make
  Me music to my sorrow.

'Alas, the sorrow of that bastard child,
  Which soweth love . . . .'

And then we were out in the Gatehouse yard, and up the maltman's passage and into Water Lane and so onto Fleet Street, past the hammering in Hanging Sword Court to the conduit where Becket held me over the water trough and swore he would drown me now, until Tom stopped his kicking and shouting. Then he set me down quite gently and sat on the edge of the trough while I squatted and played at pebbles and thought Tom may have made worse what was better mended by quiet. But that was a thought too late, as it came out after.

'Ah Tom, poor Tom,' he said to me, 'was it my fault? Did the chessplaying strain your poor brain?'

'No,' I told him, after a while in thought. 'In chessplaying I am closer to your world, for the reason that angels are not much interested by chess. Nor Tom neither.'

Simon Ames was coming towards us, looking about him, and having paid the reckoning, no doubt. Becket hailed and waved at him.

'Then what was it turned you lunatic so suddenly? Was it the rising of the moon or a planet, or something more near?'

35

Why should he notice a mere ballad singer? There is always music or singing about; every barber's shop rings with jumbled voices trying to ape the latest court madrigal, every street has its own ballad seller and sometimes several who compete like cats. Wet any Englishman with beer and he turns first to singing and then to fighting. Besides, it is a well-known fact that madness is calmed by music. I tried to tell Becket the true reason, but the Queen Moon stopped the words in my throat.

'Something more near,' I muttered through clenched teeth and then an angel put his hand on my mouth and Tom was king again.

X
Summer 1583

There are roads in England of infinite variety, many now new planted with wicked hedges depriving the commoners of their commons, most unmended since the nearest monastery was dissolved or since the Queen went that way upon progress, foul bogs in winter and dust baths in summer. Yet in summer upon a Roman road a pedlar of embroidery silks and ribbons and suchlike women's gear may step lightly enough and whistle to his pack mare in a cheery drone. The Romans were ever stone spiders and no monk's way has lasted better than their pavements. Here were no yawning great potholes to lose a cart and horse in, only some digging of the best parts and an old fort by old Sir William Fant for the building of his manor house. Beyond the poppies the haymaking was at full tilt, the mowers upon the far side of the great open field scything through the grass at a fair rhythm, like the wind made visible.

Past the fields and up a hill where one of the village copses lay, this one but a few years since cutting, and Peter Snagge the pedlar must pass by the thick growth of withies from their ancient bases, the wicker deer fences sound and unbroken and the new wood green and bushy in the sun, well flowered with butterflies. Here also were wild strawberries and brambles, and Peterkin slowed his pace. Then there was a movement that was not an animal. He caught up his stick, narrowed his eyes.

'Sir,' came the call, weakly from the thickest part of the bushes this side of the fences. 'I pray you, help me . . . I am . . . caught . . . .'

Peterkin circled cautiously closer to the bushes and then grinned, put away his weapon. There was a poor fellow caught in every man's nightmare, held by a deer trap about his left leg and his hose caught round his ankles. A basket of ballads a little way off and the penny pipe in his belt pouch spoke his trade of balladmonger.

'God curse it, to be taken like this . . . . I think my leg is broken.'

Striving to be grave-faced, Peterkin pushed gingerly through bramble vines.

'Why I know you, Goodman Dun, were you not at the Bear's Head two nights gone? I am sorry to see you in such a state.'

'Can you get it off me?'

'Oh no doubt, if you can be still enough. There is a way of the thing, all it needs is a stave in the spring . . . . You can go back to London and tell them a new way of catching coneys. Your leg might not be broken indeed, though it feel that way, and even if it is, so you live, well it's no harm to your profession, you can still sing, and I have a fine salve in my pack to cure all manner of hurts, essence of St John's wort and meadowsweet principally, compounded to a particular fineness by my wife and from her own family receipt the which came down to her by her mother . . . .'

Peterkin was feeling about with his staff for the spring lever, averting his eyes politely from the poor man's bare arse and holding his breath against laughter. Being well-known for his stories of peddling and his pillicock, he rejoiced at a true tale unlooked-for.

'If you have not fought it like a beast, be sure it will mend like new again with the use of my salve . . . . Ah now, here we have it and so . . . .'

The knife took him under the jaw, cut his windpipe and neck vein in one slash. The ballad singer toppled the pedlar's astonished body sideways to be away from the blood, wiped a few spots of it off his jerkin and stabbed the knife in the earth. Carefully he took his leather-collared leg from the wedged jaws of the trap and pulled up his hose. Then he went to find the pedlar's mare.

Sir William Fant had set his fine new house facing south-west so that the setting sun would flash on his broad windows and colour its fair sandstone frontage and knitted chimneys with a nightly pouring of gold. Behind lowered the old fortress on its hill, quarried down to stumps, a haunt of cattle and children playing at English and French. Above Sir William's great golden oak door was the carving of a strange creature, snake-nosed, snake-tailed and large to compare with the Crusader knight leading it home. Somewhere in the old castle yard its bones were reverently buried, and if the carver got his pattern from a bestiary book, well, the monk which drew that had never seen an elephant neither, and so both were well-enough pleased with it.

But the ballad singer turned aside from the door below the glorious trumpeting animal and walked about to the kitchen garden and passed through its lesser gate. He wiped his hands on the front of his leather jerkin, opened his mouth and gave forth in bronze the pedlar's chant.

'Fine ribbons, laces, points and stomachers, come buy, come buy . . . . Best silks and needles, bobbins and pins, come buy . . . .'

'Well, that is never Peterkin,' said a small fierce woman with her fists full of coriander and garlic. 'What are you doing with poor old Jenny, I know he'd never part with her. Have you stolen her, eh?'

'No mistress, Peterkin's sick of a tertian fever and being his nephew I am making his rounds . . . .'

'I never knew he had a soul in the world apart from his trull in Salisbury.'

Wishing he had known of her earlier, the balladmonger smiled. 'Alas, my father and Peterkin were no friends.'

'Hmf. Did he tell you the orders we gave him in spring?'

'The mistress has need of broidery silks, that I know and . . . .'

'Laces, by God, laces for stays, the last he brought were too short . . . . Well come on lad, come into the kitchen and bring your packs. Sam, *Samuel*, move your lazy arse over here and rub down this pony; no oats, mind, and you, come with me . . . .'

Barging past the stableboy, the little woman banged the kitchen door almost on the ballad singer's nose, and so past the pantry and the buttery to the roaring heat of the kitchen, where frantic preserve-making loaded the air with essence of raspberry. Two weary girls were grinding sugar loaves in great stone mortars, a babe crawled about in the sawdust picking up fragments of sugar to eat. In a corner sat a small fat dog on a cushion watching a haunch of beef being set upon the spit.

'Where are the breadcrumbs and the dripping?' shrieked the small woman, rushing over to it. 'I have fools, idle nithings, numbskulls and vermin to attend me, no breadcrumbs, no fat, how may the meat be cooked, eh? Stark naked on a spit like St Sebastian? You child, Mary, fetch the oldest loaf and the crock marked with three crosses, three hear me? and bring them hither. Madam, here is Peterkin's nephew in his

38

stead . . . . Not like that halfwit, or be spitted yourself, here, guide it by the bone . . . .'

A woman in a loose English gown turned away from the great pots bubbling on their trivets over the fire, her face flushed red with heat and fine wisps of red hair escaping from her worn velvet hood to plaster round her forehead. She wore no stays because she was six months gone with child and still held a long spoon and a piece of marble dripped with conserve.

'No, still not set, have you apple peelings put by, Goodwife Bickley?'

'In the red pot by the Spanish raisins, Maud, run fetch them now and take your child out from under my feet, give it raisins if you must but have him not eat off the floor . . . . The pedlar, madam, with laces I trust . . . . You boy, not on your sleeve, ay *you*, blow your snot on the ground by the door like a gentleman . . . .'

The ballad singer clutched his cap from his head, bowed low, all the while thanking God for the lucky chance of it. Here was Mistress Fant, lady of the manor, nodding graciously to his obeisance and handing spoon and stone to a grave-faced carrot-headed child in a let-out rose velvet gown behind her.

'Goodman Snagge, is your uncle not well?'

'A tertian ague.' said the ballad singer smoothly. 'Struck down by it a week gone, poor man, and too sick to move.'

'Has he seen an apothecary?' asked Mrs Fant, her brow knitting. 'I think I have some ague water still. Elizabeth my dear, go unto Dorcas with this key and have her fetch out a quarter pint of the ague water in the stillroom cabinet, which I must still some more. Have we fennel seeds, Goodwife?'

'In the pantry by the pepper, good store, now this is fine Robin, have you not learnt the way of winding up a jack yet, if I can study to learn it with my old brain you can surely . . . . Give it here.'

Clutching at his reason as well as his cap and sweating in the infernal heat, the ballad singer set his packs upon the floor and found lying at the top, thank God, a packet of long stay-laces. Next to it lay the embroidery silks, neatly wound on folded paper to save the weight of bobbins. Below lay ribbons and whalebones for stays and lace and delicate fine lawn folded about coarse linen to protect it.

'Now, I must have crewel needles,' began Mrs Fant, and ran at speed through a list to make a man's head reel. All the packs must be opened and searched through until at last she was satisfied with her little pile of booty. Putting back his wares while Mrs Fant tested the conserve again, the ballad singer mopped his brow and remembered what he had come for.

'My uncle in particular bade me give you this fine red silk, with his compliments, the best and truest dye he ever saw. He said you would know the colour, for it is like the wicked Dragon of Wales in the old tale, he said it was the colour of a prodigal son and also the colour of Rome and the priesthood.'

For a moment he thought she had not heard, or if she heard, had not understood, but then he saw the flush drain down from her cheeks. She sat slowly upon a bench near the fire, still holding the card of silk.

'Peterkin never knew that . . . .'

The ballad singer bowed and did not answer. A tumult had broken out beside them for the little dog who had once turned the spit in his running wheel had jumped down from his cushion and taken a sly bite out of the meat. Mrs Fant never blinked at the shrieking girls nor the shrill yelping of the dog after Goodwife Bickley's boot connected with his flank. The bitten piece was cut out (and covertly given to the dog by someone) and the meat hefted onto its spit.

Behind them the cauldron conversed in slow bubbles and plump Maud came puffing up at last with her hands full of dried apple peelings.

'Not like that,' said Agnes Fant sharply, awakening in time to stop her dumping the lot into the conserve. 'Put them in a cheesecloth bag first, or we must fish them out again . . . . In the chest by the window, Maud, must you be told everything like a maid? Yes, I see, Goodman . . . Snagge. Yes.'

The maidens at the sugar grinding were now casting longing looks at his packs. Mrs Fant saw them and smiled a little.

'If you would find more trade, ask the steward for a mug of beer and bread and cheese and then open your packs again in the orchard. I shall send the maids out to you by threes. What is the price I owe you?'

The ballad seller snatched a number from the air.

'I reckon it two shillings and fourpence,' he said.

'You reckon it wrongly, I think. What will your uncle say when he returns and finds you have cut his prices? Speak to the steward and he shall pay your reckoning. The girls may pay for themselves.'

She was gracious to content him before the others, but he thought her mouth was moving of its own motion, saying the right words, beneath fear in her eyes, fear and hope uneasily combined.

She nodded her head and he knew himself dismissed, made his courtesy, and threaded his way out again. Goodwife Bickley watched him balefully as he passed the table laden with fruit, daring him to touch any. One of the maids stopped her grinding to wink at him and the baby sat on a stone stuffing fistfuls of raisins into his mouth and laughing.

Behind him and watching him in a haze of sweet fumes sat Agnes Fant, born Strangways, my sister, that once was my little plump red-haired Agnes, a puppy at my heels with a stout heart to climb whatever tree I dared, in despite of her short legs and her petticoats. She blinked down at the red silk thread in her hand and indeed it was a fine shining red, blazing on its folded paper like a poppy on a field of snow.

XI
Autumn 1583

Now must we return to the *Mundus Papyri* of which Simon Ames also is a native. Sir Francis Walsingham knows his quality better than I do, for that he has been clerk and secretary to his Honour's own secretary Mr Thomas Phelippes for several years. His mind is of a sort that Sir Francis and Lord Burghley seek for, no matter what the temper of the heart, and then use as seems to them proper.

Though he is a young man still, his hair is thinning back from his brow and what is left is of a nondescript shade like dead grass. His nose is oppressed by spectacles when he works, which he keeps in his penner and ties about his head with black ribbon. In fact he is by way of being the runt of his litter and lineage, which tends to the large and bold. An uncle, by name Francisco, is commander of the English garrison at Youghal in the misted swamps of Ireland and a fine soldier, well-feared by the wild Irish. He has fourteen brothers and sisters, being a son of the Purveyor and Merchant for Her Majesty's Grocery, Mr Dunstan Benjamin George Ames, of Crutched Friars, gentleman. This, though he is a Marrano, is attested as well as any in the land, for the Queen gave Dunstan Ames his Grant of Arms fifteen years ago.

Simon's elder brother Jacob is agent to his father in Lisbon; another, Benjamin, at risk of his life, sends dispatches from Terceira to Sir Francis Walsingham, and yet another, William, is also a soldier at present with his uncle in Youghal. That Simon lodges at Seething Lane and keeps Sabbath with his maternal uncle Hector Nuñez is by reason of a great and bitter quarrel that he had with his father over the financing of the Portuguese Pretender three years gone.

Unlike William or indeed his father, Simon is neither large nor well-built nor robust nor graceful, though his hands can be deft enough. Becket once watched in amazement as he made a pen from its pristine feather from stripping to curing in a sand bath to fitting of the reservoir, all in a couple of minutes and that while talking of something else.

In this roaring world of gold and steel and sugar plate deception, he is, to his sorrow and knowledge, a babe in arms. His tailor, hatter, cobbler, all cheat him, for he longs to cut a good figure at Court, though he draws the line at padding his meagre calves. By the strenuous efforts of his Aunt Leonora Nuñez, a Jewish girl of a good Bristol family was brought to London to see if she would consent to be betrothed to him. At the meeting, Simon sat and flushed and paled by turns, while the girl gravely questioned him and he could think of nothing to ask her.

At length she pointed from under her veil at his chain of office, slim but gold that he had worn proudly to show her, and asked if it were not a chain that bound him to the Queen. When he answered lightly that perhaps it was, and that he was honoured to be held captive by such a Queen – a very courtierlike speech – she dropped her veil haughtily. Alas, she said to him in Portuguese, she would not and could not light two candles on the Sabbath with a man that was bound to another woman, nor yet the Queen. And so the girl, Rebecca Anriques, returned to her family and Aunt Leonora tutted, sighed and continued to speak darkly of the dangers for a man, being unmarried, in such work as his and such a place as London.

He is a poor coney in this world, to his father's fury, and yet, although his father will not see it, Simon Ames is a very panther of the *Mundus Papyri*. It is neither pity nor magnanimity nor a desire for Dunstan Ames's friendship that causes Sir Francis Walsingham to keep Simon so closely by him. Nor is it only his family's connections and conduits to the secret sea of money that is ruled by the Italians and the Flemings, who swim its tides and harvest its little gold and silver fish in their great ships, the banks. It is that Simon has a nose for pattern, an eye for corruption, and like a dolphin swims the swells of little signs in ink, an Arabic cabbala that destroys here and resurrects there, by pouring money on gold-droughted soils, from Genoa to Amsterdam to the Exchange in the City of London and thence to the New World and back again.

Wherefore came Dr Nuñez's packet of letters from Isaac Pardo in Rouen, who took pleasure in corresponding with a cousin he had never met, that never asked foolish questions nor misunderstood his complexities.

Once being carried to Simon's cubbyhole in Sir Francis' house at Seething Lane, it was a couple of hours' work to unfold the letter's meaning couched in a numerical cipher.

At the end of it, he held in his hands a list of all those who had cashed bills of exchange upon the bankers at Rouen. And here also was an intricate argument of Isaac's that traced some of the bills to the Spanish king's credit in Antwerp and others through the Medicis to the Vatican. Some of those nourished by the trickles of gold were known to Simon: an agent of Father Parsons' and Charles Paget, the Queen of Scot's man in France. He had been in England in September, while Walsingham was futilely busy in Scotland, but slipped away again before he could be caught. Now it seemed he was whiling away the time in northern France, with a steady and considerable need for cash. Simon made due note of the fact.

And then, among all the usual offenders was one that might have been passed by if old Cousin Isaac had not loved his work so well. It was a bill of exchange drawn upon a small Amsterdam bank of perfectly Protestant religion, but it was backed by a bill drawn upon an Antwerp bank that in turn was backed by gold at a Florentine bank.

Simon breathed deeply and smiled as he read. Here was the name of the man that drew the money, one Mr A. Semple, and here again was Mr Semple upon a list of passengers to Dover that he dug out of a chest, one of the accounts that was regularly supplied by the tunnage and poundage men in exchange for a little blindness on Walsingham's part.

Simon began writing his report in his swift clear Italic and when it was done he sifted it to the top of a pile of further papers and locked it in his chest. In his mind the shape of something was forming itself from the brute chaos of number and conjecture and again he smiled.

He prays morning and night, he keeps the Sabbath when he can, and Passover and the Feast of Esther and the Day of Atonement always. He eats no pork and discourses gravely with his uncle and his Dutch Rabbi and yet, if you would flense him to his soul, there would be found not indeed the God of Abraham, but another austere and demanding and lesser god of Number. All about him is a shifting unsolid world full of heated seekers after gold and power, which leaves him often breathless and bewildered, but beyond them and beyond also that Platonic shadow

43

of a shadow, the *Mundus Papyri*, is the purity and clarity of number which thrills his heart. He had rather read Euclid and Pythagoras and Maimonides than the Torah. In this strange idolatry, if the numbers tell him a thing is so, then in his mind, it is so. And if numbers cannot be attached to it, then is he in severe danger of believing a thing not to exist at all. This sin he shares with Philip of Spain.

His meditation upon Isaac's information was broken by a hesitant rap on the door.

'Enter,' said Simon irritably, glaring at the small scrawny man hitching at the back of his worn canions and shifting from foot to foot in the doorway.

'I am John Holder of Sir Christopher Hatton's household,' said the man. 'I heard your honour was giving silver for any tales of one called David Becket.'

'I am,' said Simon, hesitating only a moment, 'if it is the man I seek.'

'Two yards high, a yard broad, black-haired, given to drink and melancholy . . . .'

'Shall we talk over some beer?' Simon asked.

At the Green Man in Beer Lane, John Holder sucked at his drink and muttered his tale in a resentful drone, blinking at a bottle of miraculous bones hanging on a far wall.

By some means as misty and marshy as the lands of Holland themselves, John Holder had gone to fight the Spanish in the mid-Seventies, one of Prince William of Orange's many unsuccessful armies. Somehow he had mislaid himself and fetched up among a small band of deserters and dispossessed Dutch farmers roaming about the country near Haarlem. Becket was their captain, a younger, lighter man, pleasant enough to Holder at first finding. Becket had given Holder drink and food when he might have starved with his brother and fellow-deserter amongst the bleak gutted fields.

'It was all sham,' he said, glowering into his beer. 'There he was, well set up, he could have lived comfortable enough if he chose with the men he had and the weapons, but no, he had to go stirring up trouble, the treacherous bastard.'

'How could he have been comfortable?'

'Take a village under his protection, live off their tribute and keep away any others that came to take it. How else can a man live in a God-forsaken wilderness? There were troops Robin and I could have fallen in with and had a girl each and no troubles with the Spaniards to make us move on.'

44

'Were you not there to fight the Spaniard?'

Holder spat on the sawdust. 'Only fools or officers think that and even them not for long. Some captains take Spanish service for three months, or as long as the fat-arses in San Lorenzo take to send their pay and then go off to Prince William to do the same to him. Or they did. But that's the hard way.'

'Why?'

Holder rolled his eyes. 'Because they might hang you for desertion if they catch you. Jesu, where were you born?'

'But one can also go and live with villagers?'

'Live off them. That's the best way if you have enough men and arms and powder. After all, what are they for?'

Simon nodded agreeably and ordered more beer.

The tale wound interminably on, chiefly composed of complaints that Becket insisted on daily training, moans that any man who took any girl unwillingly was flogged for his first offence and unmanned at his second . . . . 'He only did it once, to show he would, did it himself too, the bloody bastard. Hicks died of it . . . .' Becket, it seemed was a tyrant, particularly when drunk, who made his men run about and build fortifications to no purpose merely for amusing of the Spaniards and worse. Then there was the final and crowning indignity.

'He *stole* a gunpowder mill?'

'Well, not stole, you could hardly run away with it, being the size of a village and the mill itself worked by wind. But we took it in the dark of a spring night in the mist and slit all but two of the Spaniards' throats that we kept for their advice and then we all must dress up as Spaniards with Hapsburg red sashes and all, we were working harder than Indians, turning out more gunpowder.'

'For the Spaniards?'

'There were two kinds. One was first grade, fine meal, and that went off north by boat. The rest was tenth grade at best, too much charcoal and sulphur, not enough saltpetre, the kind of stuff that gives a filthy stench and smoke but no power at all to drive a cannon ball.'

'For the Spaniards?' Simon breathed.

'Ay, in exchange for the saltpetre and sulphur and charcoal they were sending by barge, we sent them back bargeloads of shit.'

Simon laughed.

'What's funny about it?' demanded Holder indignantly. 'The work could kill you with no fires and soft slippers day and night and the dust getting into your food. I cannot look at a hard-boiled egg now.'

The tale floundered deeper into the marshy tracts of Holder's brain, culminating in Becket's hanging of a man for dagger-fighting in the magazine.

'It was a matter of honour,' said Honour. 'Baynes had every right to . . . .'

'But surely metal in a gunpowder store . . . ?'

'Honour!' shouted Holder, banging the table with his fist. 'It was a matter of honour.'

Here the tale descended to a bitter mumble into Holder's beer.

'There was a mutiny?' Simon asked, to clarify a little. 'Becket was thrown down from his office by the men for his tyranny and then . . . .'

'Ay, the bastard. Treacherous, murdering . . . .' Tears were forming in Holder's eyes. 'Sweet as pie by daylight, swore to abide by our soldiers' council, offered to talk to the Spaniards for us since he spoke the language, repented him of driving us so hard. . . . Sweet as a maiden, opened up his private store of wine to us, even got us Akvavit from one of the villagers and then . . . the cunt . . . the . . . the . . . .'

Holder was snortling tears back up his nose to hide them.

'He what?' asked Simon, leaning closer to hear. 'He left a slowmatch *where?*'

'He blew us up!' shouted Holder, spraying Simon with beer and spittle. 'Sky high. Lit the sky for miles around, brought the Spaniards down on us, and poor Robin and Simkin and Gateside and Bill all in bloody rags and bits . . . . Only I was having a piss, so I was . . . . Oh God.'

Thoughtfully Simon left the inn, leaving John Holder to pay the reckoning out of his generous two crowns payment, since he seemed well towards passing out there. It was about two in the afternoon and Simon's head was swimming with beer and the closeness of the inn and Holder's foul breath. After a moment's hesitation at the lateness of the hour, he set forth across Tower Street, cut through St Dunstan's Hill onto Thames Street and thence past the fair square tower of St Magnus onto New Fish Street, and so to London Bridge where the watermen gather upon the inward side to pick up those who prefer not to shoot the bridge. There Simon found a boat to take him upriver to the Temple Steps.

XII

Who would breathe easier must travel out beyond the walls where London wears thin upon the countryside, where women may launder their linen and dry the shirts upon hedges, and the city milch cows are kept and the windmills are and the market gardens to feed the milling folk within the walls. Beyond Temple gate and over the filth and noise of Fleet Street it is only a little walk up the dusty ruts of Chancery Lane, past the old house for Convertite Jews where the Lord Chancellor now is, and so to Holborn where in summer an eastern wind will bear a heavy burden of roses from Sir Christopher Hatton's garden at Ely Place. All about are gardens and sheep runs and for the work of another five minutes' walk there lies Gray's Inn, a far northern outpost of London, where rich men's sons go to learn the law and some salting of courtesy. Walsingham himself spent four years there, debating points of law after dinner in their new hall. But most of the would-be men of law in the place take no pleasure in their Arcadia of gardens and orchards and sheep and moan constantly that they might as well be with the peasants in Islington for the distances they are from any place of interest, meaning Cheapside, Smithfield, Westminster and the stews of Southwark. For indeed so did I once bewail my lot and further the price of good tailoring and half-decent ale, for none of us know when we are happy until the time has gone. There I once shared a chamber with Becket, and neither of us learnt much law for I was too addicted to poetry and he to fighting to spend time arguing points in bastard Norman French.

And here came Simon, entering humbly by the small gate onto Gray's Inn Lane, so all who even saw him supposed him a mere clerk bearing a message. He had a seal of Walsingham's as his authority, which he bore with him always, but first he walked about quietly in the fading winter light until the candles were a-lighting in the hall. Then he went back to the gate and asked for the Keeper of the Rolls and so smiling all the while, a nervous hesitant smile, was brought into the great man's presence in his inner office where the records were kept. Simon took his hat off.

Master Dawkins expanded a little, a large heavyset man with a good stomach and two chins weighing down his ruff.

'Ah well, it depends,' he said when he had listened to Simon's request. 'How far back would your master have you go, Mr Ames? We have had good records here only in the past 15 years and . . . .'

'Not so far, Mr Dawkins, a little way only. Twelve years. If I may see the rolls for 1572, I would be . . . .' A small purse containing silver was taken from Simon's belt and set down quietly upon a table, seemingly forgotten by him. Mr Dawkins smiled. 'For Sir Francis, Mr Ames, nothing is too much trouble and always a pleasure to serve him. These are the rolls for 1572 and if I may enlarge upon them, you have only to say . . . . Will you take a pipe of tobacco?'

Not to be discourteous, Simon took a drink of the smoke and gagged on it. No matter how he tried, he could not take to his uncle's medicine. In his own room was a new clay pipe and four varieties of tobacco bought at hideous expense and not one but made him feel ill.

Through the tears in his eyes he spelled out David Becket's name and noted the names of all who began their studies in that year.

'He is the man I am interested in,' Simon said at venture. 'Would you remember a Mr Becket?'

'No, I fear not, Mr Ames.'

Simon looked at the little purse still on the table and raised his brows. Mr Dawkins laughed. 'I see so many young sprigs. Could you describe him to me? Well, sir, I wish I had a penny for every tall broad hard-drinking swordschool wastrel I have seen. Went to fight in the Netherlands about '73. Ah. Yes. Becket.' Dawkins stroked his beard. 'He began the fashion, I believe, of climbing upon the walls and pissing upon passers-by. They could never get in by the gate fast enough to catch him, save one man that climbed the wall directly and fought him upon it. He had a fine skill with the sword and I saw him take his Free Scholar's prize. Never had any money. Hm. What has he done?'

Simon smiled and spread his inky hands. 'To my knowledge, he has done nothing, I am merely sent to ask. Is he a Catholic perhaps?'

'No, he came to chapel with the rest when he must and went to pose about St Paul's Walk when he need not. I never heard him have any thought upon religion at all save what manner of sword it was that Peter cut off the Roman's ear with.'

'Or one of his friends . . . ?'

'Hm . . . . The Strangways boys were recusants but no one thought much of it then, the laws being lighter and the times less straitened. We would not admit them to the inn now. But then there was Anthony Fant and Nicholas Sunningdale and Pericles Howard and the rest, all steady enough for the true religion. Even Howard was, being of a collateral and Protestant branch.'

'And what became of them?'

'The Strangways boys? One went abroad, the other went to Court which is all I know. Fant I think came back from Holland made a bad marriage and inherited his father's estate. I have seen Sunningdale since then, for he came to buy me a quart of beer a few years ago when he was at Westminster Hall in a dispute over a parcel of land his grandfather borrowed from an abbot who had no business lending it. The suit is still continuing.'

'Do you know why Becket turned soldier?'

Dawkins laughed and patted his dagger. 'Why does any man? He was no lawyer, that's sure. For the stink of the moneylenders' breath on his heels, why else, not wishing to end in the Clink. Mind it was Becket's fault he had no money, he spent every penny he had on swordschool lessons, drink and gambling and if he had no pretty little punk in some Southwark stew, it was only for lack of time to go seek her. One of them was used to write poetry that was better than the common run, not Becket, but another of his cronies. I forget which it was, but he would climb a tree and declaim from it when the drink took him that way.'

Dawkins was filling another pipe and Simon began gathering up his pens and inkbottle and scraps of paper.

'Was it Becket that dressed some of my Lord Burghley's cattle in scholars' gowns and brought them in to eat the flowers . . .' meditated Dawkins as he fished a coal out of the fire with the tongs. 'Or was that some other young drunk? I fear I am of little help to you, Mr Ames, I have seen such a parcel of fools and young gentlemen, they become as hard to tell apart as a crowd at the bullbaiting, and as noisy too . . . . I remember one . . . .'

XIII

In sickness and pain are all men made equal and no man is more alone than he who wakes in pain in the pit of the night. Jerking out of a dream of hell to find no devil spitting him for roasting upon his trident, Sir Francis came to a darker hell of a house full of sleeping folk, a manservant snoring upon his trucklebed by the door, that must not be woken by his master's moans.

They know so little, the doctors who tend to Mr Secretary Walsingham. Only the Marrano physician Nuñez has the courage to blow gently into his beard and admit he knows not why Sir Francis' humours should be so unbalanced that they make a quarry of little stones inside him where gravel has no business to be. To be sure the common folk rarely suffer from the stone in their bladders, no doubt because their humours are more robust. Some apothecaries would recommend a permanent Lenten diet, without meat, but Nuñez will have no truck with such empiric nonsense and puts his faith in purging to bring out the stone quickly.

Even the Queen's Moor in his sickbed cannot protect himself from those who love to doctor and so is he victim even to his daughter who will bring her father foul nostrums of parsley, meadowsweet and saxifrage to take when she bears in his papers in the morning.

But morning is far away, the night cold despite curtains and the pain roiling about Walsingham's vitals forbids sleep. Every time he is laid low by the stone, he thinks about cutting. There are barber surgeons who travel about the country cutting men's guts open to take out the stones. If their patient lives then will he recover completely, no more to be laid low. Lying with his fist clenched into his stomach and his teeth in the pillow, Sir Francis thought between spasms about the business. Could he have the fortitude to suffer his bowels being opened while he lay bound, and his bladder emptied utterly of gravel. Would the relief be worth the agony? And it was a gamble, he might not survive. He is not a young man and his life is of too great use to his religion, his Queen and his country. And so each time his revolving thought comes back to God and His riddling ways. If he must suffer the pain in the faint hope that he could find some doctor who could cure him with alchemical and astrological science, then why must he do so? Could not Christ who raised Lazarus, likewise heal him? He tries not to ask so impudent a question, but there it hangs between him and the tester above, limned in fire. If God has laid upon him alone the burden of fighting the machinations of the Pope and the Duke of Guise, wherefore did He not also give a body able to bear it?

And then shame strikes in its thorny tooth, for the God that gave the burden gave the body too and knows its capacities. Did He not make a mere woman into the Queen of England and then imbue her with an understanding and a knowledge and a courage impossible to women so she might be His Champion? And although she waver frequently from the true straight path that Walsingham would have her tread and although she was not and now will not marry so she may be mastered and taught her duty, still she has ruled as Queen for twenty more years than any betting man gave her when she succeeded to the throne. Thus having made almost a man of a mere woman, can God not prop up Walsingham's own frail temple of fleshly earth a few more years if He so choose, and if He choose not, then who is Sir Francis to question Him, who can draw up Leviathan with an hook?

Which manly stoicism lasts until the next fierce stab of the stone in his guts and he must turn his face into the pillow to muffle the whimper rising in his throat. And the worst of it is that no matter what the doctors do there will be more of this until at last he pass a pebble through his privy member in blood and agony and can at last be at ease.

Here is a certain black comedy, for in truth the Queen's Secretary is with child of the stone.

At last come Dawn's rosy fingers to the sky, or rather a slow winning of pale grey over dark grey and the manservant woke to light the fire and draw the bed curtains and bring his master a thin gruel that he could not touch, being too wearied with pain.

Upon this morning, Sir Francis took also some wine and a tincture of laudenum and assuaged his thirst with mild beer before his daughter entered. She was small and with the look of an Italian señora, her father's swarthy looks alchemised to ivory and ebony of her hair, a little peeking modestly from her white line cap, and her step still perky in despite of her burden. Beneath her stays lies Sir Philip Sidney's babe and an ironic thing it was too, for here she was, married in September but two months

51

before (at extraordinary expense) and at least six months' gone with child. Walsingham is very far from being a fool and can calculate: on the one hand so proud a belly so early in a marriage must be a scandal, and yet upon the other, there was a wry satisfaction to him in that his daughter had understood what was needful to bring the Queen to give her permission. If the means were sinful, yet the ends showed daughterly respect for her father: Sir Francis had chosen carefully and well for his daughter, finding her in Sidney the premier knight of Christendom, one whom scholars and sovereigns liked at first audience. Why the Queen had seen fit to prevaricate and attempt to prevent so fine a match by delaying her permission, only the God who made her knew.

And Frances was a beautiful child, a good daughter. She bent and picked up his nightcap from the floor and put it back on his head, smoothing down his damp hair. But Oh God, she was carrying a posset cup.

'Must I drink it, Frances my dear?' he asked.

'I think it can do no harm and may do some good,' she said, gravely smiling. 'This has feverfew in it with the saxifrage which I think may help the fever. Will you not take a sleeping draught?'

'No,' he snapped. 'I must speak with some men of mine. How can I do God's work if my wits are addled?'

'Why they are already, sir, if you are feverish as you look and therefore I pray you to drink this down.'

He drank, his belly heaving at the bitterness and lay back fighting to hold down the brown brew. She brought out a piss bottle from under a napkin and gave it to him, before retiring quietly.

He had a very ugly looking water ready for her when she returned bearing bags of the papers that were turned out relentlessly by his clerks, not to mention the further tides of paper that flowed in by courier from his friends in foreign lands. He took the latest batch, ruffled through them and raised his brows.

'Nothing from Mr Ames?' he asked.

She was busy tending to the fire. 'No sir,' she said. 'Was something expected?'

'I had heard from Dr Nuñez that there came a packet from Rouen. I am surprised Mr Ames has not . . . . Well, no matter. No doubt he is busy about the Mouse.'

'Poor Mouse,' Frances said. 'To be watched so closely and not to know it.'

'Hmf. He has no need to work for the Duke of Guise, he is an English-man born. He has brought it on his own head.'

'Mr Ramme, Mr Ellerton and Mr Phelippes and Mr Ames are here about the same business,' said Frances. 'My lady mother has received them and they are breaking their fast. Is Mr Hunnicutt to attend? Or Mr Dowl?'

'No. We are not to be disturbed unless the French come.' He tried a thin smile and she smiled back at the old family joke which made him think that Sir Philip was a lucky man if he only knew it. But here came another spasm and though he tried to hide it, she saw and came to give him her hand to crush. When he could speak again he saw tears standing in her eyes. She looked very gravely at him for a long time: if he could have thought of the right words in time, he would have asked her what ailed her, why she was so quiet of late? If it was the babe weighing heavy in her or had he hurt her, but before he could draw up the strength, she turned away. The piss bottle was stoppered and hidden under the napkin.

'I like this not, father,' she said. 'I will send Mr Hunnicutt's boy to Dr Nuñez with it and ask him to come again.'

She was leaving, the velvet hem of her gown making the universal song of women, a swish and a rustle and the occasional flash of feet and ankles. She had turned out so well, given his own swarthiness and her mother's ugliness, he could smile upon her again, despite the threat of the doctor's coming which would leave him drained and exhausted from purging.

And now there was Mr Ames in the doorway, framed in honey panelling, staring at him as if a question in his mouth had been popped back into his head by the strange sight of his master smiling so fondly. Then Ames came back to himself, made his bow and stood aside to leave room for James Ramme, William Ellerton and Thomas Phelippes. Ramme was a tall elegant scoundrel, Ellerton round-faced, phlegmatic and a goodly part quicker in his wits than he seemed, Phelippes was an elderly tired man above fifty with the candle-ruined eyes of most clerks and a mind that could make a secular kind of magic with the Arabic signs for number. He refused to use Roman numerals, to which Burghley still cleaved faithfully, declaring with quiet immovability that numbers which lacked a zero were not worthy of consideration.

Ramme stroked his beard, looking quietly pleased with himself. Ames however was pink about the tips of his ears and more inclined than usual to melt into the tapestries upon the walls, which was made easier for him by the ridiculous cut velvet of his short gown. Walsingham sighed inwardly that Ramme was at the clerk-baiting again.

'What is the news of the Mouse?' he asked Ramme. Ramme shrugged his well-tailored shoulder, grosgrain silk slashed with taffeta, a dark ruby red upon cramoisie, black hose, black boots, and a well-set up gentleman that had taken the Queen's eye once, only to lose it again because he could not dance and sang (as the Queen said) like a poxed pig. Ramme however was not aware of this disaster and thought extremely well of himself.

'He makes his errands as usual,' he said now, 'three this week unto the Spanish embassy. One into Blackfriars, one to Fleet Street.'

'And the French embassy?'

Ramme exchanged a glance with Ellerton. 'Sir,' he said unhappily, 'I cannot conceive we could have missed him and he has not been near the French embassy since September.'

'That you have detected.'

'There are five watchers and Mr. Fagot upon the embassy, and eight upon the Mouse . . . .'

'I am aware of the numbers, Mr Ramme.'

'But sir, he has no secret passage from the house, for we have searched it covertly, and not a soul goes forth from there that we do not observe and also follow.'

'Then he must meet someone that goes unto the French.'

'But every man or woman he meets, we also observe . . . .'

'In short, Mr Ramme?'

'In short sir, I cannot think it is the French we need fear.'

Sir Francis clenched his fists about the sheets and prayed for patience to bear with fools. 'Who was it brought death to the Huguenots on St Bartholomew's day?'

Ramme looked at the floor and began to toe the rush matting like a schoolboy.

'Who claims his niece Mary of Scots to be the rightful Queen of England?' No answer. 'Who has plunged his land deeper into the bloody swamp of civil war with every year that passes? Who is a master plotter and deceiver of men, who is in league with the Devil and Antichrist the Pope . . . . The Duke of Guise, by Christ, the bloody-handed Duke of Guise!' Walsingham was shouting and paused only because he was over-weak for anger. He could not muster enough blood for it, he thought, he was bled white.

There was a tap on the door, Frances slid her body round it.

'Your pardon, gentlemen, but my husband has asked if he may borrow

Mr Ames to be his clerk for his Accession Day entry. His cart is in disarray, he says, or the papers are . . . .'

'Mr Ames?' Sir Francis asked with courteous eyebrows.

'When would Sir Philip have me attend upon him, madam?'

'This afternoon, at Hanging Sword Court.'

Ames suppressed a small annoyed sigh, then bowed. 'I should be honoured, my lady.'

'Thank you.' She smiled at him, gracefully imperious. 'I am sure you can deliver him of his entanglement.'

'What had you planned for this afternoon, Ames?' asked Ramme nastily, 'More sword-schooling?'

Ames blushed scarlet and mumbled.

'Sword-schooling?' asked Sir Francis, as he was meant to, but then no man becomes a master of intelligencers without a good salting of plain curiosity.

'A most commendable step,' said Phelippes unexpectedly. 'Having been worsted by footpads, Mr Ames is resolved not to repeat his sorrow, and has found him a swordmaster to learn him the art of defence.'

Ramme sputtered slightly. 'A great fat ox of a man: I would I could sell tickets for the entertainment of watching them about their work, it would make the monkey on horseback a mere stale prank.'

'Mr Becket is a Provost of Defence,' said Ames. 'Perhaps you would care to play him at the veneysticks? And he has soldiered in his time.'

'Oh?' asked Sir Frances. 'Where?'

'In the Netherlands.'

'On which side?' retorted Ramme. 'Spaniard? Orange? French?'

'That is something I myself desire earnestly to discover, for if he is clean of Popery I think he may be brought to your service, Sir Francis.'

'When was he in the Netherlands?' asked Ellerton with his normal vacant smile.

'In 1573. He was among the first batch of English to go to Flushing that year.'

'Hm. Ask Walter Morgan then. He reported on the expedition for my Lord Burghley and he is a cousin of Captain Morgan.'

Ames bowed his thanks. 'And are you progressing well with your swordplay?' asked Mr Phelippes kindly. 'I found I was no hand at it, never strong enough, but I suppose it is all passadoes now.'

'Ha, no fear,' sneered Ramme. 'No doubt of it but the man is an English schooler, all sword and buckler play and none of your Italian pig-stickers.'

'He knows both rapier and broadsword,' said Ames stiffly. 'And says he gives not a fig for styles English, Italian or Spanish but practises one he calls the Bastard style which is less pretty about the flourishes but more certain to kill your man.'

Ramme laughed. 'Why, we shall have you on the boat to Holland next, a man of the sword no less, with such a teacher. If you are become a man of action, why sit you in your little den with your spectacles on your nose? When will we hear of you capturing a traitor?'

Sir Francis coughed. 'Each to his own humour, Mr Ramme,' he said severely. 'If you were as valuable a conner of ciphers as Mr Ames and he as excellent a priest-finder, then would I exchange your tasks. As it is, I am well-enough pleased with Mr Ames, and not so well-pleased with you Mr Ramme, since you have not yet found the conduit from the Mouse which leads to the French embassy.'

'Sir, I told . . . .'

'Mr Ramme, it is my guts that are stricken by the stone, not my mind, I remember what you said and I say unto you, go out and find how the Duke of Guise threatens us.' His voice had risen again and here were his fists in a knot and his jaw clenched . . . . Wherefore in God's name must he suffer these fools and obdurate halfwits who could not see where Antichrist's Champion threatened all they knew, all they held dear? The Huguenots in Paris had thought themselves safe enough.

'Now Mr Phelippes, I must have converse with you. The rest of you have my leave to depart.'

There was a dull red pain around his back again as Phelippes approached with his sheaf of broken codes. Sir Francis caught a glimpse of Ramme and Ames in the passage, Ramme making believe to draw his rapier and run Ames through with a running passado as they went by Frances.

XIV
Summer 1583

Here are sharp shards of memory, one of them mine. Agnes Fant in her chamber, by her wax candle, slowly unwinding red silk from its paper to a little carved yew bobbin, faster and faster, her fingers catching on the thread. But the paper is blank. She frowns at it, then remembers again and holds it carefully over the candle flame. A faint scent of oranges of Seville steals by her and the writing comes clear on the hot paper.

Her children standing by their nurse Dorcas: Elizabeth, Edward, Mary and an invisible gaping hole where Catherine should be but is not, being dead of smallpox last winter. Each in turn kisses her, kneels for her blessing and then they watch solemn-eyed as the groom hands her up to her pillion seat behind him on the broad Rhenish mare. At her signal the small party of horses and packponies steps out upon the road to London. An urgent matter concerning the river meadows in dispute at Westminster Hall calls her to London, though the business of summer presses hard upon the household. Her husband is at Tilbury already, brainsick of New World fever, overseeing the fitting out of a ship in which he is a partner to find the north-west passage. The steward is shaking his head: in his experience lawsuits at Westminster can always wait, the harvest cannot. But women are prone to odd fancies particularly when with child, as they usually are, and if she must go, then go she must.

I saw her come in through Ludgate and make her way to the Fants' London house, adorned by piratical old Sir William with chimneys like elephants and the same badge over the door. She was white with weariness and swayed as she stepped to the ground, but she stiffened herself and went into the shuttered house. Her lord and master was in lodgings at Tilbury and there had been no time to send ahead to have it aired.

And here at last is a man who comes striding quickly through the streets, a plain wool suit on his back and a plain hat on his head, his hair dyed from red to brown in reversal of the whore's usual progression, his eyes the twin of Agnes' own grey but colder and hotter also. In by the servant's gate and up the stairs to where Agnes sits by the window, her hands clasped upon her stomach. She sees him and her pale mask of a face melts into happiness and welcome, her arms open as she rises to greet him. But his expression stops her and humbly she kneels to her brother, ardently calling him Father and asking for his blessing. He does not correct her. So touching a reunion between my brother and sister.

Outside, hidden in an alley, I puked in a gutter.

XV
Autumn 1583

I was dancing in Fleet Street with the Lady Moon, dressed in red and white spirals, but a barbarian set upon me, beat me over the head and snatched my lady from me, which caused her to melt back into a mere barber's pole. The barber roared at me for spoiling his sign by uprooting it, made to beat me with it but thought better of that, seeing he would do it more damage. Cursing me up hill and down dale he went back to his shop and was greeted by laughter and applause from the beards and lovelocks awaiting his shears.

The ballad seller Edmund Dun that was the cause of my trouble carried on down Fleet Street, still singing his latest song, Tom O'Bedlam. And Tom and I picked ourselves up out of the gutter and followed him covertly, plucking turds from my worn tawny velvet rags. As I watched from under an awning, came a man to buy the ballad, and a girl giggling, and another man. Then a fourth that seemed in no way different, but to him the ballad seller gave a sheet also from the breast of his doublet. So it went on, and the song battered about my head so I was hard put to it to keep the reins and martingale tight upon Tom, and the Queen Moon flitted balefully above us and smiled a white smile.

'I know more than Apollo
    For oft when he lies sleeping
I behold the stars at bloody wars
    And the wounded welkin weeping.
The moon embraces her shepherd
    And the Queen of Love her warrior,
While the first doth horn the star of morn
    And the next the heavenly farrier . . .'

And here came another boy with his penny clutched tight, well dressed in a dark blue cloth livery, seamed with velvet and his linen blackworked with swans, his face pale and anxious and his hat pulled down on his forehead. He too got a sheet more than a ballad for his penny and ran off in haste.

Would we follow the ballad seller or the boy? Tom was still held fast by the ballad and would not heed my urging, so perforce it was the ballad seller that became our quarry. He sauntered on and bought a pie from a cookshop and beer in another place, and at last he came to Hanging Sword Court that still has a rusty sword hung up like an inn. Once it was a swordmaster's school, now it is a joiner's yard and rings with hammering and banging. They were bringing a two-wheeled cart in at the gates, with much shouting and toing and froing. The ballad seller stood by the gate and watched with the pie stretching out the pocks on his dark cheeks. A man detached from the throng of workmen and the two nodded to each other. Then the man turned and so I saw his face clearly for the first time in nine years, and although it was changed by a scanty reddish beard and by the years, and by the stain of Bedlam across my memory, yet still I knew him. It was like a crack of thundering light from the grey sky: this was Adam my brother, this was Lucifer, this was Cain that put me in Bedlam, this was my brother that I stole apples for, that I fought for a box of sugared plums, this was my brother that put me in Bedlam Hospital and gave the kind warders there leave to flog the madness from my mind and the flesh from my bones and the poetry from my heart. That they failed was none of his doing. Adam who once followed me about like a puppy, who hated the shame of my madness, that I taught to spit, who put me in Bedlam to rot whence I sent him the poem I became. I had not known for certain before that it had reached him.

What could I do? Down swooped the Queen Moon and ripped open my head, and out burst Tom like Athena in all his wildness and a great fit of angels fell upon me, a cartwheeling hurlyburly. Deep within I knew that capering and shouting about Lucifer at the gate of Hanging Sword Court was not the best plan, but Tom would have it otherwise. At least I could take enough grip upon my bolting brain that when ghost-faced Adam raised his arm and pointed at me and called some men watching to catch me, I fled down an alleyway and ran for the warren of Whitefriars where they lost me.

My father held to the Catholic faith in his heart, I think, but dissembled it outwardly, and went to church in the village to avoid fines. My mother was a fair trembling earnest creature held steady by a steely spit of religion and the fires of hell forever roasting at her conscience.

59

Nothing could be good that was not perfect, nor would she hold compromise with any Devil's thing. I never saw anyone work so in prayer, she laboured at it like a man digging a ditch, so she might almost have been a Puritan but for the rosary denting her plump palm. Adam she bore in pain and difficulty, and Agnes nearly killed her: I stood, a newly breeched boy of seven on the stairs, hearing her shriek and curse God while Agnes fought her way into the world. I was beaten for lying when I asked why she had spoken so wickedly of God.

When I went to Gray's Inn and then to my cousin at Court, there was still a grateful blurring and a mist over religion and besides, I was never fanatical and found it no hardship to go to church since I must. For that she cast me from her, in her last days, weeping salt over my apostasy. Adam cleaved to my mother; Agnes' faith I know not, for she went to learn huswifery with my mother's sister, Catherine Nisbet, and by then I was already losing sight of myself in the many-coloured Court.

My angels and the Queen Moon have taught us many strange things about God since the deathcart brought me out of Bedlam with Becket cursing upon the driver's seat like a broad thunder-browed Charon. Now I will go to any church that lets me in, but alas the churchwardens like me not and drive me out like the dogs and hens, and so am I bereft of God's Word entirely. God Himself, however, has not deserted me, nor never will, only stone churches and their stone priests and their strange stone words.

But the Court. . . . Her Majesty has built it into a reflection of herself, a brilliantly coloured, never-still maze, cast around and about and set by the ear by this whim and that, this faction and that, but somehow keeping a steady purpose and a steady beat about the bejewelled small woman at the heart of it, Queen Elizabeth.

I served her before strangeness overcame me, like hundreds of other young men, and I was none so bad at dancing and my new tawny velvet suit matched well with my chestnut hair. Twice she smiled upon me and gave me her hand to kiss and cast the glamour of her beauty on me. But it was not that which sent me mad, for all the sonnets I wrote protesting that it was, only the falsity of the Court itself. It was lie built upon lie but powdered and prinked to seem like a greater truth, artfully conceived by the Queen to entertain restless men. It seemed all to be a dream, with its lurid clash of silks and velvets and jewels and ruffs all in ceaseless motion through the stench of shit and piss, until it was so bad the Queen went upon her progress while her palaces were cleaned. It was a dream full of Arcadian poetry, but with no firm ground underfoot, as if the floors were made of marchpane and sugar plate and wet comfits, and so I lost my footing and fell through. In truth I know not what I did when I first fell in a fit of angels, ran stark naked through a banquet or some such no doubt.

Being in England at the time, Adam came post-haste to London and as weeks passed and still I raved, still bothered by angels, his fine drawn spotty face thinned to a blade with anger and horror of my strangeness. Five doctors pronounced my fit of angels unbreakable by music and only fit to be chained, so he was transformed into Cain, into Lucifer. To be sure, it was not that he would inherit of our father in my stead if I were lunatic, indeed I was lunatic and it was through no agency of his. But a little truth might have salved the hurt I think, a little truth and rest. Instead he had me chained and born squawking like a trussed hen to a little narrow stone cell. There he gave the Bethlem hospital warder silver and rights upon me to try whether he could beat the madness from me and if not to hold me safe until he should come again. Then, keeping my secret, telling none of my old friends how I fared, Adam took ship again for France. He never came again to Bethlem gate, only sent money twice a year.

I know not why any think that madness can be flogged out of a man: it was when I lay in pain and hunger upon straw and ordure in Bedlam that my angels truly befriended me and Tom brake forth and the Queen Moon took me into her care. All else had deserted me and left my soul to fall in coloured glass pieces like an old church window when a Reformer puts a stone through it.

Thus raving of past sadness, Tom lay in a gutter in the Temple, while Ramme sat in an upper room in St Paul's Wharf and watched a house. Once under his eyes a kitchen girl bought a ballad. Once a boy came running a message and dabbled juice from an apple tart upon the black swans on his linen. The pity of it was that Simon was too good a conner of ciphers to be there, or he might have recognised the boy. Perhaps not. Ramme did not: for all his upcurled beard and ringlets, he was not a noticer of pageboys.

At last Simple Neddy that is my near neighbour in Blackfriars found Tom capering and white with exhaustion by Temple Bar again. Being simple he had no fear of madness, so he took me by the hand and spoke kindly and haltingly to me in his thick muddy voice, and bought me a pie, and so gentled the angels from me. And yet I could not sleep as he begged me and could not drink the infusion he made of herbs to calm me. Had I truly seen Adam, or was he too a particle of my soul, broken out into the world and seen by no one else? The world is so uncertain, so apt to change.

I broke away from Simple Neddy's creaseless hands and crept back towards Hanging Sword Court, well hidden by the crowds. The gates were open, a concourse of people crowding round to see a sight. In the midst of them walked a tall slim man with a long face a little like an amiable sheep's, his hair a wispy pale brown, the perfection of his green doublet and hose and the knife-sharpness of the lace on his ruff shouting of the Court. Beside him trotted Simon Ames with a bundle of papers under his arm and his new gown not fitting across his shoulders, despite the splendour of its marten facings. I crept closer, hidden by a sawhorse.

'So you think he is pricing low?' asked the parfit knight.

'Yes, Sir Philip, very low,' said Simon. 'Mr Broom's labour costs are at the going rate, but all his materials are good cheap, to say the least.'

'Jesu, if this is cheap, God keep me from an expensive place. And two shillings in the pound is the best your cousin can do?'

'He was not easy to persuade at that level, sir.'

'Only my father in law's credit saved me, no doubt.'

'Sir Francis Walsingham's credit is always good.' Simon's face was smooth.

Sir Philip Sidney shouted with laughter. 'Which shows how little anyone knows. Do you know what he lost on the Duke d'Alençon business? No.'

'Surely Her Majesty will recompense him . . . .'

'Surely she will,' said Sidney, now turned to gravity. 'It would be a very shocking thing if she did not. I expect she will let him kiss her hand at least. Mr Ralegh is plucking all the plums this year.'

Simon coughed and looked uncomfortable. Sidney strode ahead of him to where Richard Broom waited with his family in their best clothes, and his workmen behind him, and behind that the looming skeleton of the dragon, as if it were rotting in reverse, from death to life. At the Last Trump we shall all look like that. It was still and unhammered for the first time that day.

They moved around it while Mr Broom explained how a slender strong man would be employed to hide within the body of the dragon and rise up at the right time within its neck to play his part of ferocious beast and submissive servant.

'Hot work,' said Sir Philip, narrowing his eyes at the articulation of the neck, unheaded and half-completed. 'Have you found a man willing?'

'Yes sir,' said Broom. 'A distant cousin. Very reliable.'

'Is he here?'

'I can fetch him if your honour . . . .'

'Yes, if you would, Mr Broom. I must be sure that he can do what he is required to.'

Hidden behind a stack of timber, I watched as a child was sent running to find him. Meanwhile Sir Philip caused consternation by asking if the creature would have wings and if it did, would they pass through Temple Bar gate?

'Only I should be sorry to ride a beast that must come apart in mid-procession,' he said with a smile, running his finger in the socket where the wings would go. Broom spanned his fingers across the skeleton parts of the wings lying nearby, then scratched his head and asked the width of Temple Bar gate.

'Lord, I know not.' Sir Philip laughed. 'Only Her Majesty's new coach scraped its hubs on it a week ago and was stuck fast for a while and she was very foully annoyed by it, having been persuaded to a coach by Hatton in the first place, and being made sick by the bouncing in the second. Next time she goes to the Guildhall she swears she will go by river as any sane person would, and leave new-fangled Frenchified contraptions to the poxy French, by God.' His voice swooped into a mirror of Her Majesty's tones and out again, which was wasted on all but myself for none of the crowd had heard her curse, and knew only the voice she kept for crowds and speeches. Mr Broom's cousin came diffidently from the workshop.

It was my brother again, curse his cold eyes. He stood slouching, his hat in his hands, waiting to be noticed.

Sidney beamed upon him. 'You are Goodman . . . .'

'Stone, sir,' said Adam. 'At your service sir.'

By great effort I quieted my troop of excited angels and crept a little closer to listen. It is hard for a gentleman to act the part of a workman, but Adam was doing his best. I bit my sleeve to stop myself laughing for never was a prouder boy than Adam. But here he was making jerky ugly bows to all Sir Philip's party, the perfect picture of shy awkwardness.

'Mr Ames, will you give me . . . . Now then, where is a lantern, the light is bad.'

Simon took a lantern from one of the workmen and held it up.

'Goodman Stone,' said Sidney kindly, 'I have no wish to embarrass you, so I beg you will tell me the truth. Can you read?'

Adam's mouth dropped open, shut again. He swallowed and by chance did the exact right thing, which was to look wildly at Richard Broom, who nodded.

'Yes, sir.'

'I mean, more than your name and the Our Father. Can you undertake to read anything I show you?'

'If it is not in foreign,' said Adam, finding his tongue again.

Sidney laughed. 'Fair enough. There will be no foreign in it. Then you will not mind performing a small test for me, Goodman. Will you try and read this for me?'

It was some sheet advising upon the dangers of tobacco which Simon had happened to have in his penner. Adam took it, frowned and read it in a judicious drone.

'Excellent. I am heartily relieved at it, for I must ask you to learn the script I write for this dragon. When I have spoken to your master of the things the dragon can do, we will cast up an account of its actions upon the tilting day and in the procession and so work together. Will you do that for me?'

Adam ducked his head and muttered that he would, to find himself clapped on the back by Sir Philip and invited to come and inspect the dragon.

There were decisions to be made: should the head be gilded? Yes, said Sir Philip. Should the tail move? If it could, said Sir Philip. Who would buy the horses? Sir Philip would ask my lord of Leicester's advice, and try whether some experienced horses of Her Majesty's own could be used. Otherwise provision would have to be made for the accustoming of the animals to the noise and cheering of crowds, and further, had their trappings been made? Then he must consult his saddle-makers and soon. It should be samite for the dragon's wings, of red, that they billow when they move. As Master of the Ordnance, he could certainly undertake to have slowmatch brought up from the Tower to make the dragon's smoke, indeed most of the powder in the Tower was a better bet for smoke than fire, having been stored in the damp and peculated upon by the Ordnance clerks. Would Mr Ames see to it? Simon made another note on his papers.

And now, laughed Sir Philip, all he needed to do was beat Fulke Greville soundly at the Tilt itself and everything would be well. Greville had taken lessons from an Italian swordmaster, so as to know something of the Spanish style of fighting for his part as Philip of Spain.

'I hear you have your own swordmaster, Mr Ames,' he said to Simon, who blushed. 'What is his name? Basket, was it? Mr Hunnicutt was telling me of it.'

'Becket,' said Simon, easily in Adam's hearing although he gave no sign, 'David Becket.'

'What style does he espouse? Spanish? Italian? Or is he one of those rugged Ancient Masters that love only the English style and will hear of no other.'

Simon sighed for he had been asked the question at least fifteen times before by men struggling to hide their smiles. At least Sir Philip's interest was kindly.

'He said he learned in the Low Countries that the only good style was the one that killed your man and he cares not what they call it. He says that the Spanish is over stiff and formal and he makes no reckoning of their geometry, that the English is good for sport and tilting but is too kindly for killing business and the Italian is good, but throws too much upon the running passado and putting all upon one thrust.'

'I must meet this paragon. At least he would not have me studying of diagrams and numbers as poor Fulke has been doing. . . . Will you bid him attend on me after the Tilts, for I will have no time to see him before?'

Simon bowed and then scurried to catch up for Sir Philip was striding over to speak to Richard Broom once more. Behind him, Adam stood in his rough clothes, ignored and forgotten and biting his lip.

XVI

It was on the Sunday following that Ames went to find Becket in his usual haunt. Becket had done his duty that morning and gone to church with his landlady, Mrs Carfax, and was in a foul disputatious mood at the stupidity and length of the sermon.

'To speak of the Spaniard as it were of dogs or horses, and the French too, and to say they are not men but devils and say they have no stomach to fight true English in the next breath . . . Ptah.' He spat. 'Christ, I should like to give him a pike and stand him up against the tercio of

Sicily and see how the stupid windbag likes it. This beer is worse than ever.'

'Hm,' said Simon.

'Ay, give him a pike I say if he wants to fight the Spaniard, let him try it. I give you odds of the entire Court to a pound of turds he shits his breeches and runs like a rabbit. I know I did the first time.'

'You what?' asked Simon incredulously.

'Well, I held my bowels, but I ran along with all the others.' Becket laughed at Simon's face. 'You never saw so many English lose so much piss and vinegar so quickly, and by my reckoning any rabbit would have been trampled over we ran so fast. The Spaniards nearly burst their bellies laughing. Oh never look so shocked, Ames, we all went out to Flanders thinking war to be a thing like a tourney writ large, with no wounds but upon the head and shoulder glancing, so as to bleed a little and be romantical and brave thereafter. We none of us knew one end of an arquebus from the other, but we knew God would keep the Popish cannon fire from touching us. We learned better. To see your friends shredded to meat before your eyes, now there is a good lesson in God's will.'

Simon nodded and bit down on his thumbnail abstractedly. Becket nodded as well, sighed and tipped his hat to three dice players in the corner. One of them came over to invite Becket and his Court friend to play, but he laughed and refused.

'Never play with that man nor any he introduces you to,' Becket said covertly to Ames when the bones had begun their clicking again. 'He can switch you a bale of highmen to lowmen and back and you would swear he was only scratching his head. As he is now, see. Keeps them in his hat.'

'Mm,' said Simon blinking short-sightedly at him and tapping his fingernail on his goblet. Becket sighed again, eased his broad arse back into the inmost corner of the booth and put his boots on the table.

'Wake me again when you have made up your mind about whatever is addling it,' he said, untying the bands of his ruff so his chin could rest easy on his noxious shirt. Simon blinked at him and found himself thinking that the ruff looked remarkably like a greyish caterpillar with ambitions for Becket's jugular.

'Only I know not what to do,' he said at random.

'Ah.' Becket had not opened his eyes.

'Where to begin. Those footpads you rescued me from . . . . They were not merely footpads.'

66

'Bonecrack Smith has never been anything else.'

'Yes, but someone had hired them to kill me.' Becket opened his eyes, but said nothing, only listened. 'This is to do with my work in Whitehall which I may not tell in full to any man.'

Becket lifted an eyebrow. 'Never say you are one of Mr Secretary Walsingham's men?'

Simon nodded. 'Only a clerk at present.'

'Oh ay,' Becket drawled. 'And on the good and sufficient ground that whatever a man says he is at Court, he is generally the opposite, I hereby deem you Walsingham's inquisitor general.'

Simon flushed for this was nearer the truth than he liked.

'Is some Papist Mass-gabbler after your blood?' Becket asked. 'Or a Court caterpillar of Burghley's faction.'

'If I knew the answer to that I would hardly be speaking to you.'

'Hm.'

'A message came to me at Seething Lane, I know not how, that if I would know more of the men that attacked me, I must go to Brisket's Court near Bank End this afternoon.'

'Ah. Behind the bear-baiting.'

'Yes, well, it is a place I know not and to meet a man I know not . . . . It could solve my perplexity or it could . . . .'

'Solve theirs, as it were.'

'Precisely.'

'And you need a henchman to protect you?'

'Yes.'

'How much?'

'Eh?'

Patiently Becket said, 'In what weight of silver do you price your skin?'

'Five shillings?'

'Come now, Ames, you are a better man than that. Ten at least.'

Simon looked unhappy but nodded his head. 'Five now and five shillings . . . er . . . afterwards.'

Becket laughed. 'Done. On condition that you will be guided by me.'

XVII

Every Sunday afternoon there are hordes of folk new-released from Divinity with pennies clutched in their fists and but one idea in their heads, to cross from the north bank of Thames to the south and there to throw their money away upon the bull or the bear. For which reason there is never a boat to be had upon the river and so I went round by the bridge while saner men were hearing their sermons. There are more and looser purses to charity at the bear-baiting and the bull-baiting than ever at a church door where the folk are virtuous and have been listening to the Gospel upon the rich man and the eye of the needle. The whores at the infamous Bell even gave me a knuckle of ham once when it was raining and I had eaten nothing for two days: they said I was better than a painted sign for them, since they pointed me out as a man run mad for unslaked lust.

Becket and Ames were late for the fight, having first to make a visit to Barnet, Becket's pawnbroker, and then finding no boats. They joined the tail end of the crowd about the Bank where the barkers were still telling the fight for the afternoon (Harry Hunks and Tom of Lincoln were the bears) and ballad sellers and ticket touts and orangado sellers and cutpurses and others were as busy as June bees at the harvest of a flowering field of people.

They had no hope of a seat for all the boasts of the ticket-touts by the gates, but they might have crowded in at the barriers with the dog-fanciers and risked a fight if they shouted for the bear. Becket risked a fight in any case since he was well-known as a backer of bears, particularly Harry Hunks which was the first bear that had ever won him money. Though they milled around with the others, they made no attempt to enter in past the high round walls of wildly bear-painted wood. Becket paused at the sheds to admire Harry Hunks' glossy nose and coat and watch Tom of Lincoln being led out to battle. He was wearing his brave brass collar and roaring back at the yelps of the chained dogs, all straining to be next for the fight.

Beyond the bearsheds is a tangle of booths, alehouses, cookshops and confectioners for the supplying of hungry thirsty crowds. Becket was talking to Jardin the bearwarden of the sad falling off in quality of bears in latter days, even Essex-bred bears that were supposed to be so fierce. Simon hopped from foot to foot trying to see over a group of Germans from the Steelyard into an alleyway that snaked behind the booths.

Now an angel sang to me from the roof of the Bell, and so Tom climbed a wall and from thence leaped an alley to a balcony and went up and over the roof and along a gutter to perch like a new-grown gargoyle. The crowd in the bear garden quieted for a while to hear Tom of Lincoln's pedigree recited and the pedigrees of all the eight dogs that would fight him, and the odds on each severally and together.

There was a tingle of cooking smells from the cookshops along Bankside and Clink Street that tortured my teeth with the memory of beef and onions and mutton and mint. The trumpets sounded at the bear garden as Tom of Lincoln entered, standing on his hind legs and roaring at his supporters who cheered back.

From my perch I saw Ames buy an orangado and suck on the sugary juice in the orange skin, blinking about him with a frown printed deep on his face. He wandered down the alley, Becket bidding farewell to the bearwarden and following him. The bearwarden moved to Harry Hunks' cage and lifted the grill to put the leash on his collar and change a frayed strap on his muzzle.

Across Brisket's yard a window opened and a long black gun muzzle poked through it quietly. Even above the food smells and the reek of bears and dogs came that gritty taste in the air of gunpowder smouldering. Within the darkness of the window I could see a red glow of a match that lit up half an intent face and no more.

For once Tom behaved like a sane man. He stood up teetering on the gutter with a shingle in his hand, yowled like a pinched dog, threw the shingle. Becket was coming into the yard: he looked up, stared, caught the glimmer of match and the smell of it at one and the same time, launched himself at Simon.

But he was thrown up and backwards into Ames and both went down in a windmilling of arms. The crash of the gun was sunk in all the shouting and roaring from the Gardens like iron in the Thames. I lost my grip and slid laughing down an outhouse roof and into a dungheap by a bearwarden's pigpen.

Two more men came running from an orangado seller's door, swords in their hands. Becket rolled off Simon and scrambled to his feet, his sword and dagger guarding both of them. When he saw the two swords-

69

men he kicked a spray of mud at one of them and charged at the other.

The arquebusier had disappeared from his window and down in the yard was a confused mêlée of legs and arms and blades with Becket dodging and prancing between the swordsmen, a somewhat skittish bear. Simon hovered at the edge of the fight with his dagger raised like a Court damsel at a banquet, not knowing which stuffed fig to prick. He had sat upon his sword and broken it. Becket roared. One man had caught him from behind in a hold, under his arms from behind, levering his head to his dented chest while his face went puce and he kicked and bucked and cut behind with his sword. The other man dodged his kicks, yammering in foreign, waiting until Becket should tire.

At last I stopped Tom's fool laughing, stood up, went to the gate of the pigpen and opened it, just as Simon recovered his wits and kicked in the arse the one who was holding Becket. Becket elbowed the man in the stomach and flung his crossed sword and dagger up in a guard just as the other swordsman cut down on his head. Simon was shouting for help, two whores were leaning out a window in the Bell, laughing and picking sides and laying bets on better sport than bears.

There was a peaceful snore beside me. I looked and there was a pretty little piglet asleep in the dung. I picked him up and threw him at the man trying to spit Becket on his long rapier. He bounced off the man's leg, uncurled and began running about squealing like a small exorcised demon. His dam lurched to her feet, grunting angrily.

Becket was panting hard as he swapped blows, blood blazing on his leg. Now the arquebusier reappeared, he was propping his gun on a wall ready to fire again, but the angry sow charged into him as the nearest enemy and bit him on the calf. He screamed and kicked her, she charged, I jumped up and down and cheered her on. Simon was hiding behind a pile of barrels, dodging the ferocity of a swordsman who knew his business, albeit Spanish style. Suddenly there came from beyond the yard a closer roaring than the garden.

A vast brown furry body came thundering into the yard and rose on his hind legs, his bearwarden panting behind waving the broken end of a leash and cursing horribly.

The sow turned at bay and honked defiance at the bear; the bear, who was Harry Hunks distracted from his true business by the smell of blood, roared and clawed at the arquebusier. The arquebus went off again and blew splinters off the wall beside me. Harry Hunks bellowed and caught the man in a huge hug which splintered and crumpled the gun like a reed. The arquebusier disappeared shrieking behind great furry shoulders.

Becket was bleeding from the leg, had lost his dagger and was clearly tiring: both swordsmen were now concentrating on him, having accurately judged Simon a poltroon, but failing to see that he was not stupid. He got behind the barrels again, pushed mightily and sent them rolling through the yard. One cracked its lid open and the mead washed all across the yard, scandalising the chickens in their wattle run. The sweet honey smell brought Harry Hunks away from his thoughtful lapping of the arquebusier's ripped skull and he shambled in a puzzled way towards the source of it, swaying his great head from Becket to the two swordsmen and back again. They could not keep their eyes from him and while both were glancing nervously behind at the bear, Becket ducked down deep on his haunches under a whistling blow. He came up again, catching a rapier's hand-guard with his left hand and wrenching downwards, while the blade in his right hand went up under the man's armpit and through his lung. Now he twisted his sword out and turned to the third attacker with all his teeth showing, and the man backed off and ran.

Becket saluted the bear with his red sword. Harry Hunks snuffed, grunted and then dropped to all fours and began lapping at the raw mead running about the cobbles and flagstones. The bearwarden crept up to him cooing, 'There there honeypot, there, there, babykin.' The bear ignored him.

'Now·look at him,' snarled the bearwarden. 'You have only ruined the afternoon, my master, no more. He will be too drunk to fight and have a sore head in the morning, poor sweeting. I cannot stop him having his fill now, can I? You should pay for the loss of trade, you should . . . .'

'Kiss my arse,' said Becket pleasantly, bent to clean his blade on his kill's small round cloak and paused with a grunt as if someone had punched his middle. His face whitened and his breath rasped.

'Shite,' he said, and stumbled over to a still standing barrel to prop himself. The muscle of his thigh under his ripped canions was quivering and jumping where the rapier had scored him and the front of his doublet was strangely dented. Nearby the arquebusier lay with his head mainly ripped off, while Simon blinked down at the swordsman who had coughed out his life at last and lay glaring at the grey sky.

'I wish one of them could have been alive but wounded,' he said shakily.

'Oh Christ.' Becket began to laugh and then coughed and swore, his fingers gripped around the hole in his leg.

Simon shook himself, put his unmarked dagger away and came to Becket. The other bearwarden had appeared at the entrance to the little yard with a bowl of honeycombs, trailed by a crowd of fascinated boys

71

and trulls come to see what the noise was. Not many had heard though, as was of course intended.

Harry Hunks caught scent of the honey and swung his head that way, undecided which would be better and already weaving a little with drink. The sow was nosing her piglet back into the pen; she too sniffed at the fumes about her.

There was a moment of balance and then Harry Hunks grunted happily and followed his bearwarden's coaxing to the honeycombs, leaving the sow to slurp at what mead was left, which was very little.

'There there, Harry my love,' said the bearwarden reattaching the end of the leash. 'Here's honey for you. Ahh. And you, you whoresons, you take your devil-damned fights away from here and if I ever . . . .'

Simon Ames had retrieved the dagger and was bending over Becket's leg. Now he straightened and tried to speak, but Becket interrupted.

'We'll go now, Jardin,' he said. 'This was none of our doing . . . .'

'I give not a fig for it, get your arses out of my yard or I'll set him on you, see, poor little love . . . .'

Becket and Ames limped forth and out onto the Bank through a narrow alley. By the river Becket leant against a wall and gripped his thigh while his hand rusted with blood.

Simon whistled desperately for a passing boat, waved his arm. The boatman glanced them over, saw their case and rowed speedily on. The third that came by gestured at Molestrand Dock and came in there, so Becket must up and limp over to it, past the disgruntled early leavers from the bear-baiting. Now I came up, dusting pig dung from my backside and took his other arm and so with his weight slung between us, we got Becket into the boat while the waterman watched and pointedly asked no questions.

'Where to, sirs?' he asked after a decent pause.

'Petty Wales Steps, by the Tower,' Simon answered.

The waterman sucked his teeth. 'There's the bridge to shoot and the tide on the ebb,' he said thoughtfully, 'which I would never recommend unless you gentlemen was in a hurry.'

Tom hooted and made oink oink noises like a pig in a trough as a comment on this. Simon was already at Becket's dented cuirass, the buff jerkin open and pulled off.

'And a notorious loony in the boat too,' added the waterman, leaning on his oars. 'Not but what I'm happy to take, if he is aiding you gentleman, but there will be extra on the fare for cleaning of the cushions and . . . .'

'There is a shilling waiting for you if you take us to Petty Wales.'

'One and six.'

'Christ,' snarled Becket, slapping at Simon's hands, 'I shall bleed to death while you cheapen for the fare. Waterman, take us to Temple Steps and I'll go to Mr Gifford.'

'And then there is the law against duelling,' said the waterman reflectively.

Ames's pale brown eyes glittered a little. 'Not to mention the regulations of the Watermen's Guild on charging and overcharging. One shilling if we come there whole and soon.'

The waterman spat a gobbet into the river. 'Where did you say, sir?'

'Temple Steps,' growled Becket.

'Petty Wales,' insisted Ames. 'My uncle knows an excellent surgeon that is no pomade-merchant but learnt his trade from the wars . . . .'

'God's death, that's all I need, some pissant butcher that buried his lessons in Flanders . . . .'

'And served with the tercio of Lombardy.'

'Oh,' muttered Becket, subsiding a little. 'He might be good, but . . . .'

'So which is it, sirs?' asked the waterman politely.

'One shilling, to Petty Wales.'

The waterman nodded. 'You will be wanting speed, then,' he said as he whirled the boat into the central racing current. 'Else the gentleman might be true as his word and I'll thank you to keep the blood out of my cushions, if you please, sir. Central arches I think.'

'London Bridge on the ebb,' moaned Becket as Simon strapped his soaked handkerchief to Becket's leg with his belt and pulled tight. 'Jesus God.'

'I'll thank you not to blaspheme in my boat, sir,' said the waterman.

XVIII

It was a few days later that Becket lay on clean linen in a pale golden oak-panelled room, the sweet smell of clean rushes upon the floor and a clean shirt on his back, borrowed from Dr Nuñez who was nearly as broad. His nightcap had been blackworked by Leonora to match the edging of the shirt and he sipped excellent spiced sack from a silver goblet. Simon was sitting nervously on the edge of a stool by the bed, picking at the crewel work on the curtains.

'Have you found the bastard who set the ambush?' Becket asked.

Simon frowned. 'No. The dispatch bag the message came in was unsealed and it had lain several days in Mr Hunnicutt's office, he tells me. There were several dozen could have come at it by their business and another fifty that could have done so with a little guile.

'Seek out your enemies.'

Simon shrugged and did not answer, being intent upon demolishing a worked bird. Becket leaned back on the high pillows with his eyes half-hooded and his broad face thoughtful.

'The men at the Bear Garden – who were they? Spaniards?'

Simon shook his head. 'One Flemish, one German. But you said one was trained in a Spanish tercio . . . .'

'By his drill at loading his arquebus and the way he held it. But there are plenty who have served on every side.'

'Neither of them have connections with the French embassy.'

'I said the Spanish . . . .'

'Nor the Spanish.'

'So all your enquiring has gone nowhere.'

Simon lifted his hands, palms up and let them drop. 'How do your wounds feel?' he asked timidly.

'Excellently well. I think I shall leave tomorrow.'

'Uncle Hector said he thought a full week in bed and then . . . .'

Becket laughed at him. 'Christ's blood, Ames,' he said, 'I have marched ten miles within three days of worse wounds than these – a couple of broken ribs and a pigsticker in my leg, no more – and without benefit of a surgeon too.'

'But why leave so soon? My uncle surely told you that you are welcome to stay for as long as you wish, he is mighty pleased with you for saving of my skin and my aunt also . . . .'

'Ah your most beautiful graceful exquisite aunt. I am in love with your aunt, Simon, she brings me possets and caudles and five covers of meat thrice a day and indeed I would be up and out today, only she will let me have the tasting of her French biscuits if I can stay one more night, the blessed woman.'

Ames frowned anxiously. He had brought Becket up from Petty Wales, past the Tower to Poor Jewry, bleeding copiously into the cushions of the horse litter and his breath sounding as if it passed over broken glass each way. He preferred not to think of their passage under the bridge, with the waterman whooping and shouting as he spun his little boat from one roaring rip of white water to another, the slimy stone piers with their fretwork wooden fences looming on either side like sea monsters. Simon had never suffered any kind of wound though he spent his childhood racketing from one illness to another, consoled only by a copy of Euclid. He was nervous of Becket's bravado, being accustomed to staying in bed when told to do so. But then he recalled seeing Becket stripped for Señor Eraso's work of strapping and sewing and heard his uncle growl that this one had more in his past than soldiering alone. Simon was also capable of reading signs in scars, and he had never before seen a gentleman with the marks of a lash on his back. But Becket had been unconscious, seemingly dead to the world, except for the time when he growled and struck out at Señor Eraso.

Becket was speaking. 'Eh?' said Simon.

'I asked if Tom behaved himself?'

Ames nodded. 'He ate all the leftovers in the kitchen and then slipped out the door when we were busy with you. I have seen nothing of him since.'

'So long as he fought no devils here.'

'No, he spoke kindly of the angel standing guard at the doorpost and then muttered some nonsense about Lucifer and a dragon before he went. Uncle Hector was sorry for that, he had a medicine he wanted to try on him, with a tincture of monkshood aconite in it. Why are you in such a hurry to leave if my Aunt Leonora's cooking agrees with you? She will be enchanted to cook for a man who likes to eat, she has enraged the cook already with her fussing about in the kitchen and she . . . .'

'Are you wearing the cuirass we found for you?'

'Why no, I . . . .'

Becket rolled his eyess. 'You said you would be guided by me. If you cannot track them home to their lair, whoever has made an attempt twice will make it thrice. Shall it be third time lucky for them?'

'It chafes me. And it weighs . . . .'

'Of course it chafes you and weighs a lot. It is made of metal, what else would it do? You will take a while to accustom to it, all men do, but think on it: if there had only been buff leather and doublet between me and the arquebus ball on Sunday, where would I be now? Arguing with Tom as an angel at best. And that arquebus ball was glancing at an angle and it knocked me down, bent mine own cuirass beyond help of an armourer and still brake my ribs. Wear two or three shirts beneath it, or even a padded jacket, but wear it. Besides, there is no lightness and simple pleasure like the taking off of a cuirass at last.'

Simon nodded. He understood what Becket was about. 'You are fixed on going, then?'

'I am.'

When he had taken his leave of Becket, Simon conscientiously went into the room that had once been his and put the cuirass on under his doublet, struggling and sweating with the straps, until a page came by and he beckoned the boy to help him. He already had two certain amulets from his Aunt Leonora's cook to protect him from murder, but like Becket he saw the force in putting his faith in forged metal. But beyond the discomfort, wearing such a thing beneath his everyday clothes made him feel cold and bewildered. Aside from executions and a little cockfighting, most of his knowledge of killing and violence was second-hand, belonging to reports from the *Mundus Papyri* where it could be properly docketed and filed. Now suddenly he seemed to have stepped over some hidden boundary and into the outlands of a world where swords made meaty red holes in flesh and arquebuses poked from windows. It was like knowing of lions from bestiaries and then seeing the real creature in the Beast House by the Tower.

XIX

Sir Francis was running through the night of Paris, gasping and sweating, pounding through the red mud of small crooked alleys, the howl of the mob behind and before him, trapped in a maze of buildings and sheds, tripping on corpses. Men with torches crowd through a tiny arch, catch sight of him, shouts and roars of triumph, the drumming of feet behind and he turns a corner to find a dead end. Beside him is another alley, leading away from the trap, but fear has turned him into a mere human animal, his reason lost in brute terror. He scrabbles at the wall, beating it with fists, then whimpers and screams like a woman as the Duke of Guise, his linen spotless, his fleshy clever face impassive, leaps forward to stab him in the back, the kidneys, the belly, and the mob howls around him.

'I am certain he will void it soon,' said the Duke of Guise, sprouting a beard and a long physician's robe of dark red brocade, his accent changing from French to Portuguese. Dr Nuñez rumbled in his beard. 'These spasms, the fever, the delirium . . . . All are signs that his body is working to right its humours!'

'He is on fire.' Ursula's voice above him.

'Naturally. The element of heat must accompany the dryness that forms the stone.'

'Then should we not cool him down?'

'We are working towards the crisis and it would be unwise . . . .'

Ursula's plain straightforward face, frowning with worry under her starched white cap, her white falling band under her chin, her pale skin mellowed by the mob of candles behind her. And here was Frances too, rising towards him from a river of crewelwork curtains, eyes like brown velvet, face like cream silk, lips an embroidery of pink, she should not be here, he had been negligent, she should be in England . . . .

Paris had seemed safe enough to him as Ambassador in the August of 1573. Some of the Catholics there spat on him in the street because he was English and because he was a Protestant. He pitied them because they were French and as Catholics, doomed to hell. Certainly there had been rumours that something was afoot, but at their last audience, the Duke of Guise, the true power at the French Court, had been so pleasant, so kindly, almost jocular. The talk had run upon weddings, Queen Elizabeth's and of course the wedding on the 18th August, between young Henry of Navarre and Marguerite de Valois. Walsingham had been quite sure the Duke could not know that the Huguenot Admiral Coligny was raising troops to take north to the Netherlands for fighting of the Spaniards.

It had begun slowly. Admiral Coligny was shot by an unknown assassin two days after the wedding, only saved from death because he bent to tie his patten. The King sent him men to guard his sickbed, expressing horror at the outrage.

Still Walsingham had had no inkling of the approaching storm. His wife Ursula was in Paris with them and their seven-year-old daughter

77

Frances. The boy Philip Sidney was visiting them on his way to Italy, a long gangling ungainly lad, hideously spotted, who somehow managed to make all men believe he was graceful and beautiful through simple charm alone.

Three days after the shooting, Coligny decided he would still not leave Paris. It was the feast of St Bartholomew, the 23rd August. Coligny died that day.

There had been gunshots and sounds of disturbance near the Louvre in the afternoon and although the King sent a nobleman to reassure Monsieur l'Ambassadeur d'Angleterre, no one had felt inclined to venture out of the little house in the suburbs of Paris.

As night fell hot air made a damp blanket upon the city to muffle the sounds of gunfire. There was a low universal murmur, speckled with the bright kettle sound of blades here and there, as if a Beast were clashing iron teeth. A wounded English merchant fell through the door and gasped the truth of what was happening: Catherine de Medici had called on the people of Paris to rise and destroy all the Protestants, and the rabidly Catholic mob was now destroying every Huguenot, every heretic they could find.

Time passed, a steady stream came to the door, some wounded and bleeding, most pale and shaking, their eyes blind with the killings they had seen. Some of the men wept with the horror of it, but not the women. There were few women, however: they could not run so fast as men and were easier, more attractive prey. There were tales of babes spitted on spears, children raped. Some of the fugitives were English, many only French Huguenots trusting that the one Protestant power in Paris could save them from the madness.

To Francis Walsingham it seemed as if the time of the Apocalypse was upon them, come like a thief in the night, when all would be slaughtered that bore no mark of the Roman beast upon their souls. At any time he half-expected to hear the terrible brazen clamour of an angel's trumpet above the roofs of Paris.

Ursula Walsingham broke open her storehouses and buttery to give bread and meat and drink to the fugitives, raided her stillroom for medicines and bandages. Walsingham himself stood upon the stairs, speaking more coldly than he meant, ordering all Catholics among the servants to leave at once, lest they be swallowed up in the wrath of their fellows. He did not see fit to mention that one of them might perhaps open a door that should be locked. The majordomo, M. Ricard, took leave of M. l'Ambassadeur on bended knee, swearing he would that same night, no matter what the risk, light candles to the Blessed Virgin for the safe deliverance of his master. Sir Francis nodded gravely, tactfully.

In Walsingham's own mind, this was the night when he saw clearly what he was, an instrument in God's hand, given Grace to hold cleanly to the truth. As the Beast of Paris rent and tore its own flesh, the English embassy was like a beacon of light in darkness, a place of prayer as men read aloud from Exodus of the saving of the children of Israel and from the Passion of Christ, in those behalf they hoped and hoped not to face their own deaths.

The windows were boarded, the doors barred, but all knew it was not a place to withstand siege. A torch in the roof, a battering log at the door . . . . In the hall where everyone was gathered fear grew and flourished into a thing to fear in itself, another creature stealing air and space from those hiding within. As the sounds of killing became louder and closer and there was a trembling upon an edge of hysteria, the beardless boy, Sidney, began to discourse upon notable sieges.

At first, Walsingham was annoyed by his laughing playful chatter – how they should divert the Seine and make a moat for the house, how they should make wings of the tapestries (which most appropriately told the tale of the sack of Troy) and fly back to England, how they would tether a cock to crow upon the roof and remind the Parisians of the treachery of St Peter. He had the children making a choir to practise their cock-crows; he began a riddle contest, and as the night tilted deeper on its way to morning, he found a lute and had them singing, first Italian songs fresh from court and then as the shouting outside and the sounds of flames became more distinct, Psalms that all of them knew.

There came a bold crashing on the door, a beating with a stick. Mr Hunnicutt had been one of the last to come in, dishevelled and bruised on his round face. He went to answer the knock. There was the sound of men's voices shouting through the porter's hole.

After a moment, the fog of words cleared and Sir Francis knew that they were demanding Monsieur Walseenam. Hunnicutt pretended not to understand although he spoke French very well.

Sidney was listening too, his face serious at last.

'Hide sir,' he said directly to Walsingham. 'Quickly.'

So hard to swallow in so dry a throat.

'If my presence is requested at Court, perhaps I may moderate . . . .'

'Would the King send for you with a mob? These want your head, sir, and they must not have it or we are all lost.'

He had stepped forward, catching Walsingham's arm in a familiar

79

fashion he had never used before, always in awe of him as most people are. In the rest of the hall there were men coming wearily to their feet, knives and swords being loosened again in their scabbards. A pale-faced girl with torn skirts picked up a dagger. An over-painted English merchant's wife, well-known as a crushing bore, hid three hollow-eyed children among her skirts.

'If they have me not, they might attack to find me,' Walsingham hissed at Sidney.

'You are the Queen's man. If they take you from here there is neither authority nor representation in this place. They will destroy us all.'

'I must not hide, I cannot. It is not fit . . . .'

'Listen to them, the leaders are noble, they know this is against all honour, but they are afraid of the mob. They have only promised to look for you, not find you. Mr Hunnicutt, tell them that three of their number may enter to speak with us. I pray you sir, trust me in this, I know it in my heart.'

How did he know? Yet his face so shone with certainty, Walsingham was persuaded against his own arguments, and so he hurried into another room, into a closet cunningly disguised by panelling, a jakes. There was Her Majesty's ambassador to the Court of France, crouched on the lid of the close stool with the stink of the night's fear rising up all about him. Our Father, he began in his heart, which art in Heaven, let my bowels not give way, hallowed be Thy Name, let the boy be right, Thy Kingdom come, let them not find me in such a place, Thy will be done in earth as it is in heaven, but let me not die if it is Thy Will, please God, but if I must die then let it be bravely, only let me not die . . . .

Beyond the door three French gentlemen came into the hall and asked, with bows, for Monsieur l'Ambassadeur Walseenam. Sidney, speaking excellent French, stepped forward and asked them if Messieurs had found him as the English had been searching for him all night and were now waiting for him and praying that he had not been killed in mistake by the wicked robbers in the streets. For indeed Her Majesty of England would be exceedingly angry if he had, even if it were an accident, ambassadors being protected and saved by all civilized rules of chivalry and diplomacy. She was a woman, but women were impulsive: she might even declare war.

Messieurs listened and heard the underlying threat that the boy managed to weave into his honeyed words. They thought upon it and saw that while their followers might take and ransack the house, they themselves were surrounded by men who might be pleased to do a little killing on their own account. At the end they would most likely be dead in a mere muddle of blades and furniture, no better than a tavern brawl, with no one to see any bravery they showed.

And so they bowed again and expressed their sorrow and regrets and their devout hopes that Monsieur Walseenam had indeed survived the unfortunate excitement among the people. The front door banged and was barred behind them, there was a shouted conference and then a muttering as the mob moved away to find easier quarry.

That was when Walsingham vowed that every sinew, every bone, every humour of his body would he bend to the utter defeat and overthrow of the Beast of Rome, as a thanksgiving for his unworthy deliverance.

When Mr Sidney came to find him, Walsingham shook his hand and was able to say drily, 'I pray you Mr Sidney, another time find me a sweeter hiding hole.'

Sidney laughed and then withdrew tactfully as Ursula came running to her husband, her square face chalk white, her hands shaking as she threw herself into his arms. It was unlike her, but so it was unlike Sir Francis to cling onto her in return, as if he was drowning again in a sea of fear, as if the sea he had dammed with a dike of pride had broached it and come roaring and foaming in, and she was his only rock.

Yes, I know what followed, for the Queen Moon had a hand in it. God made the flesh as well as the soul, and if Walsingham took his own wife like a trull upon the floor, all in a clogging smother of petticoats and rushes and a wild flood of joy that he was still alive so to do, what of it? But he has always been harsher on his own weaknesses than God will ever be, and even in his fever of the stone, he winced at the memory of how he celebrated his deliverance out of the lion's paw. At least he laid no blame upon the daughter who was born nine months after that night. She was always a light of his life, a symbol of his deliverance, a good gentle child. She died when she was seven and the loss has clutched at his heart ever since, for Walsingham believes God took her from him as a reminder to be about the business of fighting Popery, that it was his fault she died. But in truth he does not know this of himself and believes he no longer mourns her, indeed, he believes he is glad that she has gone to God untouched and in her innocency, with a carved white dove of virginity laid upon her short grave. He lies to himself, and God knows he lies. And so the many tears he will not shed turn themselves to dry stones and wend their way down through his body and out the wrong exit, making a riddle Dr Nuñez cannot read.

Ever since the night of St Bartholomew the Beast of Rome has spoken to him in French, the Duke of Guise has been the base enemy of Godliness. And yet, the storm of St Bartholomew fell upon him from a clear sky, when he was looking the wrong way, and so he runs again through the maze of plot and counter-plot, harried and hounded by the mob, lost and alone and a dagger in his back from an unexpected direction . . . .

The dagger shifts, probing his privy member, agony upon agony, the Paris mob howls about him, they are kicking him, stabbing his private parts, the howling rises to a shriek . . . .

And suddenly all was peaceful. His throat was sore, there was a dull throbbing below, but nothing to what had gone before. Ursula and Frances on either side of him as if he truly was a woman in childbed and they his gossips, Dr Nuñez covering a bowl and candles shining in darkness.

'It has passed,' he whispered.

'*Si*,' said Dr Nuñez, while Frances covertly wiped tears from her eyes. 'At last.'

'Thank God.' Walsingham lay like a baby while they lifted him and changed his linen and his soaked shirt and gave him another nightcap to replace the one he had shredded with his teeth. Always from an unexpected direction, always, that was the Devil's cunning . . . . He caught Frances' hand and saw his nails had left bird tracks across it, patted it in apology, but he had an urgent order.

'What time is it, what date?'

'About seven of the evening, the 4th of November.'

'Jesus, so late? Is Throgmorton still there? The Mouse, is he still in his hole?'

'I believe so, sir,' said Frances, her eyes darkening suddenly.

'Send for Norton, Ellerton, Ames. We must take him tonight, before dawn. Have them come to me at once.'

XX

Now the most apposite and physical time for arresting of a traitor is about the time of moonset, at the ebb of the tide, three hours before dawn when every man's blood flows thickly in its channels and his mind is clogged with melancholic humours and dreams. Alas, this melancholy infects the arresting officers as well, especially when they must stand about Westminster Steps waiting for a boat, with the rain soaking their hats and cloaks and the east wind chopping up the surface of the river like beaten eggwhite, tearing invisible holes in their clothes to writhe about inside with a chill finger.

The same tide that had carried them upriver to Westminster to get the warrant would take them back again. There was James Ramme and Henry Mall, Thomas Kinsley and William Henderson, being led by Mr Thomas Norton that the Papists call Rackmaster Norton, and Simon Ames also standing unregarded at the back of the group. Henderson, Mall and Kinsley were henchmen of Mr Secretary's own, large stolid men of a particular type that also makes a good dispatch rider, the kind that will stand steady if charged by the Wild Hunt and all the gods of Rome and Greece, a very English kind of Spartan.

Mr Norton stamped his feet on the thick wooden landing, and blew at his fingers, whose fingernails were as his always are, deep in the mourning of a fanatic gardener who cannot leave his precious damask roses to a clownish workman, but must dung them himself. He had stepped out of the uncertain pool of yellow lamplight, the better to see into the murk for the boat, while Henderson, Kinsley and Mall huddled up their cloaks over their ears and shared a flask of aqua vitae. Simon stood, sunk in misery, his own cloak tight about him, his nose a bright sore red with an endless drip of phlegm upon it and a fleabite under his doublet and cuirass which he could not scratch. Mall was disputing that a black cat was unlucky, having been blessed by one on his way to Tyrrel's game.

The figure of cats was a good one for such as they, he was thinking, for they had quietly watched a particular mousehole for six months while their particular Mouse trotted furtively to and fro and now, it seemed, was the time for a pounce and a little play before the hangman got his fee and the rotting heads upon London Bridge a new friend to converse with.

'Aha,' said Mr Norton, screwing his eyes into little wrinkles against the rain. 'Thank the Lord. At last.'

Out of the darkness and wet creaked the boat, gleaming sinister black on brown water, the wet of its sides catching only here and there the dribbles of light from the lanterns. At least it was large enough for all of them as well as the two halberdiers sitting in sodden miserable silence at the back.

The two boatmen brought the boat gently up beside the steps, rain-water creating a novel geography of rivers on their waxed canvas cloaks, and a Mare Novum in the bottom of the boat. Simon was last aboard, fearing the water and hesitating until he had to jump ridiculously like a goat and almost caught his new sword in the seat cushions.

'One of you must bail, sirs,' said one boatman in general. 'Because of the rain.'

It was Mall in the end who picked up the can and began scooping out water, while the halberdiers sat silent as if they had been graven in soggy felt. Simon sniffed and coughed at intervals.

The river was a rushing hissing living thing, the wind piling up the ebbing water in dangerous eddies and vortices. The one good thing about the whole business in Simon's opinion was that there was no question of shooting the bridge. He had no comprehension of the apprentices and Court bloods who shoot the bridge for fun, paying double for the privilege. At least their boatman was as expert as any other waterman, able to traverse the river at night as safely as possible. He was senior in the watermen's company, after long apprenticeship and mastery of the river, crowned by his induction, according to rumour, by heathenish rite involving some Papistical relic of Noah's Ark. He kept away from the banks where unauthorised invisible craft might be tied up in the murk, and aimed his prow with its pagan eye from one current to another to ease his labour. They could have been at sea for all they knew, apart from the occasional inkling of a great man's river steps or gatehouse where a lamp was burning. Even despite his cold, Simon caught the flat sulphurous taste in the air of the kilns in Scotland Yard, but beyond that nothing for a while.

Would his cold turn to lungfever? he wondered. There was no feeling in his fingers or toes, the tips of his ears burned despite his velvet cap rammed down on his head as far as it would go. He had fleabites round his ankles in the depths of his boots from helping Becket return to his lodgings. The fleas had welcomed them back with far greater enthusiasm than the landlady who had been on the point of reletting the room at double the price. The great brute of a rat that Becket seemed to keep like a dog had squeaked and skittered around the floor in delight at his homecoming. Becket had caught him up and stroked him, presenting him with one of Leonora Nuñez's biscuits, before setting him on his shoulder where the rat poked his nose in Becket's ear.

It might be lungfever. Within he felt as if the four humours of his body had all turned themselves to green bile and phlegm and the two had mixed together in the back of his throat to make a baleful new acid humour, unknown to Hippocrates or Galen.

Ancient trees were creaking together in the wind; they were passing Temple Gardens. Another solitary boat on the river, crossing north to south, returning a pale poxed face above a striped mantle back to the stews on Upper Ground, then lost in the darkness and the clopping water. And then they were past Baynard's Castle and at their destination, at Paul's Wharf, where the stationers bring ashore their stocks of foreign paper and ink and new type and rollers, and the ships take out printed books.

They scrambled up the slippery steps and found, for a wonder, that the men from the Tower were already waiting for them a little up the wharf, out of sight of the Mouse's hole, at the opening of Thames Street. They were a mountain range of five men, forested with halberds, fruited with lanterns. Now Norton met their leader and spoke quickly in a low voice, and Simon knew he was warning them that zeal for the Queen's cause should not blind them to the fact that live men and undestroyed papers are more use than a few mere corpses. When he finished and started up the path, all their clip-clopping pattens squelched and sucked in the straw and manure, sometimes scraping on raw cobble itself where the carriers of paper had worn a hole at a wonted place.

The house of their quarry was silent, a mousehold almost dead and seemingly empty, the door barred and bolted, the lower windows shuttered like sleeping eyes. James Ramme stopped suddenly, peered into the darkness.

'Lift that lantern . . . . . No.'

'Did you see something?' asked Mr Norton quietly.

'I thought . . . . No. A cat perhaps, or a dog. Too small for a man.'

They waited in the silence while four men climbed over a wall in the alley at the back and picked their way among hencoops. A hen woke, squawked, fluttered and then gave its deathrattle, its neck wrung for the Queen's sake, all in a few heartbeats of time.

At last Norton nodded to Henderson, who was hefting a woodman's axe, and the blade sank into the wood of the door with a great thudding crunch. Four more blows and Norton put his boot through the hole, lifted the bar inside and opened what was left of the door.

A servingman stood facing them in his shirt, wide-eyed, sheet-faced, clutching at his cods in the belief he was still dreaming.

'Master!' shrieked the man in a burst of spittle. 'Master, the Queen's m . . . .'

85

Mall's fist swung and the man tumbled over backwards, holding his mouth, still trying to shout. Kinsley blackjacked him thoughtfully. Norton was already up the stairs, two at a time, sword drawn, followed by Henderson and Ramme with his Italian rapier. Simon looked at the narrow stairs and heard the incoherent shouting and tinpot clashing of a desperate rearguard fight. He beckoned Mall and Kinsley from going up the stairs and choking them even worse with bodies and considered the very fine ceiling, symmetrically sprinkled with Tudor Roses and carved devices and all painted over in blue and rose and red and gold. The hangings upon the wall were but painted cloths of Brutus's founding of London before the Romans came, which could be bought upon Cheap Market and cost little, but the ceiling was newly gilded.

There had still been no squeal of outraged womanhood as the kitchen girl went home to her chandler father every sunset. It boded well to Simon, that they had the right place, if confirmation were needed. No woman born can keep her mouth shut, as is a well-known fact, and known to traitors as well as faithful subjects of the Queen.

Simon blinked at a very faint, light scraping above the ceiling by the door, while the noise of fighting upon the stairs grew more desperate. Norton was having a hard job of it, being hampered by the close walls and also by the enthusiasm of James Ramme behind him, trying to poke with his rapier over Norton's shoulder, and almost slicing his ear.

Quietly, Simon put himself in the shadows and nodded at Mall and Henderson to do likewise. The men in the backyard were watching the windows at the back for escapers, neglecting those at the front which were too high for a jump. Inside a carven red rose began rocking and twisting in its bed. A square of ceiling lifted, was set aside. Simon stood still, blood beating in his throat. A jerkin and cloak wrapping a sword and a dagger on a silver-embossed belt dropped to the straw.

Then came a pair of legs in good green and white paned trunk hose, wriggling their padding through the hole, followed by a somewhat over-peascodded belly of a fashionable green velvet doublet. The quarry swung and dropped quietly to the floor, regained his feet and reached for the door.

Simon's sword found a resting place among the piccardils of the man's collar. His hand twitched with tension and blood sprang from behind the man's ear.

'Good morning Mr Throgmorton,' Simon said quietly. 'I arrest you in the name of the Queen and upon Her most Royal Seal and Warrant, for the crime of high treason.'

XXI

In blackness and the smell of mice, the boy shivered and chewed his sleeve to keep silent while boots and pattens clopped about the house, searching methodically. He could hardly breathe he was so tight-packed into the space for hiding books, on his side, his knees wedged against his chest, his arms over his face and more mysterious terrifying papers hidden under his shirt.

'Ames,' came a loud confident voice. 'What are you staring at?'

'The linen press,' came a different, thinner voice. 'Its floor does not agree, can you see?'

'Too small for a man I think. Rap the boards.'

The banging came to one side of his head and passed through like a dagger. The boy froze, held his breath.

'It sounds solid.'

'I'll lever a board to make sure. By your leave . . . .'

There was a heavy thud, a sound of crunching, creaking.

'No, this is solid. Come, Kinsley has taken down some panelling and found another place, why should he have more than one. There are Mass things and *Agnus Deis* in it . . .'

'I am with you Mr Ramme.'

It went on for hours, broken by shouts occasionally when they found a thing that pleased them, and once when a cat scratched the man who found her hiding place on top of a bed tester.

The boy's stomach was growling horribly loud by the time the crashing about ceased and still he lay there, not knowing what to do. Wait until nightfall, Mr Throgmorton had said, stay there until then and if I can I will send someone to save you. If I cannot, you must save yourself and take the papers to the house you know. He had spoken so loudly and clearly and said it many times as he packed the boy into the space and locked the floor of the linen press in place.

At last it was nature that drove him out, a pressing necessity to piss. As he had been told at least three times while Corday fought desperately upon the stairs using a table as a shield, he pushed the solid block diagonally into the wall where there was a space for it. The floor of the linen press slid aside but one of the planks had been broken and it no longer went easily. He pushed and shoved, using his feet, gasping and sobbing with fear and effort until a sort of rage broke in him and the floor gave halfway.

Moments later he was out, dizzy with thirst and hunger and found a house smashed into mystery around him. He could not stand, but crawled slowly and painfully to the bed where the cat had hidden and found the chamber pot. After that he had no strength to do anything more and the room was bright with day and he was afraid of light now but more afraid of movement. Like any animal he looked for a hiding place and so pushed himself under the bed and curled up to cry himself to sleep. The cat joined him.

About the time that the boy had first begun to stir, Simon Ames sat in the dispatch room at Walsingham's house carefully holding papers up to the light and squinting at the crabbed handwriting with a plate of bread and cheese and capers forgotten by his elbow.

A woman's voice began, 'Mr Hunnicutt, I think they . . . oh, Mr Ames, I did not know you were here. I thought you would be attending on the Privy Councillors.' She smiled and bent to pick up the food he had knocked onto the floor. 'Are you quite well, you look tired?'

Hunnicutt tutted softly. 'So would you be, Lady Sidney, he has been up all night and will not get to his bed until late tonight.'

'My father uses you very ill, I fear. May I bring you a posset or some aqua vitae?'

'No. Thank you.' Even to himself, his voice sounded distant and cold. Frances Sidney sat down a little awkwardly upon a bag of dispatches and patted the dog that had roused itself out of the passageway to investigate the spillage.

'Know you what they are about, my lord Burghley and Sir Christopher and the rest?'

'Questioning the traitor Mr Ames caught this morning.'

Frances' eyes widened. 'Was it very dangerous? Did the Papist fight? Who was it?'

Simon smiled a little. 'We called him the Mouse.'

Her face changed, her hands flew up to her mouth. 'Oh no. Poor Mouse, so they caught him at last.'

'Yes.'

She was still wearing stays, he noticed, but they were loosened out to the limit of the laces. In his light-headed state he thought what strange unstable creatures women were.

Never mind their moods and humours which bent to the bidding of the Moon, but even their bodies could never be at rest, certainly if they were married and sometimes even if they were not. One moment slim as a bedpost, the next moment thickening and ballooning until they disappeared for some months and then reappeared, slim and corsetted again, with the babe either dead or gone to a wet nurse. Sometimes they never reappeared. Only the Queen herself remained always the same, but to compensate her gowns expanded and changed as wildly as any woman's belly.

Frances was moving again, uncomfortably, and now she tried to heave herself up. Hunnicutt gave her his arm to lean on because Simon was too thick-witted to think of it.

'Poor Mouse,' she said again. 'Will they torture him, do you think?'

She had tilted a little towards him, so he could see the swell of her breasts. Her skin had a gleam in it, as Aunt Leonora always said: if you would know whether a woman is with child, look at her skin first. Though with Frances there was no doubt.

'If he is wise enough to tell us all he knows without pressing, then no.'

She made a wry face. 'What do you think? I heard my lord the earl shouting when I came past the door.'

Simon put down the paper and turned to her. His own skin felt stretched against his face, as if it did not belong to him. 'My opinion is that he will not tell, he will be tortured, he will break and then he will be tried and executed.'

She pulled back from him as if he smelled bad. Stupid, stupid, he thought, she is Sir Francis' daughter, and he would have found some kind of words to soften what he had said, only she walked out of the dispatch room. After a moment, he turned back to his paper and began underlining some of the words in it.

XXII

Like Angels, Tom prefers rooftops. Even in the thinner spread suburbs beyond the walls, we who are held up by the Queen Moon can step across alleys from gutter to gutter as if over a brook, where the unangelled would look down, totter and fall. So I climbed the red lattices of the Nine Stones alehouse behind the French embassy in Salisbury Court, and strode like a giant across two alleys and a building site to come at Hanging Sword Court which is full of the sweet green smell of wood. In the centre stood the skeleton of the firedrake, half-clad with red and gilt scales, stretched across its two carts. All about it scurried men in leather aprons with chalk stuck behind their ears and truculent expressions on their faces.

At a table in a corner made by two rows of lattice-built planks sat Adam Strangways, once Semple, now Stone, always Lucifer, and the Master Carpenter Richard Broom, drinking cheap wine from pewter goblets. Before them spread out between the flagon and three offcuts was the delicately drawn plan of Sir Philip Sidney's precious dragon along with the Master's copy of the estimatio that had been accepted six months before.

"Imprimis: two carts of sound axles, one of six wheels, one of two;
item: seasoned timber, ash, elm and oak;
item: hemp rope and pulleys for the inner workings;
item: bellows for the puffing of dragon smoke and slow match to make it;
item: ii round silver mirrors for the flashing of the firedrake's eyes, made to swivel in their holes;
item: pay of one man to work within the dragon;
item: pay of one boy to work the tail;
item: viii strong cart horses, gelded, caparisoned in red silk, of Dutch breeding, to draw the whole . . . .'

The list covered five pages, marked out in a neat scrivener's hand. The sums of money were low, particularly for anything built for a courtier, where a wise master craftsman will mark up by a third to cover the time between presenting the bill and seeing any money. Master Broom had whittled his profit to the bone, creating Sidney's dragon for the honour of the thing. Or so he said to Sir Philip and also to his over-curious clerk.

I, who can peer between ill-built chimneys and see him talk with my brother Cain, I know that neither Sir Philip nor Mr Secretary Walsingham nor Mr Ames know, which is that this tall handsome old man believes he is a rightful king.

'Have you sufficient to cover the shortfall?' Adam was asking.

'More than enough,' said Mr Broom. 'Our friend is more than generous.'

Adam nodded.

After a while, Mr Broom patted the paper with his broad square hand. 'My daughter is happy that I am doing this work,' he said. 'She is proud of me, she says. She thinks me reconciled. She thinks I have forgotten my old tales as she calls them. Christ, if she knew.'

Adam smiled in agreement. 'You do not plan to warn her?'

Mr Broom shook his head. 'How can I? She is a heretic like her husband, worse than a heretic, Bible reading every day, great long sermons every Sunday, troubling her poor woman's brain with religious questions. Her children are growing the same way. They laugh at me when I tell them their ancestry.'

There is so little bar between past and present for me: squatting behind a pile of wood, part of me soaked in fear of discovery and the return to Bedlam, I could take the smell of sawn wood and return to the hall of our house when my father was having a priesthole made to content my mother. Broom came, whispered to be reliable and careful, and stripped the panelling off one wall of the parlour. He measured and considered and drew up a plan and began building the place while I slipped away from Fr Gurney's Latin lessons and Adam away from his nurse to hover about him and pass chisels and hammers and ask foolish questions.

He told one strange tale, towards the end, the two of us sitting together among blocks of wood that Adam was piling up to make a fort.

'People are not always what they seem,' he began. 'Have you ever heard the tale of Robin Hood and how King Richard disguised himself as a simple knight?'

I nodded and so did Adam.

'Now, can you tell me what is my name.'

'Richard Broom,' piped Adam, balancing a triangular block and watching it fall.

'You Ralph, do you know what Broom is called in old French?'

I thought a while, then shook my head.

'*Planta Genesta*. Planta genêt.'

Both of us sat there looking blank and he sighed. 'Do you know who was Queen before our present mistress, Queen Elizabeth?'

'Blessed Queen Mary?' said Adam, who had heard our mother talk of her.

'Good. And before her?'

'Poor King Edward who died of poison by the Lord Protector,' I said.

'And before him?'

Both of us together, echoing our mother again. 'Wicked King Henry the Eighth.'

'Never say so to anyone but me or your mother, but yes. He broke us from Rome and stole all the Church's land to give to his favourites so he could marry his trollop. Henry the Heretic. And before him?'

Again we looked blank. I could have spoken eloquently of the founding of London by Brutus the Roman and of King Arthur but this was in that middling ground between the stories of our parents and the mists of the past.

Mr Broom sighed. 'Henry VII the miser, who began as Henry Tydder, the Welsh nobody, ill-got of the Beauforts and the daughter of the mad King of France.' He spat into curls of shaved wood and Adam and I exchanged glances. 'And who was before him?'

'Brutus?' I asked.

He laughed. 'Well, at least they have not yet taught you to call him a hunchback. No, Richard the Third, Richard of York, Richard of the white boar, Richard Plantagenet.'

I frowned, very puzzled now. 'Why do you have the same name as . . . .'

He held out his left hand as a fist and I saw the gold ring, with the worn shape of a white boar enamelled upon it.

'He was my grandfather,' said Richard Broom.

'Did you ever meet him?' Adam asked eagerly, while I still groped about in puzzlement. Kings' grandsons were at the very least dukes or earls who went about in velvets and ermines and never did anything except fight exciting battles and jousts. Perhaps Mr Broom was too old for it.

'No,' he said to Adam kindly, 'Henry Tydder killed him in battle and stole his crown from him so he could be King instead. But my grand-mother was his leman and I knew her well and she told me stories of his Court and his terrible trouble and sorrow and how they brought him to a wicked sin. She knew his Queen and nursed their little boy when he died because of God's judgment, which was why King Richard lost the battle with Henry's army.'

This had lost us long ago, it was too like history, like Livy. I clung on to one trail. 'Your grandmother was not his Queen.'

'No, she was his leman. Kings may take other women if they wish, it is the custom.'

'But then your father was a . . . .'

'He was a bastard, true. But so is Queen Elizabeth since her father was not rightfully married to her mother when she was born. It seems no bar to the throne nowadays.'

His beard then was grey, not white, and his voice held an undertone which I now know was proud bitterness. The story went on and melted into the sound of hammering and sawing and his occasional grunts of satisfaction when a panel slid into its proper place. Fr Gurney came to find me and hauled me off to more painful calculations in Roman numerals. Adam stayed and struggled to carry his toolbag for him, and almost burst with pride when Mr Broom made a little hobby horse for him from offcuts. A few days later he disappeared from the house, leaving a little sawdust in crevices by the place where the priesthole was and no other sign, and that was swept out the next day with the old rushes. He went back to London in the carrier's wagon, carrying his ancient lineage and his pride in every turn of his head: he loved his work with wood and yet his grandmother had put poison in his mind, so that he could not abide the thought that he, a King's grandson, should be hammering nails and sawing wood in a small manor house for pay and not hammering heads in battle for honour. He had made it a moral tale in the end: England groaned under the scandalous oppression of a woman's rule and a heretical woman at that, all because the King his grandfather had been forced into a grievous sin by circumstances and conspiracies.

This was before our mother wasted her flesh into nothingness with the vehemence of her love for Jesus, when sin was a stealing of apples or a dirtying of ruffs.

Many years later I saw a portrait of Edward IV, Richard Broom's royal great-uncle, and saw there a resemblance, though the painting was badly done. The resemblance was still there in Broom's old age, in his height which was three inches above two yards, in the turn of his mouth and

93

the smallness of his eyes. Now as he sat and spoke to Adam, he looked very old and reverend, but his cheeks were fallen inwards with the loss of many teeth and his face had a grey unhealthy look and his bones seemed to be burrowing up through his thinning flesh.

'They laugh at me . . . .' he was saying to Adam, lines worrying his face, 'my grandchildren laugh at me, but still I would not have them touched by this. If we fail . . . .'

Adam patted his hand. 'We will not fail.'

Mr Broom stared down at the plan. '. . . I will not be here soon. The line ends with me, my daughter is no true descendant of kings, she takes after her mother . . . I will not see the end I think. Truly, I have no need of our friend's money.'

'It is here, we might as well use it to good effect.'

It was money that had traversed the sea in an egg of a paper banker's draft, money originally laid from Potosi where the wild men of the New World bleed and starve and die for its sake. Rather than risk one of the German moneychangers on Cheapside, it had been taken to Mr Tyrrel and sold at a discount.

Adam stood, Richard Broom stood, Adam touched his hat to the master in case any were watching. I scrambled across roofs again to watch my brother in his mean wool suit striding down towards Fleet Bridge with the ballad seller in his wake, and no connection between them but what mine eyes could see. If I could I would have gone to him and asked if he had lately hired an arquebusier and two swordsmen, but I dared not and I knew his answer anyway. And this was my brother, but this was also Cain, who put me in Bedlam, Lucifer with demons of certainty in his eyes, believing he served God.

And why could I not go to Simon Ames, and say to him, here is a man lately come from Spain, with silver and gold in his pocket and here he is building a magnificent float for the Queen's Accession Day Tilts and there, that place, is where he lodges? Ames would call together his English Spartans and there would be another morning raid and a search and so treason's egg would be broken and the meat spoiled. Yet how could I do so? Here was Cain, full of Lucifer's pride in his certainty and righteousness, so like unto Sir Francis Walsingham, so unlike, yet here also was my brother who would not cry when his pony threw him and he broke his arm, who sat in his baby's petticoats and listened while an old carpenter told tales of kings and lemans. And he was lodging with my sister.

94

XXIII

To an angel's eyes it will seem that when Simon goes to work with Thomas Norton upon some prisoner, he wraps himself in his mantle of ice, for a questioner must allow no touch of human warmth to undermine him. There are men who suffer from a brainsickness that causes them to delight in pain, their own or another creature's, men like Richard Topcliffe whom Sir Francis permits to operate a rack in his own home, asking no questions, hearing no lies from him because the man is an arch-getter of confessions. As Mr Secretary Walsingham works for the cause of right, he leaves the question of pity and mercy for those helpless in Topcliffe's power to Jesus Christ, who knows all causes and all men's hearts. And although Christ was Himself hanged upon a tree, Walsingham does not dread being called upon to explain himself on the Day of Judgment for all his acts have as their reason the protection and defence of True Religion against the power of the Beast.

But Simon Ames, being as they call them (and burn them) in Spain, a Crypto-Christian, he is less buttressed by faith. What he does is done in the end for the good of the realm, something which he is English enough that he takes it too seriously to think about it clearly or often. And it is further a tenet of his religion that he must serve loyally the land wherein he dwells and the sovereign thereof.

Yet there is a worm of doubt gnawing at his heart, beneath its saving ice, a snake of self-blame. Neither Walsingham nor any other of his men harbours such a thing, for they doubt not but what they do is not only for the Common Weal, but also the pains they inflict may perhaps save from Hell a poor soul now mired in the idolatry and wickedness of Rome. That which is armour to them is like sand in his hose to Simon, for it is a strange fact that a Jew may not persecute for religion's sake. But as Walsingham is blind to his own tears for his lost child, so also is Simon made deaf by his doubt. He does what he can, half-unknowing, he goes about his work as mercifully as he may. Though Norton and Sir Francis

95

both have doubts of him, they use him nonetheless which speaks well of his habit of mercy.

There is an element of the play to a questioning. In all of them that he undertakes with Norton, Simon plays the part of a mere clerk, a small man and a fearful one, a fellow mouse in the cat's den. In this Simon is well-assisted by his smallness and clerkish tendency to peer. At the time of the questioning of Francis Throgmorton he had also a plentiful issue of phlegm from his nose and a hacking cough.

It is cold in the Tower, all who have been there and survived – including our own Sovereign Lady – attest to and complain of the cold. In the round upper room of the Lanthorn Tower the combination of cold and damp is redoubled by the nearness of the water from the Thames in the moat, casting its ugly miasma full of the dirt of London upon all the poor prisoners.

Which made it damnably hard for Simon to hold a pen and hard to see also, in that the watery sun made scarcely an imprint on the dirty dim air of the room where he was working. He longed to call for a brazier, but that would have sat ill with his character and further comforted a prisoner who must be broken open swiftly, like an oyster, for the sake of the pearl of truth within him. It is true that not all oysters bear pearls, but they must nonetheless be opened, else how will you know which contain the pearl?

Francis Throgmorton was shivering and pale, inadequately dressed for the Tower in only his doublet and shirt, hose and boots. Simon was weighed down by two shirts, a padded waistcoat, his irksome cuirass, his doublet, a lined leather jerkin (the plain one without the cutwork) and a plain stuff gown daubed with candle grease. The doublet being of red grosgrain he looked like a fat robin redbreast upon spindly legs and he thought that there might be a spot of warmth near the struggling furnace of his heart.

At last he finished noting the circumstances of the arrest and the list of papers found in the house, put his pen down on the desk and flexed his fingers. Throgmorton sat before him on a low milking stool and stared down at the cold fetters on his wrists as if he had newly woken and found them there. At times he would lift them up as if testing their weight, a thing commonly done by fresh prisoners, Simon had observed.

There was a thornbush in Simon's heart. He coughed and peered at Mr Mall who stood stolidly by the door.

'Mr Mall, would you do me the kindness of asking Mr Henderson if he will send for some mulled ale?'

'Yes sir,' said Mall with a nicely judged edge of contempt in his voice. His bull's bellow echoed down the passage through the Judas hole with no alteration to his face.

Francis Throgmorton cleared his throat .

'Um . . . . Your honour . . . .'

'I am Mr Ames,' Simon said kindly. 'I am but a clerk here to take down your words if Mr Norton comes.'

'Oh. Well, Mr Ames. If I might ask . . . you said . . . Norton. Is that Mr Thomas Norton?'

'Yes, it is.'

'That wrote *A Declaration of Favourable Dealing by Her Majesty's Commissioners for the Examination of Certain Traitors?*'

'The same.'

'The one they call Rackmaster Norton?'

'Some Papists so miscall him, Mr Throgmorton. Have you read his Honour's declaration?'

'I glanced through it . . . .'

'Then you will know that only certain traitors are ever racked here and none is tormented for his religion alone. The Queen has said she will make no windows in men's souls and nor do we, only if a man is so foolish and treacherous to deny us answers to the questions we ask, then must we go about other methods.' Simon dropped his official voice, and with a nervous look at Mall said to Throgmorton, 'Which for myself I do not like. I pray you, Mr Throgmorton, hold nothing back. It was very ill to hold silent before the Privy Council as you did this morning.'

'What if I have done nothing wrong, have nothing to say?'

'Then what harm can there be in answering a few questions?' Simon smiled. 'The quicker answered, the quicker tried and the quicker out of uncertainty.'

'Tried? I am not guilty of . . . .'

'Sir, you are certainly guilty of the possession of Papist trumpery for we found *Agnus Deis* and suchlike in your house.'

Throgmorton nodded eagerly. 'I have made no secret of the fact that I hold to the ancient and true religion of our fathers. I pay my fines.'

'Truly, I am sorry for it.'

'Why? When all is ended it makes less than a fragment of a fragment of infinity, the length of our life on this earth.' Throgmorton spoke softly, as if more to convince himself. 'No matter whether we live thirty years in all or thrice thirty. If I am to be worthy of eternity in the presence of Our Lord, if silence is such a fearful thing, perhaps a little

97

fire is necessary here on earth, that it be not my fate for all eternity.'

Simon shook his head. 'I fear you are a brave man, Mr Throgmorton.'

Throgmorton said nothing, but licked his lips and swallowed.

'Mr Ames,' he said after a moment, 'will you tell me one thing?'

'What is that?'

'What date is it today?'

'The fifth of November. Why?'

'I wondered. I had lost count of dates with being so busy.'

'At what?'

'Business.'

Deliberately Simon said nothing, only he folded up his report and put it in a canvas bag to be carried to Mr Secretary. Then he sighed. The door clashed and creaked open and Kinsley came in carrying a large leather jack full of steaming ale, put it carefully on Simon's desk and shouldered past Mall once more.

Simon poured into the horn beaker hanging from the desk and let the hot clove-laden ale trickle down past the bramble thicket in his gullet, carving a path through the cold moist humours invading his lungs from his brain where they were made. Throgmorton watched, licking his lips, which had cracked already with the dryness of fear. After a moment's hesitation, Simon left some ale in the jack, came round his desk and offered it to Throgmorton with a furtive look at Mall.

'Come, I'll hold it for you.'

Watching the man's Adam's Apple bob up and down gratefully and smelling the distinctive reek of fear rising from him with the smoke of his breath, Simon was touched with pity for him. This was no innocent, he knew well, but Francis Throgmorton was scarcely a major player in the game that included the Duke of Guise, the Queen of Scots and, no doubt, Philip II of Spain. But now he must suffer for all of them since it was clearer than spring water to Simon that he knew a great deal. The greater his courage, the worse his suffering, as is often the way.

Kinsley entered again, the door opened ceremoniously for him by Mall, and gave Simon a piece of paper which he squinted to read.

'Is Mr Norton coming?' Throgmorton asked in a voice thinned by the breaking of his determination not to ask.

'No, he must make report of your papers to Sir Francis Walsingham. Most were unburned.' Throgmorton stared at his feet. 'He will have no time to speak to you this day, I fear.'

Throgmorton tensed, head lowered, like a dog not knowing whether to expect a pat or a beating. Simon stamped his feet to get the blood flowing again, and motioned for Throgmorton to rise. He clinked slowly and stiffly to his feet, Simon made way for him before, and so they formed themselves into a shuffling unmusical procession down the narrow stairs and through the musty magnificent corridors of the Queen's Lodgings and Coldharbour. Once in the daylight by Tower Green the clanging and hissing and bellows-pumping of the Queen's Mint between the walls sharpened on the ears, an eternal infernal noise that bounces about the stone of the Tower all day from sunrise to sunset.

Throgmorton wanted to ask another question, that was clear, but dared not, would not. Simon said nothing, only nodding to one of the Clerks of the Ordnance who was hurrying by to the armouries in the White Tower. This man Throgmorton was no idealistic would-be martyr, he reminded himself, who had studied in a seminary whose walls were painted with scenes of ugly martyrdom the better to accustom the would-be priests and missioners to their likely end. This was a messenger, a co-ordinator, working in a matter that Throgmorton, like the others, prayed devoutly would change the kingdom. In the way of such changes, some would rise and some would fall: Burghley and Walsingham could hope for the favour of the hangman's axe, Leicester, Hatton, Ralegh and all the Queen's favourites would do well to die in battle. Simon and his family might end by being burned as Jews, but Throgmorton would find the chance of power and riches of his own. He might dress his treason up in Romish vestments, but at base he had the same tincture in his blood of any other fashionable struggler at the Court.

They walked around the side of St Peter ad Vincula and once more within the stone walls, down more steps to the basement, full of the smell of rising Thames water. They paused at the doorway of Little Ease, Throgmorton eyeing the heavy door with its Judas hole, his teeth chattering. Simon was sure the air was colder within than without. Mall unbolted and opened the little door, showing the short tunnel with its carpet of mould and a few wisps of stinking straw. It was a kennel would have been disdained by a street hound, though further into the blackness, beyond the reach of Mall's lantern, it opened out into the tiny cell four foot six inches at its largest, by four foot by three foot high. Absurdly, Throgmorton, who was five feet eight inches tall, relaxed a little, under-estimating as do they all why Little Ease is so named. The clanging came formlessly from the Mint, multiplied and distorted by quirks of stone.

Simon gestured for him to crawl in and untangled his leg irons for him as he did. Mall pushed a bucket for his necessities after him, one that Kinsley had cunningly holed with a stiletto at the side. As if on an impulse of kindliness in that bitter place, Simon picked up an old blanket and thrust it in after Throgmorton who muttered some words of thanks from his hands and knees. If you would break into a man's soul, first you must humble him, but also you must give him an opening of seeming mercy, an illusion of escape. Also, in general, fleas and lice prefer blankets to cold floor. Mall slammed the door, locked and bolted it loudly.

Simon coughed and dabbed at his nose with his third sodden handkerchief. Mall went ahead with the lantern and put it out when they returned to daylight.

'Mr Norton is in the Wakefield Tower and wishes to see you sir,' he said. 'It seems someone was missed in the search.'

XXIV

The boy had woken under the bed, his mouth like parchment with thirst. The papers still crackled against his skin and the cat had moved to the warmest spot by his stomach. She mewed indignantly when he rolled over and crawled cautiously: although sunlight was still falling through the broken shutters, he cared nothing for that, he must find food and water and be rid of the terrible papers.

He went to the window and peered out, avoiding the trapdoor hole in the floor. A man was walking about in the courtyard. He opened the casement, climbed onto the roof and half-slid, half-crawled down the slope and up the next one. No one saw him go, nor did anyone remark on his dusty face and hair and suit, for boys will be boys and attract dirt to themselves. He had the sense to walk once he reached the ground: he knew it was important to walk when carrying papers, he had had that principle beaten into him. And he knew the house he must go to, which in his fear he named to himself as the House where the Men Speak Strangely. It was in Southwark and he crossed the Thames by the bridge. He dared not think of the place truly as the Spanish Embassy. Even he knew what that must mean and why Señor Mendoza welcomed him.

About the time that the servingman opened the kitchen door to find the white-faced English boy outside, a second pack of searchers saw the place whence he had been reborn and the fresh piss in the chamber pot and the place where he had slept. Simon Ames arrived an hour later as the sun set and inspected the place with his face set still in cold fury.

'A small man, a woman or a boy,' he said to James Ramme, who nodded.

'No doubt of it but it was a fine hiding place,' Ramme said, excusing both of them, then fell silent at the ugliness of Simon's eyes.

'Next time we will have every floorboard up,' was all Simon said as he stalked out.

Once in the square, he stood for a moment at a loss, ignoring the singing in the midst of the crowd that had gathered to watch the sport. Over by the red lattices of the alehouse on the other side he saw a broad familiar shape at ease on a bench, a wooden trencher laden with stew and bread on one knee, a jack full of beer in his fist and a long clay pipe in his mouth. Becket waved him over, and cross-eyed with tiredness and hungry as he was, he walked over and sat down.

'Christ, Ames,' said Becket, 'you look like a ghost. Where have you been? Was it you at the notable storming of a Papist's nest? Did he get away after all then?'

Ames nodded. 'Someone did. We know not when nor who it was.'

'You will never catch him then. Have you eaten this day? No? Here, boy, the ordinary and a pint of best.'

Becket in possession of money was a fine expansive sight, which confirmed Simon's suspicion that his uncle had rewarded his saviour in gold. He took the plate of stew and had eaten half before the unfamiliar salty taste won through to his mazed mind. 'What is this?' he asked Becket.

'Bacon, peas and carrots,' said Becket, making eye-talk with a handsome pigeon-breasted young shopwife. 'Why, do you not like it? Then give it here, it tastes well enough to me.'

Simon drank beer to quell his queasiness. His head was singing and his eyes kept shutting of their own will. He thought of going down to the river again and finding a boat to take him back to Seething Lane, but he could not find the strength of will to do it. Instead he sat there and drank some tobacco smoke with Becket, and sipped his beer and watched the scurrying of the booksellers' men as they finished the lading of a ship ready to catch the tide. Idle notions rose to the surface of his thoughts like scum.

'What is the best way to find . . . to be sure of finding anyone hidden in a house?' he asked Becket once.

'Set fire to it,' Becket answered, and he nodded in agreement that this was certainly the surest way.

They walked through Ludgate just as the Watch were shutting the gates and the curfew bell rang, heading in the wrong direction towards Becket's favourite haunts along Fleet Street, where he was once more welcome now he had paid his debts. It was plain foolishness to play dice with Becket at the Green Lion and then again at the Cock and once more at the Globe tavern in a slow progress of taverns and boozing kens. Once a woman apparently named Sweetbush Julia told him he could have her at double the price since he was so bony and some other time Becket rose up like a mountain from a bench and leaned over a boy who had almost knocked Simon spinning.

He fell asleep twice with his head resting on sticky tables and was drunk enough to mutter assent when Becket told him that he might as well pass out on a bed as on a floor. Once in Fetter Lane, Becket whispered that Sweetbush Julia was as poxed as any Winchester goose and besides Ames had lost all his money to her, what he had on him, and so there was no money left for an inn. They propelled each other up Mrs Carfax's stairs and this time, like a true gentleman, Becket gave Ames the narrow bed and himself took the floor. As he let go his grip on the world, Ames wished feebly for a way to kill the snorting creature nearby, and then remembered that he might not have slept so well on his clean linen at Sir Francis' house. Here at least there was no unspeaking presence of Throgmorton and all his plots, no Christian prayers to end the day, no business unfulfilled nagging him from his chest of papers. The words of his usual prayers floated unconnected before him and the whirling of his head was . . . .

XXV

All this day I was in the midst of a great fit of angels that took Tom over half of London, I think, and brought in a few shillings' bribery for Tom to cease declaiming of dragons in one place and begin again in another. I dare not take my usual begging place by Temple Bar for the reason that it was so close to the firedrake's spawning place, and further my song of madness was being sung by ballad sellers there which struck to my heart every time I heard it. The chorus was not mine, but every other part was, and each verse held the seeds of my trouble, being ripe with the dreams that plague me. Wherefore not, when I wrote it? And Cain it was who had taken it and abused it. Above me the sky broke open continually to show that shadow-drake of treason and anarchy taking shape in his mirror-egg of stars.

I awoke in a field hours before sunrise, cold and stiff and wetted through with rain, though the Queen Moon had given me some covering of bracken and leaves. Four cows wearing the bear-brand of my lord of Leicester were blinking at me kindly from under an oak. I climbed to my feet and reeled from hunger, my belly clenched up under my breast-bone and aching with it, my head pounding from it. The Queen Moon laughed at my plight from behind her veil of rainclouds and told me the answer and so I went to the cows. While she gentled each one, I milked their teats into my begging bowl and so filled my emptiness with warm sweet milk. They lowed at me, thanking me for easing their udders a little. With luck the cowherds would blame hedgehogs or Robin Good-fellow for the smaller yield.

The Queen Moon pointed and nodded at the way I should go: I climbed the gate and squelched south down Gray's Inn Lane towards Holborn. Here was a true time of angels, in the silence and cold of the dark raining pool of night where the sun hides his head before his awakening, yet was I now as cold and lucid as a Secretary to the Queen. The walls of Gray's Inn gardens gleamed in the drizzle clear and sharp where the lantern light fell, and every sound cut through the air like a knife.

It was still an hour before dawn when I came at last to Fetter Lane by a short cut behind Rolls House and Clifford's Inn. There was a clattering and a roaring and crying out in the lane and shouting for water. I peered from behind the garden wall and there was a house afire, smoke rolling from the thatch and flame licking and cracking the windows. Down in the street milled men in shirts shouting at each other and Mistress Carfax in her night rail and cap and cloak, beating her breast and weeping. Some of the men had formed a long bucket chain up from the conduit in Fleet Street, no mean distance, while others were working the well behind Rolls House as fast as they could.

Tom loves a fire and he laughed and cheered the devils dancing in the sparks on the roof and swinging merrily from one rafter to another.

There were two particular devils, one large and broad, the other thinner and smaller and less nimble, both black-faced, that had clambered through a small window in the attic and were clinging to a ledge. Their neighbours in the street were using the long fire hooks to pull out the thatch, while urchins darted among them cheering the two devils, cutting purses and shouting advice.

The two on the ledge inched their way along to the gateway that constricts Fetter Lane a little way along. There the larger devil stepped down onto the upper part of the arch, clinging to some headless carvings of saints, hung by his fingers from a moulding and dropped the last few feet into a soft midden heap. He was followed in a scramble by the lesser devil, who plumped down upon his bum and coughed his guts up there and then. The greater devil stood with his hands on his hips, coughing sometimes, watching the burning roof intently and an ugly look under the soot and sweat blackening his face.

God sent the rain to come down harder and so between the buckets and the sky the fire guttered and smoked and fell at last to a sullen smouldering, leaving the house unroofed but still standing and Mistress Carfax weeping and sniffing upon a gossip's bosom.

The cobbler across the way had invited Becket and Ames into his house where there was a crowd drinking beer and talking loudly about the good fortune of the rain and the notable bravery of Jemmy Burford who pulled down the worst piece of burning thatch himself, and the right way – much disputed – of forming bucket-chains. Someone brought Becket the sword and cloak that he had tossed down into the street from the window, but Ames had lost his second sword in a week. On the other hand, Becket had lost all he had that was not in pawn, save what he wore. His black ringlets were plastered to his neck by heat and rain and fear. As the grey daylight seeped its way out of the east, his face grew uglier, even after he had washed it in an ewer of water brought by the cobbler's wife. He and Ames coughed by fits and turns like a madrigal of crows, but Ames seemed to have lost the power of speech and sat in a corner by a heap of calfskins and some labelled lasts, holding his elbows together and blinking at his singed boots.

When the Watch at last came tottering in and quavered out their questions, it was Becket answered them one word at a time, miserly between coughing.

No, the fire in the grate had not been burning, for the reason he had nothing to feed it with and had not got around to buying any more. No, he had not gone to sleep with a taper still lit. He knew not how the fire came about, being asleep at the time and his friend too, and no, neither had been the worse for drink, both of them God-fearing men.

Then Becket caught sight of me, eating half a sausage. He stepped away from the folk asking questions and took me by the elbow, backed me into a corner by some half-finished roses and pompoms and leaned his face fiercely towards mine. I could see his tongue darting behind the gap left by a long-ago loss of one of his eyeteeth.

'What do you know of this, Tom?'

'Nothing,' I said, trembling. 'Nothing, I have been dancing with angels and . . . .'

'I know that,' he snarled. 'You came prating to me yesterday of some man you had seen that you took to be Lucifer, and more nonsense of a firedrake. What do you know of *this*?'

'Nothing. Is it a mystery?' I asked, trying to unscramble my thinking and recover the beautiful clarity of the cows' milk. 'Could angels have done it? No. Angels never set fire.'

'Ah, but *you* Tom have set fires to my certain knowledge for you set light to an awning with a torch once when you said a devil was hiding in it . . . . Well?'

'Not this,' I said. 'No, not this. Your own angel would have stopped me.'

'Pfft,' he said in disgust. 'And you saw nothing in the lane neither?'

'I was not there. I came when I heard the noise.'

'From Blackfriars?'

'Gray's Inn.'

Seeing the country mud on my feet he grunted and let go my arm, leaving his prints upon it.

'If I find you have lied . . . .'

'No, David,' said Simon Ames, speaking like a sleepwalker and not moving from where he sat still shivering by the lasts. 'I saw an arrowhead caught in a beam and by it an open wineskin. Would Tom have the wit to throw painter's spirit or turpentine on a roof and then fire flames into it?'

'Christ, no,' said Becket, rubbing his blood-rimmed eyes with grubby knuckles. 'No, he would never do that. Why did you not say before?'

'I did not wish to speak before the Watch. I fear I have brought you into mortal danger again, David, for which I am heartily sorry. What was it wakened you in time?'

'My little rat dancing on my chest and nipping at my nose. If it were not for him we would be as crisp fried as Latymer and Ridley now and no crown of martyrdom for payment. He ran into the wall and away, or I would have brought him out with us. Jesu, I pray the poor little rat is not burned saving his family, I have not seen him yet.' And he rubbed at his scorched eyes again and looked as sorrowful as if he had lost a dog.

XXVI

When he had stopped shivering and eaten bread and cheese, Simon had the cobbler's wife brush the worse of the soot off his gown and then went down to a shop on Cheapside to buy a new shirt and ruff on credit, before going straight to the Tower. There Throgmorton's servant with the broken teeth and the lump on his head was the dish preserved for the day. Throgmorton's friend had died of his wound in the meantime.

The serving man was scarcely an oyster, for he opened at once and after a great deal of dross with nary a pearl, confirmed all that Simon and Walsingham's other followers had found out since they first began to study Throgmorton. Indeed he was so anxious to be agreeable it was hard to tell dross from gold and gem from glass in any of what he said. Some of Throgmorton's more mysterious wanderings were explained, at least, Simon found. He had been gambling and was lucky as well, according to his servant, although it was never a passion with him as it was with some at Court.

By the end of speaking to him, Simon's head was throbbing with evil humours and his poor nose like a beacon upon a headland. He spent some time with a glowing dish-of-coals, carefully heating Throgmorton's papers one by one, even a few stray balladsheets, to find if they had writing in milk or orange juice on them and that made his head worse. At last he put the final paper aside in disgust and walked out, with a curt nod at Mall to come with him as a bodyguard, and the sour catching smell of burning still clinging to his clothes.

In Fetter Lane he found the unroofed house with builders' men poking about the rafters to see if they could take a roof upon them again or must they come down to be made anew? Mrs Carfax was sorting her belongings out of the ground floor and crying over the hangings and clothes that were spoilt and asking of her neighbour how she would ever find money to pay for the house to be roofed again and now that big black bastard Becket, who had no doubt set the fire himself, had gone and vanished like smoke with three weeks' rent unpaid. This money Simon paid to her, to her considerable shock, and then he walked down Fleet Street to the Gatehouse.

At that place Goodwife Alys was friendly enough to him, but none of the company had seen Becket nor heard of him since the morning, nor knew where he might be, which caused some suspicion to Simon, rightly surprised at such agreement in such a company as the Gatehouse's regulars. He ate the ordinary and left the place saying he was sorry to have missed Mr Becket, but must return to the Tower now, and so left them congratulating each other on having coneycatched him.

Now upon Fleet Street he stood while Mall waited patiently, his square face graven in stone, and Simon thought hard on how he could find Becket in that forest of London.

Seeing the conduit with its little lantern over it, he was reminded of me and Tom, and also knew where we at least might be found. Beckoning Mall to follow he stopped on over Fleet Bridge, up Fleet Hill to Ludgate and through the old gate just as the watch were a shutting of it, and then round the wall and down to Blackfriars. All the way he walked unknowing past packs of city wolves who were daunted by Mall and his size and his half-hidden blackjack.

Ames found me at length, rapt in contemplation of a window of God, a fragment of the old church that they pulled down for to build houses thereof, and it was a head and crucified shoulders of Christ bound in a rough-hewn new window. The face was fine drawn and the hair and thorns a pain of blood to look upon and weeping angels upon either side of it. A whore had saved it out of the ruin and put it up in her window-space for its beauty. Tom likes to look upon it and so do I, for I think never was a man's agony better and kindlier made in glass and lead. Simon saw it too, for it was the whore's habit to put a wax candle by it, and he stood to look awhile. Mall loitered against a wall, paring his nails and muttering of idolatry.

'It is well-done,' he said to me, after a while.

'It is,' I said to him. 'What shall it profit a man to gain the world if thereby he loseth his soul?'

He stiffened as if I had shot him with a dart, and looked alongside at me.

'Why do you say that?' he asked.

'You were thinking it,' I told him, and regretted it for he paled. The gifts of angels always made men afraid.

'How did you know?'

I shrugged and ruffled my hair back and forth with my hands. Ames gestured at the grief-lined face. 'It was done by one who knew the face of pain,' he said, and then 'What kind of religion is it, that centres about a man tortured to death?'

'Is it better for the centre to be triumph and glory and the destruction of enemies?' I asked, with Tom's favourite angel nodding upon my shoulder.

'To glorify suffering, and make it a prize to be desired,' he muttered, not speaking to me, rather to himself. 'And then force its creation upon others who do the will of the martyrs and suffer also, although they are cursed.'

'Bitter speech.' I said. 'If you like it not, do not do it.'

'But it must be done,' he said, 'And I think I do it better, and cause less suffering. What burned us out this morning were more of the same, worms infecting the Commonwealth, that will gnaw it to death if they are not cauterised.'

'What is it you do?' I asked, although of course I knew.

'I break men open,' he answered bleakly, 'so they give me the secrets hoarded in their hearts. Most are silly, dirty little things, these secrets, but from time to time, we have one who has a vital part of a greater secret and knows it not. Or knows it and revels in it. What must I do? Be merciful, avoid the rack, shun the screws, put no pains upon him and so risk the destruction of this realm and the death of men, women and children in foreign war or civil strife? Or shall I lay on like Topcliffe and perhaps damn my soul to eternity for the finding of the secret as Christians believe, but save the realm? Walsingham suffers none of these doubts, nor Thomas Norton, nor any of them. I wish I could see as clear.'

'Is there not a worthy part for a goat,' I said, to comfort him. 'Even a goat to have sins weighed upon him and be driven out and killed and so the sins gone also.'

'That is the Redeemer's part, I believe,' he said. 'To speak Christianly, I am the one that kills the goat. If you like, Tom, I am Pontius Pilate that wash my hands.'

He spoke low, hardly to me or Tom at all, his voice from far beyond the grim river. I could not answer him, nor could the angels, for they are not permitted to say whether Pilate screams in Hell or loves Christ now in Heaven. I squatted down instead and began making patterns of the dragon in the dirt by the cloister wall. Mall stamped his cold feet and sighed as he changed hands on the torch.

Ames put back his little flask of aqua vitae, blew his red nose and squinted blearily at me.

'So Tom,' he said heavily, 'have you seen Becket? I must speak with him.'

'I have seen him with a piece of cheese in his hand, shouting and calling for the rat that saved your lives,' I said.

'When?'

'This morning.'

'Where is he now?'

I lifted up my shoulders and waved my arms and flapped my mouth like a fish to show him I knew nothing. He shook me and shouted at me but that told me no more and so I could tell him no more and in the end he cursed in Portuguese and walked away.

XXVII

It was the churchwarden of St Dunstan's in the West that found Becket, sitting in a pew which was not his at the back of the church, dead drunk and weeping. Knowing the man and having more sense than to go near him when he was in that state, the churchwarden stood worrying his pockmarked lower lip for a while before he crossed over Fleet Street and spoke to a woman that kept a second-hand linen shop, by name Eliza Fumey. She was a friend to Becket the churchwarden knew, for he had seen them conversing after the service on a Sunday. She listened to his tale frowning, left the shop in the care of her boy and came bustling over with her apron still on.

She found him still stinking of smoke and now of booze, with tears running in channels down the half-wiped grime of his face.

'What is it?' she asked. 'Is it the fire?'

Becket shook his head and hiccupped, mumbling incoherently.

'Is someone dead?'

Becket nodded.

'Who is it? Tom? A girl?' Becket shook his head, heaved a great sigh.

'You will laugh,' he said thickly.

'No, never.'

Becket's fist opened to show a crushed piece of cheese.

'Poor little soul,' he whispered. 'Poor creature, burned to death.'

'Who?'

'Saved my life and the Jew's. Did you know? We would have burned had he not woken me. See here? He nipped my nose. I tried to take him with me but he would go back for his family.'

'Who do you mean? A dog?'

Becket shook his head again. 'My rat.'

'Rat?'

'Ay, rat. Better friend to me than most of humankind, by Christ.'

'No doubt,' said Eliza drily, 'but have you seen his body?'

'No, but he comes not when I call and would never . . . .'

'Well then, he is afraid because of the fire and has removed to a safer place. I would count no man dead until I had seen his corpse, and how much more with a beast that can creep between walls and hide under roofs.'

'He would come to my call. He always has.'

'Ay, but he is a rat, David. A better creature than many men I grant you, but for all that he has no reason.' Eliza looked up at the church beams for inspiration, shook her head fiercely at the churchwarden who was hopping from foot to foot in the throes of curiosity. 'He may have run so far from the fire he cannot hear you.'

Becket's shoulders shook and he started weeping afresh. 'Then I'll see him no more . . . .'

'Better that than thinking him dead.'

'He was my friend.'

'So he was if he braved the fear of fire to waken you . . . .'

'Even when I had no meat for him, he was pleased to see me, I could tell and each night he would come and . . . .'

'Jesu,' said Eliza under her breath. 'David, I will lay you good odds he lives yet and has but gone too far away to hear. Now come with me and wash your face.'

It took a little more coaxing, but by the time the rain had cleared to cold greyness, she had him out of the church and washing his face in the conduit, which was not enough to keep him upright, so she brought him back to her house and up the stairs to her bed. There she stripped him and covered him up and took the grey remnants of his linen to give to the rag and bone man.

Becket snored out the day there. At sunset Mrs Fumey sent her maid up to lay and light a fire for him. An hour later she went up herself with a posset and a mess of eggs and Becket's newly brushed and mended hose over her arm. She found him sitting on a stool poking the fire with the coverlet wrapped round his nakedness, Roman fashion. He winced when she shut the door, though she shut it gently.

'Oh Christ, why do women bring you food when your head is like to fall off?' he grumbled ungraciously.

'Because it is good for you. Drink.'

'What is it?'

'Poison.'

'Oh ay, some sovereign bloody cure for a man being distempered of drink no doubt, owl shite dissolved in horse piss with a seasoning of nightshade or some such . . . .'

'Wine, hot water and spices and citron, now drink it.'

He did, meekly. She left the mess of eggs by where he could smell it while she rummaged a clean shirt for him out of her chest.

'Was it you came to me in the church?'

'Yes.'

'And thinking me half a Bedlamite to be crying for a . . . .'

'I think no less of you, David, that you mourn for a friend, even if the friend had fur and a tail. Besides, I wept more salt for my little tabby cat than I did for my babes that died, and so if that is madness, I am afflicted too.'

Becket had discovered the eggs and was throwing them into his mouth absent-mindedly. When Eliza found a shirt that she thought wide enough, she brought it to him and measured it to his shoulders.

'I shall go to Pickering tonight,' Becket said with his mouth full.

'Laurence the King? Why? I thought you swore to have no more to do with . . . .'

'I can think of none else can help me.'

'He was sorry when you left him, I heard.'

'Was he angry?'

'No, he knew your reasons, and you did it gentlemanlike, but even so . . . . You swore you would not go back.'

Becket shrugged.

'Is it in behalf of the Court Jew you have been teaching swordplay?'

'Somewhat. Someone is trying hard to kill him in a matter that touches his Court work and this morning they near as a whisker succeeded.' His attention wandered, remembering the squeaking and biting upon his chest and his struggling out of the beer fumes into the blindness of smoke and heat.

'You were not so hot for revenge after you were wounded.'

Becket stretched forth his leg from his toga and looked at the purple scar. 'No, for that was done in the way of business when I was guarding Mr Ames. Last night. . . . Why burn my lodgings? They could have waited in ambush for Ames when he left in the morning. No, they wanted to kill me too . . . . Which annoys me. If a man wants my death he should come and get it openly, if he can. I cannot pay you for the shirt, Eliza . . . .'

She tapped him on the cheek. 'Hush. Did I ask for money? Besides, I paid nothing for it myself.'

Becket grinned and kissed her on the mouth, and then under the ear. She shut her eyes.

'I must be respectable, David,' she said. 'The goodwives watch me for any slip, any hint of . . . .'

'Pfft to respectability,' said Becket, kissing her other ear.

'But what if . . . .'

'We may all die of plague next week. Pickering may have me slit like a fish tonight.'

'But the sin . . . .'

Becket kissed her on the mouth again, laughed a little as she swayed her hips away from his hands, though she did not push him off. 'Sin be damned,' he whispered. 'If you will not pity me, must I go to some Winchester goose who will?'

She cuffed his ear half-heartedly, then sighed and caught his head and twined her fingers in his hair. Becket was making heavy weather of the lacing of her bodice, tried main force but was defeated by stout canvas and whalebone and must wait meekly while she unarmoured herself one-handed, unbuttoned her smock.

'Ah Eliza,' he said, happily muffled, 'you have such beautiful tits . . . .'

Well, well, there is a sudden desperate hurry which takes some men before they go into the valley of the shadow of death, to play the game of the two-backed beast, to foin something before they die, and for this reason is much rapine committed by soldiers. After all, Laurence Pickering was unguessable and not known for his kindness to those who left his employ. Others by fear are struck with a sorrow that drives all power from their privy parts like witchcraft, but Becket was not one of these.

I myself find that the company of angels has gentled my animal nature and kept me from impure thoughts, though at night sometimes am I troubled by the she-devil known as Succubus whom I must battle until I am rescued by an angel or by dawn.

In the warm afterglow of their sin, Becket left Eliza to lace her stays and refasten her bodice again, and picked the clean shirt she had brought him from off the rushes by the fire.

'When was you whipped?' Eliza asked, of mere womanly curiosity while he was brushing meadowsweet flowers from it. 'Was it in the Low Countries?'

'Yes. When I was a young lad with no sense and too much love of dice.'

'For dicing?'

Becket laughed uneasily. 'No, for rioting and drunkenness and destroying of a tavern.'

'Lucky not to be hanged.'

'True. I think I was born to be drowned.'

'And the second time?'

This time Becket's face went blank. 'There was only the once.' Which was a lie, as she could see clearly, but she nodded and made herself busy with retying her bumroll.

'And you, were you ever whipped?' Becket asked as she disappeared under her petticoat.

'Oh twice, in the old days. But I paid the man and he hardly marked me at all. The goodwives were sorry for it.'

'That you were whipped?'

'No,' Eliza laughed. 'That there was no blood. There now, you look a proper man again. Why do you always wear your shirts until they rot and fall off your back.'

'Idleness and the company of wicked women.'

Dressed and with her cap primly fastened on her head, she went downstairs and fetched his doublet that she had mended and steamed and sponged and lastly aired with a stick of burning perfume so it was as well as ever it was likely to be. Her two children sat eating bread and milk and apples in the kitchen and watched her wide-eyed while the maid said nothing at all.

While he waited, Becket looked at the hangings that were painted with the marriage of Cana, and Penelope weaving at her loom. She had always been a cleanly whore and now she was a respectable widow. Her rooms sparkled like a Dutch woman's, not a single rush upon the floor older than a week and well scented with meadowsweet and lady's bed-straw from Simple Neddy's garden.

He had been sorry when he returned from the Netherlands and found she had long married out of her trade and had two babes that lived. He was sorrier still when he at last persuaded her back to his own bed and found the scars and marks of a stick no thicker than her husband's thumb on her haunches.

The husband was found dead in an alley a month afterwards.

Now Eliza was a widow of substance that most of the hedge-pickers in London resorted to when they had a good haul of someone else's washing, and she instructed them in the better kind of linen to pick. Becket liked her even more as a sturdy widow than he had as a plump businesslike whore, but she saw no sense in putting herself under the marriage yoke again, even for so good and kind a friend as Becket. Considering how hot and lusty all women are by nature, which is a well-attested fact according to all good authorities, it is strange how many of them bloom in widowhood when they have no man to guide and protect them.

'Marry me,' he said nonetheless when she came back and held up his doublet for him to put on. She laughed, shook her head. 'I am not so ill a match, even drunk. I could turn respectable . . . .'

'If I wanted a respectable man I could marry half a dozen that want their little fingers into my pie of silver. Did I tell you that Mr Custance asked me after church a few Sundays ago.'

'But he . . . .'

'Ay, once upon a time he was a-dipping of his wick unwed and no lacking of enthusiasm. He was the one that cast down and broke the little crucifix that Molly gave me from Blackfriars. He said it was idolatry and wickedness.'

'What did you say to him of the marriage?'

'I told him I could never wed a man well-known by all to lust after whores and left him to wonder how I knew.'

'But did he not recognise you?'

'How should he, with no view of my gear?' She laughed at Becket's puzzled expression. 'Why, David, sweeting, one thing that made me take a liking to you in the old days was that you look upon my face every now and then . . . .'

Becket kissed her and would have spoiled all her work at making him neat but she cuffed him with intent this time and slid out of his grip.

'When will you go to Pickering?' she asked.

Becket shrugged. 'Tonight,' he said. 'Why sit about waiting on it?'

'His price may be high to help you.'

'No doubt of it.'

'If he ask you to do it, will you kill for him?'

'Why not? I have for lesser men.'

'That was in war.'

'So? The men were dead.'

Becket would have no more of the conversation and she brushed him down and stood to look at her handiwork and smiled on him as if he were indeed her husband.

'Go to,' she said. 'I think you were wise to fear Laurence the King. I hear he has hardened.'

'I do fear him,' said Becket reasonably. 'There is no shame in fearing one who might break every bone in my body on a whim and then fail to kill me. I would fear the Queen herself no less.'

XXVIII

From Blackfriars Simon Ames made his way by Water Lane down to the river to find a boat, which Mall did for him at that late hour, being possessed of a kind of sixth sense for the watermen. Once at Seething Lane, Simon made for his chamber and called upon his manservant to attend him.

'Why would he ask the date?' Simon asked of no one in particular, forgetting that his man was lighting the fire.

'Who sir?'

'Ah . . . a man in the Tower.'

'Hm. Throgmorton.'

'It is supposed still to be secret. What is that racket?'

'A page being beaten for running away. Well it is, sir, none of us would dare let on to an outsider.'

'Well then, Throgmorton. Why did he ask the date?'

'To know what it was, sir? Phew. Sleep too close to the fire, did you, sir?'

'What . . . . Oh the smell. I had forgotten. So long between sunrise and sunset, I sometimes . . . . Yes, there was a fire, but no harm done, to me at least.'

'Thanks be to God.'

'Indeed. If you cannot take the smell out of them, I suppose you had best give them away . . . . No, leave me the book and the candle, I am not sleepy yet.'

The servant waited outside the door until he heard the quiet muttering of prayers cease and Simon's reedy snoring, then crept back within to out the light and draw the bed curtains.

Meanwhile Becket was out in the black night of London, still coughing now and then from the catching of smoke from the fire jostling in his lungs. He went carefully, slipping from alley to alley and keeping a curved path as it were drunk, but in truth full of choppings and changings to see if any followed him. By theory there is curfew in the City through the night, and by theory it is impossible to enter or leave once the gates are shut. In practice there is the broad highway of the Thames striking through the centre and besides that a man need only walk a little north-wards of Ludgate into the rookery of Amen Corner and duck down an alleyway, to find broken and stolen places in the old wall which would scarcely stand a siege of well-armed rabbits and fieldmice.

Yet there is still a slight fault to the City in that the Watch walks about it, and the absence of many folk on the streets makes it hard for the evil to mingle among any but their own kind. Laurence the King himself lives in the suburbs, in a good tall house, with his wife and children and two manservants and a cook and a tiring woman for his wife. He holds court in a number of places, each day different, and does his business now from this warehouse in the Vintry, now from that yard in East Cheap, and bases much of his power upon the convenable fact that his own sister is wife to the London hangman.

Becket headed north through Old Bailey, Gifford Street and Pie Corner, to where the ruffians shout and fight in Smithfield on the grass. There he asked at the Cock alehouse whether Pickering had a game open that night.

At last he found a man he knew to be of Laurence the King's faction while he was hiding from one of Tyrrel's party. He made a petition for an audience that night.

A little later two men stopped him as he passed again down Long Lane.

'Mr Becket,' said one, 'the King wishes us to bring you to him.'

Now mark you the trust in Laurence the King's name, for Becket instantly allowed the two to take from him his sword and dagger and even the little knife in its sheath at the back of his neck. It is because all London rogues know that the man who takes the King's name in vain must expect a death no less bloody than the man who does as lightly with her Majesty the Queen's name, and so is good order and governance maintained in any realm.

They brought him to a fair large house in the Strand, and at the end of the upper room by a good fire of coals, his pipe in his hand, sat Laurence Pickering, the King of London. For those who have never seen him, he is a small plain-looking man, with a round bullet-head, his clothes as rich and dark as a Cheapside goldsmith's, and happy small eyes set deep and brightly gleaming in his head.

Becket uncovered his head and made his bow, which tickled the man's vanity. He had Becket sit beside him (a little closer to the fire and upon a lower stool than Becket would have liked) and ordered him to be brought a pipe and a silver tankard of best Canary, and so did him honour.

There were pleasantries to be exchanged, as must be the case at any audience, politesse and courteoisie marking out the Prince from the common herd as well as the swords of his soldiers and the nobility of his blood (which Laurence the King hath also, coming of a very ancient family of thieves and murderers).

Behind them in the room velvet and samite crowded on slashed leather and dark brocade as men fought politely over the dice and cards, with Lady Luck as their hoped-for champion. There were rush-mats on the floor so that no dice could hide there and no covers on the polished oak tables, and men of experience as artists with weighted ivory and marked cards watching all. The stakes were gold. In this, the best game in London, Laurence Pickering the King makes guarantee that there is no coneycatching, no thieving, no footpadding of winners and no cheating. Which brings in the Court gallants and their oozing honeypot purses in plenty, and forms a pillar of Laurence's estate. He will even grant credit to some, at a price would make Simon's cousin Senhor Gomes the pawnbroker stretch his eyes, and he levies a tenth penny on all winnings as the price of honesty and safety.

Becket had been there before and had no fear of the wearers of embroidered silk or cunningly tufted velvet. He sat square on his little stool, overlapping the edges on all four sides and causing it to creak sadly, his broad hands on his knees.

'Someone in London is attempting to kill a friend and patron of mine, a Mr Simon Ames, Sir Francis Walsingham's man. I know not what their quarrel is with him, but it seems they have included me in it. This morning we were burned out of my lodgings and I . . . I take exception.'

Laurence inclined his head and puffed on his long pipe. Becket counted off the other attempts upon his fingers, but omitted the detail of the rat.

'What do you want of me?' asked the King, affably.

'This is one that pays others to do his killing, in Spanish gold or French gold, we know not which. At least, he must be a foreigner and against the common weal. Let me hear of it when he next hires men, or the next time someone is paid.'

'Does Mr Ames know you have come to me?'

'No.'

'And what will you do for me in return?'

Becket spread his hands. 'A favour sir, whatever is within my power and not against my honour. I am a poor Provost of Defence, without even a school, not a penny of capital beyond my sword and my best buckler which is still in pawn. Alas for me, I cannot . . . .'

'Spare me,' smiled Laurence. 'I have always had a liking to you David, and was sorry when you left me before. But I think this service you ask of me is more to the benefit of your friend than yourself, and so it were justice if he were to . . . carry the debt.'

Becket looked worried. Laurence leaned forwards and tapped his knee. 'No very great burden, believe me, David. Here, I will lay it out for you and you may put it to him and so decide. And in earnest of my good faith, I will enquire a little for you, whatever his decision.'

Becket waited while Pickering tapped out his pipe into the fire. 'Have no fear, all I ask is an audience with Mr Ames' master.'

'With Walsingham?' Becket asked, astonished.

'With Mr Secretary Walsingham, yes.'

'But . . . .' Becket's mouth was round to form the question 'Why?' when he thought better of it and swallowed it. 'Of course. I shall ask him as soon as I may.'

'No. Wait a little. Put it to him when he is feeling grateful. You will know the time. Now, if you have need of money this night, David, you may stand guard for me here as you used to.'

Becket made a little open-handed gesture of thanks, and when his own pipe and Canary were finished, he took his place among those who prevent the uninvited from entering the game and inspect those who enter for sinful dice.

Which was a bad night, in truth, for Becket. The riddle for a man such as he, who made no fortune out of war in Flanders, is not how to come into Laurence the King's employ, but to get out of it without a halter about his neck and a tilting ladder at his feet. A thing he earnestly wished to do and had tried to do, but was now thwarted. The audience with the King was in the nature of a defeat, and both knew it.

XXIX

For Throgmorton the day had been far worse. While Becket snored in Eliza Fumey's bed and I spent my strength on vain prophecy and warning, Throgmorton was haled out of Little Ease and hustled into the basement of the White Tower among the barrels and the broken pikes and the pairless greaves. There, in a corner under an arch hung with armour, they married him to the Duke of Exeter's daughter and stretched him a little while Mr Rackmaster Norton hectored and questioned and Simon Ames, in his part as Judas, made pretence at being his friend. Simon had estimated the man to be made of a baser metal than he proved in the end, for he spoke nothing but the word Jesus no matter what the cruelty of the rack.

In the end Mr Norton gave up the business as a bad job and Ames had Throgmorton carried to a cell with a dry floor and good deep straw upon it in the Lanthorn Tower. Then he brought him a tincture of poppies and held his head up to help him drink.

'If you will give me a little word or two,' he whispered, tempting like Satan in the poor man's ear. 'Something or nothing that seems like something, I may prevent the next racking.'

But even this counterfeit softness got nowhere for in truth Throgmorton was too far gone to hear him, and so Simon left him. When he came outside Henderson asked what had disagreed with him, and got a very foul and cold stare for his kindness.

Simon went to a little room within the hardly used Coldharbour building that he had begged of the Records Clerks. He wrote his report by candlelight for the greyness of the day, his borrowed spectacles further

119

oppressing his nose and making his gritty eyes water. He imparted his reflections upon Throgmorton's determination, which was unexpected. He thought, perhaps, the man was waiting for something. He also recommended there be no more racking for a goodly while, or he thought Throgmorton's joints might burst and so he might die of the bleeding. Which was a kind of kindliness.

XXX

If the City of London be likened unto a man, and its heart is, in the figure, the great Church of St Paul's, then is the heart of London full rotten. St Paul's squirms with as many thieves and money-changers as ever fouled the Temple of Jerusalem which Our Lord scoured of the same with a rope's end. Who has a new cloak that cost ten villages or a doublet that cost forty must run unto St Paul's and walk up and down and round about, past the food stalls and the stationers' stalls, and the men in search of work by the serving man's pillar. Those who have spent all their lands to get fine clothes may likewise walk about and at dinnertime continue and listen to their bellies rumble by Duke Humphrey's tomb.

I myself flew through the nave, borne upon angels' arms, speaking to the faces carved upon the roof bosses and the still whole saints in niches too high for Reformers to reach.

Tom capered below and got some pennies for amusing of a Queen's favourite with an argument that it was possible to weigh tobacco smoke. Becket was there, standing with his thumbs in his belt by a headless statue, his heavy lids half-shut to watch the eye-curdling parade of red and green and buttercup and violet. He smiled to see me dancing about the thin bars of sunlight from the holes in the roof and splashing the puddles among the stone flags and brasses on the floor. The rain comes in at the place where the spire was before God struck it with His bolt. At the time the preachers ranted that this was a manifest sign of His anger at a woman presuming to be Governor of the Church; even the bishops were a little concerned. Now it is only as it has always been, and the temporary roof they put up after the lightning become older than many of the new flowers of the field that flaunt their vanity below.

I was making good money with my larking but when I saw three of the churchwardens foregather with their staffs, pointing narrow-eyed at me, I bowed, scooping up my earnings and trotted out into the churchyard among the awnings and booths of the booksellers and stationers. There I saw the small pockmarked ballad singer that killed Peterkin and left him to rot in a ditch. He was taking up a new load of songs, with Tom O'Bedlam still among them but ousted from his pre-eminence among the sheets, and that place taken by *A New Song of the Hatter's Daughter from Islington*. As the balladmonger left the churchyard and began to sing, a ragged boy and a man left at the same time, one before, one behind, and nothing to show any connection.

I think it was no angel that pulled me eastwards, away from mine own haunts, to Old Change in the City. It was a house I knew well and had watched often from cover and loved well for those that dwelled there. Now its high pointed roof and fair diamond windows and the worn grimy elephant above the door lay under the shadow of Cain, or Lucifer, the pink of its bull's blood wash become an ugly pale clot on its walls. This I could forgive my brother least of all: that being come into England in a matter of treason, he should take shelter with our sister.

It happened as I came through the gateway that led from St Paul's Ground into Old Change, I saw the boy I had marked before, in his livery of blue and swans upon his linen, running in at the kitchen gate, and I followed him which I had never done before. Tom was now settled firm and immovable in his madness so I could not resist. I had no wish for Agnes to see me in such a state, yet I squatted by the kitchen door where he went in, and shook my head at the boy when he came out again.

'Here is sadness, here is harm,' I whispered to him. 'Speak not to Lucifer, for he will up and eat your soul if he can.'

The boy stopped and stared at me, long lashes fringing his intense blue eyes.

'Here is poor Tom of Fleet Street that speaks with angels, come to warn you of Lucifer, and keep away.'

He shook his head, slipped past me though I made no attempt to catch him, and trotted on down Maidenhead Lane. A stone hit my shoulder and I turned to see my aunt, Catherine Nisbet, upon the kitchen threshold with her hands upon her hips and her face full of anger.

Her mouth was shaped to shout at me, but she stopped, full of doubt at the ghostly familiarity of my face.

'Now then Aunt Catherine,' I said peaceably enough. 'My duty to you. Is my sister within?'

Her pale watery eyes bulged and her face turned as white as her ruff. There was a gargle in her throat, which the singing of angels hid from my ears, since it was my old name that must be kept from demons.

Never before had I done this though it would have been easy enough. I had found the house by a chance glimpse of Agnes' husband, whom I knew well once, when I followed him home. I had watched my sister coming and going, marshalling the packhorses and carts to traverse back to their home in the country, riding at their head with her steward, back and forth she went, pursuing her husband's interest at law through the courts in Westminster Hall. Aunt Catherine had generally drooped behind her, riding pillion with a groom and fingering her beads covertly. Once there was a wet nurse as well with a babe puling and puking behind that. But never had I dared come so close nor speak to one of my family, for fear they would hale me back to Bedlam.

Now Aunt Catherine had one hand to her throat, her other crossing herself wildly. I thought there might be a demon choking her and so rose to my feet and went smiling towards her, holding out my hands to help strike it from her throat. She shuddered, threw the other stone she had in her hand, then swept backwards with a swirling of her skirts and slammed the door. I stared upon it and went up close.

'Tell Cain I forgive him Bedlam.' I roared through the wood, and to be sure they must have heard me in Fleet Street. 'Tell him Mr Secretary's men will come, he is in danger.'

There was a shriek of voices within and a scuffle of nails on flagstones, a low growling bark. I backed from the door and as it opened wide enough to let out a dog, I skipped backwards like a hart and was down the lane and through the gate into Paul's Yard again, his teeth snapping at my heels.

Oh it was hard to run with my eyes full of water and a stone stuck in my breast. Tom was dashing tears away as he came to Ludgate and ran through, while an angel asked in amusement why I was weeping. What did I think would come of it? Aunt Catherine had mourned me dead in Bedlam of plague years gone by and no doubt had quietly thanked God for a merciful release. My sister had surely forgotten me entirely. Who would welcome a ghost in rags and tatters, a man of shadows and angels breaking out of his reported death and forgetfulness, the brother who had brought shame to their name with his wildness and turning of the Queen's banquet upside down? Adam would never do such things.

No doubt it was hunger that brought on the new fit of angels. Another afternoon went missing to join the flock of my lost days in the locked belfry of my mind. When I conquered Tom once more I was by the whore's beautiful Christ-window again, with Simon Ames shaking me and Henderson holding up a torch to light him from behind.

'It is like talking to water and wind to get sense of you, Tom, I know not why I came back. Nor will I come again if there is no fruit to this, and so you may tell Mr Becket, if it was he that sent you.'

He was tired and unwell, his face gone thinner and black circles under his eyes, and a cold sore under his nose where he dabbed at it too much.

His guardian Henderson was backed to the wet wall, the patience of a saint carved on his face. Behind his face ran his thoughts, and he and his fellows all thought Simon Ames was next for Bedlam and the begging bowl, with these purported assassination attempts, besides playing in dangerous waters with David Becket.

On which thought, like the Devil spoken of, came Becket himself, at first nothing but a looming of black at the gullet of an alley running into the whore's little yard, beyond the grasp of Henderson's torch, but with his own torch on one side of his width and a large bundle in his other hand. As he came closer so the bundle became a man, much battered about his pocked clever face and his arm broken from the way it hung useless.

'What is this, Mr Becket?' Simon demanded while Henderson straightened up and dropped his hand to his veney-stick.

Becket swung his arm and the man crashed against the wall and slid down to a moaning heap. Crumpled sheets of paper fell out of his doublet.

'There,' said Becket, breathing hard, 'that one works for the man that paid to burn us out.'

'Hm.'

'Tell him your tale, bastard, or I'll piss in your mouth.'

The ballad seller crawled to his knees and began to babble at venture, that it was nothing to do with him and he worked only for those who paid him and he asked no questions and knew nothing at all of nothing. This last caused Simon to narrow his eyes. He crouched down to the man, trailing his gown in the mud.

'What were you paid to do?' he asked quite gently.

The ballad seller's eyes rolled at Becket who was lowering over him with a dagger in his fist.

'Put your knife away, sir,' Ames said curtly. Becket did so. 'Now tell me what you were paid to do?'

'Follow you, your honour, follow and mark where you lay, no more I swear it on . . . .'

'His pack stinks of turpentine,' said Becket. 'And he has a small crossbow also, a fowling piece. And I have marked him speaking to one of Tyrrel's men upon the Bridge in time past.'

Ames gazed at him a long while. The ballad seller shivered, his head and shoulders were wet and stank of a gutter which no doubt was where Becket had half-drowned him, but under the skin of his face which was so twisted with fear and humility, still he was thinking and planning.

'Have you been upon Tyburn?' asked Ames in a grey neutral voice, 'when they execute traitors? Did you see Campion die? Did you see how they hanged him but a little time and then cut him down quick and still breathing and slit open his bowels? There was a song made of his treason and men such as yourself selling it to the crowd, singing it also. Were you there?'

Here again was Ames all clothed in his protective armour of ice, intent upon his prey, while Becket stood still and Henderson also, caught by the magic of fear he was weaving upon the ballad seller. He nodded once to Simon's question.

'You were there. So you saw them strip out his guts in his sight, like butchers making sausages? You saw them take his manstones and throw them on the fire? I think he did not cease shrieking until they cut him in four. It is wonderful, is it not, how much it takes to kill a man, so it be done right?'

Edmund Dun nodded once. He was a man of as long lineage in singing and travelling as Richard Broom was in power and killing, his dark skin and eyes came not from Egyptians but from Languedoc in the days of heresy. Alas for a lineage long decayed and brought to poverty by printing, and a bitter burden of pride in the man that none now valued his skill at holding hundreds of complete ballads in his brain.

'Speaking for myself, I was glad when he was dead, Fr Campion.' Ames continued, 'I pitied him. It is a death I would wish on no man, no matter what his crime. And yet I think he preferred it to life after we had finished with him, in the Tower.'

Here was a long breath, like a sigh, from Becket, but only I heard it.

'Tell me where Mr Semple lodges.' Ames said quietly, coaxingly, 'It is all I desire to know.'

The ballad seller closed his eyes. After a long moment, he whispered and when Ames bent closer to listen, he shouted, 'The house with the elephant over the door, in Old Change.' Now came many things, all crammed into the same heartbeats. First the blood drained down from Becket's cheeks as Simon stood up straight again, removing the signet ring from his finger.

'You heard that, Mr Henderson,' he said crisply. 'Go at once to Mr Recorder Fleetwood, show him this ring and bid him meet me at Paul's churchyard south gate with a good force of men immediately.'

But as he spoke, a Romish devil was whispering in Dun's ear, and he lurched to his feet and charged his shoulder into Ames' side, knocking him into a puddle. He ran down the alley clumsily, his feet in their tattered shoes and chipped broken pattens turning sideways on themselves, slipping in dog turd, barking his broken arm on the wall and mewling in pain.

'Stop him!' shouted Ames. Becket seemed to awaken, ducked his head, put his hand to his neck and threw narrow-eyed. The singer of songs went down on his face with a smooth-handled well-weighted little knife sticking from his back. By the time they reached him, he had vomited blood and died.

Ames stood a little apart whilst Becket set his boot against the man's ribs and twisted out his knife. He wiped it carefully on the ballad seller's hair to clean and grease it before sliding it again into its nest under his own ringlets.

'I had not meant him to die,' Simon said after a moment.

'No?' said Becket while Henderson looked among the man's many papers.

'Nothing but ballads here,' said Henderson.

'Put him in the Thames then,' said Ames, shaking himself a little, stepped over the ballad seller like a cat and began leading them towards Water Lane. Henderson departed to find Mr Recorder Fleetwood, whilst Becket and I took up the body and followed down to the river where he slipped sadly into the water with hardly a splash.

Ames watched, warming his hands in the sleeves of his gown.

'Will you come with me, Mr Becket?' he asked civilly, 'since you have worked so well on my behalf.'

Now David Becket need not have obeyed. He could have melted into the night and never clapped eyes on Simon Ames again, with a little care. But he did not. And yet he knew as well as I did what he had done.

I am afraid of Becket when he kills for an ugly mood comes down on him. He was full of danger and indifference spilling out of the dark places in his soul. Men are strange how they will take vengeance upon themselves.

He turned to me and lifted his hands as if asking my forgiveness.

'At least bless me for a good shot, Tom,' he said.

What could I say? I was crouched against a wall, my hands holding back Tom's ravings in my mouth.

'You may come if you wish, Tom,' said Ames, ignorantly.

I laughed at him. In the choice between darkness and ice to numb me, I chose neither of them. Instead I went out and up and walked about among the stars, leaving my animal part to rave below, while I trod the dark gritty clouds of London, the star daemon in my soul conversing pleasantly with the Queen Moon and the Seven Governors of the Sky.

XXXI

They treated my sister with all courtesy, seeing she was a woman and seeing she was great with child and near her time. They permitted her to dress herself and wait in her hall with all her servants gathered, while Simon Ames and Recorder Fleetwood and their men went through her house like an army in a sacked city. One by one Ames spoke with the servants, privily in a little solar behind the hall, and also with Catherine Nisbet who wept and cried that they all had been betrayed by the zany. And the loud-voiced cook swore and cursed that none among them would ever tell him anything, no, nothing and besides Mr Semple had gone away, gone for good, sweet Jesu be praised for it.

He waited upon Mistress Fant last of all. She sat in her husband's carved chair to receive him, her long wax-white fingers folded upon the dome of her belly, her chin rested on the white folds of her ruff, her gown an old green velvet one in the loose English style for her stays were put away now until she was delivered of her burden. So she seemed as it were something from before the King's Great Matter, a few vagrant wisps of red hair as always escaping to startle the black velvet of her French hood, and her linen cap beneath it as lacking colour as her face.

She had not studied to put Simon at disadvantage, but did so by instinct only, by the operation of ancient blood which goes about its business subtly. For my father's lineage was too new and fine to be very old, being indebted to the Queen's grandfather for his gentility, whereas my mother's could stretch with neither effort nor boasting back to one of William the Bastard's ruffians.

When Ames entered she had but one candle by her on a table, a breviary laid near it, the fire low and the fresh rushes still smelling sweetly under his boots.

She looked at him and waited for him to speak, saying nothing that would put him at ease. When he spoke that was itself in the way of a small skirmish lost in a new and deadly war.

'Madam, I must tell you that we have found Mass things and *Agnus Deis* within your hiding place by the stairs.'

She inclined her head a little, kept silent.

'Who was the man calling himself Semple that has been staying in this house these past weeks?'

'My brother.'

'Did you know he is a Papist, one that works for the Duke of Alva?'

'I know he is a Catholic,' said my sister quietly, 'as I am myself.'

'Did you know he is a traitor?' asked Simon. Again silence, for she folded her lips like the shutting of a book. 'Where is he now?' Still nothing. Simon took a piece of paper he had found and shown at venture to all the household, held it out to her. 'Who sold this ballad to you?'

Agnes glanced at it. 'It is the ballad of Tom O'Bedlam,' she said. 'If you will arrest every household that has a copy, you have a busy night before you, sir.'

'From whom did you buy it?'

'To be sure, I bought it not. Ask of the kitchen girls or one of the grooms perhaps.'

'Madam I must press you on the matter of your brother.'

She shut her eyes momentarily. 'That I am as you term it, a Papist, a believer in the Faith of my father and grandfather and great-grandfather, that I freely admit,' she said. 'I keep the Mass things and have heard Mass, that too I admit.'

'Which is against the law.'

'Yes, it is. But that is all. Besides the matter of religion, I am Her Majesty's liegewoman and as true loving subject as any minister's wife. I am no traitor, nor any in my house.'

'Seeing that God made the world, what is there that can be beside the matter of religion, madam?'

Agnes smiled. 'Whatsoever the Queen wishes, surely.'

'Then what think you of the Bishop of Rome's Bull of Excommunication upon Her Majesty? If Alva came with his army, which would you pray for, the Queen or the Spaniard?'

'Ah. The bloody question. I would pray for all English men and women, sir, indifferent, as I do now.'

Simon was silent himself a moment. 'Where is your husband?' he asked.

'My husband knows nothing of my brother's sojourn, nor of the Mass things, being lodged at Tilbury this past six months. He goes to church every Sunday and pays my fines out of love for me.'

'Then you are a most evil wife to him,' Simon said coldly. Agnes bowed her head.

'Yes, I am,' she said, 'but he knows nothing. He is at Tilbury overseeing the building of a ship for the exploration of the north-west passage and the lading and unlading of his cargoes for Muscovy and the Hansa. I scarcely ever see him save in winter when the seas are closed. I am in London upon business of a lawsuit.'

Simon went to the fire and laid his hands upon the mantel to warm them a little.

'Madam, I have already sent to Tilbury for the taking of your husband. In addition, although I am loath to do so, I fear I must bring you to the Tower. Would you prefer a horse litter or to travel by boat? Speak your desire and I will arrange it.'

Agnes smiled and steepled her fingers, no tremor in them.

'I desire not to go to the Tower at all,' she said. 'As you can see, I am not like to run away from you. I was about to take my chamber and wait for my hour.'

Simon inclined his head. 'Nevertheless I must require it of you.'

'A pretty thing, a woman brought to bed of her babe in the Tower.'

'You will not be the first, madam,' said Simon, 'nor the last, I doubt. I shall see to it that there is a midwife to attend upon you.'

'If you are hoping that my brother will come back to this house tonight, I may tell you now sir, you will be disappointed. He shall not return.'

As this was indeed one of Simon's hopes, he did not answer.

'I will wait upon you when we have the horse litter ready,' he ended as he turned by the door, while Agnes looked into space, eyes hooded. As he crossed the threshold, she lifted her chin and called out to him in a rush.

'Be gentle with my husband sir, I pray you, he is choleric and not well and he knows nothing of my foolishness . . . .'

Simon bowed. She did not return the courtesy and the eyes of all her people bored into him like awls as he passed by them to speak to James Ramme, that moment come from the Queen's household and still gnawing on a baked goose leg.

XXXII

Two of Mr Recorder Fleetwood's priest hunters were measuring the passageway as he wandered into the kitchen. There he found Becket building up the fire. Two pokers rested in the embers, two tankards sat on a bench waiting to be mulled.

Simon came to a halt and stood watching as Becket busied himself, nervously hitching up his gown on his shoulders and scratching at the sore place made by his ruff under his chin. Becket turned and grinned at him, at which Simon near turned and fled because he saw the man was drunk.

'Come, friend, drink with me,' said Becket flourishing a poker before he mulled the ale with it. Simon sat down gingerly on a bench, listening to the ale hissing and bubbling and smelling the spices. He took the tankard, forebearing to remark that it was not Becket's kitchen for all he was making himself at home, and sipped carefully. Becket sat down next to him, causing the bench to creak in protest, cradled the tankard, and elbowed him in the ribs.

'It was gold I brought you, with the balladmonger, eh?'

'Indeed,' Simon agreed peaceably, 'though alas, we came a little late.'

'Tell me the tale.'

Here was the smell of old sweat, old smoke, booze and fear so strong that Simon coughed. He blew his nose again on his handkerchief, all the time pinned to the bench by David Becket's over-bright eyes. He thought it might be better to talk a little.

'The man we seek came into England under the name of Semple, but his true name is Adam Strangways, for he is Mistress Fant's brother.'

Becket spat into the fire, drank some more.

'He is known to be a friend of Charles Paget, that is the Queen of Scot's man in Paris, who was here himself in September but slipped away before we could lay hands on him. Strangways we know was given private audience with the Spanish King early this summer.'

Becket raised his brows. 'What was said?'

Simon spread his hands. 'That alas we do not know.'

Becket tutted, finished his ale and went to draw some more from the cask in the buttery.

'I have been overpressed with business, these last few days,' Simon called. 'It has been concerning one called Francis Throgmorton whom we have in the Tower now.'

Becket appeared in the doorway, swaying. 'Was he put to the question?'

'Ay.'

'Did he speak?'

'No.'

Becket snorted and drank without the ceremony of mulling. Simon sipped again.

'We took him, but I fear we miscarried upon it. There was one hiding in his house that we never found, who later slipped away and no doubt took with him whatsoever Throgmorton would not have had us read.'

'I know.' Simon rushed on, unwilling that Becket should misunderstand what he was about.

'Walsingham was certain that this was a Guisan plot and that therefore we should look to the French embassy as the source of it. Behind all of them is the King of Spain to be sure, because he hath the money to pay for all, but prime movers we thought were all in France. Yet it seems from what papers we found that little Mr Throgmorton has been running messages not merely between Guise and the Queen of Scots, but also unto the ambassador of Spain, Mendoza, that we had thought could not dare to be so directly tangled. In other words, they have been less cunning than we thought them and so have fooled us. This was not a Guisan conspiracy. We were casting for the scent in the wrong coverts entirely.'

'And the . . .' – Becket waved his hand at large in the air – '. . . the end and purpose of these foul foreign plottings?'

Simon pressed his fingers flat to his mouth, shut his eyes a moment and thought for the third time that he must visit a barber the next day.

'Sticks and straws show where the wind blows. I see a footprint in mud, and like Electra, I know its owner although it is but a mark in the mud to anyone else. But where Electra saw Orestes, I see a host armed against us, the King of Spain massing his armies against us. Yet there is so little to prove it with.'

'If Alva invades in behalf of the Scottish Queen, surely all Her Majesty need do is lop the woman shorter by a head,' said Becket, with the throat-slitting gesture of the streets. 'Lord knows why she has not done it long since.'

'Ay well, there is proof that you know nothing of policy, David,' said Simon. 'Think upon it. The Scottish Queen stands between Philip of Spain and the throne of England, which she inherits by right of descent before he does by his marriage to Queen Mary. We had hoped he would be less inclined to invade when it was in her behalf rather than his own. It seems we were wrong. And this lopping business is not so simple nor so easily done, there must be due cause. The Queen is very loath to kill another anointed Queen. I would say she has a horror of it. Davison has often said that whoever brings her to do it finally will destroy his career in her service, for she will shrink from him ever after. And then there is another point.'

'Which is?' prompted Becket, coming to sit beside Simon again as he seemed to grind to a halt in mid-flow glaring at yet another foolish elephant carved above the fireplace.

'Why, that our Sovereign Lady will find it hard to kill Queen Mary if she has been first killed herself.'

Becket winced.

'There is an army planned to come from the Netherlands, that we know,' Simon went on, 'but all has seemed premature since they cannot come across yet, nor for at least a year. They have nothing ready, no boats, no fleet, no supplies, though the Prince of Orange is in desperate case once again.'

'He has the worst luck of any soldier I know . . . .' said Becket taking breath no doubt to begin some tedious tale.

'An army cannot be whipped up like a syllabub hot from the cow, nor a fleet neither. But all of England and our unity hangs upon a single slender thread and if it be . . . .' Simon made a pinching movement with his fingers and then shrugged.

'Why not do the snipping when the army is ready?' Becket asked, at last distracted from his drink.

'So we thought. But reflect upon it a little; if the Spaniard is at the gate and the Queen is killed, that will rather inflame the English than

131

dismay them, there will be no squabbling until the foreigner has gone.'

Becket pupped with his lips. 'True. Even the bloody Earl of Leicester could lead us.'

'But cut her off now, with no outside threat to hold us together. . . . Would you follow the Earl of Leicester? What of the Scottish boy-king, James? What of his mother? Which would the Council choose? There is no heir of Her Majesty's body nor ever will be now. The realm would burst asunder. And then comes Philip of Spain with his army when it is ready in a year or two when we are bloody and wearied with fighting and London a smoking ruin, and so he makes peace between us all.'

Becket looked about him. 'It seems impossible that . . . .'

'David, you have seen the Netherlands that were so rich. Learned you nothing there of how delicate a thing is the rule of justice in a realm, how easily unseated?'

'Ay,' said Becket, heavily, glaring down into his tankard as if hunting for Spaniards in the lees. 'But . . . .'

'But? The Almighty will protect you? The Almighty, being English (blessed be He) will not permit such a thing to come to pass?' Simon was sneering at him. 'Tell it to the Portuguese or the Dutch, yea, tell it even to the Bohemians. It is not so hard a thing to kill a Prince. The way to do it is to send a single man that cares not if he live or die, but that he gain a martyr's crown. Which I think they have done. But to catch such a one is like hunting a particular fish among the cod on the Newfoundland banks.'

'But you are a . . . a little closer now,' Becket said at last, 'are you not?'

'Oh we are.' Simon spoke wearily. 'Your finding of the ballad singer was a fine trick. How was it done?' He asked the question delicately, nervous of Becket's mood and jumped with fright when Becket cracked out a laugh.

'Why, I went and spoke to the King,' Becket explained. 'And he received me and gave me audience and in return for a little service, he found out who had been hiring of Spanish-trained arquebusiers and foot-pads such as Bonecrack Smith. It were no great labour.'

'The King? Do you mean the King of thieves?'

'Who else would know such things?'

'I had heard of him, but not believed . . . .'

'Oh come now, Simon, where there is gold and power and no law there will come first anarchy and then at last a King.'

'And what was the little service he asked for his help?'

'He desires an audience with your master.'

'With Sir Francis?'

'Yes.'

'You never spoke to me of it before.'

'He wished me not to do so until you had cause to be . . . grateful.'

Simon looked long and hard at David. 'Hm,' he said at last. 'He has certainly rendered me a favour. You may tell him that I shall speak to my master of it, if I may know his name.'

'Laurence Pickering.'

Simon nodded, then sighed, picked up his cooled tankard and drained it. Becket elbowed him in the ribs again, nearly knocking him from the bench.

'Why so melancholy, Simon? Is this not in . . . in the way of a victory for you?' He had slurred the words, swayed a little as he spoke, too jovial.

'It saddens me when a friend will not tell me the truth.'

The Almighty help him, he had not meant to put it so baldly, the words had tumbled out of his mouth like naughty boys out of school. Becket froze, glaring at him.

'Do you give me the lie, sir?' he demanded.

'No, no, not exactly.' Simon strove to placate, 'I am truly grateful for your work in this, but . . . .'

'But?' Becket's face had darkened with blood under the skin.

Simon swallowed hard. 'But . . . I wish that you had told me of your own free will that you know both Anthony Fant and Adam Strangways.'

Becket said nothing.

'I am as you know, of Sir Francis Walsingham's household,' Simon struggled on. 'He is a most worshipful man, but . . . suspicious else he could not do what he does. We all of us become as suspicious as he, we must for there are indeed workers in strange corners, men to suspect. Treachery flowers easily among men who grasp after power and gold . . . .'

'Are you saying I am a traitor?'

'No sir. It is only that . . . I have given you many chances to tell me that you know the master of this house and that you know the man I seek, and you have not done so and . . . it saddens me. You were at Gray's Inn with them after all.'

Oh how reedily his voice trailed off. This was not what he had planned at all.

'Will you . . . will you tell me anything about them that you know?'

'Should there not be a clerk here to note down what I say? And perhaps Mr Rackmaster Norton with his toy to teach me honesty?'

Ames met his eye, passed a hand across his face again. 'You have not been arrested. You need say nothing to me if it please you not. I ask as a friend.'

'And if I say nothing? What then? The Tower? I see you have sufficient power to roust the Recorder of London out of his bed. No doubt you could find a warrant about you somewhere and have me into Little Ease before morning, eh?'

A cold thought entered Simon's mind, that it was odd to see so big a man struggle so fiercely with fear, though he hid it well.

Suddenly there was a smell of violence in the air, that if Becket thought himself about to be taken, he would not go quietly, that he would rather gamble all, beat Simon down with a poker and run. In seconds he had gone from friendliness to the brink of fury.

How can I reassure him, Ames wondered, when I am not certain myself of his trueness? If I prevaricate I am surely dead.

In the kitchen passageway there was a sudden banging as the searchers began to remove panelling. Becket jumped a little but never took his eyes from Ames. Here I was talking to a friend, Ames thought to himself sadly, that I was only a little doubtful of, and now he is become like a beast of the forest that I must calm.

Becket had shifted a little on the bench, freeing his sword. His hand had dropped to his dagger.

'I am not a Spaniard,' Simon said in a rush, hearing foreignness in them as the words came without a plan. 'It was Spaniards put you to the question before, no?' Ask no questions, warned a voice within him, and he answered himself. 'Ay, it was.' Simon's mouth was dry, felt sticky inside with fear. 'All I have is my dagger. If you think me so false and forgetful a friend as to arrest you, then do what you plan. I will not fight back.' Somehow he managed a smile, though his lips stuck to his teeth. 'I know well it would be a waste of time and sweat.'

'I may go?'

'David, I know so little of you, I wish . . . . If I must lay my life on it that you are no traitor, then I will. But if you trust me not, then go at once. I doubt you will be missed.'

Becket stood up, looming massively over Simon's hunched thin shoulders. Very slowly and carefully, he moved to the carrier's door, picking delicately and silently over the flags. As he opened the door, he said, 'I believe you, Simon.'

And then he was through and into the little kitchen garden and past

134

the jakes and out the privy gate, leaving Ames to take a long slow breath. I have never been so close to death, Ames thought to himself, with a kind of cold wonder, and then his shoulders sagged and he coughed and weariness fell on him like a cloak of mail. He longed for sleep but wondered despairingly where he could be safe. For Adam Strangways was still at large, though with luck he was in hiding and unable to act without his ballad singer go-between. Yet he might have set on pursuers earlier who still hunted Simon.

Ames found he no longer cared. He waited until the horse litter came for Mrs Fant. Then speaking habitual words he did not hear himself say, he walked out of Anthony Fant's townhouse and down Old Change to Knightrider Street, where he found that the Crusader Inn would open its door to him, although it was long past curfew.

Perhaps his luck had turned. The landlady greeted him with a kiss and the sheets were clean linen. She put a warming pan in for him while he undressed and when she had taken it out again and bidden him God bless, he climbed into a nest of warmth in his shirt and netherhose. He said his prayers unworthily, paying out mere words like beads on a string. With the bed curtains tight shut, he could believe in his safety as a kind of lesser fiction, and sleep like the dead.

XXXIII

Within every head upon each pillow lies a world, with its cities of thought and its forests of dreaming. Deserts and mountains have we all of us within our skulls, with only the cities to bring light and learning to the savage country. My cities are all broken and destroyed like the stone forests of old Rome, but even in those whose minds are as populous as the plain of Flanders, come the night and sleep, the Queen Moon mounts her white horse and rides jingling her bell bridle over the forests and heaths, and beggars and creatures of rags and patches come dancing from their hiding places. London at night swarms with dreams so I am hard put to it to pick my way safely between the shadows of the true world and those of the truer one beyond where I dwell daily and all men

135

visit nightly. Now here is Walsingham twitching in his bed while the rabble of Paris hunt him through the maze of his own mind and there is Simon Ames at table with the Spanish pyre of his uncles blazing before him, too fearful a thing to recall in the morning, as are all his dreams. Becket had found himself a greasy little boozing ken to drown out his own fears, safe in the liberties of Whitefriars, and snored like a pig with his head on his hands, dreamless.

The Royal Mint, which girdles the Tower between the inner and outer wall, begins its work well before sunrise in winter, with a hideous hissing and bellows-pumping of the furnace and then the round bright rhythmic clanging of die upon metal. Picture after picture of the Queen spills from their unmusical work, pennies, groats, shillings, half crowns, crowns. Is it the magic of the Queen's face that lends them their worth, or the silver in the higher ones?

Within the Salt Tower, the clanging brought cannon into Anthony Fant's dreams. He woke with sweat freezing to him, and stone walls around him, the agony of an arm smashed by an arquebus ball running through him like fire and jerking him ten years into the past. Christ have mercy, was it all to do again? and he reached with his right hand to feel for his wounded left and found nothing there. He had been through such awakenings before and so swam back into the waking world where amputated arms do not miraculously regrow in a night. With his own eyes, after all, he had seen the stinking black swollen horror that was once his hand and arm tossed into a bucket and heard the red-hot iron steaming and sizzling in his blood. He often wondered at the clarity of his memory: he could remember how he had bucked and fought against straps and wrapping arms, how the taste of the leather in his mouth had gone through his head and become imprinted there with bile, how he had still possessed a particle of sense buried deep in the animal which wondered why he did not faint, and yet he had no memory of the pain, only of what he did while it was there. The pain that came and went in the ghost of his lost arm was a different thing; his memory of losing it had been mercifully censored by a mysterious God who had not let him faint at the time.

Which same merciful God had now caused him to be put in the Tower, discreetly and courteously escorted from his lodgings at the point of going to his bed by a well-dressed plain-faced young man and two others and brought at once upriver. He knew no reason why, except that his wife was a Catholic.

Fant sat up and looked about him in the darkness, at a small empty

136

round room with a covering for form's sake of elderly rushes on the floor, a bed with a thin pallet on it and nothing else. Starlight coming in at the barred window glanced off walls ominously roughened with carving. It was the musty damp smell and the hardness of his bed and sleeping in all his clothes, these had taken him back to Haarlem where his arm lay (would he have to go back there to look for it on the Day of Judgment, he sometimes wondered).

Something his wife had done had brought him here. No doubt she was also in the Tower, listening to the clanging. For a moment he felt anger at her foolishness and disobedience and then he sighed. Until someone came to question him he could do nothing. All was in God's hands, in whom he trusted mainly out of unbreakable habit. Had not God delivered him out of the Spaniard's paw for the purpose of making the New World English and not foul Spanish? Had not the very loss of his arm saved his life? He climbed out of bed, knelt on the floor and thanked God for his life so far, asked mercy for himself because he was a sinner and for his children because they were innocent and, if possible, for his wife because she was only a woman and could not help herself. Then he climbed back onto the pallet, huddled his gown up about his ears, put his hat on his face and went back to sleep.

Agnes meanwhile had woken to find Catherine Nisbet bending over the fireplace and weeping salt tears into her skirt because she had laid the fire and now could not get the tinder to light no matter how she struck flint to steel again and again. The babe kicked cruelly at Agnes' ribs and she must haul herself up by using the curtains because the bed was old and sagged in the middle. The cold struck at her as it had at Nisbet, but found her armoured against it by the little furnace of the child within. She rolled cautiously to put her feet in her shoes and waddled over to the fireplace, where she took the flint and steel from Catherine's shaking hands, found the tinder to be damp, no doubt from tears, fetched another scrap out of the box and had the little stub of candle lit in a few minutes more. With the fire curling through hay into the wood, she went back to the chest where her clothes lay.

Mrs Nisbet stumbled over to her in the dark to assist her to put on her hose since she could not reach her feet except sideways, scolding all the while that Agnes should not be cold when her time was so near, it was invariably fatal, and Walsingham was wicked and cruel to do so to a woman in her state. She would speak of it to that meagre little clerk and demand better lodging.

Agnes watched Catherine Nisbet's breath make curls dragonlike in the air and let her complaints run about unresisted: she wondered at how calm she herself was, how she had known at once on waking where she lay and why, and yet it had brought no stab of terror to her heart. Was this how God had helped the martyrs of Rome? She had dreamt of Edward, Mary and Elizabeth waving farewell to her as she left them in the summer, and in her dream Catherine was there also in her new petticoat.

When she left she had hoped to be back in time for Edward's breeching, but Dorcas their nurse had seen him out of his child's skirts and into his man's hose, with a proud (and blunt) little sword to complete the picture of a gentleman. Edward himself had written to her about it, very carefully, with only one small blot, signing himself her most dutiful and loving son. The girls had put their marks to the paper also and Mr Carbury the tutor had penned an elegant and incomprehensible report of their doings, their achievements and the great day when Edward was breeched. She had shown it to Adam, longing to be able to present her children to him for his blessing, but he had only glanced at the letters and asked if they were being brought up in the True Faith as their mother would have wished. She had asked him hesitantly if it would be possible for him to come and give Edward his First Holy Communion, but he had told her severely that his work would not admit of it.

'Oh, they have taken our rosaries,' wept Mrs Nisbet. 'How shall we pray?'

Agnes blinked at her stupidly, to find she had finished her toilet, dressed, pinned her hair, put on her cap, all while she was thinking of her children. She made a wry smile at Mrs Nisbet's distress.

'There are worse things they could have taken,' she said and then softened her severity. 'We can pray on our fingers as they used to do under Diocletian.

Becket in his boozing ken, meanwhile, awoke when a scrawny child tried to wipe the table around his arms, and lifted his head like a bear. His hands had gone numb and tingling, his back and arse ached and his head pounded from bad wine and beer. He rose like a man long dead of old age, while the child dodged and backed against the wall. Ignoring her reedy cries about the reckoning he pulled himself out the door. There was too much sunlight for all it was only dawn and so misty, he screwed up his eyes and wavered to the conduit, where he broke the ice and dunked his head and gasped as if he was wounded. Then he sat down upon a stone lion's mane and moaned gently to himself.

He had had worse awakenings. Slowly his mind waded like a lost traveller in a swamp back to the end and origin of his drunkenness and found there Simon Ames and a sudden turning of Anthony Fant's kitchen in ghostly wise to a small Dutch farmhouse where he had lain bleeding and gasping on the well-scrubbed floor of the locked pantry.

'Christ,' he said and dug his fingers at his eyeballs, trying not to puke at the memory and what happened after. But the drink had not scoured it out of him and nor could his distemper afterwards, for in Simon's English tones he had heard that clever old Spanish soldier Julian Romero asking gently and remorselessly what message exactly he was to carry into Haarlem.

He lifted his head and looked about for an inn that might be open, but when he felt his purse he found that the reason why it had not been cut was that it was empty. The coldness of the water made his nose throb when he drank it, and then he set himself on his two legs and began to walk down Fleet Street to Eliza Fumey's linen shop which was the nearest place he knew where he might find paper, pens and ink. He gave no sign of noticing the slender clever-faced man with a wheelbarrow of fruit who paced him exactly upon the other side of the street. I saw him as I also saw Agnes upon the other side of the city, shifting her knees on the cold stone and trying to turn her wandering mind back to the five Sorrowful Mysteries of Our Lady while the coiners of the Mint stamped and struck at their precious metals and the Clerks of the Records and the Ordnance came hurrying in streams through the Lion Gate and the Watergate, and the river mist made of the stone Tower a cunning ship sailing on the air.

XXXIV

A stone dropped in the fair diamond puddle wherein I was considering of these things, and broke it to shards. Tom would have lashed out angrily at this spoiling of his play, but I prevented him and glanced up at the one who had done it, with the misty sunlight turned to pillars and rainbows in my eyes.

A boy stood there, scratching languidly at his cods, with a fine red silk slashed and watered doublet of a size to fit a fullgrown man which drowned out his poor thin shoulders and arms.

'Gabriel,' said I, for I knew him well. He is a wild rogue, born on the road to the daughter of one of King Henry's spoiled nuns, and reared entirely in mischief and thievery, and bidding fair to be the King of London in Laurence's place, when that one dies or is hanged.

'Which is it?' he demanded suspiciously, with his long narrow fingers at his knife. 'Tom or the Clever One?'

'The Clever One,' I said peaceably, 'for the moment. Why do you trouble me?'

For answer he caught my hand and pulled me behind him from the alley and into Fleet Street, through Temple Bar and along the muddy disgrace of the Strand where the rich men's houses stand. Those same rich men are too mean to pave their road over because they take the river when they must traverse east to west. Then he dived down another little alley hard by Holywell Street.

A naked boy was squatting there, his back against icy stone and the skin staring on him like a plucked chicken, his eyes wide open and seeing nothing, and his bruised arms clamped tight upon his bruised knees.

An elder boy in oversized velvet rags lolled against the stone, paring his nails with a comically large knife. He stood up straight and sheathed the knife when he saw Gabriel, swallowing nervousness. Gabriel made his name by killing an upright-man that beat a friend of his, and he has wounded those who follow him if they fail to obey or show him respect.

'No change,' said the other boy with a poor ducking bow. 'Sits as still as a stone, save for shivering.'

Gabriel looked at me and then nodded at the naked boy.

'What do you make of him, Tom?'

I sat down on my haunches next to him and waggled my fingers close to his eyes, touched his hands which were cold and clammy. He might have been dead but for the shivering and blinking. Another boy came running up the alley, holding a shirt and blanket with twigs from the hedgerow still stuck in them, thrust them into Gabriel's arms and ran off again.

'I brought you to him to know if he is mad.' Gabriel said, 'Is he? He looks as if his sense has gone flown away, and speaks nothing.'

'Come boy,' I said, 'stand up and we will dress you.'

To my surprise he stood, put his arms up like a small child or a nobleman accustomed to being attended at his dressing. There were old bruises and scratches of a birch-beating on his backside. I dropped the shirt over him, where it hung about and flapped, and wrapped the blanket on top. This was different gear to the fine shirt with the mute swans upon it and his blue livery suit that someone had despoiled him of in the night.

'What is your name?' I asked, 'I am called Tom of Bedlam, which is not my right name, but you may call me by it.' He nodded his fair head and smiled a little shyly and I knew then his sense was not so far gone that it could not come back in at the windows of his head. He knew me from the time I had followed him in his errand to Agnes Fant's house, and warned him of Lucifer.

'Give us your name,' Gabriel said harshly. 'Who are you?'

The boy turned to me, making 'Ung ung' noises like a dummerer that would have you think he is speechless, the better to beg, but when he opened his mouth wide and pointed, we saw he was indeed a true dummerer, for his tongue was a quarter its proper length.

'God's guts,' said Gabriel, catching his chin and peering in. 'Was it cut?'

The boy had shut his eyes, shame staining his pale cheeks crimson. I shook my head. 'No, I think not. I saw a printer once that had his tongue cut for slander, and it was all gnarled into scars from the searing iron, though he could speak a little with it. The boy was born so, I think.'

Gabriel's eyes narrowed and he surveyed the boy up and down like a farmer considering of a milch cow.

'Too fat and well-kempt,' he said, 'but with a few spearwort plasters and a little less lard . . . .' He grinned. 'If he is abram as well, so much the better.'

'I am no physician,' I said gravely, now understanding his embroidered mute swans for a sign and a signal, 'but I think he has had some great shock which overwrought him. Do you know who it was robbed him of his clothes?'

'None of mine,' said Gabriel, 'though it was a hard night. I will ask of the palliards, but I doubt we can find the duds. Why, were they good?'

'Ay, worth a few pounds I would say.'

'Do you know him then?'

'No, but he has been errand-running about here before. Did you not mark him at all?'

'Of course I did,' lied Gabriel, 'I wanted to know if you done so. He could be worth some mint. Will you keep him until I come for him then?'

141

I hesitated. What if Tom should return and do him some injury? But then, left as he was, he would starve or freeze and if he had food in his belly, he could always run from Tom if he must.

'He must be clothed better than this,' I said, 'which I cannot do. And nor can he beg yet.'

Gabriel reached in his codpiece and pulled out a couple of shillings.

'There,' he said, 'let him not die and see if you can learn what he was and where he came from. And if you will be counselled by me, feed him nothing until he is thin enough to earn his pannam at the begging law, and beat him well so he pays you mind, if you will be wise.'

Gabriel slipped away with his henchmen, dissolving among the morning crowds upon the street. I turned to the boy and smiled at his fright.

'Ah, but I am Tom,' I said, 'and notorious for my unwisdom. Come.'

XXXV

Great men's barges sail upon the Thames like swans amongst the lesser breeds of ducks. In the one sits Burghley, lapped in sable and black brocade, in the other stands my lord of Leicester, tigerish in tawny and black velvet, a half-cloak over his shoulder and his gloves alight with topaz, rubies and amber. Half his mind is preoccupied with the cost of silk flowers, since Her Majesty hath taken a fancy to appear as Proserpine upon her Accession Day and now expects that the bower will be decked with blossom of spring, whereas the flowers that would have graced it have been eaten by mice and must now be replaced within a week and at no cost to the Court.

Walsingham, living hard by the Tower in Seething Lane, need only walk with his attendants around to the Lion Gate and so enter, but nothing may begin without the Privy Councillors.

Meantime, in the Wakefield Tower, Simon Ames sat behind a small desk, dabbing cautiously at his sore nose. Kinsley brought in Anthony Fant with a flourishing rattle of the door, and Simon saw with a little jolt of surprise that the man had only one arm. He was tall, running to flesh, with a round red face and thinning black hair, in a fine-woven well-tailored suit of murrey wool, the left sleeve pinned back neatly. He stood and stared down at Simon, ignoring the stool that Kinsley pointed to, before he said in a deep voice, 'I assume you will explain the meaning of this, sir.'

'Yes, Mr Fant, I will.' Simon gestured again at the stool, which Fant ignored, his whole body a study in dignity of a gentleman. 'You will be brought before the Privy Council to answer unto them for your harbouring of a traitor.' Kinsley blinked at such openness with a prisoner.

'What kind of traitor?' Fant demanded. 'Some damned priest?'

'No sir. Your brother in law who has . . . .'

'That bastard? I had hoped he was dead.'

'No.'

'Why do you want him?'

Simon took a deep breath. 'Mr Fant, I will be clear with you. I believe he has come into England to murder the Queen. Your wife harboured him in your house on Old Change.'

'Christ Almighty,' said Fant, sitting down on the stool at last.

'Will you help me find him, Mr Fant?' Simon asked quietly. 'I understand from your wife that you are no Catholic. And this is no mere matter of Jesuits and printing presses, this concerns the kingdom and the Queen's life. I beg you will help me.'

'In my house. Adam Strangways. God damn it, I cannot believe Agnes would . . . . Her brother, of course. Hard for her to refuse, but Jesu . . . . When he . . . . Jesu . . . I must speak to her.'

'Speak to her?'

'Yes, by God, I want to speak to my wife.' Fant was reddening and swelling before Simon's eyes. Ames remembered what Becket had failed to tell him, watching coldly to see if Fant's anger was an act or no. If it was the man knew how to flush to order.

They made a procession along the wall-walk, climbed the stair and found Agnes Fant and Catherine Nisbet breaking their fast with bread and cheese and small beer. When Agnes rose and made her curtsey to her lord, Anthony Fant stood straight and stony. There was a vein beating in his neck under his ruff, Simon noticed, and his one fist was clenched.

'What is the meaning of this, madam?' he demanded. Agnes swallowed, laced her fingers over her belly and stood still watching a cockroach scuttling along the wall. 'At our very wedding I gave orders that your brother was not to be seen by you nor our children if he ever came into this land again, not for the reason that he is a Papist which you know I will not use as a stick to beat a man, but for another reason, good and sufficient. Did you not swear this to me?'

'Yes sir.'

'He comes back to England, curse his guts, and straightaway you give him shelter in *my* house, feed him *my* food, put *my* children in peril because he is a traitor, a foul evil man. What do you say, madam?'

The cockroach had found a crack and slipped into it. Was this to be her punishment for envying Dorcas that her children ran to their nurse first when they were hurt, not to see any of them again? Agnes had never seen Anthony in such a rage, she had not known he could be so angry because she had always tried to please him, as a good wife should. She thought she had been a good wife to him, until the strange pedlar came in Peterkin's place with his thunderbolt of silent paper. Her mouth was dry, her throat stopped up, he had never berated her publicly before, Catherine Nisbet was staring at him with her mouth open, indeed, he had never berated her at all. He had always been a gentle and kindly husband who would sometimes in the night put his head on her shoulder and smile in his sleep, as if he loved her.

The silence was as heavy as an anvil, but she could not speak. She had not been entirely innocent. Adam had met a ballad singer who looked uncommonly like the one who came with the message; her steward had written to tell her of the rotted corpse in Peterkin's clothes that the men had found when they went to take down the deer fences. There had been the strange zany, more like a bale of twigs than a man, who had screeched a warning of Walsingham's men and Adam had left the place within an hour. And Walsingham's men had indeed descended upon them that evening.

She swallowed again, sickness and heartburn in her throat still rendering her dumb, and beneath her fingers she felt the sharp shifting and prodding of the new baby's feet against its swaddling of flesh.

'You kept me ignorant,' Anthony said at last. 'You used my house but you told me nothing.' To protect you, Agnes wanted to say, but could not. 'If it had been some priest, any man but Adam Strangways, I would . . . I would try to help you, Agnes.' Were there tears in his eyes? No, surely not. Yes, he was trying to ram one of them back with his forefinger. It seemed as if the stuff in her throat would strangle her, and her legs felt strange and far away. Why could she not say at least that she was sorry, when she was indeed sorry? She opened her mouth again, but nothing came out.

Anthony turned away from her, waiting while Mr Ames knocked and

144

the man outside opened it and the procession trooped out again. Agnes stared at that door for a long time after it had been shut and bolted, until Catherine Nisbet came fluttering round her and led her to the single chair and sat her in it, all the while complaining of Mr Fant's hard usage to her.

'Be quiet,' she snapped at last, her voice returning when she had no more need of it. 'He was a good lord to me and now I have hurt him sorely.'

'But for the Cause . . . .' said Catherine with her foolish pale eyes filling up with her meaningless easy tears.

I come to bring a sword, Christ had said, and He spoke no more than the truth. She wished she could pray for guidance but she could not.

Upon the wall-walk, Anthony Fant glared over the shining moat, newly skinned over with ice, at the smoking roofs of London.

'I believe you, sir,' he said. 'My wife is a truthful woman and finds it hard to lie. Had she denied anything, I would have believed her before I believed you. But in her silence hides her guilt.' He stopped, blinked out at a wagon making its precarious way down Little Tower Hill. 'If you will take me to Old Change I will make sure you have missed nothing that may be hidden in my house. And then I will help you in any way I can.'

Ames chose his next words with care. 'What was it Strangways did that makes you so hot against him sir?'

'He is a traitor, you told me so yourself.'

'You have only my word on it, sir. With respect, I am not usually so easily believed.'

'No. Hmf. Well, if he is not dead in a ditch somewhere, seek out a man called David Becket and ask him.'

'I am asking you, Mr Fant.'

Fant turned his head to look at him, but Ames could not read his expression.

'Whatever you know, I pray you will tell me, sir,' he pleaded. 'My lords of Burghley and Leicester are making their way here to examine you and your wife, if I may have something to show them . . . .'

'Privy Councillors waiting upon me?'

Simon coughed. 'Er . . . no, only I am assured that a woman so close to her time should not be carted about from place to place, it would not be seemly.'

'Hmf.'

'You said you would help me find the man.'

145

'Ay, I did. But it is not so easy to unstopper a tale I have never told before.'

'Perhaps we might go to my office.'

With Kinsley and Fant's assigned Yeoman standing guard at the door, and bread and cheese and small beer divided between them within, Fant ate in morose silence, drank, then sat back and glared at his one hand resting on his thigh. Ames was too wrought up with tension to eat more than a bite of bread, and found the beer to be sour.

'Were you among those who went out to Flushing with Captain Morgan in 1572?' he prodded gently.

'Walter Morgan reported on it for my lord Burghley, did he not?'

'Yes.'

'He boasted he was doing so. Have you read it?'

'Indeed, yes.'

'He is the Captain's cousin, but not quite as great a fool. Well, if you have read it you know more than I do about the expedition.'

'It seems you were not altogether successful . . . .'

'Successful?' Anthony Fant laughed nastily. 'Christ, it was a God-forsaken joke, a pack of gentlemen wastrels and ne'er-do-wells prancing over to Holland to save the poor Dutch burghers from the stupid Spanish, sack a few rich cities and prance back again by Christmas, well weighted with gold.'

Simon held his peace.

'Upon the journey to Flushing I know one young fool that was brought to tears by seasickness and the fact that the seawater spoiled his new velvet suit and so he would not cut quite so fine a figure when he landed.'

Fant blinked at the frost damascening the window behind Simon's head. 'To this day, I cannot eat stockfish.'

'Stockfish?' asked Simon.

'Flushing, or Flissingen as the butter-eaters call it, is a fishing port and there they make stockfish to ship into England and down the Rhine into France. The whole town stinks with fish, every yard is decked with fish and littered with salt barrels, and what they cannot sell, they eat. Nine or ten months we spent there, God help us, no pay, notes to buy food and never anything to buy but fish, and the damned French in all the best billets. When the news of St Bartholomew's eve came we cheered, God forgive us, for the French that were in Flushing were Huguenots. Becket got his stripes then, from Roger Williams.'

'Oh?' asked Simon in neutral tone.

'He began some drunken brawl in one of the few inns that would still serve Englishmen, was well beaten and so he set light to the place in revenge. Williams made an example of him. At the time I was shocked to see a gentleman flogged.'

'And now?'

'Now? I would have hanged him and saved much grief. But then I muttered of mutiny myself along with his other cronies, until the French-men left and the Spaniards came.

Simon held silent. Fant banged his hand on his knee, turned on him.

'You know what became of us, if you read Morgan's account. You know the fine show we put up against the Spanish tercios.'

'Why, think you, did they win?'

'Oh count the reasons, Mr Ames. Imprimis, they were veterans, we were raw. Item, they knew how to load and shoot their arquebuses and we did not. Item, they knew how to hold their pikes and we did not. Item, they knew which end of a cannon the ball comes out, we did not. Item, they had commanders accustomed to command and impose discipline, and we had Gilbert and Morgan that quarrelled with each other from dawn to dusk and then drank from dusk to dawn.'

'But surely the English are the finest fighters upon the sea,' said Simon, more naively than he was.

'Oh to be sure, Mr Ames, upon the sea. But put us upon the land in some muddy little pack of hovels . . . . We were well enough when we raided them, when we went out to kill the Spaniards in their beds and amuse them a little, but set us up against a tercio in battle array, pikes levelled, artillery firing and we broke and ran. Gilbert went home with his tail between his legs and most of his martial men with him.'

'Not you?'

'No, I was too great a fool. Becket gave me the notion for it, damn him: he said he would go to fight for the Prince of Orange in Sassenheim because he could not leave the Dutch to think that all an Englishman can do is shit his breeches, turn tail and flee. I agreed with him. About one hundred of us went to the Prince.'

'Did you not know that Becket was hiding from his creditors?'

Fant looked down his nose. 'Of a certainty I knew, I was the one that told him Tyrrel had taken out a writ against him for his debts.' He smiled. 'I advised him to go home, confess all to his father and ask for his mercy and help.'

'And?'

'As I understood it from Becket, his father gave his third son an unscriptural beating, broke his nose for him, booted him out of his house

147

and Becket stole his favourite horse to bear him back to London.'

Simon hid a smile.

Fant sighed. 'We chose a fine time to join the Prince. That was the year when the Spaniards were running through the rebel provinces toppling our towns like a boy breaking mud forts with his feet. Then . . . where was it? Naarden tried to come to terms but the Capitano del Campo, Julian Romero, he got into the city under a flag of truce and they massacred all the people in their own church.'

Fant passed his hand over his eyes.

'What do you know of Haarlem, Mr Ames?'

'Little enough,' said Simon untruthfully. 'A town parallel to Amsterdam and controlling the westerly routes to Holland.'

'No one thought it could hold, not even the Prince who hoped it might. The walls were too high and thin, no earthworks to speak of, a port on the Haarlemmermeer. They say it was a fair city and it was rich.'

Simon poured him some more of the beer to wet his throat.

'Jesu, why make an Iliad of it. The Spanish found it a tougher nut to crack than they thought, but they took the city in the end.'

'Were you there?'

'Yes, Becket, Strangways, Balfour that was at least an honest bastard in his perfidy. At the end he convinced the Spaniards, Christ knows how, that if they let him live he would contrive to kill William of Orange.'

'He did not, though.'

'No, no, when they let him go he went straight to the Prince and told him of it and dined out on the tale for years after. Now Balfour was a cunning man, a Scot. He got us into Haarlem and to be fair he told us clear that it was a foolish thing and likely to lead to our deaths. There were above thirty thousand Spaniards round about the town, but with the lake frozen and winter mists so thick, they could not stop the supplies coming in. We ran one hundred and seventy sledges loaded with food and gunpowder into Haarlem right under Julian Romero's nose, it was a famous deed.'

He fell silent and Simon coughed again. 'What happened after?'

'It was a siege. The Spaniards dug their siegeworks, we raided them for food, we worked like peasants to keep the walls buttressed against their artillery. They mined us, we countermined them and set off their petards, and they beat the Prince's relief forces again and again. And in time we learnt of new things to eat such as horse and dog and rat and that tulip bulbs may be eaten if well soaked and salted first to take out

148

the bitterness. By the end there was but a quarter pound of bread per diem for the men and that mostly sawdust. It was a vision of death, Mr Ames, to see a city with no children in the streets and the few that lived gone into old age in a few months. There was one I knew – she was the daughter of a woman that Becket and I were billeted upon, a wealthy woman she had been once, but her husband died in the Christmas attack Don Fadrique made on the Gate of the Cross. She had lost her other children before, this was the last. When Becket was laid up with a sword slash on the leg, little Anna taught him Dutch.' Fant shook his head. 'This was her plot. She desired to teach Becket her tongue to further his suit to the widow her mother, since she liked him better than she liked me.'

'Eh?'

'You would scarcely credit it, but Becket and I were nearly at daggers drawn over that Dutchwoman. I think he might have won her, but. . . . Come the spring when the ice melted and the Spaniards got control of the Haarlemmermeer, Ilse put Anna to bed and Becket would spend hours reading her tales from the Bible – Genesis, Jonah and the Whale, Tobit.

'Then Balfour asked him to take a message to Sassenheim, begging the Prince to try again to relieve the city. Balfour knew he spoke Dutch, you see, and could pass as a Fleming with a little luck. Becket agreed to it, and we made another attack for horses to eat, and he slipped away during the fighting.'

This time Fant was silent for a long time, and Simon heard the shouts and clash of halberds as the Privy Councillors came in by the Watergate.

'And?' he asked at last.

'He never came back. Anna took a fever and died. When Count Batenburg came with his puny raw army, Romero knew the day and smogged out our signal fires with green woodsmoke, he knew the direction and laid ambushes and cut them to pieces as they blundered about in the smoke. We watched from the walls.

'Well, Orange told us by pigeon to surrender. But the Haarlemites would not, they swore that since they must die as the townsfolk at Naarden and Zutphen had died, they would rather die fighting and fire the town behind them. In the end, Duke Alva was so puzzled he made a merciful treaty: he would kill only the garrison, the officers, the Protestant pastors, the town council and all who led the fight against their lawful King. The rest might live and he would not sack the city although he had spent nearly a year in taking it.'

'But you – were you not one of the garrison? How did you survive?'

'It was in the treaty, that all the garrison must give themselves up or the Spaniards would sack the town. I would have surrendered and been put to the sword or drowned, but I had taken an arquebus bullet in my arm in the attack that gave Becket his chance. The wound sickened and the night before the surrender Ilse brought a barber surgeon to cut it off. When the soldiers came, she convinced them that I was her husband, shot upon the walls. I know not how she did it since I was near death at the time.'

'But . . . how did Romero know when the relieving force was to come?'

'Must I spell it out for you like a tutor? Adam Strangways had turned his coat months before, when he disappeared after one of our sorties and went to serve Romero – he was a Papist and liked not our jests with Mass things and idolatrous images that they think so sacred. Julian Romero kept him by to serve him and advise him. And when Becket came back from Prince William, he met Strangways and betrayed the date and direction of the relief force to him.'

Simon let out a breath. 'Becket turned his coat as well?'

Fant shrugged. 'How else did he live after the Spaniards caught him?'

'But . . . I heard Becket fought the Spaniards later, he raided them, he took a gunpowder mill from them, I have had letters from informers in the Netherlands that say the Spanish feared him.'

'So he turned it back. Once done it is easy to do again. Roger Williams did the same, only less foully.'

'No, but I . . . Well. And you? How did you fare after the siege ended?'

Fant smiled, a warmer smile. 'I married the Dutchwoman, when I was well of my arm, since it had pleased God to spare me to her. We planted lime saplings in her street to replace the trees that withered and died when we ate their bark. I had no notion that my elder brother was dead of sweating sickness or I would have returned, and my father thought me dead. As I told you, Ilse was wealthy, she was a burgher's wife and although she had fought with the women's troop, the Spaniards let her keep her property. She was a good match and . . . we were fond enough.'

His face became bleak again. 'I would be living there now, only she died miscarrying our child and I inherited her wealth. Which was as well when I sold up and came back to England and found what state my father had brought our lands to. With both his sons dead, as he thought, he had no stomach to business. Thank God he lived to see me return.'

'Mr Fant,' said Simon, 'I am indebted to you for this account, but I must be clear upon one thing. You say that Becket betrayed the relief force to Strangways and Strangways passed the intelligence on to Julian Romero. How do you know?'

'Balfour told me.'

'He could have lied.'

'Ay, but David Becket told me so himself, years later. He came to me at home one night, drunk, dressed as a beggar, wanting money of me, and I would have shot him if I could have found a bow or an arquebus. I asked him then if he could deny what Balfour said, and he did not, so I gave him a shilling and had my reeve throw him out.'

Simon chewed the skin of his chapped lips and blinked down at his chapped fingers, then drew on his gloves.

'Sir, I must hurry and wait upon my lords Burghley and Leicester and my master. I will tell them that you have helped and will continue to help me and that I think there is no need for you to be brought before them, but will rather save time by rendering a report in writing. Your wife however must be seen by them.'

Fant looked away. 'She is no longer my wife.'

'Have you told her this tale?'

'No. I had no wish to distress her. She loved her brother greatly as a child.'

'Might she not have refused Strangways shelter if she had known.'

Fant's round pleasant face was cold. 'As my wife I expected her to obey.'

Simon said nothing, but made his bow and left.

XXXVI

It was one of the better rooms in the Wakefield Tower, hung with old moth-eaten tapestries brought out of storage in Coldharbour where they had been put since their fashion was of the Queen's grandfather's time, with wooden ugly men and snakelike sinuous women with white pudding faces and complex foolish plants. The fire burned brightly, heaped up to make attempt at warming the Councillors. The crystal sunshine breaking through the window made a mockery of these poor attempts and the room looked better in the shadows where Simon's desk was placed, though he had need of a candle. Sir Francis was seated at a heavy old table reading a report, when Ames entered and bowed.

'If I may speak with you a moment, my lord . . . ?' he said timidly. Sir Francis looked up and raised his brows. Simon rushed on. 'This capture was achieved with the aid of information from a . . . person by name Laurence Pickering.'

'Ah. The King of London, no less.'

'Yes my lord.'

'And?'

'He begs the favour of an audience with you, sir. I have promised only that I will convey his petition.'

'Hm. And the place?'

'At your pleasure, sir.'

'Then he may come to me at Seething Lane upon this Saturday evening, if he will, Mr Ames, and may bring with him one attendant in tribute to his . . . ahem . . . rank.'

'I will see he is informed, sir.'

As my lord the Earl of Leicester entered and my lord Burghley, Simon withdrew silently into his shadows and stood throughout the morning, seeing them as it were a second tapestry placed upon the old ones, the woman alone before the full weight of the Privy Council.

They began by speaking kindly of her natural foolishness as a woman, inviting her to unburden herself of her guilt by a clear and open exposition of her brother's doings, and ended with my lord of Leicester pacing the room like the lion at the Tower roaring that her silence was as guilty as sin, and showed her a plain and pustulant traitor and they would have her on the rack by God.

At which she raised her head for the first time and spoke with anger crackling in her voice.

'I know no crime that the babe within me has wrought, my lord. Even women that are convict of murder may plead their belly to the noose.'

'Are you playing for time, madam?' asked Sir Francis coldly.

'Yes, my lord. Once the babe is born, you may do as you will with me and indeed no doubt you shall. In the meantime, I pray you, my lords, do not demean yourselves with this unseemly behaviour.'

The Earl of Leicester's mouth fell open and he fairly gobbled with rage. Simon bent his head as he dipped his pen, to hide his smile. They got no further answer of her and in the end Kinsley led her from the room, where she promptly fainted upon the stair.

'Pray God it has brought on that damned babe,' said the Earl coarsely as he drank his goblet of sack. 'Christ preserve me from her kind, though no doubt she is more pleasing when not heavy with child. How may a man reason with such a creature?'

Once dismissed, Simon hurried first to see that Mistress Fant was recovered in her cell, where Catherine Nisbet had put her straight to bed with her feet higher than her heart and was bubbling a posset upon the little fire.

'Mr Ames, I must require a dish-of-coals of you, how may I tend to her with nothing to cook upon? And I must have wine to calm her nerves also and ginger and galingale and a little, a very little, pennyroyal mint and . . . .'

'Please mistress, write me a list and I shall see to it. Is she well enough to . . . .'

'No, sir, she is not, she has been kept standing this five hours and more and I must rub her legs and so I will thank you to draw the bed curtains and shut the door as you leave.'

The day was gone into the afternoon before he could win back to Anthony Fant once more, waiting patiently in his own tower room. He was far too proud to ask how his wife had fared before the Privy Councillors but smiled a little when Simon told him anyway.

'Did they think to overawe her?' he wondered. 'She has been in Westminster Hall often enough in pursuance of my lawsuits and she is a most tenacious woman, that I know well. You will get nothing of her that way, but Mr Ames, I have been considering and I believe I may show you other hidden places your searchers may have missed.'

'We are very thorough . . . .'

'Nonetheless.'

With a shrug Simon made the necessary arrangements and they walked, discreetly escorted, through the city to Old Change. There Anthony Fant only blinked a little at the wreckage Simon's men had made of his house, and led the way to a place that had been one of the first to be found.

'I think he was working here. Yes, here it is.'

He rapped the side of the cubbyhold revealed behind ripped panelling, and it sounded dull and solid. Simon looked quizzical as Fant felt about within and at last there came a click and a thick piece of wood, deeply padded with bombast and old linen, turned about on itself to show a long deep hole. Simon stopped him from reaching in, and did so himself to bring out a small box that was locked.

It broke open to Mall's crowbar and within lay the little blessed discs of wax known as *Agnus Deis*, a rosary and a roll of parchment. Ames took it, glanced at the seal, stopped and looked again, and then opened it to scan the lines of Latin.

Fant had taken one of the little discs of wax. He held it up to the light, squinted, rubbed his finger over the figure of the Lamb of God and then clenched his fist so the wax broke into crumbled shards.

'Mr Fant, I am in your debt,' said Simon, breathing hard with excitement. 'Are there any other such places?'

'No,' said Fant, drily, 'I think you have found all the others. Where did he keep the Communion wafers?'

'We found none, only Mass things and some holy water and a couple of bones in a bottle chased with silver that no doubt were relics of some sort.

'Catherine Nisbet's gear.'

'My master must see this at once, it confirms all I had feared.'

'What is it?' asked Fant. Simon hesitated, but told him.

'A plenary indulgence from the Pope,' he said. 'It says that no matter what Adam Strangways does and no matter what sin he commits in furtherance of his mission, he does not sin since what he does is to the greater glory of God. Thus murder is made a venial sin.'

Fant looked as if he wished to spit, but could not bring himself to do it inside his own house, even wrecked.

'It tells you nothing you did not know before, though. I told you Adam Strangways was a traitor.'

'This confirms it. I had not been certain before if he were a chimaera or a true danger or in some way concerned in mine own difficulty. But now I know, I may narrow the search. Do you know who built this cunning place?'

Fant thought for a long while.

'Agnes knew him, a tall bitter man, well-built, what was his name . . . Gorse? I cannot think.'

'No matter. We are making progress, Mr Fant, distinct progress.'

XXXVII

Now of all this I knew nothing then, seeing that I was well-occupied with my new apprentice. When Gabriel had gone about his business, I took the dummerer boy by the hand and led him out to the Strand. He cowered against the house walls, I thought for shame at his unclothed state, and so I brought him into alleys until we came to Barnet's the pawnbroker where I bought him shoes and a brown suit of trunk hose and a doublet that was made for a page his size, near enough. It had so much age upon it that the fashion was twenty years gone and the velvet worn down clear to the cloth nap on the front and the back. Then with the rest of Gabriel's wealth I bought bread and went to a cookshop for peas pottage and an end of bacon and so brought him to my little hole in Blackfriars. We sat by the pool in the cloisters that the iron air was forging to iron also and we ate well, which the boy did carefully and slowly, not to dribble. His manners came from some great lord's house.

'Can you read or write?' I asked him, and he blushed and stared at the ground and shook his head. It seemed passing strange to me, seeing how dainty he was in other things.

Boylike he was greatly interested in the cloisters and when he was done, he rose and wandered about, shying stones at the ice on the pond and peering at the hens as if he had never seen such monsters before. His hair was golden, his eyes were sharp blue, like the winter's sky above us. His face had none of the old-man's hardness in it of Gabriel and his henchmen, but was soft and innocent and eager. Only from time to time he would mind him of something, and sit down as he had been when I first saw him, with his arms clenched about his knees, staring into space.

'Now I must have a name to call you by.' I said to him, 'What was it? Can you write that at least?' Again he blushed and shook his head. 'Why then, I shall call you Ralph.' I knew not why I picked that name, only it seemed a pleasant and comfortable one that I should not forget. The boy shrugged. 'Then Ralph it is,' I said, reached over and tipped the lees of my beer in his hair. He jumped up brushing furiously at his head and

I laughed as I said the baptism for those of the begging law. 'And I hereby stall you to the rogue, that you have leave to beg and thieve for your living, so help you God.'

After a while he laughed too, not understanding, but willing to take a joke since he must. I looked about the cloister: there was the sun shining down and the damp frost-tiled roofs about us glistening and drying slowly, a pleasant day with no need to go begging for I had sixpence to feed us on the morrow. And further, it was always a place of learning and had the essence of words in its stones, another cause for liking to live in an old cloister that was crumbling to the dust like the monks who walked it once.

'Shall I teach you to read, Ralph?' I asked.

Such a succession of expressions on his face. First the blush and a boy's eager nodding, then sullenness and a casting down of his glance to the earth and shaking of his head.

'Why not? For that you are a dummerer? So? You understand me, wherefore should you not understand the written word? Oh there's a trick to it, but it's not so hard.'

He tapped his head, made his jaw go slack, shook it again.

'What do you . . . ? Is it that you think you are too stupid?'

He nodded fiercely, sadly.

'What manner of ape told you that? There are astonishing many fools that not only read, write and reckon, but teach it also to boys your age. Now I am a fool, it is true, but I think you are none, only misfortunate. Come.'

I had seen no angels and could not ask their advice. This seemed to me a fine thing to do, to offer the boy a key to open up the walled city of his head, albeit he would have little use for the art as a beggar. Still, he might choose to be a scribe in the shadow of St Paul's and might be well-regarded as such since he could not make half-witted suggestions for the improvement of his customers' style and the polishing of their phrases.

Yet this that I call the Clever One was not so clever neither, or I would have thought further on it, on those who had taught him to mop his mouth nicely with a cloth, but not to write, and why they had not. *Mea culpa, mea culpa, mea maxima culpa*, was it pride that blinded me?

He and I thought nothing of it then. He suffered me to lead him up to St Paul's churchyard where I found a stationer in his stall that had not forbidden me to read his books when I was in a sane humour. On the way there I was planning how the teaching might be done, for the boy Ralph could not speak his lessons aloud but must do all inwardly.

And so I begged spoiled scraps of paper from my friend the stationer who laughed heartily at the joke of a madman turning tutor to a dummerer, and half a broken slate and a hornbook that had lost its paternoster from being spoiled by rain, though the alphabeta was clear enough, and found chalk in broken pieces by another stall. Then back we went to Blackfriars and I set about my new trade of schoolmastering.

Did my old friends the monks gather about my shoulder to watch? I know not, for I saw nothing but the staggering walnut tree by the pond and Simple Neddy piling dried bracken on his tender plants to save them from the cold.

I spake the letters aloud to Ralph, and we made a row of things or pictures that he could point to and show he knew which letter I asked him, as an apple for A and a brick for B and a cat (that walked off and so must be drawn on paper) for C and so on.

By the end of the day I could point to any letter in his hornbook with my schoolmaster's twig and he would point at the thing that it stood for. As we worked, so my anger grew at what had been done to him, for his softness, his eagerness, his cleanliness, all spoke of his being used to ease and wealth, and yet none had thought to enquire if he had a mind that was whole despite his quarter tongue. Still I never questioned if it could have been left so deliberately.

When evening came on, we ate the rest of the loaf and some cheese I had by me, and finished the beer with Simple Neddy. In honour of the occasion and his tender upbringing, I made a fire in my little room and burned another broken desk and some panelling. It happened, alas, that there was paint on some of it still, and briefly as the wood settled, the face of a woman veiled in blue shone out of the fire with painful beauty and then blackened and peeled and was gone before I could save her. In her ashes we roasted apples and then I showed him my pallet and we lay down under two cloaks near the fire while the frosty stars bit down on London like little prickling insects.

He huddled close, put his arms about me, and I thought he was only cold. Then I felt his hand at my points, unlacing of them right speedily, and then about my privy member. For two heartbeats I lay there with understanding growing to a foul black flower within me, and then, with what gentleness I could muster, took his hand from my parts and sat up, and laced myself again. Without a doubt he wished only to please me as he had been taught, to show his gratitude as he had been taught. Alas my face was bleak.

He had shrunk back against the wall, staring at me, tears in his eyes, shaking. 'Ung ung,' he said, shook his head in frustration and wept like a maid.

I stood also, shaking also but with rage, that this should be an explanation. If a man is warped to love boys and not maids, that is sin enough. But here was a far greater one: for some rich man, being warped so, had taken him a catamite that could never tell who had corrupted him, taught him ease and wealth and courtesy, but never given him the printed and written word that he should forever be a sealed vessel, a locked casket, unable to speak of nor threaten his master. And then whoever had done this, I thought, had tired of his toy or found fresher meat, and had thrown him out to die upon the street, like a dog. And this was why he had been so shocked, so lost, for whoever had brought him up to sin innocently had then broken his world asunder.

'Did you not know it is a sin for a man to lie with a boy?' I asked him, clasping my hands together that he see not my anger and be afraid.

He stared at me open-mouthed, a very dummerer. I tried again. 'Do you know what it is to sin?'

Now he nodded eagerly. He picked up a piece of wood, glancing about him as if in fear he should be caught, hid it under his doublet, then stood and crept away. Then he put it down and came to me, opening his arms, with his head on one side like an amorous girl.

I took his hand, clasped it that he should not think I hated him, and caused him to sit down again.

'Now Ralph,' I said, 'you must listen right carefully to me, for what I say concerns your soul. Know you what your soul is?'

He nodded, linked his thumbs by his breast and flapped his hands like wings. Then he shut his eyes, lolled his head, and flapped his hands away from his chest.

'Ay, then you are not completely heathen,' said I. 'Hear me. The man that was your master before, did he bring you to his bed and . . . and use you as a man does a woman?'

His brows wrinkled deeply and he stared at me in puzzlement. I breathed deep and mimed as best I could, and he smiled and nodded.

'Know you what God is?'

He looked insulted, pointed up at the ceiling and mimed praying.

'You master did not tell you this for he wished to have what he wanted of you and not be prevented, but God hath said that it is a sin for a man to use a boy so. Indeed it is wicked.'

His face clouded, fell, his mouth began to tremble and he shook his head violently.

'No, not that *you* are wicked, for you must know that ye sin before you *can* sin, but he was wicked, your master, for that he used you so and also that he kept you in ignorance of what he did. I will not do so with you Ralph, for I am mad not wicked. You have not seen me when Tom comes and wrests me from myself and speaks with angels. Tom does strange and foolish things then, but I think even Tom will not commit this sin. And while I am in my senses, so I will not. It would be evil in me to do so.'

He put his face in his hands and made a low moan. I could not think what ailed him now, but then when he stood and went drooping to the door, I saw his thinking.

I upped and brought him back to the fire. 'Listen to me, Ralph. That I will not lie with you is not for the reason that I do not like you, nor that I will cast you out on the street as your master did, but only that it is wrong and besides, I prefer women to sin with, if sin I must. You may stay here as long as you wish, although it is poor enough compared with what you are likely used to, and although I have little enough, all that is yours also.'

He stared at me, tense as a cat that must pass a dog.

'Do you understand me?' I asked. After a moment he nodded. Then he reached out gently, gingerly, took the tipmost ends of my fingers, brought my hand to his face and kissed it reverently.

For all the cold of the night, we slept on either side the fire. I slept hardly at all, because instead of two covers above both we had one each. But we could not be bedfellows any more than if he were a girl, until he was weaned from his sin. He was exhausted and slept, turning his head once and calling out without words, an ugly sad sound. I thought about him and wondered in the depths of my anger who had been his old master.

XXXVIII

Tom slept dreamless within me while I kept the boy Ralph as my apprentice. He had a boy's bottomless hunger and the money and food were soon gone, so I took him out upon the begging cheat with me the next day, though he wept like a girl and shook his head so frantically I feared it might unship itself and fall off. I shook him and shouted that he might like to feel his belly cleaving to his backbone, but I liked it not, and we would make better profits with him than without, which was as well since he ate three times as much as I. It breaks my heart that I was angry with him for he had good reason to be afraid. But being a man and he a boy and schooled to obedience, I won the contest bravely, and he stood sullenly by me in the street and hung his head, while I cried his misfortune like a Smithfield stallman. Hunger lent wings to mine own tongue and I told a fine tale of how he was born with but the rump of a tongue, so to speak, and words were lost to him, and how he was of good family but cast out therefrom when his mother that protected him died, and so he was double unlucky in that he had known easeful life and had now lost it. This is something I know myself, that it is far harder to bear the loss of wealth than it is to be brought up to harshness and hunger and find wealth later on.

Once a fine neat merchant's wife of the City stopped in front of us and berated me that I had myself cut the boy's tongue out the better to beg with him.

Ralph flushed with anger, stepped between us shaking his head fiercely, made a good deep bow and opened his mouth. When she saw no scars she tutted and dropped a groat in the bowl, and stalked off.

So we ate well enough thanks to other wives and the boy's bashful manners and soft sad face. Once we had food for the day and a faggot of wood for the night, we stopped and turned to lessons. Teaching him to read was no easy thing – for without him being able to recite his lesson, how could I know he had learned it? Soon all the cloister courtyard was snowed with little pieces of paper that titled the tree TREE and the hens HENS and Simple Neddy's garden GARDEN. Sometimes I changed the labels about and bade him set them aright, or I wrote him a message on the slate, telling him to take off his cap and scratch his nose with it, and so on. It was hard for him, being unable to sound letters aloud and so find the riddle of a word's meaning, but he had been encompassed about by men who could read and did so and he was apt to the work. Indeed it was like putting water on drouthy soil, whatever of learning I gave him was sucked and swallowed up.

As evening fell, I was moved to take him into St Bride's church and up to the great Bible that was chained there. He knew well of churches for he doffed his cap reverently and never spat nor coughed while he was there. At the lectern upon its hard eagle I opened the Bible at venture, to see what would be a text for him, and found it at the place where Christ saith, he who believes in me shall not die, but live forever.

The candlelight lay like a shadow's shadow upon his grimy face and he smiled at me and nodded.

'Here is simplicity.' I said to him, for I also am a lily of the field, that toil not neither do I spin, 'Here is comfort.'

He nodded again and then jumped from the shout that came out of the unlit rear of the church.

'You two! Begone! Ay, you, out of this place.'

Well, it was a churchwarden bustling between the carvings, waving his staff and bellowing at us. We ran out again into the dark alley and so onto Fleet Street, where I took a fit of laughing at the man's furious face and frightened eyes, while Ralph frowned and punched his boy's fist in his palm. I patted his tense shoulder.

'Think you that a Man acquainted with sorrow would know him?' I asked. Ralph frowned until he placed the reference and then smiled grimly as he walked.

I chanced to look up and saw Becket at an upper window of Mrs Fumey's shop, lit from behind by a fire and a tallow dip, the unmistakable lour of his shoulders.

His shape disappeared and on a whim, no doubt from an angel clouting my suddenly dense head, I took Ralph's hand and led him to the tables of a boozing ken opposite, where we sat on the bench beneath the red lattices. Ralph was impatient, but I gentled him.

Soon Becket sauntered from Mrs Fumey's door, looked at the sky, spat, adjusted one of his pattens, wandered towards us as if hearing the beer calling and then suddenly turned and walked the other way.

A tall well-dressed man behind him almost collided with him, excused himself and found Becket's hand at the front of his doublet, was lifted two inches from the ground and carried backwards through an entrance into a court.

Daring three horses and printer's wagon, I pranced across the street followed by Ralph, and slid in at the entrance.

There was the sound of a knife being drawn by the man, a little flash of metal and eyeballs and then the dull thud of Becket's knee in his victim's groin. Ralph started forward, but I held him back. Becket had never to my knowledge descended so low as to become a footpad.

He waited for the man to cease whimpering on the frozen mud and then leaned close. This time the knife was in Becket's hand.

'Who sent you?'

The man only moaned and retched.

'Speak or I'll make cutwork of your ear.'

'No need.' I called in the dark, 'I know him, David.'

'Is that Tom?' he called, cautiously.

'No, the Clever One.'

Becket sighed. 'And what do your angels tell me this time. That this faggot is a dragon with a deadly eye or some such garbage.'

'My angels say nothing of him, only I have seen him with Simon Ames.' I said nothing of how, since the Clever One had heard of tact. 'His name is James Ramme.'

'Is this true?' asked Becket of his prey.

'Yes, God damn you, I am sent to give you a message.'

'Oh indeed? And wherefore then did you skulk about in corners and play act a fruitseller if you were but a messenger? I would have greeted you more kindly had you spoken to me direct and given it me like an honest man.'

Ramme, who had hoped to find Ames's strange friend conversing with Spaniards or attending Mass, rose creaking to his feet and tried sorrowfully to brush the mud off his grosgrain and little round velvet cloak. Becket had backed off somewhat, his dagger still in his hand.

'Speak your message,' he said.

'His Honour, Mr Secretary Walsingham will receive your liege the King of London at his house in Seething Lane, the morrow evening.'

Becket's eyelashes dropped half across his eyes at Ramme's satirical tone and he smiled gently.

'Well, I have a message for Ames, but I think I will not use so flighty an Hermes. Who knows what strange fate may overtake it?'

Ramme was sullen and said nothing, still trying to repair the damage to his fine Court suit and making worse what would have been better amended by drying and a stiff brush.

'James Ramme?' asked Becket, 'Hm, I recall Mr Ames speaking of you, sir, that you are somewhat of a swordsman. Are you also a gentleman?'

Ramme lifted his chin at the insult. 'I am sir.'

'Indeed then, Mr Ramme,' said Becket jovially, sheathing his dagger, 'I fear I owe you a blow.'

'You do sir. I must demand satisfaction of you.'

'Well, well, let us not duel upon it, to be sure, as I would not wish to cause Mr Ames grief by killing you nor myself grief by hanging for it. Perhaps we may compose our quarrel in fair exchange? You have taken a blow from me, now I will stand and take a blow from you and then call it quits, eh?'

'Done,' said Ramme through his teeth. All would have been well if he had but struck back at Becket with his fist, but no, he was foolish and also dishonourable. He drew his long rapier and charged at Becket, who blinked, side-stepped and tripped Ramme as he went past. Dagger and sword appeared in Becket's left and right hand, and as Ramme recovered himself and returned to the attack, he made a double beat, trapped the thin Italian blade at the crossing of his own two, twisted and broke Ramme's weapon in half with a flick of his wrist. Ramme stared in dismay at the ruin of his expensive cutlery after the previous ruin of his silken clouts, and further at Becket showing his teeth and tossing his sword and dagger so they passed each other in the air, and back again.

'Tut tut,' said Becket softly. 'Mr Ramme, I fear you are no gentleman and no swordsman neither.'

Ramme was backing away, his half-sword held up before him pathetically. I saw the gleam in the dimness as Becket glanced at me and away again, and who knows but if we had not been there as witnesses, Ramme may have ended his days there and then for his petty treachery. Perhaps not. It would have depended upon Becket's mood and the level of his choleric humour and so forth.

Becket spat at Ramme's feet, sheathed his blades.

'Run beg your mother to wipe your arse for you, Ramme, and come and call me out when you are fullgrown. And give Mr Ames my duty, but if he send any other message by you, it will never reach me. Good night to you, Tom.'

There was another movement and the courtyard was of a sudden empty of any but James Ramme, breathing hard and shakily, and a sleeping pig, whereas Ralph and I hurried back to the boozing ken and then onwards to Blackfriars. In the bone-aching cold of the night, I felt a little warmed that still my angels took care of me and mine, although it caused me great disquiet that I could no longer see the Queen Moon as she rode her swirling horse closer and closer to London.

XXXIX

Since the night before her Coronation when she lay there of ancient usage, the Queen has never lodged in the Tower and her unused buildings there rot and moulder unheeded. Which can be no surprise to any man who knows the nature of her memories thereof, the place where her mother died and she herself was cooped up by her sister. Yet even had she never felt its chill as a prisoner, Her Majesty would have more sense than to sleep there, for by day it is noisy and clangorous with coining in the Royal Mint, and clerks swarm about it and the armoury is there and also a steady rumble of carts to and from the Mint, and by night it is no place for the unangelled.

Agnes Fant could sleep there, with a pile of pillows at her side to take the weight of her belly, a little musty-smelling though they were, as well as sleeps any woman in her ninth month which indeed is never too well, for the effort of moving and the many times she must up and resort to the chamber pot under the bed.

Catherine Nisbet, however, could not sleep at all, she thought, no matter how many Ave Marias and Paternosters she muttered to herself. She lay blinking in despair at the worn moth-eaten tester above them, her niece tormenting her with deep and even breathing of sound sleep beside her. And the bell paced slowly through the night, giving the hours she lay awake, picking witlessly at her sin and her weakness.

In her silly youth, when girls will tease themselves with heroical pictures of martyrdom for Christ, she had never imagined such cold and bleakness and such tedium as she found in the Tower. Could she have spoken to a priest of it, she might have felt better, she thought, but that was impossible though there were priests within a few yards, behind more stone walls. They may as well have been in the New World for all the use they were to her. All that kept her from weeping aloud was her hope that her covert speech with Mr Kinsley might bear fruit.

The day following she sat at her needlework by the deep window, no girls to instruct, no cook to supervise, no steward to consult, no purchasing to be done, no accounts to bring to Agnes for casting, no legal men weaving smooth unimpeachable word webs for her mistress to unpick, no gossips to exchange the news, nothing. She stitched and stared and stared and stitched. Agnes rested on the one good chair, her own work making a white mound of black-embroidered linen for a child's nightrail on her stomach, and her feet on an old worn footstool with the Dudley arms upon it. Neither could work well for their fingers were cold and stiff despite the fire, for the Tower is too chilly and damp in its stone soul to be easily warmed by mere wood and flame.

When at last the bell tolled noon, Agnes heaved herself up and knelt stiffly upon the stool to say her Angelus, meek before God. Catherine found her knees too painful to kneel, and so stood. Before they had finished the door was unlocked and Simon Ames entered, with Kinsley behind him bearing a tray of food, mutton and a baked pheasant, farced with chestnut and berries, and good manchet bread, and wine in a pewter jug, and a sallet of a few winter herbs. Kinsley's face was stolid, but he stole a glance at Catherine and nodded almost imperceptibly.

When Ames saw they were praying, he motioned Kinsley to stop and stood waiting until they had finished. Then he came forward and offered Agnes his arm to arise once more and conducted her to her seat and brought up a little table and set the meal down upon it with as good a courtesy as if he had been her steward. Mrs Nisbet longed to speak privily to Kinsley but dared not, only she noted that he had carried the tray ostentatiously to their clothes chest and set it down there. Did she hear something drop to the floor?

Kinsley continued in stately fashion to the door, called to have it opened and walked through where he stood just visible through the Judas hole and nodded at her again. With her hand clenched at the place inside her stays where her little gold cross should have been, Catherine went to move the tray and sit down on the box. When she peeped down, there was a blessed little black leather bottle lying in the dust.

'Oh,' she said, 'I have dropped my needle.' Her knees were not so stiff she could not bend down and feel about and hide the little bottle with her body until she had got it safely under her skirts and into the pocket in her petticoat.

Standing up she made a great play of her aching back and for good measure clapped a hand to her head.

'Madam, alas, I have a megrim.'

'Perhaps some meat would settle it?'

'No, no, I think I must lie down.'

Agnes watched quizzically as she went to their bed and lay down and drew the curtains.

Simon Ames raised his brows. 'Would you like another woman to attend upon you, madam?' he asked. 'I could arrange it if you wish. Another of your own household, perhaps.'

'No,' said Agnes, with an edge of annoyance in her voice. Then she smiled a little. 'I never know whether to rejoice in your kindness or fear it, sir.' Ames inclined his head and sat upon the footstool by the fire while she said her Grace. He folded himself up neatly, with his gown tight about him, and his new velvet cap pulled down out of its shape to half-cover his chapped ears. As ever his nose was issuing phlegm, which made Agnes long to wipe it like a child's, and his eyes were red and circled with shadow. By the evidence of her hand-mirror, she thought he looked more the prisoner than did she, but perhaps that was womanly vanity.

She tore off some pheasant breast with her little knife, nibbled on the bread, drank sparingly of the wine which she mixed with the good well-water in the earthenware jug. Then she stopped.

'Come Mr Ames, I like not to eat alone. If Mrs Nisbet cannot bear me company, do you share with me for the babe takes up so much of my belly I cannot eat above a quarter of this.'

Simon hesitated, then drew up his chair to the small table and used his penknife to take some of the pheasant which was a little tough.

'Have you spoken to Father Hepburn about me?' she asked after a while. 'I wish very much to make my confession before my hour comes.'

Simon shook his head and gulped inelegantly at some meat.

'Father Hepburn is willing enough, it is my master Norton that likes not the idea.'

'Ah,' she patted her lips with the napkin. 'There is a man strong for the new religion.'

'He is a Puritan, true.'

'Poor Mr Rackmaster. How strange to be so certain sure of the purity of a thing only fifty years old, built upon the word of Luther the spoiled monk, and a madman . . . .'

Simon raised his brows in question, his mouth being full again. Deep in cipherwork he often forgot to eat, and had found a better stomach to his food than he expected.

'Calvin, I mean, the Switzer that has outlogicked Aquinas,' explained Agnes.

'Is God then, not logical?' Simon was surprised to hear this.

'God created logic, but he is not nor cannot be bound by it, being infinite.' Simon nodded. 'Calvin says that there can be no free will nor redemption by our own acts because God knew in the beginning, with his first speaking of the Word, which among us will be saved and which damned, and therefore is all laid out, with only His foreordained Grace to save us.'

'It *is* logical.' allowed Simon doubtfully.

'But not sensible. Here are we two: say that you are among God's Elect and I am damned, as Mr Norton believes, what a counsel of despair is this! For you need do nothing and try nothing to remain of the Elect and I can do nothing nor attempt nothing to become fit for Heaven. All is coldly separated now and forever: a melancholic prospect and a faith leading to melancholy and madness.'

Simon observed, 'I have seen madness and melancholy among Catholics too madam.'

As indeed have I, but Agnes had been too young to remember our mother in the year before she died, when all about her were devils trying to steal her soul. So Agnes smiled and leaned forward as far as she could, her pale eyes shining.

'Ah, but there is always hope for me. No matter how black my sin, I need only turn my face back to God, confess my crime and gain absolution from the priest, and God His Grace and my soul's hunger for him will catch hands and so swing me blithely up to Heaven. To love so gentle a God is not hard, Mr Ames, nor is it strange that He who made the world can turn bread and wine like these here into His Body and Blood. None of it is strange, none without hope, there is hope shining through all the world like the course of the Sun.'

She was smiling as she spoke, and perhaps the babe within her caught the infection of her joy, for there was movement in the velvet of her gown as the child kicked. Simon looked aside.

'I do not ask you to turn from the Almighty.' Simon said, 'I would ask that of no one. Only turn aside from the Pope which is not the Almighty but a man that has too much power and too little holiness.'

'But God appointed him, he descends from St Peter. You speak of such a little step . . . .' Agnes smiled. 'But then one step leads to another, and so again on to damnation.'

There was silence between them, more sad than tense, as of two who speak with bars between them so that they cannot meet.

Simon cleared his throat. 'Speaking of the sun,' he began awkwardly, 'have you ever read Thomas Digges, his *Perfect Description of the Celestial*

167

Orbs? No? I shall bring it to you, for it was a true wonder to me.' He began to set out goblets and little pieces of bread to display to her the wonder of Copernicus' universe, which so cleanly and beautifully to a mind like Simon's, makes resolution of a vast heap of puzzles. With one simple step, a change of view, it cuts through the Gordian knot of cycles and epicycles and epi-epicycles. To Simon who had puzzled at the ugly complexity of Aristotle's world that centred upon the earth, the cleanliness of Copernicus that turns about the Sun in his glory was thrilling to the heart.

Agnes too saw Simon's true intent. 'Is this then your faith?' she asked, when he had come to a halt. 'A faith in the answering of number and the arts mathematical. You seem not to have that hectic certainty of salvation of Mr Norton. Indeed it is a puzzle to me that you do the work you do, for you are not poor, I think, and not besotted with cruelty neither.'

Simon blinked and stared at the orderly crumbs of bread before him. 'No,' he said, twirling the strap of his penner in his fingers. 'By birth and nurture I am a Jew.'

Her mouth opened wide before she noticed and shut it. Nor did she draw her skirts aside, though the impulse was clearly there before she quelled it. She flushed instead. 'I . . . I had not met one before.'

Simon laughed, hand to hair. 'As you see, we have no tails nor horns and I must assure you, I have never tasted baby.'

For a moment she whitened and then laughed too. 'How come you here then? Do you attend church? Is it not also blasphemy for you?'

'Some might say it is. I have a dispensation from the Queen gained by my lord of Leicester, that I need attend only at Christmastide and Easter, which my rabbi says is permissible, and I must not make converts which I have no desire to do. My family are from Portugal, but all thrust out from there by the Inquisition of Spain which burned two of mine uncles.'

'Then how . . . .'

'How can I be part of another inquisition?'

'Is it revenge?'

'No. Less noble. It is . . . self-preservation, fear.'

'Fear of what?'

'Fear of this land being swallowed by Spain. Fear of my family's last safe harbour being taken and sacked by an implacable foe. Coming into this work was a slow matter, madam, and often I lie in bed and think of that slowness as a kind of curse, like the snail's course of leprosy. By my arts mathematical I have skill in ciphering and the breaking of other ciphers, in the piecing out of documents, the connecting of one with the other, what my master Sir Francis Walsingham is wont to name the *Mundus Papyri*, wherein all things have their shadows, and wherein knowledge moves slowly, sluggishly like a sick serpent, but leaving ever its tracks upon the page whereby it may be followed.'

'Then why not cleave to that trade?' Agnes asked, coldly. 'It seems a cleaner thing than this.'

'But the one led naturally to the other, for knowing the patterns and plots within the *Mundus Papyri* I was better able to frame what questions should be asked. And when one is obdurate, then if he is racked, so must I question him under pains, and so . . . .' He spread his hands, not looking at her, as if a supplicant appealing to her mercy.

'And this is done not for the safety of religion, but for your own safety?'

'Religion is part of it, madam, although it is not mine own faith. The Queen hath woven the two together cunningly so if one fall, falls the other also. And the Queen's Grace is the lynchpin, the foundation stone, the golden chain whereon hangs a most heavy, a most beautiful and bejewelled realm. One single narrow chain and if it be broken then falls the jewel to the ground to be swept up by Spain, its diamonds and rubies broken out of it and the gold molten to pay for Inquisitions and priests and the destruction of the Netherlands. It is so easy to kill a man or a woman, we are all such delicate, brittle, fragile creatures.'

Agnes was sitting back again, her hands clasped on her stomach, her eyes narrowed. 'So for the safety of the realm, you ply your bloody trade like a soldier?'

'I would make a very poor soldier.' Simon said, 'though if the Queen is killed by this new Guisan plot, and Spain invades, then will I take up a gun and fight as a true Englishman and a Jew.'

'As would I, although I am but a woman.'

'Would you, madam? And yet you are a part of the plot.'

'I have nothing to do with . . . .'

'Oh indeed, you are but a simple foolish woman, that only attends Mass secretly said by Jesuits – yes, madam, I know that most of them truly have no dealings in treason overt – and who but gives shelter to her poor brother, lately returned from Spain, with the intention of killing the Queen.'

Agnes had stiffened, her expression cold. 'I am right to fear your kindness,' she said. 'What makes you so sure that it is my brother you must seek.'

169

'The Papal Indulgence your husband found for me in a place you thought we would not find.'

'The Papal . . . . May I see it?'

Simon hesitated. 'It is being examined, but I believe you may. And then perhaps you would enlighten me, madam. You have spoken to me most eloquently of the Almighty and His infinite goodness: how then can you accept this – to bind Him with paper and kill with dispensation?'

She said nothing. Simon sighed. 'In the meantime, I have here a report of your husband's dealings with Adam Strangways, which he has signed upon each page. I pray you Mrs Fant, read it and consider of it carefully.'

Wordlessly, Agnes took the papers. Simon stood, made his bow. 'Madam,' he said, 'I pray you again, think on this land ruled by Spaniards.'

'I had not thought you would put a woman with child upon the rack.' Agnes said thoughtfully, 'but that was before I knew there could be a rack made with words.'

'If I knew a better way to find your brother, I would use it.'

'He, however, could not plead his belly to the rack.'

Simon left her then and the door was locked behind him.

XL

Upon the Saturday, Becket paid a visit to the Nuñez house in Poor Jewry, bearing a letter that had taken him hours and many attempts to compose, for all its brevity. The house was quiet and reverend for the Sabbath and while he waited for an answer to his knock, he wondered at a strange sight he saw at the window.

'What is that?' he asked the pretty fair-haired piece who came at last. She blinked at it.

'Why, it is a candle with a pot over it and a hole made in the pot.'

'I can see that,' said Becket patiently, 'but what is it for?'

'How should I know?' said the girl. 'I am no Marrano. What did you want? None of them will come.'

'No need,' said Becket, 'only give Mr Simon Ames this letter when he can receive it. And . . . .' he smiled winningly, his foot wedged in the door, '. . . tell me your name and how I may serve one so fair.'

'Hmf.' said the girl, snatching the letter, stamping on his toe and slamming the door shut a half-inch from his nose.

That same evening, and unwitnessed by Becket who was bargaining with Sweetbush Julia at the Cock on Fleet Street, a small man that looked to be a successful merchant of the Staple or a sergeant-at-law, rode smiling and talking merrily to Seething Lane. He rode a handsome chestnut gelding, well-caparisoned, but to a country eye must have seemed strange in that he was clearly of quality and yet had no attendants riding about him or walking at his stirrup. To see a wealthy man with none around him, entirely alone, might have made such a homespun-clad farmer stretch his eyes indeed. A Londoner might have noticed that the lane was overfull of beggars and large servingmen, whereas Becket or Henderson or Mr Recorder Fleetwood would of a certainty have questioned why Turling the hedge-picker and Hogg of Smithfield both found it essential to be in Seething Lane that day. Not to mention Cur-face Mitchell, Long Jack, Enderby, Pratt the Clown and a dozen others.

'Enough men and we could sweep London bare of footpads, coneycatchers and filches,' said Ramme with a gesture at the window. 'But Becket, alas sir, is not there.'

Walsingham nodded once, watching through his window as Laurence Pickering dismounted.

'I had not expected him.'

'Hiding at the Widow Fumey's no doubt.'

'Hm.'

'Shall I have him taken?' Ramme was over-eager and cooled at Walsingham's glance. 'Only I like not his dealings with Mr Ames.'

'Do you not?' said Walsingham. 'I like them well enough. I shall receive Mr Pickering in the library.'

The King of London was conducted by a pageboy and smiled cheerily at Ramme as he went past.

Within stood Sir Francis, engrossed in reading a book. Pickering waited the space of five seconds to be noticed and then grinned, bustled forwards and laid a bundle of papers on the table.

'There sir,' said Pickering. 'In earnest of my good faith.'

Walsingham closed the book, replaced it and took up the papers, leafing through in silence.

'It is no concern to me if a man gambles,' he said at last.

'Of course not, sir,' said Pickering happily. 'A very restful and pleasant pastime for those who have the means.'

'Quite so. And it seems that these notes of debt are not made out to you, Mr Pickering.'

'No, I rarely accept notes for any game. I prefer to deal in wholesome gold or bankers' drafts. But not all are as scrupulous, sir. Mr Tyrrel took these from Sir Edward Stafford, as you see.'

'And?'

'And I have it on excellent authority that a Señor Mendoza paid them.'

'Can you prove this?'

'These notes sir, were stolen from Snr Mendoza's office. Alas they must go back . . . .'

Like a ray of sunlight striking through an overcast sky, Walsingham's face caught fire with delight and was transformed.

'Mr Pickering, I am astounded. I will tell you plain, I would gladly have given all my fortune to place a man at Mendoza's side this past year, but I have never achieved it. Can you at least tell me your means?'

Pickering was rocking back and forth on his toes. 'Yes sir,' he said affably. 'To you I will gladly tell it. Of what station were your men . . . .'

'Clerks, secretaries, manservants. One was found in the Thames.'

Pickering shook his head. 'Shocking.'

'And your man?'

'Who sees the nightsoilwoman?' said Pickering. 'And where may she not go?'

'Has she any other . . . .'

'Alas, she cannot read, only she knew what these were from the shape of the writing and brought them to me in case they were of value to her.'

'Can she put them back?'

'I shall have her carry them in on the morrow well-covered with shit and have her say they fell in the pot.'

Walsingham said nothing for a while as he examined the papers, and noted the amounts in a ledger. Pickering smiled again, plumped up and down on his heels and surveyed the room admiringly.

'A magnificent sight, your honour,' he said at last. 'So many books, so much learning. A man who had read all these books, he must be wise indeed.'

'I rarely have time to read for pleasure.'

'I am sorry to hear it, sir. With your many duties . . . .'

'Shall we come to business, Mr Pickering?'

'With pleasure sir.'

'I am indebted to you, twice over now. I am in hopes that my debt to you may increase. For instance know you aught of one called Adam Strangways or another by name David Becket?'

Pickering shook his head sadly. 'I have been seeking Strangways, but have found him not. Becket I know well but have seen him neither. No matter, I shall continue the search.'

'And?'

Pickering waved an arm expansively. 'Sir,' he orated, 'I am by no means a poor man and nor am I in want of power. What little I have done in your assistance is done for pure love for the Queen, God bless her, although I can never . . . .'

'And, Mr Pickering?'

'Well then, sir, if you are hot to repay me, which I take very kindly, sir, then simply your smile shall weigh against gold in the balance.'

'And my blindness, no doubt.'

'Yes sir. Your countenance, your goodwill. And as you say, your blindness. On occasion.'

'Upon what manner of occasion?'

Pickering rubbed the end of his nose with his forefinger.

'Surely it is a very wicked thing for an Englishman to sell Sir Edward's notes to a stinking Spaniard?'

'Very wicked.'

'And it seems that Andrew Tyrrel did so.'

'So it seems. Mr Tyrrel is no friend of yours then?'

Pickering laughed. 'No sir, no more than is King Philip a friend of her most Gracious Majesty the Queen.'

'Do you compare yourself to her?' Walsingham's voice was suddenly cold.

Pickering opened his bright button eyes wide. 'Why sir, that would be rank rebellion and treason. I have heard Tyrrel do so, but I myself . . . I am Her Majesty's most humble and loyal subject . . . .'

'Then it is untrue that men call you the King of London.'

'Over-zealous servants and followers, sir, I check them for it when I catch them. And to be sure, I can be no King whilst another claims the title with the help of money from Spain.'

'We have but one Prince in this land.'

'And very right and proper too, no realm can be at ease when it has two Princes in it. And if any call me King be sure it is from ignorance and foolishness . . . .'

'Which may lead to misunderstanding,' said Sir Francis with emphasis. Pickering coughed slightly.

'There will be no more of it, your honour.'

Sir Francis nodded and poured two silver goblets of sack. He handed one to Pickering, and sipped his own at once.

'This sack is over-dry for my taste, Mr Pickering, you may prefer your own drink.'

Pickering's eyes gleamed and he drank half the contents of his goblet in a gulp. 'Why it seems very fine to me, sir,' he said. 'In fact, I have never tasted better. You do me too much honour, sir.'

'Do I?' asked Sir Francis. 'Concerning Mr Tyrrel. I will have his papers. Your good health and fortune, Mr Pickering.'

XLI

We were begging by Temple Bar while the Sunday morning crowds passed by to their churches, to be instructed of the benefits of *caritas*, and love for their neighbour. I was not working the begging law too hard, for I know better than to beg of holy folk that know themselves to be of the elect: catch them when they can feel a few seeds of doubt niggling them like wild barley in their hose, and then will they make attempt to bribe their way into Heaven. Little Ralph was studying of a ballad sheet that praised the Fair Eliza and was regarding the frosty glass sky that seemed so empty and fearful, when I saw Gabriel come swaggering out of Chancery Lane and into Fleet Street, with the two boys his closest henchmen at his shoulder. They were glancing about themselves and fiddling with their daggers to seem more manly.

Gabriel marched up close, his chin lifted.

'Have you taught him the begging law?' he demanded of me, waving at Ralph.

'He is not apt to learn it.' I said, 'It comes ill to his nature.'

'I heard you do well enough.'

'Ay,' I sighed. 'What is it Gabriel? Must I tithe him to you?'

'No,' said Gabriel, 'I will have him myself.'

'Why? What for? He was never brought up to this life, he would be the hangman's firmest friend if you tried to teach him the cutting of purses.'

Gabriel put his hand on my stomach and pushed me backwards to the stone of the Bar until the carving pressed my spine.

'There is one will pay me money for him,' he said quietly, 'and I found him, so I keep him.'

'Money for what?'

Gabriel spat sideways. 'For his old trade.' He leered up at me.

'You know he was some rich man's catamite?'

'God's Blood, Tom, what else could he be with that face and hair? There's one that will pay me double for his being silent.' And he grinned and tapped the side of his nose. 'Has he done nothing for you then, to pay for all your care of him? Eh?'

Fire and hard-eyed vengeful angels rose up from my belly, and I laid his cheek open to the bone with my fist. And then hands held me from behind and small fists beat a drumbeat on my ribs and belly until I must keel over for want of breath, and be kicked. In the distance I dimly heard Gabriel shouting, 'Don't kill him, lads, it's bad luck to kill a lunatic, only teach him.' And then further in the distance, a sorrowful tongueless cry as my boy Ralph was stolen from me.

Sometimes angels are merciful, even Tom can be merciful, carrying me away from the pains of my body and the pains of my mind. Indeed, I have found pains of my body at times almost a blessing for they release the star-daemon trapped in my soul to walk about where he wills, leaving Tom to gibber below. In the dung and dirt of the alley where they left me, Tom lay broken and weeping, bleeding from Gabriel's knife where he cut me judiciously upon the cheek in payment for his wound, bleeding in my heart also for my poor Ralph who now knew he sinned. Perhaps it would have been better had I not taught him God's law, but then an angel stood beside Tom and berated me, saying a sin forced upon one who wills it not, is also no sin. This differs from what the Divines speak of it, but I think God is more merciful and gentler than most of his party upon the Earth. But then I am only poor mad Tom and know nothing, and indeed, if God is merciful, wherefore do the innocent ever suffer worse than the guilty?

XLII

And here was Becket, beard trimmed, clean shirted, his doublet and buff jerkin brushed and sponged, his boots clean and polished, his sword clean and oiled as always, and a new hat upon his head, sitting glowering into his beer in the Gatehouse common room. He had gone with Eliza Fumey to St Dunstan's, and heard a sermon of inordinate length upon the vexed and vital subject of the old argument between *homousion* or *humoiusion*, or some such, only one word in three of which he had understood. He had eaten his way stoically through the Gatehouse's Sunday ordinary of beef, roast on a spit and bedded on bread sippets, and peas and turnips and a sallet of elderly winter herbs, and a bag pudding with currants and a hard sauce of sack and butter and felt bloated and at peace, as to body.

In his mind he had eaten the meal before his hanging and made it as good as he could find. When Simon Ames entered and peered about him, he sighed with relief for he could never abide waiting.

He noted without surprise that three large hard-faced men entered with Simon, one remaining by the door, and that the other two went severally to stand by the entrance to the kitchen and the window on the street. Goodwife Alys dropped her hand to a veney stick she kept by the aqua vitae keg and watched through narrowed eyes. Becket from long habit and intent was sitting with his back wedged in a corner on the far side of the room. He awaited Simon, who wove nervously through the crowd of eaters and stood before him.

Becket planted his legs and rose. Before Simon could produce whatever warrant he had sworn, Becket said, 'I wish to speak with Mrs Agnes Fant who is presently your prisoner, sir.' Her clapped his hand to the buckle of his swordbelt, ready to do the thing properly, but Ames forestalled him.

'Keep your weapon, sir. You are not under arrest. I shall take you to Mrs Fant forthwith.'

They threaded past the Fleet Street dunghill and turned down

Crocker's Lane, through the dark passage beyond the entrance to Noon Alley, down Temple Lane and round about the cloister and so to the Whitefriars Steps where Simon had a boat waiting.

To traverse the river west to east is no easy matter with all the traffic going north to south to the Sunday afternoon bear-baiting, and then they must circle on foot about the Bridge and take another boat at Fish Wharf before rounding the forest of ships about Billingsgate and so into the Tower by the Water Gate. It was a beautiful day, a day made of adamant with all sounds striking through the air like daggers. On such a day even the stench of London must give place to the sourness of frost on the air and above the Bridge, each halt to the water had made for itself a ruff of dirty ice. There were mudlarks wading about in the mud by the quays and a flurry from some German ship guards when they found that a boy had got aboard their cog and was throwing cargo off to his waiting friends.

'Think you we shall have an ice fair this winter?' Simon asked, dabbing gently at his red nose. Becket shrugged and he gave up the attempt at conversation.

At the Tower, filled with Sunday silence, so that the ravens could be heard arguing upon the midden, Ramme and Mrs Fant's appointed Yeoman were awaiting the boat. Ramme looked askance at Simon when he saw Becket still had his sword, but Simon and Becket both ignored him and so he said nothing.

'Shall all this rabble be present when I speak to Mrs Fant?' asked Becket without bothering to lower his voice as they passed between high walls to the Wakefield Tower.

'I shall be a witness since one there must be. The others may wait without.'

'You have spoken already to Anthony Fant?'

'Of course.'

'No doubt it was a very ill tale.'

'I would rather term it sorrowful.'

'Hmf.'

'Speaking of Strangways, there can be no doubt that he is the assassin now. We have found his Papal Indulgence that makes him free and clear to murder the Queen.'

Becket said nothing for a while and then, 'Have you told her I am coming?'

'No.'

When the door opened they found Agnes Fant and Mrs Nisbet finishing their own meal. To Simon with his nerves stretched out to breaking point, Mrs Fant's flush almost tingled in his own cheeks.

'God in Heaven,' she said slowly as she rose to stare at Becket. Catherine Nisbet crossed herself. 'Is it David?'

Becket bowed to her and she returned the courtesy.

'I think there is more of you than when we last met,' she said with a gleam in her eyes that surprised Simon, as did Becket's laugh.

'Ay,' he said. 'And of you I think, madam.'

'So to speak,' said Agnes merrily, giving him her hand which he kissed very loverlike. 'Must we stand like courtiers or may we be seated, think you?'

Unobtrusively Simon brought up her chair to be by the fire and Becket found the stool and placed it before her. Catherine was busily setting about the plates to scrape them off and pile them up, before she retired to the bed and drew the curtains. Simon looked about him for a place to sit and found the clothes chest. The door was already shut, but the Judas hole was open and he glared at Ramme's eye appearing Cyclops-like behind it, gesturing him one-handed to depart. The cover shut with a snap and Simon pictured him with his ear pressed tight to the wood.

Becket seemed in a strange mood. On the one hand his face kept breaking into a boy's grin, on the other he hung his head with contrition. It was a foolish thing to see a grown man look so coyly on a woman. Agnes smiled steadily on him and seemed always on the point of laughter which never came, so that Simon felt a slow sting in his chest, as if her smile were an injury to him, instead of an assistance.

'It grieves me to see you here,' Becket said at last which caused Agnes to look away, 'as it was I that brought you here, you know. I must confess it to you now. I never . . . .'

'But how did you know?'

'If I had known indeed, I would not . . . . Well, I might have thought first of what I did. I was hunting some men who had paid to have me killed, myself and Mr Ames both, and when I found one of his creatures and got the story of him, it was your house he led us to.'

Agnes looked down and shifted her swollen feet in the rushes.

'No doubt this is one of your ploys, Mr Inquisitor Ames?' she said to Simon. 'A cunning variation, I think.'

'No, Agnes,' Becket said before Simon could answer, 'I came here of mine own free will. At least hear me out. In the first place I wished to ask your pardon for having brought Mr Secretary Walsingham's men upon your household.'

'It is granted.'

'And in the second place . . . Adam is your brother, flesh of your flesh, and nothing more natural than that you should want to protect him. I am come here to . . . to tell you a tale, only so you may know what manner of man you are protecting. Once my tale is told then will I press you neither way, not to protect nor to reveal, since that must be a matter for your own conscience. Only you must know why he paid to have me killed. And as God is my witness, this is not a thing I do lightly nor wantonly, I have thought upon it and consulted my . . . friend upon it, and am decided it is for the best.'

'Does it concern the fall of Haarlem?'

'Then Anthony told you of it?'

'Not until this week. I have read his account of it. I had known he was married before in Holland and that his wife died, but not the circumstances.'

Becket shut his eyes and fell silent again. 'I had not known,' he said heavily. 'So he and Ilse . . . Well. Well.'

He was quiet for so long that Simon grew uneasy. At last Agnes reached out clumsily and touched the hand that rested on his knee.

'You were one of those that ran the supply sleds into Haarlem. Will you tell me of it?'

Becket smiled briefly. 'Why it was like flying through black milk, the town was like a place in a nurse's tale, all battlemented with fog. It was winter . . . Holland is a strange place in winter. No flies, no ague marshes, all turned from green grass and brown mud and grey water into white steel, all that was soft alchemised to rock. They move their heavy gear in winter, not summer, if they may, and the children bolt about the ice like waterbeetles on their ice skates.'

'Those are the Dutch pattens with blades upon them? I saw some last winter and Edward clamoured to have a pair.'

'Edward?'

'My son.'

Becket laughed. 'Did he so? Then you must buy him some, they are the best sport for a boy I ever saw. The children in Holland are all bred to them and at the festivals they run races and . . . .'

'Adam was there also?'

'Oh ay, he was there. I think it was he made a pretty figure of the enterprise, now how did it go? Yes, he said that the plan for bringing the sleds past the Spaniards might be a parable of religion. That each of us, our souls, were like such sleds weighed down with worldly goods and near-blind in the fog of the world, and if each followed faithfully the one before we would surely find the City of God. Which was a pleasant fancy, but then Cut-the-Rope said that for the figure to be complete each sled must have bright lanterns of the Word of God to light their way. And anything other than dark-lanterns were madness for our enterprise and Adam liked the simile less then and so left it.'

Agnes nodded. 'But did you not care that he is a Roman Catholic?'

Becket shrugged. 'He was English, he had fought the Spaniards better than many of Gilbert's hot-worded minions. And it was not so deeply a matter of the Reformed against the Pope then, it was more the Dutch in arms for their ancient liberties against the oppression of Spain and their tenth penny tax. Or so the Dutch said. There were Catholics in plenty among the Germans; Roland Yorke was Catholic also.'

'Who was Cut-the-Rope? Did I know him?'

'No. There were the three of us, friends of old from Gray's Inn, Fant, your brother, myself – Ralph had gone to the Court by then. Cut-the-Rope Johnstone was a Scots Borderer, with his brother Black Will, and they were there because they had more foul bills waiting for them in Carlisle than need serve to hang them and there was famine in Scotland. We were five to a sled, nine hundred in all, with scouts and forerunners and rearguard.'

'And the siege?'

'Where would be the profit in speaking of it, Agnes? It was a weary sorry time. We fought and starved our best and in the end it all came to naught. The Spaniards spoke discourteously of the Dutch, saying they were fat peasants jumped up to be burghers, but they were valiant men and women all. Even the women fought which was something I never thought to see.'

Agnes stayed quiet and watched as Becket gathered himself internally.

'Well, it was I that brought all their labour to nothing, you know that I think. Myself and your brother, Adam. With him . . . if we had opened our eyes, we might have seen it coming: he was angry so much of the time we were besieged: he could not abide to see what the Iconoclasts had done to the churches, nor the way we piled broken saints and carvings as bulwarks to strengthen the walls against cannonfire. When we made a few little japes with vestments and Mass things upon the walls to annoy the Spaniards, he was not to be entertained for he called it blasphemy. The Johnstones and he had a great bitter argument about it that lasted the better part of a day and he brooded for a week after. Then we made another night attack for food and he never came back with us.

180

We thought him dead, we mourned him, said prayers for him, and forgot him, as we had others of our friends that died.

'Then the weather warmed and the ice thinned and melted and still the Prince had not been able to relieve us. The Spanish ships took control of the Haarlemmermeer and the rations were halved and halved again. Men began to drop and die from simple hunger, not requiring a wound or sickness to bear them off, and the children . . . . Jesu, I will not tell you of the children, Agnes, it would make you weep to hear it.

'And then Balfour asked me to go a message to the Prince of Orange to tell him that if no relief came we would yield to the Spaniards and hope for a little mercy. That was in summer. I had learnt some Dutch, you see, enough to pass.

'And so I went out upon a raid and hid behind a wagon and took a red Hapsburg sash and a Spanish-cut jerkin from a man I killed, and when morning came, before they mustered, I slipped away southwards.'

Agnes had clasped her hands. She admires him, thought Simon inwardly, and felt the ugly sting in his chest deepen to a burn.

'No doubt it was half in hope of feeding I went,' Becket said, unwilling to be admired. 'Haarlem was become a city of the dead, all populated with skeletons like an old image of the Dance of Death, save for those that swelled up in a kind of hunger-sickness and looked well-enough fed until they died suddenly of it. I was tired of dreaming of food – God knows, I dreamt of every meal I ever had, so even stockfish made my mouth flood. I dreamed of comfits of Seville oranges and dates glistening with gold and pounded pearls and I dreamed of hot puddings and good plain white meats of cheese and eggs and butter and bread, which all were swallowed by birds in Spanish ruffs before my eyes. To dream of food and to awaken with your belly clinging tight to your backbone, I am no saint to rejoice therein. It was the thought of food that pushed me on, I tell you now, lest you think me some hero, but the Spaniards had few enough rations themselves and no livestock left I could steal. The country round about Haarlem was eaten bare.

'I talked my way past the Spanish and Walloon pickets and when I was out beyond the siegeworks, the mud and the stinking trenches, I found the road south and swung along it boldly. Balfour had told me that to skulk and hide is to attract attention and it was good advice. It took me two days to escape from the ravaged lands, like walking from famine into plenty, from Tartarus to Arcadia. For the Netherlands is a very Arcadia: where the marshes have been drained and farmed, they are green and fair and the cattle . . . . Agnes, you would not believe the cattle, for they are twice the size of any English beast and give twice the milk, as much as a gallon and a half per day. Yes, in very truth they do, I have seen it with mine own eyes.

'I met a little girl on the road who was driving two great fat cows and she cried out upon how I was a poor man that was sick to death, and she milked one of her kine there on the road and gave me half her loaf of bread as well.'

'Was she frightened?' asked Agnes, frowning.

'No, I was afeared of her. After Haarlem it seemed unnatural to see a child with pink cheeks and plump arms and a loud voice and no swollen belly. And why should she be afraid of me? I was a shambling poor creature that she could have outrun with ease, or set her giant cows on me if she wanted. But she was kind and gentle to me and would take none of the store of gold I had for the journey, and she gave me Godspeed.'

'But you came to Sassenheim in the end?'

'Oh yes, I came to the Prince. I saw his troops and thought them raw but that they might be sufficient, given how weak the Spaniards were themselves, if we sallied out of Haarlem to help them. I showed his Grace by mine own person how desperate was our case. He was kind to me also and had his doctors examine me and gave me meat but alas it was too tough for my poor teeth which were loosened by the scurvy, and I lost an eyetooth in a piece of pork.'

Becket showed the empty place, Agnes tutted, then he sighed and ducked his head, as if bracing himself against a heavy weight he must lift.

'If I had been wise I would have stayed in Sassenheim where I was safe. But I could not, so Prince William told me his answer to Balfour. I loaded up a packhorse with food and thought if I were brazen enough I might slip through and gain the meer's shore and swim across by night, perhaps . . . . Well, it was foolishness, I was a half-witted zany to believe it. Perhaps feeding made me less cunning or I had used up all my store of luck for that month. Or perhaps Balfour was right when he hinted that he did not trust those about the Prince. I know not, only I told the pickets that the food was for the Capitano del Campo, and the packhorse had the Prince of Orange's brand on him, and Christ forgive me, I never saw it.'

'They caught you?'

'Ay, and I was still too weak to fight them. I wounded only one and they would have killed me, which was my desire, only the Capitano Romero saw us and ordered them to stop.'

And there were Becket's great square hands gripped tight upon each other.

'They put you to the question?' Agnes had her hand to her mouth.

'They made a few attempts but none so bad I . . . .'

'They hung him up from a gibbet by his wrists with weights on his feet,' said Simon calmly. 'When that failed, they flogged him.'

'How the devil do you know what they did?' snarled Becket.

'I read the signs on your body when Señor Eraso was strapping your ribs. After you had saved my life. And this is material to your tale, that Mrs Fant should know . . . .'

'Whose tale is it, Ames, mine or yours?'

'Yours, of course, Mr Becket.' Simon thought: and nor will he be pitied.

'I could have done it, Agnes, I would have held out for the few days before Count Batenburg was appointed to come, I was counting them for all the time passed so slowly, it was not that I was weak, in truth it was not . . . .'

'David, I would never think you weak.'

'But they tricked me. And I was too much of a fool to see it, too innocent . . . .'

'And weary.' said Simon to himself, but neither heard him.

'After the second day they cut me down again, in the evening, I think. They said they would try fire next. They locked me in a storeroom, and late that night one came to the little window that I . . . knew. The chain was long enough so I could . . . get close enough to hear him. He whispered to me for an hour, he said he could not save me, but if I gave him whatever message I was bringing to Balfour, he would see that it reached him.' Becket swallowed. 'And I told him.'

And here was silence, only the fire speaking to itself quietly, Agnes's hands folded on her stomach, Becket uncomfortable on his stool, shifting, looking up at her.

'He was Adam,' she said calmly.

Becket nodded.

'And after?' she asked, 'Why did the Spaniards not kill you when they had what they wanted?'

'Too busy at first. And then your brother again, perhaps he felt some pricking of his conscience. He fed me while they dickered over Haarlem. And then, two weeks after they marched into the city, the Spanish troops mutinied for they had not been paid in over two years and were not permitted to recoup themselves by sacking the place. The burghers had made their bargain well: they had Alva give his word as a gentleman of honour upon it and not even a Spaniard will break that.

'Romero was shut up in his tent while the soldiers' council talked with the Prince of Alva and by that time I was healed enough to walk, and so I broke away. I remained in the Netherlands a few years, fighting the Spaniards and living however I could, trying to run Romero and Strangways to earth. But I lost track of Strangways and then Romero died in a fall from his horse, may he rot, and so at last I came back to England, and here I am.'

Agnes put her cheek on her hand, her eyes were shut.

'I . . . thank you for telling me your tale, David, for all its heaviness.'

'Will you tell them where Strangways . . . .'

Her eyes opened, blazing with anger. 'From you at least, Mr Becket, I expect no inquisition.'

David shrank from her as if she had struck him. She shook her head wearily. 'I must think on it now.' Becket rose, went to the door.

'I have done what I came to do,' he said with a few remaining shreds of dignity. 'God be with you, Agnes.'

'And with you.'

Simon began to hurry after him, but then minded him of an important thing.

'This is the Indulgence I spoke of, Mrs Fant,' he said, turning to her and taking it out of his penner. 'I recall I promised you a sight of it. Did your brother not show it to you?'

'No.' She spoke abstractedly. 'He said I was a woman and could not understand it, though I had a good tutor and I read Latin well enough . . . .' She frowned at the writing. 'This cannot be right. Have you forged this, Mr Ames?'

'No madam,' said Simon, annoyed, 'I have no need to stoop to such tricks. This was found in a box within the second hiding hole, the one within another hidden place. In the hall. Can you not see the Pope's seal on it?'

'But it does not name him priest, it names him plain Adam Strangways.'

'Yes it does. I have never believed he is a priest.'

Agnes pressed her lips tight together, handed the paper back to Simon.

'It was our mother's especial desire, even I know it that was so young when she died. It was why he went overseas in the first place. Work upon this again, Mr Ames, to be sure you can do better.'

'Madam, I swear to you by . . . by the Bible, this is no forgery. Can you not see the Vatican's watermark in the paper?'

She held it to the daylight, squinted, and gave it into his hand again. Then she turned her back on him, went to the chair and sat slowly down upon it, picked up her work and began to embroider a baby's biggin.

Simon sighed and followed Becket onto the stairway, and Kinsley shut the door again and locked it.

XLIII

In all this time, where was poor Tom lying in his privy trough of despair? I think it was Simple Neddy found him, for once I looked up and found his odd Chinaman's eyes and thick lips hanging as it were a suspended moon above me, his smooth brow all cluttered up with concern.

Somehow he must have brought me to Blackfriars from Temple Bar to my little leaking room there, and made a fire out of more rotten wood broken from the far end of the cloister and perhaps some secret store of his own. He put dried woundwort on my sliced cheek and scattered sweet-smelling leaves, and then because I was still unseeing and lost, he brought and put in my arms his own true treasure, which was a ragbaby wrapped in motheaten wool, its face crudely sewn and worn thin with kissing. Alas, it could not mend me and so I lay like a post that day with it in the crook of my arm, the blood drying and clotting on my cheek and my ears burning with Ralph's last cry to me. When Simple Neddy came back and sat by me helplessly stroking my matted hair, I could muster enough sense to say,

'Find Becket for me, you know him?' He nodded with a frown slowly forming on his face. 'Find him. He might find the boy.'

It was a hard thing to put upon his few wits, but he nodded his grey head again and left with determination on his face, and I lapsed back into darkness.

As it happened, Simon Ames was himself bearing David back to Whitefriars Steps, having an appointment with Sir Philip Sidney for the inspection of his dragon. Besides there was nothing more he could do at

185

the Tower in unravelling the plot. He would come back to study his reports and papers and begrudged the time spent in Hanging Sword Yard, but saw no help for it if he would please Walsingham and his beloved daughter Frances.

Becket was morose and at the steps turned at once to the red lattices of a poor boozing ken at the corner of Water Lane. While dragons of danger leapt out of the foggy air about my dreams, the thing itself was growing in Hanging Sword Court, of wood and metal formed to a beast from the old stories of King Arthur. Perhaps the Queen Moon rides upon such a dragon on the days when she fares forth to battle; it would seem a fitting mount for her.

Simon Ames came into the yard a little breathless with hurrying and made his apologies to Sir Philip who was already there.

Sir Philip waved a hand nonchalantly. 'My father in law told me what you are about. Now here are some horses of the Queen's own stables – hush, Titan, steady, when did a harness ever bite you, eh? – and better-experienced wiser horses are there none in the Kingdom.' He slapped the broad brown neck beside him familiarly while Simon sidled back and away from its vast yellow teeth. He had no quarrel with the general run of horses, though often they had a quarrel with him, but the vast creatures that pulled the Queen's progress wagons and triumphal floats seemed unnatural to him somehow. But they were well-used to crowds and noise and cheering and Latin speeches and the smell of fireworks.

Dragons with carved and gilded heads they had not encountered before, however, although there had been giants for their parents at Kenilworth. Yet they were peaceable enough and allowed their grooms to lead them up to Master Broom's masterwork to be introduced. None did worse than sidle and snort. Then they were hitched to the traces, which they liked not because the leather was new, and all eight made essay to try if they could pull the weight of the dragon, which they could.

Adam was there, observing, wearing a workman's suit of clothes and his hands scrubbed clean. At a nod from Sidney, he slid within the scaled barrel body of the dragon and lifted up the head and blew the horn mounted within, and flashed the mirror eyes and even lit some slowmatch for the beast's breath.

Then must all come to a halt before they could rehearse, for the wings had been altered to fit past Temple Bar and now one broke its internal rigging and flapped brokenly to the sawdust. Mr Broom climbed up to see the cause of it and found a place where the rope chafed a pulley and so must the pulley be replaced and all about was that bustle and smell of panic that men make in the days before a great procession, when all know that nothing can be ready in time. They were still painting the tail and the gilders had not come for the reason that the leaves of beaten gold for the gilding that they needed were not come either. And then Juno took a dislike to Minerva and so all the horses must be unhitched and moved about to separate them and rehitched.

To all of which, Sir Philip stood at his ease in his second-best suit of armour. He was wearing it to see if his appointed seat could be reached while it was on or if the weight was too great. And also because he was intent on defeating Fulke Greville squarely and was wearing his armour to accustom himself to its weight of eighty pounds.

Simon had gone upon an urgent errand and came hurrying back to say he had found a goldsmith on Ludgate Hill who could supply beaten gold the next day and Sir Philip clapped him on the narrow shoulder and bade him sit down before he fell, and have some sack, and not to be concerned for all was well forward of Sir Philip's expectation, being long experienced in these matters.

'I trust your attending on me does not prevent you from working about Sir Francis' business. He hath told me that it is a matter of great moment. Mr Phelippes is making another search of the city for Throgmorton's friends this very night.'

'And for our man?' said Simon. 'At least we have his name and his looks.' He was in fact near frantic to be dealing with foolishness such as tilting dragons at this time. 'With God's help we will find him.'

'Still London is a mighty antheap. I had heard there was a woman in it, a fair lady.'

'Ay sir, very close to her time to have her babe so we dare not press her. Nor Throgmorton who may die of it.'

'Hm. What of the Accession Day Tilts, will the madman make his trial then, think you?'

'I have been over the plans with Sir Francis and Mr Ralegh and of all the times when Her Majesty is in danger for the reason she is abroad among crowds, there is least danger then. She goes not upon the ground at all, but sees all the sport from her gallery and the only ones about her are her own folk, with the crowds well back. My lord of Leicester will see to it that her bower is well searched and her food and drink twice tested.

'No, we think he must mean to come as a petitioner to her, not caring whether he live or die and so kill her from close by.'

'Therefore they have been annoying petitioners at Court by searching them.' Sir Philip nodded. 'Good. And how is your swordplay progressing? Will you try a passado or two with me?'

Simon flushed. 'Sir, I am a most inept pupil and no credit to my swordmaster, besides which I have not had time since we took Mr Throgmorton and have not . . . .'

Here came Master Broom to say the dragon could begin now, and so all scurried about for to rehearse the speeches and the movements.

Dragons of danger indeed, alas, for here was the cunning of it. The Kingly clerk Philip II in his fair study all lined with tapestry and lit with gold, he had seen that there could be no loss to him in the enterprise. If the attempt by Adam succeeded, why so his worst enemy was dead. And if it failed, it would still ruin her foremost and wisest adviser, his worst adversary across the tiltyard of the *Mundus Papyri*. Sir Philip Sidney was Sir Francis' son-in-law: all his house and party would be suspected. And Walsingham had no lack of enemies to make the suggestion that he took gold from Spain, for all that many who might make the hint, themselves took gold in fistfuls from San Lorenzo.

Poor Neddy could not find Becket at all that evening, for David had gone straight from the boozing ken to Laurence Pickering's house upon the Strand and was locked in council with him over his own plans for the Accession Day.

XLIV

In the Tower, behind black walls, Catherine Nisbet fought her demons which she could scarcely name. For all their stink she went to the jakes as often as she dared and drank from the black leather bottle Kinsley had refilled in exchange for a ring of hers. Agnes seemed not to notice anything: she was staring into the fire, sometimes stabbing her needle in her work, sometimes idle. When it came to suppertime she ate nothing and drank but a little mild beer.

Encouraged by drink, Catherine once began a speech upon firmness in adversity and the martyrs of old and was chilled to her sore bones by the paleness and stillness of Mrs Fant's glare and the cold words she spoke, that she would consider and make up her own mind. She threw Catherine into a misery of weeping, who could remember hardly anything of what she had heard of Becket's tale. She climbed muttering to herself into the bed and drew the curtains and made an attempt to pray, but all the while her black bottle sang to her and at last, unlike Odysseus, she unstoppered her ears and went to it.

And yet to be just to the lady, she would not have done so had she known what Agnes knew. All day she had felt griping in her belly, aching in her back and although well-experienced in childbirth, she had hidden from herself her own knowledge of what such gripes portended, being gripped in an indecision near to stone.

Perhaps some of her distress lay in what she guessed but had not heard of the child Anna, the Dutchwoman's daughter. Thinking of it made her heart quake within her: any woman must look to lose babes, for when a soul is new come to the world its grip is uncertain and a puff of wind may dislodge it. Agnes thanked God she had lost only one that died a little after his birth, long enough to be baptised. It is only to be expected that babes and old people die; yet the death of children is scarcely less common and so much more grievious, for then has liking and loving grown and the children made some growth to their full adulthood. Small Catherine her youngest had taken the smallpox in the year before, and died of it, and the tears filled her eyes to think of it, though it was becoming an old wound. Agnes had paced out the nights by her bed praying, as do all in such a case, that she herself could take her little girl's suffering upon her and die if need be, and not her bonny babe that laughed and loved her new rose-coloured petticoat. And yet, although the child died, it had been God's commandment that she should, a thing beyond her mother's help. But to have her daughter suffer and die so ill a death as by starving and it to be by the agency of man, that was a far worse horror.

She winced for Becket that he had spent so much courage in resisting torment, only to have his secret cozened from him. To Adam it must have seemed that he did aright, to save his friend and regain the city from the Reformers. She too liked not the thought of japes upon the walls with Mass things and vestments. A pity that it had to be also to the benefit of Spain. Her brother was a great man to her, so painted on her mind by Cathering Nisbet that brought her up after our mother died. As for my tale, she barely knew it, being so little when I went to London to study law and then on to the Court and then madness in the lordly lofts of Bedlam hospital, a secret, unmentioned shame to all about her, like a disease in the privy member.

But . . . the Indulgence. She no longer doubted its veracity, yet it did not name him Father. And yet he had permitted her to kiss his hand, he had let her think he was ordained, he had let her make Confession to him . . . . So complete a lie. It turned her world upside down. Her cheeks burned with shame when she thought of confessing to him. To mountebank the sacred station of a priest . . . . If he had lied in that, what else had he lied in? Could it be true that he was come to kill the Queen? If he was, should she not tell whatever she knew to the little powerful clerk, Ames?

Here were questions to which neither God nor the saints gave her an answer, but must she hammer one out for herself, and now in overplus to it, Pelion upon Ossa, came the strident demands of her new babe to be born.

At length she could make fantasies of wind in her bowels no longer, for she was pacing about the darkened stone room and leaning up against the wall when the pains came and then pacing again, like the caged lion in the menagerie by the moat, only with even greater urgency, as if the babe was far away and thither she must walk to find him.

She called and then swept open the bedcurtains and found a new betrayal, for Catherine Nisbet lay upon her back snoring, and would not waken though she shook her and slapped her. When a new gripe had gone, Agnes hurried to the door and banged upon it and shouted for the Yeoman Warder set to guard her. When he came, wiping pork grease from his mouth, and she told him her state, he was so affrighted at the thought that he left the door unlocked while he ran to find Simon Ames. Which at least made her smile: for all her pacing she could have gone nowhere and Mrs Nisbet was dead drunk upon her bed.

Simon had but a little while since climbed from his boat and come up to Coldharbour Tower to find some food and break his fast, with his ears echoing with Sir Philip Sidney's rousing speeches and the creaking of dragon's wings and the stink of gunpowder from the slowmatch still itching his teeth. When Henderson came running in white-faced and stammering of a woman in labour, he could only sit and sag for a while, that he had not the strength to deal with this also.

But then he pulled himself back from musing and sent the man on to fetch the midwife, and hurried to Agnes Fant's captivity, fumbling a lump of cheese for sustenance into his penner as he went, and trying in haste to recall what little his uncle had told him of women's travails,

190

which was small enough as no physician likes to meddle with a woman's work.

At the door he paused to see it open, then knocked timidly, entered, and found Mrs Fant kneeling by the trundle bed with her gown all darkened and dirtied with her waters.

'Where is your woman?' he demanded indignantly, and when Agnes gestured speechlessly at the bed, tried himself to waken Mrs Nisbet and failed.

God cursed Eve that tempted Adam, and bade her bring forth her children in sorrow, and Simon said after to any who would listen that he knew no reason why women ever bore more than one babe unless they were forced. And yet to Agnes it was no worse than any other of her travails and better by far than her first, and between her pains she could tell him what he must do to comfort her, as to rub her back and wipe away her sweat and undo all knots in the room, including those upon Catherine Nisbet's stays, to make the babe come free more easily, and build up the fire to keep it warm once it had been born.

When the midwife came she brought the birthing chair upon her back in a stained cloth, being a little scrawny woman with small hands marked with another birth she had attended that morning. Her face was wrinkled and brown like a walnut, her black and grey hair in wisps under her cap, her apron bloodstained.

'They never come but in sixes and sevens,' she said as she unlaced her bodice sleeves and took them off and rolled her shift sleeves out of the way. 'Begone with you now.' And Simon went gladly, his stomach roiling for Agnes that was always so cool and white and knowing her own mind, was now sweat-soaked and grunting like a sow in a farrow.

There was a whore I came upon at birthing once, and held her hand in the darkness by the cloisters, a poor little thing, not long from the countryside, and she wept and screamed and groaned all night long and at the end of it there was a little blue baby like Simple Neddy's treasure. It breathed long enough so I could christen her with puddle water, and then died. They say these go straight to heaven, being new washed from their original sin, but it seems strange there must be so much Hell before. A Divine would say it is woman's lot to expiate the sin of Eve, but men may sin and sin again like Adam and yet go unpunished as Mrs Fumey is wont to remark. And I have never understood wherefore the gift of Knowledge of Good and Evil should be so ill a thing, for without it are we but brute beasts indeed.

Yet Simon could not walk away. He paced about upon the wall walk, between flaring torches, until the midwife bawled from the barred window that she must have another woman to help, another pair of arms.

Of a certainty he could have found someone in the kitchens or the Mint households, or some noble lady, but Simon's mind was emptied of all remembrance of women. All he could think was that he had brought Mrs Fant unto the Tower and he had permitted her woman to be supplied with spirits to weaken her and perhaps loosen her tongue, and that he owed the lady recompense. So he ran up the winding stair and entered breathlessly, saying, 'There are none, I will do it.'

The midwife straightened her back, still keeping hold of Agnes to steady her on the stool, and cursed that there were no attendants for the poor gentlewoman, nor relatives, save one that was drunk, God curse her, and this was a thing unfit and wrong and what was he thinking of for how could the poor lady keep her modesty and she would be shamefast to think . . . .

'Stop your croaking, you fool.' gasped Agnes, 'I care not.'

And so was Simon become a man-midwife, a gossip for his own prisoner, helping her upon the stool as she writhed and worked and gasped and screamed and sweated and her face turned purple with effort.

'Jesu,' muttered the midwife, with her hands in Agnes' privities. 'This is a big babe and awkwardly lain . . . . Easy mistress, easy, go slowly . . . .'

There is a scream that men and women have in common: for men they make it when they go mad in battle and rush upon their enemy to kill him, and are filled with magical strength that knocks away all obstacles, and loses itself in the blood of death. And in symmetry, women make that scream when they bring forth a babe. The stone of the Tower let not the scream Agnes made enter it, but bounced it about from wall to wall, having no place there.

The midwife caught the head and eased its shoulders about and then there was a pale slippery bloody scrap in her hands. She breathed into his lungs and breathed again with her finger clearing his throat and at last he opened his little triangular mouth and let out a great many scratching roars and so lost the blue and gained the red. Then she wrapped him in cloths from the trundle bed and gave him to Agnes.

There was a time of peacefulness before the afterbirth was born, and in it, Agnes rested her head upon Simon's breast as he knelt beside her and he pushed the salty tails of hair from her eyes. And once the cord was cut and the afterbirth gone, the midwife took the slop basin and took it to the candle stand and gazed at it like a Roman soothsayer reading a liver, shaking her head and clucking. But then she smoothed her face and came back to Agnes to clean her and with Simon, help her into the bed with her babe. Catherine Nisbet they pulled out and rolled without ceremony onto the trundlebed, still snoring.

And now with dawn broken through the sky full of clouds, there was a concoction of herbs to be made, to clean Mrs Fant's womb, and a wet nurse to be sent for and the cradle and swaddling cloths brought out from under the big bed. The midwife wrapped up the babe upon his splint to keep his limbs straight, muttering charms while she did. Agnes watched solemn-eyed and took the babe upon her breast in the crook of her arm. The midwife forbade that she should be troubled to change her stained shift and so Simon pulled up the sheets and blankets and the old counterpane to warm her and rolled up her old English gown of green velvet that was now spoiled with her waters. The midwife kicked away the sodden rushes and heaped them by the fire for burning. Simon paid her silver for the live birth, and Mall escorted her away from the Tower.

XLV

Simple Neddy sat with me that night and when I asked him again in the morning to find Becket for me, he went out and as I heard later marched up and down Fleet Street shouting his name. At last Mrs Fumey came from her linen shop and scolded him, and when he had stumbled out his reasons, she took off her apron and went herself to find David.

By which means Simple Neddy returned to me in triumph with Becket looming worriedly behind him, who sat down beside me and gave me wine with bitter-tasting herbs in it.

'Do not spit,' he scolded me. 'This is recommended of an excellent apothecary that said it has qualities to soothe distracted minds which yours is, God knows.'

I smiled at him and drank it, meek as a maiden.

'Is it true that Gabriel was the one beat you? The tale was all up and down Fleet Street when I came.'

Now he was taking his pattens off and setting them by the coals of the fire to dry the mud on them. He had brought a whole faggot of fine dry wood.

'Was it Gabriel indeed then?'

'Yes.'

'Why? What had you done to offend him?'

'I hit him.'

'Well, that would have offended him. I am surprised you are still living. For what reason did you hit him?'

'He took my boy Ralph from me, my poor boy Ralph that had no tongue.'

'What? Ralph? What are you talking about?'

With many tears I told him the tale after which Becket sat back on his bolt of wood and raised his eyes to the Heavens.

'Jesu. And no doubt you want my assistance in finding him, eh?'

'If you are not so very overpressed with business, David,' I said humbly. He sighed and patted my hand.

'Come now,' he said. 'I know where Gabriel may be found if you will bestir yourself Tom. Up you get. Are you wounded any place else? No, ay then, up and on your feet, it was only a beating.'

We went to a boozing ken in Little Bailey where I had not been before, up beyond Ludgate Hill. There seemed a strange press of boys about it and Becket shouldered his way into the common room with me in his ruffled wake, batting cheeky boys from his purse with his new hat.

We sat down in a booth and called the potboy. Becket spoke quietly to him and his spot-specked face which was at first all pulled and bunched in a sneer, froze over like a plaster saint on a tomb. We sat quietly waiting and Becket took a bale of dice from his purse and began throwing them idly, counting under his breath. One was a highman and one a lowman as it came out, and a naughty imp sitting on each when they came to rest. I was about to warn him against the sin of cheating at dice when the potboy came back.

'He says he will not come.'

Becket raised his brows, scratched his black beard that was new trimmed and elegant. 'Oh? Am I so fearful to him then?'

'He says he never knew Tom was a friend of yours and says he will not be blamed.'

Becket considered. 'As I understand the battle,' he said without a trace of a smile, 'it was Tom struck him first. Gabriel may have my safeconduct if he wants.'

'He says if it concerns the boy with no tongue, then he's gone to a bawdy-house on the South Bank and we have him not.'

I put my head in my hands to squeeze back the tears.

'Poor Ralph.' I said, 'I told him . . . .'

'Hush,' said Becket impatiently. 'At least we know the boy truly exists in this world, of which I had my doubts. Wild geese I will chase willingly for the fine eating of them, your phantasms, no.'

The potboy was still at Becket's elbow.

'We truly have him not, sir,' he said. 'You know we would deny the King's man nothing he wanted.'

'Hmf,' said Becket. 'Name me the place and I'll give good report of you to Mr Pickering.'

The potboy looked embarrassed and rubbed his hands behind his back. 'Well, there is only one, sir. Of the kind.'

'And? I am not educated in these matters.'

The potboy waited. Becket sighed and produced a couple of pennies and then a groat. The potboy flickered them away with his fingers.

'The Falcon's Chick, hard by Paris Garden Stairs,' he said.

We came into the city by Ludgate and were passing by the curved walls of the Wardrobe on St Andrew's Hill when Becket stopped and clicked his fingers. He struck off into an alley that leads to Blackfriars and strode through the cloisters and into the old Refectory where Rocco Bonnetti holds his swordschool.

Bonnetti is small, nimble, swarthy and a lover of boys, being Italian and corrupt. The Ancient Masters of Defence hate him devoutly, in particular John Silver who longs to beat his brains to a pudding in fair fight. Bonnetti steadfastly refuses to fight with Mr Silver since he maintains that he is a gentleman and Mr Silver a commoner and it would be beneath his dignity. Silver burns with fury at the insult but can gain no satisfaction. Now Becket had fought his prizes under the laws of the Ancient Masters of Defence and has gained from Scholar to Free Scholar and thence to the dizzy heights of Provost which permits him to instruct men in the old arts of broadsword and backsword and sword-and-buckler fighting. Indeed, he is a feared opponent on Smithfield. But he has made study of the Spanish and the Italian styles and so will have converse with Rocco, the better to cozen him, he told me.

We walked in by the whitewashed walls to find Bonnetti blazing in black and violet velvet and shouting at a plump courtier that his passado was as limp as his prick. Becket and I made our bows to him and sat upon the bench against the wall until the lesson was over, and the courtier gone hobbling away.

'Signor Becket,' cried Rocco with much flourishing of his feathered hat, 'I am happy to see you, it is a long time you have not been here. Is your scholar deserted you, ah, what sadness but I think he was *come se dice*, not well ept for it, eh?'

Becket smiled and escorted him to a private corner where they spoke a while and I made sport with the veney sticks, throwing them up and catching them. Jerome, Bonetti's own boy, ushered in the next pupil, a better set-up man with a grave face, and they both stood watching me throw and caper. At one point Bonnetti put his hand to his sword and Becket grinned nastily and prodded his chest with a finger, and indignation and cowardice made sport with each other on the foreigner's face, until he seemed to sag a little and nodded.

They returned and Bonnetti spoke rapidly to Jerome in Italian causing the new scholar to protest in the same language that he wanted the master not the boy, but was mollified by the offer of an extra free lesson. And so the three of us won from Blackfriar's maze and into St Andrew's Hill and so down to Puddle Wharf to find a boat, leaving behind us the clash of polearms.

Now I have found that there are a great many worlds, temporal and spiritual, all jostling upon each other within the great compass of God's creation. Perhaps my trouble is that the walls betwixt the temporal and the spiritual worlds are for me the thinnest gossamer and for the sane, of hardest rock. Each man's brain is of itself a world and beyond spun from many men's brains and composed of many, lies the *Mundus Papyri*. There is a false sugar plate world of the Court and there is a dirty ugly world of streets and dungholes and beggars. As it were, in Copernicus' metaphor, a moon to this last world is the world of those who love men not women, boys not maids. I knew the Falcon Inn at Southwark, being a most respectable place, full of clean pleasant whores newly brought up from the country who are ever kind and ready with their purses. The Bishop of Winchester owns the freehold and collects the rent (most strictly) which is the reason they call whores the Bishop of Winchester's geese. However, what I had not known was that the boy-lovers' world was here in conjunction with mine own that love girls, for the Falcon hath a chick that she likes not well to acknowledge and that I had never heard tell of until the potboy told us in Little Bailey. In that quiet house are fresh-faced country boys new come up from Kent and Suffolk and Essex to seek their fortunes in London, where they are harvested by such as Gabriel and shown that their fortune lies in a far different place from where they thought to seek it. To be fair, for many it requires some weeks of cold and hunger before they can be brought to it, but hunger is a hard-faced dominie and most will learn at last.

Bonnetti walked up to the unmarked door and rapped a brisk double note. His face being inspected by the doorkeeper and some explanation made of ourselves, we were admitted, Becket muttering all the while about shoving a clout of cloth up his arse to keep it clean in such a place.

Once within we sat upon padded benches in a pale panelled room with a good roaring fire and a clean smell of polish and herbs from the rushes. A sad-faced middle-aged man entered in stays and a farthingale, most delicately pale lavender velvet was his gown and his linen wrought with blackwork narcissi. He had that circular line about a prim mouth that often at Court marked one who was rumoured to love men. In stately fashion, as if he were the mistress of a well-found inn, he kissed all of us upon the mouth, which was a surprise to me, to find beard stubble prickle about a soft dry pair of lips. Becket wiped his mouth covertly.

'My friends,' said Bonnetti 'have a small favour to ask of you, a special request, Signor Hardy.'

The woman-man put long fingers against his chin and turned courteously to us to listen. The false front upon his petticoat was embroidered with a fair tale of Ganymede.

'Please,' he said, 'I am at your service, gentlemen.'

'I have . . . hrm . . . I know a gentleman who wishes to buy a boy you have in your keeping, to be his page.' Gravely Mr Hardy nodded his face on the long stem of his hand. The painting of his face was well-done I thought, if a little harsh. Becket shifted about on the bench, unable to look straight at a man in woman's dress. 'A boy very fair of face, blue eyes, golden hair . . .' Mr Hardy smiled understandingly. '. . . and dumb. He has but a quarter of his proper tongue and cannot speak.'

Mr Hardy's smile fell off his face and he sat up, dismay in every rustle of his skirt.

'Now,' said Becket, 'I know you have such a boy here and I tell you none other will do since my gentleman has taken such a liking to him . . . .'

'But sir, sir,' said Mr Hardy in agony, 'alas and alack, he is gone. He had run from his master and is now returned unto him by the agency of another man. I truly regret . . . .'

'And can you tell me his master's name?'

Mr Hardy was shocked. 'No, indeed sir, it would be improper. Besides I know it not, I have always dealt with this gentleman through the agency of someone else. The one who came to collect the page was new to me, but he bore a letter of introduction and the gold.'

'Will you perhaps tell me his appearance?'

Mr Hardy was unhappy, but Becket placed a crown of silver upon the table and he picked the coin up and turned it about his fingers.

'Sir, he was tall and slender, with red-rooted hair badly dyed to brown, a fine pale visage and poorly habited for his speech. Other than that . . . .'

I felt as if he had punched me under the ribs, gasped and paled.

'. . . ay, perhaps a little the look of your . . . ah . . . your henchman sir,' finished Mr Hardy.

There is a family resemblance between us to be sure, but what did Adam want with Little Ralph? Why? And then I thought and thought again and all my thoughts running and jumping about my poor skull and turning whirligigs and playing football and I clutched my head and groaned. Becket saw the symptoms and rose, bustling me and Bonnetti from the room whilst Mr Hardy fluttered behind us as we went through the passage, asking if he could do us any other service and would we like to see the boys, many very sweet-natured pages he had there, and well-trained from country-ways, and had supplied many at Court with them also, and so on. Becket grunted at him discourteously and let the door bang behind.

Rocco said that since he had done his part he would go down and see how the bulls were faring. Becket took a grip on my arm, hustled me down to Paris Garden Stairs and hawked and spat mightily into the Thames. Then he washed his face and hands carefully in the brown murky water and made me do likewise and each time I began to lament, he shook me or slapped me lightly to make me desist until I began to be angry with him.

The boatman that bore us back to Blackfriars Steps again saw that we were morose and made haste to recommend a place where we might recoup our bull-baiting losses by putting any money we had left upon a certain cock named Achilles at the Westminster cockpit (whither he would take us himself if we liked) which was certain sure to win, because the other cock had been fed poisoned corn in the morning by his nephew.

Which blatant piece of coneycatching Becket treated with smiles and agreement, but said that alas all the money he had left in the world was the price of the fare over the water.

At the Blackfriars Steps we clambered out and David tossed him the money. Then he led me to the cloister where we could be quiet but for Simple Neddy, and there he sat me down upon the wall.

'What was this boy?' he asked. 'Tell me the whole of it.'

I stared at him and laughed that he did not know. Becket reached out to shake me, and then held his hands back.

'Have you *seen* Strangways?' he demanded. 'That was the man that took your boy from the Chick, was it not? Do you know where he is? Or what he is doing? You are so much changed, I find it hard to recall he is your brother, God have mercy on you. Have you helped him?'

I laughed harder at the thought. 'And return to Bedlam for my pains?' I said at last, when I could. 'I saw him when he was with my sister.'

'That is now in the Tower for harbouring of him?'

'I know.'

'How do you know so much, Tom?'

'This is the Clever One. Why, I have told you often enough, David, my angels show it to me and the Queen Moon instructs me, and I see through shadow walls and into shadow houses for all about us is shadow, this very wall is shadow, the whole world is the moving shadow of a thought in God's heart and . . . .'

Becket rolled his eyes, clinging to his temper with the fingernails of his mind. 'I mean *truly* how do you know? Not by angels, but truly . . . .'

'It is angels. In very truth it is. As I see the great dragon of danger, so I see Adam, so I see Agnes, and where Adam has become Lucifer and Cain, my sister must be the Lamb of God, for so she is named, but all I see is true, David, all of it. But I cannot see Ralph, I know not where he is, although he was a messenger between them.'

'Between whom?'

'Why, between the ballad seller you killed and my brother and others also. He had mute swans upon his linen as a sign he could not speak, and ran most diligently between them for love of his old master, that I also cannot see.'

'He was a messenger?'

'A very Hermes, but safe.' I said, 'For he could never tell what he saw or heard, and therein lay his value.'

'But could he write?'

'No, they had not taught him. Yet could he learn it well enough.' I said proudly, 'I was teaching him myself.'

199

He was quicker than I at fathoming the wickedness of the world. I saw that he was appalled and that he understood what had become of little Ralph and that he tried to hide his knowledge, and I saw his face change and pity slip over it, and even my addled wits could at last piece together what I had done. I had indeed given Ralph the key to open the locked casket of his mind, a mind that was brimful of secrets, and if those who had left him locked ever learned of his new skill . . . . Why they would smash the casket in pieces rather than permit it to be opened. My brother had him in his keeping now, but it was I who had killed him.

An angel laughed behind me. I turned to speak with him and he was a devil, one of Lucifer's own, for horns brake out upon his brow and a tail upon his bum and he laughed at me. I turned back to Becket with my hands on my eyes and Becket too was growing strange, melting back and forth into my brother. Such things happen to Tom, not to me, and Tom himself stepped out of the gate into my last remaining city of thought, and we laughed and cried and clapped and danced upon the lichen-furred cloister wall.

Becket shouted, his face twisted with concern, but Tom laughed and the devil laughed, and the Courtier and the Queen Moon laughed and my poor Clever Self screamed, and in all the racket none of what he said won through to my besieged brain, and so he left me.

XLVI

So Tom ruled the brute democracy of my mind which foul thing, as any gentleman will know, means rule by demos, the mob. All of you whose minds are a gentle commonwealth ruled by the Great King Reason can never guess at the horror of such a republic, forever swayed back and forth by the outcry of the mob, now one humour become the leader and now another, and King Reason dethroned and ever fighting to regain his proper rule. So was I and so did Philip of Spain mean to make a madman of England, with our Sovereign Lady torn from us.

I sat among the rooftops and gazed out across the fantastic leaf-clutter of the London roofs, across three miles of crowded ground and more to the Tower where Mrs Fant lay with the babe now in a cradle by her bed. Catherine Nisbet sat in a corner by the fire enduring bands of iron about her head and an acid retort in her stomach and the fires of hell in her heart for her wicked dereliction of her duty. The babe slept sweetly now, a little discoloured to yellow as new babes often are, but my sister slept ill, turning her head, moving her hands, her face flushed with fever. Anthony Fant had sent the wet nurse from Old Change that they had brought with them to London, a sturdy stupid woman related to Dorcas by name Joan.

Being so disordered by heat, Agnes' eyes were opened to me and to Tom's angel, and she cried out in fear while I sought to hide myself amongst the shadowy stones of the walls. Catherine came to her then and gave her water and aqua vitae mixed to drink, trying to soothe her.

Simon Ames entered then, being brought by Joan, who then went to the solemn-faced sleepy babe and set herself down by the fire to open her stays and feed him. Ames set his candle down by the bed, and drew up the stool. After a while, he took Agnes' hand and cooled it in his own and she smiled upon him. And if this seems strange in an inquisitor, then can I only tell what I saw with mine uncorporeal eyes.

'Mr Ames,' she said, 'I have a favour to ask you, as I asked it before. I long to see a priest of mine own religion.'

Catherine Nisbet snuffled hard and retreated to the fire again, to let the tears run down her face.

'Hush,' said Simon. 'I have sent for my uncle, a very learned physician that attends also upon my lord of Leciester.'

'But who will pay the fee . . . ?' she asked, fretting at the sheet with her fingers. 'My husband should not be . . . .'

'No, if there were fee to be paid, which there will not, then would I pay it,' said Simon, 'since it was I brought you to this pass.'

She opened her eyes wide then. 'I think you should not blame yourself,' she said. 'If I had been in mine own chamber at home, all hung about with damask and attended by three midwives and all my gossips, yet still might I have taken a fever.'

Simon shook his head. 'Nevertheless,' he muttered, and for an occupation to his hands, he dipped the cloth Catherine had been using in the pewter bowl of rosewater upon the table and cooled her head with it.

'All for nothing too,' she said. 'I know not where Adam went, not at all, only I was glad he left me at last because I thought he was using my house for a safe harbour for the paying of villains.'

Simon never paused. 'What villains?'

She moved her hips uneasily, caught the sheets as the afterpain went through her, then relaxed. Simon dabbed the new beading of sweat from her lip.

'I know not. A very pockmarked man, a boy . . . a zany . . . . And he talked of great changes, of a great benefit to our religion and there is his pardon from the Pope. Oh alas for it. What should he need such a thing for save a very great sin that must mean his death?'

'What indeed?' murmured Simon.

'I wish I could see clear what to do, Simon, I am so uneasy in my mind, I must make my soul in a fit state to meet my Maker . . . .'

'Hush now,' said Simon. 'No need to think so. I would send you home now if I dared move you. I wish I had never brought you here.'

'If wishes were horses all beggars would ride,' she said, and smiled crookedly.

Henderson knocked, escorting Dr Nuñez who came in wearing his physician's gravity and wisdom like a further gown upon his long sober one of brocade edged with marten.

He did what he could, bleeding her eight ounces from the arm to try and relieve her body of the poisoned blood infecting her womb, and giving her a draught to make her evacuate any other poisons about her gut. But whenever a woman comes to birth of a babe, she and the child step into God's hand, only leaving when she is churched, for if she has survived so long then is it likely she shall live to bear another babe, in accordance with Eve's sentence.

Ames and Hector Nuñez left her with the wet nurse and Mrs Nisbet to void herself upon the jakes and went to Simon's little room in Cold-harbour that was already piled up with papers and ciphers. Dr Nuñez found Simon's abandoned cuirass and raised his brows at his nephew.

'I thought you were still wearing this?' he asked in Portuguese.

'It is heavy and it wearies me.'

'Time enough to sleep when you are dead, Shimon. Wear it, so I can tell Leonora that you do.'

'Mrs Fant?'

Dr Nuñez pulled out a pipe, packed it with tobacco and lit it with a coal from the fire, before offering it to Simon who took it reluctantly.

'Is she a Papist?' he asked. Simon nodded. 'If you would be merciful to her then, nephew, find her one of her own priests.'

'Is it so bad?'

Nuñez puffed upon his pipe. 'Were you the husband I would speak of hope and prayers to the Almighty for her deliverance.'

'Her husband has disowned her.'

'Very wise of him, seeing where she is. You however are not her kinsman and to you I will speak the truth: if a woman takes fever in her womb within a few days of childbed, then she may live indeed if she is strong and hale, but she is more like to die. In every ten that sicken I find one or two that live.'

Simon bowed his head. 'Will your treatment help?'

Nuñez shrugged. 'I have known it work, sometimes. But I think she is sad in her heart of another matter, and that is not good. Where the spirit is strong and loves life, then I have seen men recover of the plague, but here . . . . Ay well, look not so sad yourself, Simon, take more tobacco, for it also drives away melancholic fumes from the gall bladder.'

Simon drank the smoke obediently and coughed. 'I cannot take to this medicine,' he said. 'It makes my head giddy and my lungs short.'

'Yet persevere, for it is an excellent herb, new to us but ancient among the wild men of the New World.'

'Will you attend upon her still?'

'Of course, since you ask me. And I have often wished to see the sights of the Tower, although I have never done so before. These cases proceed quickly. I think I shall visit the Jewel House and the Menagerie at least which will fill the afternoon. Would you send a man to guide me so I am not coneycatched at every turn?'

Nuñez's treatment did not halt the fever which ran through Agnes' body like an army pillaging a town while Simon slept exhausted on a borrowed truckle bed. In the afternoon Simon sent a message to Mr Norton asking that he might bring a priest to Mrs Fant, and then, seeing how swiftly she was failing, went of his own authority to the cell of Father Hepburn. He was an old and holy man that was ordained priest under Queen Mary and in the Tower since the mid-seventies.

He was one that greatly desired to see an angel, but had never caught sight of one, which seemed to me a sad thing, seeing that I am daily plagued with them unwilling. But he is too well-seated in his reason to find them save in his sleep. There I believe he hath nightly converse with them, only to forget in the morning, from which it may be guessed that angels too love to sport with those who love them best.

He had no holy oil to anoint Agnes, but he took his breviary from a hidden place by his bed and came at once with Simon.

Henderson was deep in disapproval, muttering of Papistry and idolatry and a soul lost to the true Religion, until Simon turned upon him and snapped.

'If it should ease her soul and make its flight sweeter, then I shall do this and take the consequences, idolatry or no idolatry. There is idolatry enough in your pure Religion, it seems to me, idolatry of men's words.'

At which Henderson left off muttering of Papistry and protested indignantly that he should reason with her and try and save her soul.

'No. She will not be troubled. You showed little enough interest in her until she was dying: Christians are all the same, spiritual kites every one.'

Which led Henderson to mutter of Hebrews who knew not their place. To be certain sure that Mrs Fant was not disturbed while she made her confession, Simon himself stood watch at the door to her Tower, sitting on the wall walk and blinking into the courtyard. At last, frozen with cold as the sun set in brazen triumph and his chilblains throbbing, he knocked and entered with a fresh candle, and found Father Hepburn sitting upon the stool, with his head bowed and Agnes unmoving and unbreathing upon the bed. Catherine and Joan the wet nurse were weeping over the babe in the furthest corner, whither they had gone so as not to overhear her confession.

'I must speak to you in private, sir,' said the priest, rubbing his eyes. 'Poor lady, her heart was sore burdened.'

Simon gestured that the priest should go before him to his own little room, where the fire had burned out and the ink frozen again. On their way, the priest looked about him curiously, freshening his eyes upon the cobwebbed old-fashioned magnificence of the Queen's unused corridors. Henderson was sent to fetch more wood and coals, tutting and shaking his head and while they waited to be warmed, the priest told Simon the most important of the things that Mrs Fant had bidden him say, which was but a sequence of numbers.

'The poor lady asked my advice in this,' he ended, 'and it was a thorny question; I think you know its nature sir, whether to tell you the few things she knew of her brother's conspiracy or to hold silent as her brother forced her to swear. I told her that as she was cleft between two evils, all she could do was choose what she thought was the lesser with an honest heart, and God would surely pardon her the other. Which she has now done. Her other affairs are in order: she made her will before she left home and the rest is matter only between herself and God.'

Simon sighed. 'Why could she not have told me this before?' he asked. 'Why?'

'She had sworn to her brother that she would not,' said the priest, 'and being of gentle blood, prized her given word. But I advised her that if it touched upon the Queen's safety, then she had a larger duty than to her brother or her honour, and if she failed out of mere pride, then God would require it of her soon.'

'Does not this go against your Religion?' Simon asked, after Henderson had lumbered resentfully in and laid a very ill fire and lit a candle. 'So to help me in my task?'

Fr Hepburn's face settled into its lines of repose, his eyes watery, and the fingers tangled together by habit. 'It is a hard question,' he said midly, 'and I make no pretence to have answered it, for where indeed does our duty lie? But Christ hath said, "Render unto Caesar that which is Caesar's, and unto God that which is God's." This I know: that God hath made Princes for our ruling, and that as He made Queen Mary, so also He made Queen Elizabeth and He knoweth all things, to the innermost heart of even so riddling a Prince as our own Sovereign Lady. And so I cleave to the old thinking: that to make and unmake Kings and Queens is not within the compass of any but God. If, as Mrs Fant said, her brother plans to shed such sacred blood, I care not which cause he says he does it in behalf of, it is not mine and I will aid him neither by deed nor word nor silence. And further, Mr Ames, I will not willingly see any foreigner sit upon the throne of England.'

'Yet our Sovereign Lady has kept you mewed up here these ten years and more.'

'If the case had been opposite and I a Protestant in her sister's reign, of blessed memory, then would I have burned like as not, and I am not one that hungers for true martyrdom. A little cold and discomfort will suffice.'

'Sir, you put me to shame,' said Simon, after a while.

'Good,' said the old man with a smile. 'I have always wanted to do so. If I must suffer bodily, it is only fair that you should suffer in the mind.'

'I think I will quit this work and do some other thing to serve this land,' Simon said all in a rush.

'She said you were an inquisitor, though you treated her gently enough.'

'It is true.'

'Were you one of those who questioned Father Edmund Campion?'

'I was.'

'He, I think, was not treated so kindly.'

'No sir, he was racked.'

'To any effect?'

'We found his printing press, if that is what you ask?'

'How was he broken, was it the pain?'

Simon paused. 'No sir, I think not. He was a clever witty man and he thought he could outwit me. But he could not.'

'And was he plotting against the Queen?'

'No. Only so far as any priest must plot against the Queen, by trying to turn her subjects away from the religion she has ordained for them.'

'Can any King or Queen rightly do that?'

'Can the Pope?'

'You then uphold the doctrine "*Cuius regio, eius religio*", as the King worships, so shall the people?'

'It seems a sound and simple thing, conducive to good order.'

'And yet Mrs Fant said you are a Jew.'

Simon bent his head. 'This is a thing that greatly troubles me, sir. It was not for his religion that we racked Father Campion. It is forbidden to me to do so in any case: for us it is a sin to persecute for religion's sake. Only we do not know beforehand which Papist we catch might have knowledge of a Guisan plot. I have often thought on this. If we put none to the question, then will hidden treason fester and flourish until it break out, murder the Queen and destroy the realm. We are afraid. We dare not risk permitting even one that seems to us tainted to escape unquestioned, lest by so doing we let slip the one who will kill her.'

' "We are afraid".' repeated Fr Hepburn, 'Do you find much truth upon the rack? Or do men lie to you so you will abate their pain?' Simon did not answer. 'Do they not accuse any whose names they can recall, only to stop you hurting them? Is this not as unreliable if not more so than mere clever speech and cross-examination and outwitting them? Surely they lie?' Fr Hepburn smiled. 'I have never been tested so, but I too have thought on it, and I know my weakness: I would name every name I could as a dangerous traitor, cause untold suffering to the innocent and guilty alike, yea, conjure plots from the air, if only you would not test me further. Am I the only cowardly priest you have found?'

Simon was silent and Fr Hepburn narrowed his eyes. 'As to religion, Mr Ames – I think you are an honest man, but surely what you say is naive? I doubt not but that the Queen is a merciful and gentle Lady that loveth all her subjects, Catholic and Protestant alike. But Walsingham? Topcliffe? Norton? Are these men not of the sect called Puritan? Do not other Puritans gather together to speak of altering the realm? It seems to me that they are harsh men, deep-dyed in heresy, that hate the rule of bishops and bitterly resent the governance of a woman. And tell me, sir, how many Puritans have you racked?'

Simon looked at him for a while, his lips pressed tight together and then rose and thanked him courteously and escorted him back to his own cell and the care of his anxious Yeoman Warder.

On his return, dizzy with suppressed thinking, Simon searched out amongst his many papers, my own ballad of Tom O'Bedlam, in its manifestations with Throgmorton, Dun the ballad seller and Agnes Fant and began applying the simplifying art of number to it. A quarter of an hour later he left Coldharbour at the run, grabbing his hat as he went, and scurried down to the Lion Gate.

XLVII

Mr Hunnicutt was taking the evening air in Seething Lane having but an hour before left the most important meeting of his life, when he saw Simon Ames, the clever little Marrano, come running heavy-footedly round the corner from Tower Street, puffing and blowing like a horse ridden post.

'Mr Ames, Mr Ames,' he cried, blocking the man's path. 'What is the matter sir, what is afoot?'

'Sir Francis . . . .' gasped Ames, trying to dodge past. 'Is he there? I must . . . we have no time to waste, none . . . .'

Cold coils of suspicion began to constrict the pleasant remains of Mr Hunnicutt's dinner.

'Why, he is at Whitehall, Mr Ames, did you not know? Her Majesty summoned him but two hours ago.'

There followed an explosive string of Portuguese, which Mr Hunnicutt supposed were oaths, and Ames threw his velvet cap on the ground, then picked it up and tried to dust it down.

'Thither I must go then.' He turned away, returning down Seething Lane and no doubt intending to go to the Custom House Steps.

'But Mr Ames . . . .' Hunnicutt hurried after him, plump hands out-stretched to slow him down. 'What is wrong?'

'I have untangled the elements of Mr Throgmorton's plot, which I may say were staring us in the face, and I must see Sir Francis.'

'Well, well, permit me to help you, sir, permit me to come with you, I shall find a good fast boatman. . . . But the tide is at the ebb, surely sir, it would be better to gain upriver of the Bridge and then find a boat.'

Ames paused and looked distracted. 'We need horses.'

'Stay there, catch your breath, you shall run yourself into a calenture. I will fetch mounts.'

Hunnicutt bustled in at the stable gate, caught hold of a groom he knew and within minutes, two tall rangy horses were saddled and waiting. He mounted one with a heavy upward flip from the groom, and trotted down Seething Lane, where he found Ames hopping from foot to foot and wrenching his hat about. Ames was in the saddle with extraordinary speed and urged his horse to a reluctant trot and then to a heavy-footed canter. There were still folk about on the streets, although the curfew had sounded, and they looked curiously at the pale red-nosed and insecurely seated man in the lead, and his rotund companion trying hard to keep up. Then any in their path cursed and swore and must leap for it because both were riding far too fast for the city crowds where a trot is a difficult matter thanks to the press of people. Hunnicutt's horse pecked at a hole in the ground, Ames found his way blocked by a pedlar's cart full of newly unloaded Seville oranges, set himself and jumped the whole affair to Hunnicutt's horror and astonishment. They swung off Tower Street to circle about St Dunstan's in the East, from there into Thames Street, still heading west, at which point Ames struck his hat on the horse's flank and kicked the bad-tempered gelding to a true gallop. Romeland and St Magnus' church whipped by Hunnicutt in a blur, they crossed the busy intersection with New Fish Street with nary a look nor a check, skidded to a trot as they passed the entrance to Old Swan Lane and the regulars at the Old Swan Inn stood and stared to see Ames urge his astonished horse through the narrow lane and down to the Stairs.

'Do you, Mr Hunnicutt, take the horses back to Seething Lane, while I find a boat,' said Ames curtly as he slid down from his horse without a tremor.

'Ah no, no, Mr Ames, I insist, I shall bear you company, we may need the horses to return . . . .'

'I expect to be at Whitehall all night.'

'Well, there may be messengers, no sir, take the horses to Old Swan stables to rest and I shall find a boat. Remember, despatching is my trade, though I must say I never thought to . . . .'

'Do it.'

Fortunately by the time Simon Ames sprinted back Hunnicutt had found a suitable boatman and primed him well with gold. For the first time in his life Simon jumped into a boat without hesitation and Hunnicutt nodded to the boatman who leaned his thick-muscled arms against the rip of the tide to bring them clear of the Bridge's turbulence.

'Perhaps a horse were faster,' Simon said, gnawing at his lower lip and unknowningly ripping a small piece from his penner.

Hunnicutt leaned forward and patted his knee comfortingly.

'No, Mr Ames, this is my trade, depend upon it, a boat is faster, even against the tide.'

Darkness was coming down thick and fast, a sour smell of snow on the air. The boatman had his regulation lanterns ready lit fore and aft and the water-strewn lights from his and the other boats glittered on the great buckler-sized badge on his arm and his worn red coat.

'What is it that Sir Francis must hear with such urgency?' asked Hunnicutt coaxingly.

'It is for his ears first, I fear.'

'But sir. . . .'

'If you must know, Mr Hunnicutt, I have found out the date when Philip II will make his attempt upon Her Blessed Majesty's life. Now if you do not regard that as sufficient cause for haste, sir, I know not why you serve Sir Francis . . . .'

'Of course, of course,' murmured Hunnicutt. 'How dreadful a thing . . . .'

For all his brave badge, the waterman was having trouble with the tide in the centre of the river. They were not much above the bear-baiting when Hunnicutt nodded and the boat spun suddenly about on itself.

Simon lurched, caught the side. Hunnicutt fell hard against him, stabbing with the long knife he affected at his belt, the boatman backed water and Simon tumbled, mouth open with complete astonishment, into the black water and sank like a stone from sight. Two large bubbles came up and Hunnicutt relaxed.

'Back to Old Swan Steps,' he said.

XLVIII

In my distraction I had a purpose, and Tom also, which was to find little Ralph. I knew the places where bodies may be left, or where they fetch up, and with the Queen Moon to support me stepped blithely from gutter to gutter and roof to roof while men sometimes caught sight of me and cried out that I was a hookman or a prigger of linen.

At last I stopped to piss, which even the mad must do, and wondered at the number of pigs and dogs all gathered about a white bundle. By means of a balcony and an awning and an open window I returned to terra firma, hoping it was no more than another beggar gone to the cold, but this time it was not. Is it the Earth itself that breathes out evil, or does evil come from some black fountain within ourselves, or is there a more terrible thing, evil all encompassing like the night sky with only here and there the little lights of good in it? When I gained the ground and saw what lay there, all about me were angels mixed with devils and barking dogs and pigs that I drove away with stones and sticks and rage, Tom howling like a wolf.

He was dead right enough, poor boy, that could never have asked mercy save with his eyes, dead a while and his flesh gone to wax, a bruise along his back where he had lain, unbleeding where the dogs had ripped him. I have seen death often enough, and felt him too, come creeping up behind me in the cold and snow, full of treacherous warmth and ease, a false friend as Adam was to David Becket. But never did I see so grievous a death as this. Tom howled and wept and clutched himself about his ribs where his heart would have escaped if it could, and I could see no reason in it, no purpose, no answer. Yet was it I that killed him? For I had given him a key to open the locked casket of his mind and as Becket had suspected, someone, Adam, discovering it had broken him entirely, had taken him at the neck and squeezed until he was dead, leaving his face all blue and purple. Commonly those that die of strangling like felons on the gallows that are not given enough drop by the hangman, their faces are particoloured and their tongues are black and stick out, making them fools and satyrs in their death. Not Ralph. Blue-faced Ralph in that respect was decorous.

A woman banged open her shutters and shrieked at me to shut my howling, God curse me, and she emptied out her jordan but missed me in her anger.

I took up his body and first I wandered about, weeping, not knowing where to go, while that sweet smell of death choked up my mind with its fumes. All about I was crowded with angels and devils that melted into one another, so which dare I trust? Appearance is no guide to the wisdom or goodness of angels. At last one rose up and beat off the others, ordered them to silence and then said that I should put down the body of Ralph and take thought.

Shall I take him to St Bride's and ask the priest to bury him? I could pay with the golden dish I found in the old abbey, and there could be mourners paid sixpence each and a coffin and a grave in holy ground and perhaps candles to light up his darkness.

No, said the angel, for they can see he was killed and did not die, and you being mad will be their clear first suspect.

At that I was troubled worse than before: did I do so indeed, in some fit? but the angel smiled and said my madness was of another sort and not to be a fool.

But he could not lie upon the midden and his blood licked by dogs, like King Ahab, poor boy, that had lost all he had and then his life.

But this is only the clay that held the coals of his soul, saith the angel, do you think he cares now he is in Christ's keeping what befalls his mortal remains? Only you care, wherefore take him down to the river, and pray for him, and then put him into the stream and let the river carry him to the sea.

But the fish will eat him, I said, weeping again.

So will the worms eat him if he is buried: have you never heard the Bible, nor the prayers of a funeral, that of dust ye came and to dust ye return.

But what of the Day of Resurrection, if he is not buried in sacred ground . . . .

The angel sighed kindly at me. Think you that God whose Word made this world and all the firmament of stars and all things unto infinity shall be troubled or bound by the nature of the place where he rests? Funerals are for the comfort of the living, not the dead, so now give him an easy gentle funeral and find an end to it. A churchman would term this rank heresy but angels need have no fear of Archbishops and it sounded wise enough to me.

So I went down to the river, where it welled cold and black with a little fire spangled on it here and there, the lights from men's windows become jewels upon the hem of God's night. When it came to pray, I could think of no words, and so climbed down the steps and put him softly into the water.

At once the current took him and turned him and covered him, sliding him towards the Bridge and onwards. For a moment I was dismayed at the thought of the bridge whose rushing and gushing might break him further, but the angel had the right of it after all.

And yet a devil whispered that it would be easy enough to step from the boatlanding and die in the water likewise, and I crouched for a time thinking of it, but then it seemed to me a coward's flight. When Death comes for me finally I should be ready to meet him, but would not go out to find him, nor bully him to take me. Which was an argument I used to Becket when I fished him dripping and drunken from the river, that self-murder is the basest kind of cowardly dishonour. I was a gentle-man once, and heir to lands and some wealth and good kin, as indeed was Becket also though not heir to any lands being a younger son. No, I said to Tom, I will not go with Ralph. Yet I could find no ease for the pain in those thoughts, so took a nail and scratched my arms with it, to let out the pain and the fumes in my blood.

Still I could not move from the boatlanding, but stared down at the pattern and feathering of the water about its weed-garlanded posts, gazing deeper and deeper through the folds and melting in the water, and heard the cries of men and devils ringing through the snow-flecked night.

There Becket found me in the morning and he demanded to know if I had seen Simon Ames who had disappeared. His uncle had missed him at his house and as everyone in the God-cursed city seemed to do when they had lost someone, sent for him at Pickering's through Mrs Fumey and Christ knew he had enough to concern himself with at present without hunting high and low for a fool of a clerk without enough sense would keep a beetle alive . . . .

I had no words for him, no speech.

'Well, if it is true that your angels tell you the truth, ask them to find Simon for me.' Becket said with his face thrust up to mine and his breath foul from a morning tongue well-furred by a night of tobacco-drinking and beer and argument. 'No? Hah! No use in them, is there then?'

My brother's fingers about Ralph's throat had choked mine off also, although I at least could breathe. I hurried after Becket in the hope Adam's grip should relent, and I followed him down to the next boatlanding to ask of the boatmen what they might have seen or heard in the night.

XLIX

In all of England is no stranger nor finer sight than London Bridge, the glory of the City, with its serried fleet of piers against the onrush of the Thames. The best drapers' shops in the land are on it, arching across it, enclosing those who care not that they get their cloth good cheap, but only that it be fine. There may be bought silks of Cathay and cottons of India, velvets and damasks of buttercup and viridian and violet and crimson and strange fancy colours like Dead Spaniard that was begun as a putty shade. There may you also find lawn that will pass in its entirety through a wedding ring and tissue of cloth of gold, cloth of silver and delicate leathers made to a buttery softness by the tanner's art. And all the colours and the textures are heaped up and arrayed by the great drapers in mountains of white samite and deep valleys of cramoisie and forest green so it be pleasing to the eyes of the folk that pass up and down and hither and yon beneath the Drawbridge Gate and the Stone Gate with its traitors' heads upon it and their attending ravens. The people choke Gracechurch and New Fish Street and Long Southwark as they bend their paths to the bridge, and slow at the old Drawbridge to gaze east upon the lower side at the sturdy Hansa cogs and the graceful ships of Venice and the brave and beautiful English ships.

I was right to fear its piers on Ralph's behalf, although they saved Simon Ames' life. Being knocked into the water and sinking down, he learned what an uneaseful death is drowning. He had felt not Mr Hunnicutt's knife, though he had seen it, because it had been turned aside by the cuirass he was wearing again. That same cuirass nearly killed him as he sank down into the black river. Raw terror possessed him, he was swallowing huge rocks of water, but then his fingers found his dagger and drew it and slit open the front of his doublet. He cut a side strap of his back-and-breast and by reason of his thinness was able to shrug the thing off over his head and kick hard for the surface with his lungs on fire.

Bobbing on the current and gasping among the stars in his head he was turned and twirled by the ebb current until he heard the louder roaring of the Bridge and rolled about the white waters, pounded against the barnacled stone and protective wooden beams until his skin was scraped raw and his shirt was tattered. He glimpsed and grabbed and clung onto a ring bolted to the stone of a pier. There he clung gasping and coughing and puking. Above him there were calls and a dirty pair of hands reached down to him and pulled him up out of the foam. Voices above him talked and he felt a pulling on his hands as his rings were taken and his slim chain of office that had somehow survived his entanglement with cuirass, and his boots and when he feebly protested and tried to fight them, a boot thudded into his side and he whirled down into darkness again. When he came back into the lesser darkness of the cold night, shivering and still coughing he said: 'I serve . . . the Queen, find me Becket . . . . Dr Nuñez in Poor Jewry . . . . Gold for one who helps . . . Simon Ames . . . .'

A bigger shadow kicked him in the mouth and Simon held his broken lip and mewed with despair.

The talk was hard to understand that went on about him, being mainly in thieves' cant, but he heard Becket's name and Pickering's and then the larger one that did the kicking said, 'I'll cut Tyrrel the bene whids, keep him clinked . . . .'

He lay trying to recapture his lost senses, his wet shirt clinging about his sore shoulders and the cold stone striking up from below and the freezing air striking down from above. He dare not move for fear of kicking.

In a long frozen while the large ragged creature came leaping back to the world beneath the piers and a knife shiny in his hand,

'Tyrrel says, kill him, there's lour for his . . . .'

He had a heartbeat's time for his benumbed mind to understand the words, to teeter between despairing acceptance and red rage and to find his heart leaping in him and somewhere strength coming into his legs so he could roll and climb to his feet and dodge along the pier side beneath the bridge's arch, where there was a narrow ledge and the brown and white foam roaring below. His feet were bare and the stone cold hurt them, he slid along with his back to the stone, hunched over as the arch rose and bent, his toes gripping desperately at the slimy ledge, his mind battered and numbed by the bellowing of the prisoned river.

Tyrrel's man was too broad and tall to dare the ledge, and leaned inwards, stabbing wildly with his knife. Anger flared in Simon again, unbidden his fist came forward and struck back, trapping and hurting the man's hand against the wall so his fingers opened and the knife rang into the water. Terrible curses and shouts for a pole to knock him off echoed distorted under the arch.

'I cannot remain here,' he thought quite clearly, the world somehow slowing about him as his anger became transmuted from the red to the white, how dare they make attempt to kill him, how dare they threaten the Queen's life that sheltered his people from Spain, by the Almighty there shall be a reckoning . . . . Above him his now dark-accustomed eyes could make out the blacker shadows of the bracing beams between the arches. London Bridge was old and needed shoring up and oak timbers helped brace the tight arches to support the weight of all the finery above.

He reached up, clamped his hands around the beam, scrabbled a toe into a hole between the stones and heaved himself up and onto the broad beam on which he lay lengthwise catching his breath. And then he crawled long it over the teeming bellowing water and swung down again onto the fellow ledge upon the other side, rocking and terrifying himself, but clinging on by his toes and fingers. He was in horror of slipping back into the waters: he dare not rest, but inched sideways to gain the better footing of the pier. Once there he blinked about, cowering as the full force of the wind struck him.

He knew that there was one place on the bridge where the drapers' houses did not rise sheer from it, crowded together into a single block of commercial wealth on the most valuable thoroughfare in England. That was upon the old drawbridge that could once be raised to permit a tall-masted ship to pass upriver. It was sharply fenced but the melancholic could sometimes be found leaning on it and wondering at the waters – indeed, it seemed Becket had jumped from it and Tom as well, so perhaps it could be scaled the other way.

The drawbridge was in the middle. Where was he? There was no smell of putrefying brains from the traitors' heads on the Great Stone Gate but the wind was cutting sharp from the east and might have blown it away. Simon blinked toward the bank and tried to think: if he gained the land, Tyrrel's men might be there, but they would not expect him to climb . . . .

There was a shout, a pole came swinging at him and he ducked, jumped sideways. Someone had found a waterman and made him brave by the magical application of gold or fear: there he was sculling desperately in the white waters, while a large ragged man chopped at Simon with a rusty halberd.

Simon ducked again, dodged the backsweep of the wicked axe blade, bruising his feet on the rubble infill of the pier, fell flat as it whistled over him. Becket's voice came to him: 'Fighting a man with a pole or pike, strive to come in close . . . .' And again: 'Arm yourself, Simon, catch up a stool or a rock if there be nothing else, arm yourself and attack, it is the only safety . . . .' His scrabbling fingers found a loose half-brick, slick with crawling creatures on its underside; he threw it awkwardly, at venture, heard the clatter in the boat, then came up to his knees and managed to block the wood of the pole with his forearm as it wavered ('Not with your hand, fool, you will have your fingers broken!'), grabbed it to his chest with the axehead scraping the stones behind him, and threw his weight against it. The upright man in the boat clung, swore, let go and sat down suddenly with his legs in the air, near upsetting the boatman as well who lost his hard purchase on the current and was swept on into the Pool of London.

Simon was left clasping the halberd. Only a month before he would have had no notion what to do with such a thing: his notions were still of the haziest, but he had at least seen the two-handed grip and he knew that the sideways strike might break armour but was slow whereas the hard jab with the point would pierce flesh and was swift. 'It is the argument of the rapier against the broadsword,' came Becket's voice in his head again, 'speed against power and each may be right in its place, but in general, choose speed first for in speed is also power.' Becket was much enamoured of philosophising over war especially after his second quart and Simon had listened as one might to a sailor that had seen El Dorado and the savages of the New Lands.

But Becket was no doubt drunk in some boozing ken, and Ames was alone. The darkness freighted with wind closed on him. His exertions had warmed him but now he cooled quickly: the gusts flapping his shirt bore frosty teeth, he was soaked with stinking river water and he started to shiver, his teeth rattling in his skull. He set his back against the brick of the bridge, facing outwards, and tried to take stock.

Firstly, it seemed that his name was known to the creatures who make their hiding place beneath the land roots of the bridge. Their anxiety to kill him in such a way as to keep his body rather than simply knocking him back into the river spoke of money to be paid for his corpse.

Detachedly, he wondered how much, in what weight of silver had they priced his skin?

And there were many mighty implications in what had happened, cobweb shrouds of inference to be woven, from which his mind could not refrain. Tyrrel would seemingly pay for his body, but the end and inspiration of that transaction must be Hunnicutt, whose own knife had scraped harshly on Ames' hidden breastplate. Here then was an answer to Simon's original riddle, the one he had spoken to Nuñez about and then almost forgotten in the hurry of later events, his suspicion of a spy at the heart of Walsingham's work. What better place to put a spy than in the dispatch room?

Hunnicutt, not Adam Strangways, must have been the one attempting to kill him, at least at first, using footpads, mercenaries . . . . What madness to use Adam's servant, the ballad seller. Was he so short-sighted, so self-important that he could not wait upon the more important mission? But men in mortal fear of the rack will often jump before they should, and it could not have been easy for Hunnicutt to find another safe conduit into the world of men who kill for money. And he had not done so badly after all, thought Simon bitterly, with the only man who knew his treason and the day of the attempt upon the Queen, freezing to death on a pier of London Bridge.

The wind was blowing harder, the frost coming in like iron. When Simon moved his shirt crackled, starched by ice, shreds of it frozen into the blood of his cuts and grazes, and he shook like a man with the ague. He tried banging his arms around his body, which hurt him, and he looked up at the nearest lantern, burning feebly high above him, and his face was stung with the first whirling little dry flakes of snow. He coughed when he breathed in. No doubt there would be a frost fair on the Thames this winter and oxen roasted on the ice and men doing a roaring trade in Dutch skates and metal pomanders made to hold hot coals and incense – he still had one in his clothes chest from last year, wrought like a pomegranate.

He must escape. Above him the wall of the bridge rose sheer, the houses of merchants and drapers with their windows gazing directly out upon the river that was their wealth, to see their ships pass, full of wealthy folk snoring in embroidered shirts and caps, pillowed and blanketed in linen and wool, guarded by bedcurtains from draughts, inured to the tumble of the waters beneath and deaf to any cries for help. He shaded his face from the snow, screwed up his short-sighted eyes: perhaps there was a ledge near the lantern? He squinted again: it was narrow, but yes, perhaps there was a ledge. Once on it, he could break a window . . . .

He leaned the halberd against the wall, squeezed his fingers into a long crack in the brick work, bruised his toes into another unmortared seam, hoisted himself up a little, spreadeagled like a spider against the wall, his face squashed sideways. He pushed up a little higher, his fingers scrabbled for a purchase but could find none, his toes gave way and he fell. Picking himself up, he moved along to a rougher part, set himself, tried again. His mind yammered on within, as he inched himself up the cruel bricks: could he shout for help? That would attract the ragged man, the clapperdudgeon, one of authority among beggars. Surely he could offer the man more in ransome money than he would get for Simon's corpse? How? And why should the man believe him? Why should he come near? He had only to wait and the wind and cold would do his work for him.

He had climbed perhaps five feet from the pier, but his fingers and toes were bleeding, the bricks filmed with frost. His calf muscle cramped agonisingly, salt sweat went into his eyes, he paused, slipped, clawed, slipped again, and fell once more. The breath was knocked out of him and he blacked out.

He came to once more with a new thought: there was a band of white stone running along the bridge wall, just below the lantern poles and first high windows, which marked the height of the arches for ships. He had mistaken it for a ledge that he could climb to.

He moaned in despair and turned on his side, curled up. The evil wind wrapped itself round him, the snow fell on him, he was a mass of bruises and his mouth hurt, he was alone in Becket's nightmare, marooned at the centre of a broad river, and cold, cold. There was no escape. In the morning they would find his corpse and his soul would be gone, flown away from the ice. It would be a relief, he thought dully, trying to shelter his head with his arms, an ending to coldness and confusion.

Oddly he was starting to feel warm again, even comfortable and sleepy. It would be good to sleep. If he shut his eyes and concentrated he could imagine that they had found him, that he was tucked up in bed with hot bricks at his feet and Uncle Hector had put ointment on his hurts, and there were warm blankets and no more need to struggle or fight . . . .

He dreamed he was a child again, peering up at a table set with clean linen and unleavened bread upon silver dishes, and a cup of wine overflowing and a dish of herbs and another of salt. He knew he was meant to ask an important question, but he had forgotten it while all his family stared at him for betraying them. Outside the Angel of Death was pushing on the door.

What was he supposed to remember? He knew the words, he could hear his mouth saying them, slurring the Hebrew, making nonsense of his prayer, an empty garble though he knew them so well, they were words of power and importance, fit words for his last breath. But the wind stripping the life from his bones had also stripped memory and understanding from his mind, if he had ever really understood, and he had not. In truth, scraping along the bottom of his soul, he knew he had not, and he struggled to think, to remember, belatedly to learn.

This was a matter between Simon and God, nor will I presume to tell it as a tale. Let it suffice that at last, in the cooling furnace of his heart, as softly as the first sight of the sun, he remembered.

It was a simple enough thing, and no secret. Beyond and between all is one Lord God. Not Simon's god of number, not Walsingham's god of logic, nor yet my brother's burning god, but one single, simple God, beyond all our walls of words, who keeps us company. And at last Simon need not flee nor hide from confusion.

Perhaps the wind changed a little, perhaps his heart found some fresh fuel to burn. It was a hard thing for him, requiring all the remaining dregs of his courage, on a single thought like a mustard seed to turn from false warmth and into cold like a dagger in each vein.

I am dying, he said to himself, and struggled to open his eyes, blurred, dizzy, saw his hands before his face blocking the dark snowflakes. No, but I should be dead, he thought and found himself smiling a little in triumph that he was not, yet.

He pulled his hands away from his eyes, and uncurled himself, came to his hands and knees, staggered like a new-born calf to feet which he could hardly feel. There was a clatter on the stones and he blinked down at the thing that fell there, short and stubby, fletched at one end, sharp-pointed. Why, it was a crossbow bolt . . . .

Simon reacted like a mummer in a comedy. He stared at the bolt, blinked owlishly through the stinging murk at what he thought was a gleam of metal on Old Swan Steps, no great distance. There was the creak of a jack winding up the crossbow anew.

He had been about to surrender to death, but now the fear of it sent the blood into his veins again. He grabbed his weapon, ducked under the arch, stepped back on the ledge above the waters, balancing on numb slippery feet above the fading ebb, still with the halberd clutched in his hand. He thrust it up and over with all his strength and by a miracle it stuck, hooked over the beam. And then he was scrambling up beside it, pulling halberd free, eeling along the beam on his belly, hooking the halberd again between the beam and the wall and climbing down again on toes and fingers with the halberd shaft as an aid.

As he looked out onto his new pier a crossbow bolt slammed into the bricks above him: he winced, crouched, scuttled round to the next arch. He did it once more and then again and again, his mind fogged and confined in weariness and fear and cold, but some newly deep-dyed thread of obstinacy forcing his body doggedly to save itself, himself, all the world lost to him save his aching arms upon the rough slimy oak and the wet bricks and his toes cramping upon the narrow ledge . . . .

At last he stopped in the middle of crossing the torrent on a bracing beam, and he knew he had no more coin of strength or courage to spend, there was nothing left in him. He peered down through a blur of sweat and ice at the Thames. He would stay where he was. At least he was sheltered from the snow and the biting wind, he would be damnably hard to shoot or hit with any weapon, and he was in a place where he would be afraid to let go of his mind and sleep again. Even if he were not afraid, the magnified roar of the river would help prevent him. It was the best he could do, the very best. Now he was in the hands of the Almighty.

He folded his arms to rest his chin on his ruined hands, coughed, and began to consider of a problem in chess-playing.

L

Well it was I that led them to him, for it was I that saw his seal ring, the one he had sent in sign of his authority to Mr Recorder Fleetwood, it was I and an angel saw it in the window of a shop well-known to deal in such things by St Paul's. When I whooped and leapt and pointed, Becket left off his questioning of a stationer and came and looked. One minute later we were within the shop, the man's grill had given to the lever of Becket's sword, and the shopkeeper himself was backed up against his furthest wall, trembling at the length of steel Becket was threatening to wash in his unworthy blood.

'No, I . . . I . . . your honour . . . I would never . . . sir, I beg you . . . . It was an upright man sold it me . . . . I will tell you sir, of a surety, he wishes a third of the . . . . Yes, he shall have it . . . er . . . well, your honour, sir . . . . It is in my ledger . . . . If you will permit . . . .'

He sweated no less when the blade transferred its position to the place behind his ear where two inches will suffice to kill.

'Capperdudgeon Mick Reynolds,' he said at last. 'That is upright-man to the beggars by the bridge . . . . Sir, do you not want the ring . . . .'

I plucked the ring off the counter where Becket had made a dent when he slammed it down and cartwheeled after him. At first we thought it a foolish quest for there seemed to be no beggars on the bridge at all, and certainly no sign of Simon. Becket stamped to the fences on the draw-bridge and roared 'Simon Ames', and we heard a faint answering cry.

An apprentice ran delightedly for a ladder and the drawbridge was groaning under the weight of sighseers, experts all, by the time it arrived. Some urged waiting on the Watch, others would have the Mayor and Aldermen sent for, and in the meantime Becket lifted the long ladder over the fence, set it firmly on the nearest pier in the sugar-dusting of fresh snow, climbed the fence and began his descent. I held the ladder for him and shook my head fiercely at the naughty imp that said I should topple it over to watch him swear.

Shaded equally from night and the sun by the weight of the bridge above him, Simon had not realised day had come and that the glittering pattern of water reflected on the stones was not the glitter of a distracted mind. He thought there might be some beast burdening his back and searching his ribs with a fiery icicle but he heard his name called and answered. A little time later he looked up and saw sunlight streaming past the black broad shape of Becket, peering round the pillar and under the arch at him.

'Jesu, Simon,' said Becket. 'What are you doing there?'

'I thought they could not reach me here,' whispered Ames a little complacently. 'Nor did they.'

'Well, I cannot reach you either if you got up from that little ledge, my fat arse will not permit of it.' Ames smiled feebly. 'So my friend, you must climb down yourself.'

'I cannot.'

'Die then.' said Becket harshly. 'Would you have me run a boat beneath you to catch you as you fall? Come, if you got so far, you may come further. Move along, slowly, gently . . . .'

He came to the place where he knew he must swing himself down, grip with his toes and transfer his weight to the tiny ledge. How had he done it in the dark? Now he could see what he was about his heart quailed in him.

He tried gingerly twice, but the second time he nearly fell and gripped the comforting width of the main beam like a woman.

'I cannot,' he gasped hoarsely. 'No, David, I . . . .'

'Can you hold still then?' demanded Becket.

'Ay,' Simon whispered shakily, 'that I can do.'

'Wait there.'

Where would I go? Simon wondered pointlessly. He heard shouted orders, much thundering on the bridge, saw a thick rope dangled uselessly from the other side of the bridge, Becket return to his pier.

'Stay still no matter what,' shouted Becket. 'Hold tight. A boat will come through . . . .'

And in a little while it did, sculled by a delighted waterman with another balancing in the prow. Simon was too short-sighted to see clearly how it was done: as the boat came racing in between the piers of his own arch, the waterman that was standing caught hold lightly of the rope that was trailing from the bridge, let it run through his hands as the other waterman tossed his frail craft from white eddy to rushing stream and then threw the end of the dripping coil to Becket as he passed. Becket meantime had hammered a strong hook into the far pointed end of the pier. He pulled the rope taut, passed it about the hook and then dusted his hands.

'There is a good way about this and a better way. The good way about it is to clasp your arms across the rope so and push off with your feet and slide down to me. But that will burn your arms cruelly and you might leave go for the pain.'

Simon nodded and tried to concentrate through the fog in his mind and the stabbing in his back. Had the crossbow bolt hit him after all and he not noticed in his numbness? Listen, pay Becket good mind, he knew what he was about . . . .

'The better way is to take the halberd you have with you hooked on the beam there, grip hands close on that across the rope and let the halberd shaft bear the pain of burning on the rope. Do you understand?'

Simon nodded, reached for the halberd, in terror lest he drop it in

222

the water and end up burning his arms. Burning might be better than freezing . . . . No, better the halberd.

It was heavy, heavy as his head. Infinitely slowly he passed it under the rope that stretched below the beam, just touching it, gripped tight with both hands, swallowed hard in a burning throat, set himself and let himself slide over sideways from his precious beam.

The jerk on his arms almost unloosed him and the end of the halberd struck sparks from the stone as he slid down it and his legs trailed in the water which he could do nothing about and the breath had been blown from his body but Becket had knelt and spread his arms wide to take the force of his arrival and he was clamped tight and being hauled up and onto the pier again.

He tried to rise to his feet but his animal part had used its last strength and he was crowing at the frosty air. He fell again, crumpling up, and found himself lifted up on Becket's shoulder, very inelegantly and arse foremost. The ladder creaked ominously as Becket scaled it while the sightseers about cheered and clapped.

Byt the time he reached the top Simon had gone silent, his eyes half-shut in his trodden face and his breath barely whistling and creaking under his grazed ribs. Rather than wait about finding a horselitter, Becket slung his own cloak round Simon and carried him through the streets at a long angry stride, straight to his uncle's house in Poor Jewry trailing a clamour of nosy small boys and dogs. There all was a flurry of hot bricks and blankets and his Aunt Leonora magnificent and imperious calling orders more rapid than a file of arquebusiers in Portuguese and English combined. A boy ran to find Dr Nuñez who had gone out to attend upon a goldsmith with the gout.

Yet ever Simon lay still and cold and so Leonora called up one of the boy-children and bade him get into bed and snuggle up to his kinsman to warm him out of his deathsleep, which was a heavy thing to put on a child. Yet he did it willingly.

Dr Nuñez returned, breathing heavily from running up the stairs, took Simon's pulses and pronounced that there was not a one of his humours that was not so dangerously low, but that he felt letting blood would further unbalance them. The day passed and gradually the warmth came back into Simon and the child was bidden out of the bed again and downstairs to eat his supper. Simon tossed and turned and a flush began to burn high on his cheek and he suddenly broke through the skin of sleep and clutched at Dr Nuñez's sleeve. When Dr Nuñez soothed him he croaked louder, first Portuguese, then English, angrily.

'Tom O'Bedlam, ask Tom O'Bedlam, there's the answer, when they will kill her . . . . Listen . . . the number is one, three, four and seven. . . . One for God, three for your Trinity, four for your evangelists and seven seals upon some book of the Apocalypse, there is the key . . . .'

Becket came down the stairs two at a time and stormed into the kitchen to find me, eating pottage with the children by the fire. He lifted me up by the front of my doublet and made it tear.

'What do you know, what have you not told me you half-wit zany, you counterfeit crank . . . .'

I curled up and held my arms over my head, but I knew from my angels what his question meant and began to sing as the ballad singer had done once, before Becket stopped his song forever.

> 'From the hag and hungry goblin
>   That into rags would rend you,
> And the spirit that stands by the naked man
>   In the book of moons, defend ye.
> That of your five sound senses
>   You never be forsaken
> Nor wander from yourselves with Tom
>   Abroad to beg your bacon . . . .'

Dr Nuñez was behind him, rumbling an order, Becket was staring at me thunderstruck.

'The ballad of Tom O'Bedlam. How do you know the words?'

'I made it,' I told him, straightening up and unloosing his hands from me, driven sane with anger that the last good spawn of my brain should be bent to treason. 'I made it, I wrote it in Bedlam on stolen scraps of paper and sent it to my brother. All but this part.'

> 'Alas the sorrow of that bastard child
>   Which soweth love will make me wild,
> And if I must die so on I moan
>   'Till her Moon's face become mine own
> And sorrow has ceased on a silver feast,
>   Hey diddle, sing diddle, hi diddle I drone . . . .'

And I spat to show my opinion of Adam's doggerel chorus which the song needed not.

'Sing it again,' demanded Dr Nuñez, clearing a space next to a fascinated little girl and opening his penner. I sang, he wrote while the little girl dutifully held his bottle of ink, and then he went among the words, plucking them out with underlining and muttering the numbers under his breath.

'The . . . bastard . . . will . . . die . . . on . . . her . . . own . . . feast.'

And I laughed at the simplicity of it, to make a date for murder and rebellion upon the Accession Day and to pass the knowledge of it about under guise of a ballad that every child in London could sing now and was already tiring of.

'It is the dragon,' I shouted. 'The dragon of danger, rising up in his house of secrets, and Lucifer within to shoot her down, seek ye the dragon . . . .'

Becket growled impatiently. 'Be silent,' he barked and I was, for I was afraid of him.

'We must warn the Court.' Dr Nuñez said, 'I will ask audience with my lord of Leicester this night . . . .'

'No, no!' I shouted again, unable to bear it that they should be so near the truth. 'The Queen Moon will never call off the Tilts, seek ye the dragon in God's name, the firedrake of the deadly eye, like unto Basilicon that kills with its glance, yea, seek it by the sword of Damocles . . . .' Why was a devil hanging on my tongue to whirl my words into an egg froth of foolery? 'Find the dragon and you shall find Cain that is also Lucifer . . . .'

Becket swatted me aside like an importunate fly. Dr Nuñez took his cloak, and they left, leaving the children gazing solemn-eyed at me. Above Simon sweated and turned and his spirit leapt the fences of this world to dance about the daemons and Angel Governors of the sky, that he believed not in, and played in a cooling cascade of number and swam the waves and troughs of that foaming mathematical sea that maketh the storm of stars above us. Below I bowed to the angel in the doorpost and then took up a kitchen knife before the horrified eyes of the cook, put it in my belt and left the house.

LI

I cannot speak as Adam, for I cannot understand his world, how it could be so harsh and clear and simple to the mind's touch, how truth could be one thing and one thing only and that the truth of Rome. I was brought up in it myself and think that for all the ancient Fath's bloodiness it hath a gentler, less rigid nature than the Reformed. For those who cannot speak with the Queen Moon, Our Lady the Blessed Virgin Mary is a kinder holiness for prayers of the weak than that stern Christ of St Paul and St Augustine and John Calvin. But what do I know? To me the world is a thing of mist and truth also is doubtful as its shadows; to Adam all was illumined harshly, unkindly, by the bright light of his Faith. The world is much the same for Sir Francis Walsingham and his great enemy the King of Spain, the Kingly Clerk, and who am I to say such mighty worshipful men may lie? Is not the world of mist and the world of paper moved here and there and about by those who think so harshly? When men burn each other, always it is the ones that hear no siren singing of the Queen Moon who light the faggots, the ones who see clear and know the truth and intend that all shall be well because they shall see to it, they are the destroyers. I would have the world a veil, a tissue of fairest rainbow silk and you would have it a damascene sword blade, and we both know which is the harder and which cuts. And which is stronger and fairer?

My trouble comes to me from our mother who wasted herself to nothingness and the image of the grave by her fasting and penances that England should return to her Truth, as if by her suffering she could turn the world about. Agnes was still at wet nurse, but Adam. . . . She left him for a greater Truth, as she said, and so has he held to that Truth all his life, and would now finish her desire by the steadiness of his aim. He would destroy the Protestant Jezebel, the bastard of England.

Cozening the key to Haarlem from Becket ten years ago, that was one thing, dirty but understandable and expedient. To seek to kill the Queen of England has a splendour in it. But to strangle a boy only because he had the means to reveal him – not for any cause that he had done so, nor even considered it, but because he *might* – no, I cannot comprehend how straight-edged, how razor-sharp and single must the world be to him, that Adam could do it. Had he no regret, no fear that the Pope's forgiveness paid in advance might not suffice to clear him of it before the Judge?

Well before sunrise upon the Accession Day, the river was thick with boats of folk going unto Westminster for the Tilts, and others lining the Strand for the great procession, and banners hanging from windows and hawkers selling woodcuts of the Queen, and ballad sellers doing hot trade with new-made songs of Eliza the Fair. As the Queen had growled the night before to the Earl of Leicester, it was as much as her throne was worth to call off the Accession Day sport, and nor would she for a mere riddle in a ballad sheet of a madman. So all of Simon's haste was set at nought.

Adam was in his place within the dragon with all his accoutrements, covertly winding up his small crossbow in readiness where it was placed to shoot from the eye, when there came a rapping on the trapdoor. His heart stuttering and his hat over the weapon he opened it to find Sir Philip Sidney smiling up at him, his silver and blue tilting armour burnished to dazzling, holding out a silver flask of wine.

'To warm you, Goodman,' he said. 'It will be a long day and I would have you strong for it.'

At sunrise the firedrake wheeled ungainly from the gates of the Hanging Sword yard, to have its wings better folded and strapped for their passage through Temple Bar. Here Broom, wheezing with excitement and an unhealthy colour of flush on parchment, also looked in at the trapdoor and nodded. Adam smiled at him: it was a thing he did rarely, even as a boy, and it was an easy thing to behold and broke open his sealed face for a moment.

The horses set themselves in their traces, ridden by a boy in olive green velvet, and began their long trek, turning into Fleet Street and passing through the Temple Bar. Then there was a delay whilst the wings were unfurled and Adam must work at the central winch to be sure they could still flap. Sidney had caused to be removed part of the Fleet Street midden's overspill, so that he could pass and the horses snorted at the tottering heap of ordure that neither the City of London nor Westminster would remove, it being, as each side insisted, upon the other city's land.

And then all went into the Strand at a crawling pace, the joints creaking and Richard Broom dancing between them with oil and tallow to ease them. At Charing Cross they waited for the others in the procession where the final tweaks were made by anxious masters of ceremony, of horses caparisoned as unicorns and a multitude of children being the Children of Discord, marshalled by schoolmasters with hoarse voices and nervous whips. These were the dragon's allies and after his taming by the Queen, they would fight in her behalf with paper roses.

There was a minotaur also and harpies, and a great shambling beast made upon carts like the dragon, which was the Beast of the Apocalypse. It was very hairy, having consumed a strange quantity of goats, and foul-odoured, being scented within by burning flowers of sulphur and honey, and had for its head the Pope's face and crown, with a necklace about it of three sixes to be sure none could mistake it.

The Beast had been made at St Giles in the Fields and was ridden by Fulke Greville in disguise as the King of Spain. It came with a clashing of cymbals and blowing of bagpipes and comical clownish monks beating each other and singing cod Latin that he and Sidney had made up over a quart of sack. The dragon also had his consort of instruments in a further cart behind, but they were harps and viols although playing untunefully at variance as part of the metaphor.

When the procession finally went its way down Whitehall towards the vast concourse milling about St James's Park and the fields near the old lazar house, great shouts were thrown up to see such magnificent sights. Adam was working hard, puffing smoke with bellows out of the dragon's mouth, flashing the mirror eyes and with his legs working a drum machine from a playhouse for the dragon's roaring. Now Sir Philip rode up on his fine grey tilting horse, all caparisoned in blue and silver, and his tilting helmet now capped with a dragon enamelled in red. The crowd roared to see him, and the silly maidens in it screamed in a most disorderly way. The music fell silent, and Adam too.

'Here is the Dragon of Discord!' (Loud blowing on trumpets and banging of drums, so Sidney must pitch up his voice a notch) 'He late hath marred the Kingdom. Shall I ride him?'

Some in the crowd shouted 'Yea!', others shouted 'No!' which was not in the script so he ignored them.

'Ye tell me yes. Then I shall essay it!'

Adam was sweating already in the belly of the dragon. He turned one winch to make the wings flap their red samite and another to move the head. The tail being on the smaller cart behind was moved by a boy hidden underneath.

Sir Philip Sidney made to climb up the side of the dragon, but with Adam's conscientious pulling on ropes and winding of winches was in truth thrown off.

'This drake is too wild for me,' he cried, and the crowd roared at the pun. 'Yet will I lead it and hope it shall follow me to one who may tame its mighty rage and humble its uncouth pride.'

This was done three times in the procession to the Court Gate so all could see it. Fulke Greville had his piece to say also, which he did with a Spanish accent and approval of the Dragon of Discord.

There in the enclosure were the courtiers who could beg or buy or steal a space sufficient to stand upon and no more, all in their finest broidered velvets and silks. It was many days' harvest of lilies of the field from St Paul's, and every shade of colour beginning in black and deepest violet, verging on the treasonous, rising up through cramoisie and crimson, slashed with tawny, now hopping over the rainbow to emerald and viridian with a pause at citron and buttercup, and on through rose and blush and salmon, London Bridge ransacked for blazing finery, even pale peachy cream for those whose skins could withstand it. None dared white, the Queen's colour. And every cloak was overburdened with small flowers and wildly looping vines, every stomacher engulfed in coloured thread, every sleeve wildly puffed and slashed and pinked, and every chin craned high by a newly starched white or yellow ruff.

Upon the other side, beyond the smoothly raked tiltyard, stood the common populace of London on rickety stands, shouting and craning and drinking and singing lewd songs back and forth regarding bears and dogs and Eliza the Fair. Uncompared with the lurid brilliance of the Court, they would have seemed a very flower garden of folk.

Now came the procession down through a lane made by the Queen's Gentlemen before the Court Gate, with Sir Philip speaking like Stentor: 'Way there, way for the Dragon of Discord and all his company!'

Leicester has doubled the guard, I thought. But the Beast of the Apocalypse had lost a pin from the axle and so must stand while a sweating carter pounded in a new one and prayed it would hold. Then went the procession through another gate in the fence to the tiltyard itself where the Queen's Majesty waited at her accustomed balcony above the yard. It was all fringed with black and white hanging samite, and vines, and speedily wrought silk flowers so it seemed a bower of the Queen of Spring.

As Proserpine she stood on the dais, a shimmer of white velvet and satin with a single pomegranate worked upon it. Light cast back softly from the creamy pearls and brilliantly from the diamonds and rubies all set about the colours of her kirtle, which were black and white and cloth of gold. There was a jewel upon her breast of the Snake Wisdom and another upon her sleeve of the Pelican, that giveth the blood of its breast to her young.

Now a boy descended in a basket, dressed as a cherub with golden wings, shivering in the sharp air and his skin staring on him, to orate upon the sorrows of a land beset by the Dragon Discord, whilst Sir Philip dismounted and took off his helmet and then stood before the dragon, head flung back to gaze upon the Queen her beauty.

She listened as she ever does, with her head on one side and rapt attention on her face, as the boy rambled piping through his speech which had not been made by Sidney and was the worse for it.

I, meanwhile, went to crawl between the legs of the crowd to fight through them and surprised two cutpurses in the plying of their trade. Both were of Gabriel's flock, I knew.

It so happened that Adam also was in straits, for with fear and excitement wrought up tangled in him, along with Sidney's kindly wine, he longed to piss, and had forgot to bring a bottle with him. He aimed into the silver flask in his haste, and had barely finished when Sir Philip began upon his own speech.

'Alas,' he said, 'for this poor realm, not only oppressed by the pride and untameable wrath of this Dragon of Discord, hath also been threatened from without. Here is the Guest Beast, ridden by a Prince of Darkness and all unknowing our Dragon maketh common cause with him, yet all the while loathing. How may we defeat such a Beast that comes against us when Discord rules our hearts? Yea, for is it not in the prophecies of Merlin written that a Dragon shall fight a Beast . . . .'

The horses drawing the carts, themselves clad in red samite, must pull forward a few paces to allow the Beast of the Apocalypse its place. One lifted his tail and unleashed great copious quantities of manure, for all the drench he and his fellows had been given by Sidney's horse-coper the day before to empty them out. The other beside him began to stamp, frightened by the glimpses of the hairy beast he caught beyond his blinkers.

Adam sweated to draw up the moveable part of the dragon's head to its highest extent, then climbed quickly up inside to where the crossbow was ready nocked with a poisoned bolt, aimed through the firedrake's eye and now straight at the Queen's heart.

He wedges his feet on the ladder to steady himself, draws breath to aim at the woman a few feet from him. But the horses stamp their feet again, snorting: they have seen a thing at last beyond their experience and wisdom, a strange creature bursting from the crowd, a scrawny jumping bundle of sticks wrapped in tawny velvet, a creature with his hair and beard in elflocks and blood streaking his tattered arms and hands where he had scratched them with a nail. It was all I could do, to deny him a firm platform to take aim, to confuse and bedevil his one clear shot at the Queen. What else could I do?

The horses snort and stamp at the smell of blood and when the creature throws aside a Yeoman and leaps the fence to caper demented before the grave giants of horseflesh, first Jupiter shies and then Titan and Juno, and then all back and start forward together, moving the dragon in jerks, sidling and bumping it and neighing in panic. The nearest to the cart begin to kick backwards at its front board.

Some of the urchins in the crowd are cheering; the cherub still hanging in his basket and blue with cold clutches the rope and starts to cry, and the head of the dragon sways back and forth.

Sir Philip sees disaster looming at the corner of his eye: embarrassment, humiliation. The capering lunatic punches a groom that runs up to control the horses, who are now throwing their weights at venture into their collars and are determined to escape, if need be with their burden behind them. Another begins to kick at the traces.

Dropping half of his carefully composed speech, Sidney launches into its finale.

'And now celestial lady, fair sister to Artemis and Aphrodite, incomparable Queen and most reverend Prince, only vouchsafe to turn your most imperial and beauteous gaze upon this rebellious dragon . . . .' The crowd laughed at his wry expression, making a comedy of his difficulties, as to say, what can you expect of a Dragon of Discord? '. . . If you will but bend your diamond eyes to his, so his Discord shall be tuned to a sweet harmony by your great glory.'

The Queen smiled graciously, with a wicked twinkle in the aforementioned eyes, which are not diamond indeed, but snapping and black. After a moment, as the script dictated to Adam, the high swaying head of the dragon lowered and a puff of submissive smoke escaped. In the cart behind, the musicians who had been playing as they pleased and against one another, slid very aptly and gracefully into harmony.

Sidney smiled sweetly in that moment when all eyes were on the moving dragon and I danced a little incautiously near to him. He took two steps forward, caught Tom's arm in his mailed fist, and stunned me with a great blow to the side of my head with the other. I could hear the laughter and cheers rolling out of the crowd who had seen as he dropped me down, considerably away from the horses' hooves, and turned again to mount the steps of his Dragon of Discord.

'Sir Philip,' called the Queen, leaning over her balcony, 'must you also fight with Bedlam beggars?'

'Why yes, Your Majesty,' he answered straightfaced, with his helmet in his hands. She raised her brows severely. 'For this was a part of the pageant vouchsafed by God, being the Spirit of Unreason and Melancholy, which I have now defeated in fair and knightly combat!'

The Queen laughed once more and inclined her head as Sidney stood up on the dragon's back and shouted, 'So end all who trouble the Queen's Peace!' The crowd roared.

LII

In the finances of the ungodly, Accession Day bulks large. Where there is such a press of people gathered together, there also will be the cutpurses, the nips and foists, and in the alleys for the unwary the footpads. If there had been one there with eyes to see, he would have wondered at the fact that all who mingled with the holiday crowds were of Tyrrel's party and paid their tithes to him. None of them were the followers of Laurence the King, which must have been a sore loss to him.

No matter. For a greater gain he was willing to take such a loss. Pickering himself was at the front rank of the common folk who watched the Tilts, raising his voice from a growl to a yell as the knights in their gleaming armour set their horses and charged towards each other, until with the clash at the centre all the audience shouted and cheered. Next to him sat his wife and upon the other side her sister and beside her the hangman of London in festive dress of red with little skulls to be his buttons.

Behind them all in the city, round about a large house not far from Old Fish Street, was a gathering of his men, and at their head Becket that had been so busy for the past few days. In one fist he held a shotted dag with the wheel-lock ready wound, in the other a broadsword, and behind him were three men with crossbows likewise wound up tight, ready to fire.

The first of Tyrrel's men to fall to their bolts were his guards upon the door. Then up came four big men with a small swinging ram that had been practising in an old house of Pickering's to break the door down. Axes thudded into the wood of the back door and Pickering's raiders were into the house and piling up the stairs, Becket roaring at their head.

It was Tyrrel's affectation that he had no need ever to leave his house with the Watch in his pay and his partisans all about him: but to a fierce frontal assault at a time when all the apprentices were out of the city to see the sport and the Watch likewise, to this he had no answer. The fighting boiled through the house and fat Tyrrel swept up his dagger and launched himself into it, but Becket took his aim coolly and shot him dead.

With that his men began to lay down their arms, but snatched them up again when they found that for all Becket's shouting, most of Pickering's soldiers had no notion of giving quarter to their hated rivals for London's gleanings, and so within an hour all were dead or dying of their wounds, and Becket's strategy was proven with but two men lost to him. One poor creature that jumped from an upper window to shout 'Clubs!' in the street was picked off with a crossbow bolt and the only one that answered his call was a sour-tempered old woman that had no use for Tilts of any kind and threw an apple at him.

Under Becket's baleful captainship, every scrap of paper in the house was gathered up into three chests and packed onto ponies he had brought for the purpose. First they would go to the Strand to await Pickering's advantage and then they would go to Seething Lane for Walsingham's perusal. As the spoils of war, aside from Tyrrel's treasure which was now Pickering's, all else in the house belonged to those who had taken it and by the mid-afternoon there was nothing left to take, even the panelling ripped off the walls in search of secret hiding holes had been gathered up for use somewhere else. In the middle of the ruin Tyrrel's body lay belly up and a broad hole in his chest.

LIII

The dragon died soon after it had paraded thrice about the tiltyard and flashed its eyes and flapped its wings, with Adam sweating and cursing in his close confinement, and his crossbow still virgin beside him. The schoolboys of London were belabouring each other with paper roses, some containing cunningly concealed stones, and their shrieks rose above the crowd's laughter. Poor Tom, meanwhile was shaking and rubbing his head and staunching the sticky blood running from his ear. There is no justice: here was a dreaded threat to the Queen her sacred life, which he had thwarted by his timely capering and all the thanks he got for it was a clout on the head from a mailed hand.

Adam's mind was a broth of confusion and wrath and incomprehension. Had not his whole enterprise been blessed by the Pope, was it not in the service of God and the Truth? Could the bastard Queen of England truly possess the witchcraft rumoured of her mother?

Circumspectly he waited until the dragon was retired beyond the tiltyard in the stableyard, and smiled and took Sidney's gold. All about him the while his sharp-edged world quivered and shook like air above a dish-of-coals. When all had been so clear, how could he have failed?

He tried to push among the people from behind, to become part of the crowd, trying to sidle and move back and deeper into it, counter to the press of those who leaned forward as Sidney and Greville made their first pass.

He stood like that unseeing and unknowing, his world in tatters, trying to understand wherein he had failed while the tilting went on and the noise rose and fell with the horses' hooves. Tyrrel's empire had fallen to sudden assault and Becket mounted a strong cob gelding and drove it through the almost empty streets from Old Fish Street to Knightrider Street through Carter Lane and Creed Lane to Ludgate and then down the hill and over Fleet Bridge and so onto the Strand, all empty of people to clog his way. Only when he reached Charing Cross must he slow to a walk until the men he had stationed there could meet him. They made a pack about him and shoved through the crowd until he could cross into St James's Park and come at the stands from the side. All this he had planned, ready for the day, Balfour having taught him the value of foresight and rehearsal. During a pause in the tilting he came to Laurence Pickering and made two signs – thumbs up and then a throat-slit with his finger and Pickering smiled and nodded gravely.

Adam knew none of this for he thought he had read the riddle, and his world steadied and stilled. Was it that God required of him the martyrdom he had sought to avoid, did He in truth require the blood of His faithful soldier to accomplish the sacred deed?

In the face of such failure to so careful and painfully worked a plan, there could be but one answer. Adam stood stock still, his face blank, swaying a little with the press about him as they craned with their eagerness to see the thundering horses and the shining armour and the clash of weaponry, hoping for a dreadful accident and some blood to marvel at.

If he must be a martyr, how could it be accomplished? He had on him only a long poignard dagger. How could he find the means to gain close enough to the Queen?

For all of the tilting, which she greatly liked, loving to see handsome well set-up young men show themselves off, the Queen remained in her gallery the better to see the bouts of arms. Adam's eyes lighted on the crane with its cherub-basket and knew that his God was still with him. He shifted back the way he had come, treading on toes and drawing curses, but most were too busy laying bets and gasping as the blows rained down in bright shields to pay him any mind.

The cherub had been wrapped in blankets and patted on the head for a clever boy that had remembered every word. Adam walked by his bench and spoke to the Yeoman by the crane's side.

'I am come to make the crane fast.'

'Eh?' said the Yeoman, preoccupied at the sight of his month's wages dodging and swinging on the raked sand. 'What was that?'

'I must tie the crane back, else it might sway and damage the Queen's bower.'

'Oh. Ah. Very well.'

Adam ducked inside the crane's body and began climbing its internal ladder. The Queen's gallery was built onto the Great Close Tennis Court and the crane had been brought up upon its left hand side by the Park Lodgings. As Adam was climbing, Becket chanced to look that way in mid-critique of Fulke Greville's Spanish style and froze to see his old friend and enemy so close to the Queen. In a moment he was up and

235

running across the frontage, drawing howls from the spectators, vaulted a fence, dodged two Yeoman convinced that they had found the assassin and began pursuing Adam up the crane's ladder. Adam looked down once, climbed faster.

'Beware!' roared Becket, 'Ware assassin!'

The Earl of Leicester's broad red face appeared peering between his silk flowers, caught sight of Adam and turned to shout an order. Behind him a tall dark man with a black beard, in red and tawny silks, moved up smoothly to the Queen, his hand tightening on his sword hilt, his body between Adam and his mistress. If the Queen heard or saw the ruckus she gave not a single sign of it, though some of her ladies bobbed and swayed. She moved to the other end of the gallery in stately fashion as if it were part of her plan, to wave graciously at the people and smile upon a triumphant Sir Philip, who had finally bested Greville and was smiling up at her with his hair plastered to his head with sweat. While her gentleman blocked her from Adam, a knife-throw would be a useless gesture. He was almost blind with rage and despair to be so close and fail again.

Becket grabbed at his foot, Adam kicked viciously backwards, put his knife between his teeth, grasped a rung of the ladder with his hands and dropped down with his free foot onto Becket's fingers one rung below. Becket gasped, let go, almost fell, dodged Adam's boot again, and the crane bucked and swung. Becket scrambled out the throwing knife behind his head and threw, but it was an awkward target and he missed because a Yeoman that had climbed up after him chose that moment to grab his boots and cry out that he had caught the villain.

To be martyred and yet fail to kill the Queen, that was intolerable: Adam climbed to the very tip of the crane which creaked ominously under his overburden, heard Becket roaring at the loyal Yeoman, and then before David's furious eyes saw the escape route of the basket and its rope.

Adam leaned out over the crowd, caught the rope, made it fast, slid down hand over hand to the little basket. He clung there for a few seconds, measuring a ten foot drop into an upturned blossom of faces, before dropping into its midst. A broad woman broke his fall, but he rolled from her tangle of bumroll and skirts and crawled into the forest of legs.

Becket meanwhile had kicked the Yeoman from the ladder, slid down and plunged into the crowd in pursuit of Adam. Another Yeoman blocked his path, was felled with a blow to the belly, and his fellow

236

accidentally hit a courtier rather than David who had rammed through a knot of excited women fluttering with ribbons and posies. One of their husbands tried to knock Becket out with a wooden rattle and caught a Yeoman instead when he ducked, and within seconds there was a heaving fighting throng upon the left side of the gallery whose interest in the tilting had given place to the usual English lust for battle.

Knowing my man, I waited for Becket upon the rim of the confusion still finger-drilling my ears in search of the buzzing from my head. I heard him first.

'Jesus Christ!' he roared, 'God damn him to the Devil, may he rot, that whoreson bastard . . . .'

He was shoving aside a game little Court-tailor who was swinging wild punches unnoticed at Becket's chest, and came stamping out of the fight, pounding his fist in his palm, beside himself with rage. He caught sight of me cowering, grabbed the torn front of my doublet and lifted me up again.

'God damn you, Tom!' he bellowed, making my ears buzz even more. 'Why did you not tell me? Where the devil was he? How did he mean to do it?'

'He was in the dragon,' I wailed, 'the dragon Sidney rode. I tried to tell you, David, I truly did but you would not listen and devils rode on my tongue for the confusing of me, it was the dragon, he was hiding inside with a crossbow only I saw and I danced a little dance to entertain the horses and make them shy and so he could not take aim, I have done my best, God knows, I have done all I could when I am so beset with angels and sorrow and . . . .'

'Do you mean the dragon that Simon Ames was helping to build, the one Walsingham will pay for?'

'Yes, yes!' I shrieked. 'What other dragon is there? Dragons do not burst from the clouds, you know, they must be built, they must grow from the egg of their idea and plan into the full blossoming of their beauty and strength . . . .'

'He had a crossbow inside?'

'Yes,' I said, 'to shoot her with.'

'Show me.'

It took a little oiling of palms and argument with an anxious Yeoman but we gained behind the stable blocks where the dragon was waiting for his return journey. Becket opened the trapdoor and looked and I heard his long string of oaths when he saw how close we had been to disaster. He grunted a couple of times then came out.

'This was built for a man narrower than I am now. Do you rise up inside and unhitch that weapon. Carefully, mind.'

I did as he said and brought it out to him. He trapped the string with his thumb and took out the bolt, then released the tension.

'Only a bird-bolt but from a narrow distance when the dragon reared up high . . . .'

'Yes, yes,' I said. 'And the bolt is dipped in poison to be sure, it need only scratch her skin, he carried the poison with the gold.'

'What gold?'

'The gold that paid for it.'

'He must have been in league with whatever carpenter built this dragon?'

I nodded frantically, making windmills of my arms.

'Think you he may return there, asking aid?'

I nodded again. Becket took my arm, tried to rearrange the front of my doublet, drew me a little aside.

'Tom . . . .'

'This is the Clever One.'

'Ralph then,' he said, looking straight at me. 'Will you bring Adam to me?'

Did my heart freeze then or was it frozen before and in that moment began to melt?

'If you go to him and offer him shelter, wait for him where they made the dragon . . . .'

'Hanging Sword Court,' I told him wisely.

'Say you so? Jesu. Well then, wait for him by the back gate and when he comes, say all is discovered and you will give him shelter in the Blackfriars liberty where none will find him. Then bring him to me in the cloisters.'

'Why not tell the Queen what . . . .'

'Ralph my friend, think. Imprimis, how may such as I accomplish that? I am no courtier. It would take me weeks and much gold to reach her. And item, say that I do so, that I fling myself in her path on my knees and gabble out the plot. Whose is the dragon, who rode it?'

'Why Sir Philip Sidney . . . .'

'And whose son in law . . . .'

'I know this,' I said impatiently, 'Walsingham. But will she not trust him . . . .'

'Either she will trust him and not believe me or else she will believe me and never again trust him. The only man who could have gone between us was Simon Ames and he is sick to death in the City. We dare not let Adam alone, he is a proud man and I think brave enough: he will of a surety try again and they say third time is the charm. We know where he will be and so I say . . . .'

'But to betray my brother . . . .'

Becket said nothing to that. He put his hands out, palms to the sky, shrugged and let them fall. I would have spoken to mine angel if I could, but he had flown away again and I could not hear his voice nor the voice of the Queen Moon. With the use of my demon-threatened name, Becket had worked a magic on me I think. I could take advice of none but myself.

I shook my head and hid my eyes and tried to still the buzzing in my ears. Becket's heavy hand fell on my shoulder again.

'Listen Ralph, I will not try to persuade you. But I will take a boat now downriver to Blackfriars and there I will wait until the morrow morning. If you come bringing him, sing the ballad you made, the Tom O'Bedlam song to warn me.'

'I will not have him shot in the back.'

Becket sighed. 'So I am not taken unawares,' he said. He left me then, taking a wide circle about Westminster and buying an overpriced pie from a big-breasted girl on the way before he came round to Westminster Stairs by the hall. There were a few boatmen there, who had drawn short straws, to keep guard on their fellows' boats during the tilting, and for double the fee he found one that would take him whither he would go. As the waterman pointed out, he would get no fare coming back, since all the City was in Westminster now.

LIV

My brother was ever a sagacious boy and became a man who thought many times. He milled about with the other crowds, attaching himself now to one group, now to another, until he had scouted about enough to know that there was no hue and cry for him yet. And then when the fireworks began and the sky filled with golden flowers and starbursts and all the air was tinged with gunpowder, still he contented himself and

239

ohhed and ahhed. He took up a boy on his shoulders to give him a better view at the request of the boy's mother, a sturdy boy not much younger than mine own little lad had been. He smiled and exclaimed and when the last rockets had shot off the last praises of the Queen and the human shortlived stars had given place to God's own pavilion, only then did he drift with all the other happy Londoners to the river and argue over boats. He shared one that was going to Temple Steps with a rabble of young lawyers, all well-mellowed with sack and each proposing a further pleasaunce to the evening and a great moot taking place about him as to where they should go.

He bade them farewell and joined some other folk walking up Water Lane, expounding on the meaning of the procession and how the Queen might take its sermon. When he paused at the rear of Hanging Sword Court where the privy door was shut for the night, he looked about him with great care.

And I unfolded from a corner and said, quite low, 'Brother?'

Had he seen me I doubt if he would have recognised me, so changed was I from the elder brother he had known. And from the raving creature he had ridden post to London to visit. It was my voice stopped him in mid-stride.

'Is that you Ralph?'

To hear his voice so cautious, it might have made me weep, but it did not. Becket's magic with my name had worked its charm.

'Ay, it is,' I said, coming a little closer. 'Enter not in there.'

'I thought you . . . .'

'Dead? So I had hoped. You see, I liked not the lodgings you found for me, so I feigned death and left them and all this time you have been paying silver for nothing.'

I saw his teeth as he smiled. 'You are recovered then?'

'Quite.' I lied. 'It was only a matter of a little rest and feeding and to be in a place where men spoke the truth. I am well-enough now, though poor.'

'Why should I not go in there?'

'Have you business with Mr Secretary Walsingham?'

'N . . . no.'

'His men are there, awaiting someone. I think it well not to meet with such gentlemen but if you have business with them I shall call them . . . .'

'Er . . . no, keep your voice down. I have no wish to see them.'

His mind was working, his heart was beating too fast, he thought he had had a narrow escape, he had been on the point of scaling the wall. And all my reproaches and questions and sorrows were boiling to my lips but the new-awakened man in me that was Ralph held a dam behind my lips and struck away the devil who sits on my tongue. I would have asked my brother why he gave the jailers leave to beat me, and why he lodged with Agnes when he came on a treasonous mission, and why he betrayed Becket and why . . . . But I only asked, 'Did you become a priest then?'

Let him lie to me, I thought, and I will strike him down myself. He looked at the ground, stepped over a pig's turd, and walked on up Water Lane to Fleet Street.

·'No,' he said at last. 'No, I applied to the Jesuits and even began their training, but . . . they would not take me. They liked not my vehemence, I suppose, for I never understood it . . . . And I would not take a lesser place.'

He was worried, walking hunched over.

'Where will you go?' I asked.

'I know a Mr Tyrrel . . .' he began and stopped when I shook my head.

'He is dead,' I told him. 'Murdered in a brawl this very day. I know it by the man who killed him for he was greatly hated.'

'Jesu.'

We walked a little further, and at Fleet Bridge I ventured, 'Have you nowhere to go, Adam?'

He laughed a little. 'Is it so manifest?'

'You may lodge with me. It is only a little hole in the Blackfriars priory, but it hardly leaks and it is within the liberties. No one will mark you and none will ask questions if you come there.'

He laughed again, happily, and clapped me on the shoulder so I nearly stumbled.

'Right gladly, Ralph, if you will show me the way.'

Now the heat of anger was draining from my heart as I led him up beyond Old Bailey to the rookery of Amen Corner and through the motheaten old wall into the city. All the boozing kens were full of singing, some of it tunable indeed, and there were winestains about a conduit that had been paid for by a merchant to run with wine. Among the men at their shouting and the women at their singing, sorrow rose up in me that I was betraying him and yet I felt I must. An angel broke through and waggled a finger at me and then another nodded and I perceived that my angels were as much at a loss as I. He was faithless, but I was not. I had never betrayed anyone but myself . . . . Alas, for are not the betrayers mainly those who are rich . . .?

It is easy enough for angels who see directly God's will. If they were perplexed, so was I, as Agnes had been. It would be justice to betray the betrayer, but justice was not my province and once he was my little brother that I fought and rode with upon our proud new ponies and who tended my sparrowhawk all the time I had smallpox . . . .

We were coming near the cloisters. 'Did you receive my ballad that I sent you, Tom O'Bedlam?' I asked him fondly.

'Some outpouring of madness came to me that rhymed well-enough. Was it you sent it?'

Oh he had struck a dagger in my heart. 'Yes, and I made it too. It was to give you a taste of my distraction.'

'I have published it.'

'I know,' I said and my heart began to boil and scald again that he should boast of what he had done with my poem. But still he was my brother. . . . I began to sing it quite loudly and the tears were running down my face. He was still my brother . . . .

'Run Adam,' I said. 'Becket is waiting for you here, run . . . .'

In the starlight I saw his face change, not to fear nor sorrow but to a cold stark fury. There was a little flash in his hand, he caught my shoulder, yanked me close and I was puzzled and thought he meant to embrace me. Embrace me he did but as he did, there was a thump about my midriff and a kind of broken coldness and a great wash of blood that was cold and then galloping in a long time later, a huge yawning chasm of pain that broke my breath to a rattle and poisoned my legs so I must fold up against the cloister wall and choke slowly, while the tear in me worked and yawned and the cold blood flowed.

'God damn you,' said Becket's voice. 'You shite, he warned you . . . .'

If my voice had not slid out of me with my blood I would have warned Becket not to waste time talking, but he was angry and in that moment, Adam leapt the cloister rail into the courtyard and threw a chicken coop at Becket. Surely Becket was blinded by rage for he chased Adam across the courtyard and when Adam seemed to cower against a wall, struck with his sword cross-handed for Adam's neck. It is an old trick: Adam dropped at the last minute and Becket's blade hit the wall and broke in pieces and his right hand was numbed by the shock, and Adam had tumbled against his legs and brought him down.

They ruined Simple Neddy's garden as they fought across it, dagger to dagger, a silent vicious fight that could not compete with the rowdy noises of drinking and laughing from the hundred boozing kens all about the place. Nobody came to watch or lay bets or give assistance as they struggled. They were evenly matched for all Becket's weight and strength, because Becket was in a red rage of grief and guilt and Adam had the reach on him and was moreover clear-headed. And the beer and tobacco were telling against Becket's wind.

Becket yielded first blood to a well-judged slash by Adam for his eyes, which scored his cheek and made him yet angrier as he broke away and rolled to his feet. His dagger flashed in the air as he switched from his bruised right hand to his left and Adam jumped him when the blade was still in flight. Becket slammed against the wall, Adam beating his dagger hand on the stone. Then Becket headbutted him and kicked him off.

The stars and the moon gave clear sight of them as they circled and breathed hard and Becket's stinging face cleared his mind a little of the fog of anger. Adam nearly tripped on Simple Neddy's spade under its canvas cover. He threw the canvas at Becket, trying to entangle him, swept up the spade and chopped left-handed with it to crowd Becket onto his blade. But Becket had plucked the flung canvas out of the air, took the blow from the spade on his shoulder, closed in and trapped Adam's knife with the stout cloth. Then he threw his full weight onto Adam, though the knife blade razored through to his side, and stabbed Adam in the guts and then again, viciously, in the throat. My brother arched his back, laughed blood and died.

Becket rested there a moment, then climbed to his feet crowing for breath. He stood gazing down at Adam, watching for movement, until his breathing had eased and the full pain of his wounds crowded in on him. Even through the canvas Adam's dagger point had scored his side cruelly, his right arm hung down uselessly from the damage the spade had done to his shoulder, and he could not move his hand. The blood from his cheek was soaking his new ruff and his face was swelling and burning. From sheer force of habit, he cleaned his dagger blade on Adam's jerkin, sheathed it and then stumbled over to me with his left hand gripped to his side.

As for me – it had seemed to me while they fought, that a cold tide of blood was rippling about my feet and rising to engulf my knees and my hands and my elbows and my hips, and a tearing agony blazing in my stomach. My breath walked on thornbushes each time I breathed and so I breathed less and less and at last, as the cold tide reached my heart, I had no more need for air.

Now all my pain was gone. Becket found me, found the black blood and the hole whence it had come and saw my eyes so shining and starstruck that they had no more use for their lids and so they closed not at all. He sat down wearily beside me on a stone and wept.

LV

It was Simple Neddy that found him half dead of cold and loss of blood in the morning, and Adam's body and mine also, and had the sense to run and find Eliza Fumey.

Between them they brought him staggering into her house, and then dared to send her son for Dr Nuñez. When the good doctor came, he brought Henderson and Kinsley with him, who hurried to Blackfriars to collect up the bodies there. Becket had passed out by then, and so they put him on a horselitter against all Mrs Fumey's protests that she could nurse him where he was, and brought him through the city to Poor Jewry.

There Becket was surgeoned by Snr Eraso again, who strapped up his shoulder and hand and put honey and rosewater in his sliced cheek and side, before letting him a little blood against infection. In another room Simon lay propped high on pillows, fever blazing in his cheeks and eyes as he raved reedily in Portuguese and English mixed, and struggled to breathe against the ill-omened humour filling up his ribcage.

The first time Becket opened his heavy eyes he thought he must be feverish also, for there stood the Queen's Moor, a pillar of black velvet and white linen, his face graven with concern. Words were spoken, he thought he heard Dr Nuñez enquire about Throgmorton and heard Walsingham's answer clear through his weakness.

'He broke when we showed him the rack and told him the date. He had hoped that the Accession Day fireworks were the first shots of the civil war he had plotted to bring us to, and was sorely disappointed. Think you that Mr Becket can understand me?'

Nuñez shook his head. 'A pity,' said Walsingham. 'I had wished to thank him in the matter of the papers from Tyrrel's house that have come to me. And also in this. Is he like to die?'

Nuñez chuckled a little. 'I doubt it, sir. Unless one of his wounds

244

sickens, he will do well enough with rest and good feeding, and I have no doubt he has lived through worse than this.'

'Will his swordarm be well again?'

Nuñez shrugged. 'I think you should speak to Snr Eraso concerning that, for it depends upon how well his collarbone heals.'

'And your nephew, doctor? What of him?'

Nuñez sighed. 'Sir, he is in the hands of the Almighty, blessed be He.'

Sir Francis nodded. 'It would grieve me to lose such a man, for he hath proved himself right worthy in this matter, both quick of brain and dauntless of heart.' Nuñez looked at the ground.

'We must trust in the Most High.'

A little awkwardly, Sir Francis reached out and touched his arm.

'Doctor, would it offend you if Christians prayed for his deliverance?'

Nuñez almost smiled. 'Sir, how could I be offended?'

'Then we will pray for him twice daily at Seething Lane.'

'Yet we are all subject to the Lord's will and so must abide.'

Sir Francis bent his head a little and left him standing there. Becket could no longer keep open his eyes with their weight of lashes, and so plunged once more into darkness and sleep.

The dragon was taken away and stored in Whitehall, ready to be brought out for another entertainment. Master Richard Broom died a few nights later of the carpenter's canker in his lungs, in great bitterness and sorrow, knowing that his daughter would have him buried in the Protestant rite and there would be no Masses said for his soul.

Still no man knew what had passed between Simon and John Hunnicutt, who continued at his work in Seething Lane and mouthed prayers with the others for Mr Ames's safe deliverance under the Will of God.

Simon burned and raved in his fever, his scrawny body overwhelmed with pillows and counterpane, and infusions coaxed between his battered lips occasionally by his grim-faced Aunt Leonora. Other shadows alternated between a likeness of his father and that of his mother. He wished to reassure them all, but found he had no breath to do it.

Washed up by the tide of number and geometry he found himself once again climbing amongst the pillars and piles of a vast bridge, a very mouse on God's masonry. Below him roared the river, but here it was a river of flame that rose up toward him, snatching for him with golden

245

and crimson hands, and then ebbed again. Something hard and heavy gripped his chest, weighing him down.

The face of the goddess that he crawled upon became flesh, and she spoke to him, taunting and commanding.

'If you would rise, serve me.' she whispered.

He had reached such a pitch of delirium that it had turned to clarity, and he looked at her gravely.

'I think I have served you enough.' he said, took off the gold chain about his neck and threw it away. The goddess became white marble again and he felt light and cool.

He climbed on up towards the distant sky.

LVI

The messenger came to Seething Lane from Poor Jewry a little before dawn, as Walsingham was preparing to lead his household in prayer. Receiving him within the hall of the house, with all his folk awaiting, Walsingham took the piece of paper, unfolded and read it, and bowed his head and sighed. He led the morning prayers in as firm a voice as always, in the voice, did he but know it, with which he also invariably addressed the Queen – that of a faithful servant who will be heard. At the end he paused.

'I have sorrowful news to impart,' he said. 'We have been praying these past few days for the life of a man of this household, Mr Simon Ames. Alas, he hath no more need of our prayers, for he died of his sickness this morning at the turn of the tide. ". . . The glory of Israel is slain upon the high places . . . ."'

Immediately afterwards, he went to the Nuñez house, which was shuttered and quiet, to be met by Dr Nuñez and another well-dressed middle-aged man whom he knew slightly as Dunstan Ames, the Queen's Grocer, Simon's father. His words of condolence were interrupted and he was brought swiftly into the house and up the stairs to the end of a passageway. There he paused at the threshold of a door to find Simon white as linen, lying propped up on his bed, but breathing and moving his head to look.

Hereat you may see Walsingham's true worth, for he throttled back his instant rage at the lie which had grieved him more than he wished to admit. He merely stepped forward to seat himself upon a stool beside the bed, where he put his hands on his knee, raised one eyebrow and said nothing. Dr Nuñez and Simon's father withdrew.

Before Simon was more than halfway through his whispered discourse, Walsingham was pacing about the room, white with anger, the hotter and drier for being unexpressed.

He was like a man who has ridden a horse merrily home one night and then returns in the day to find he was riding at the very edge of a sheer cliff. Hunnicutt's treason had caught him and his family neatly in its coils, and he could bring no arguments against it for which Simon had not an answer.

The worst of it was not that he had paid for the dragon which was to be the engine to kill the Queen his mistress, nor that there had been a channel of the Devil directly into the heart of his household and service. It was that his intelligence could scry further into it than Simon, and there see that Hunnicutt must have been using his daughter against him as well. There were parts of the riddle for which it was the only resolution. There was the report of Simon's drawing attention to Strangways' arrival in England as Semple, which never reached him. There was also the scant warning Throgmorton got of his arrest. Hunnicutt must have found a lever to shift her from her filial duty, possibly the scandalous means by which she had brought the Queen to allow her marriage with Sir Philip Sidney. To have his gentle daughter used so brought Walsingham to a shaking pitch of fury and yet he must calm himself and consider. As Ames pointed out in his weakening breathless voice, if Hunnicutt were arrested it would be a fearful blow to the Queen and her trust in him, at the best. At worst his enemies in the Court would bring him down in a fever of suspicion, he might even find himself standing trial with Hunnicutt for treason. He had no lack of enemies to see the opportunity and seize it.

He stilled his pacing, his busy mind weaving possibility to probability, and stared at Ames appalled.

'I have thought . . . on this and spoken with . . . my father . . . .' said Simon almost inaudibly, '. . . and I see no . . . cause why Hunnicutt . . . must be arrested.' Simon paused for breath, licked his swollen lips.

A little awkwardly, Sir Francis brought him a silver cup of rosewater that stood near the bed and helped him to drink.

'It seemed to me . . . sir . . .' breathed Simon, '. . . that Mr Hunnicutt must wish me . . . dead and if he . . . believed I were . . . dead . . . he would think himself secure . . . and would continue his work . . . .'

Sir Francis stood completely still. He began to smile.

'With a little care . . .' Simon creaked, but Walsingham held up his hand.

'I am with you, Mr Ames. With a little care, some duplication and expense we may have them know in San Lorenzo whatsoever we wish them to know . . . .' The smile became wolfish. 'Yes, I think we may make shift. Mr Ames, sir, I am greatly in your debt, though I am grieved to see that I must lose you after all. Unless . . . ?'

'My uncle says my health will not permit of it.' said Simon quickly, all on one breath. 'I must . . . regretfully . . . leave your service, Sir Francis.'

'It will be a sorry loss to me.' said Walsingham, 'I must say I am loath to be without your advice and subtlety, Mr Ames, though I see why it must be so. Will you require any . . . assistance?'

Simon smiled a little, his eyes half-shut with weariness.

'I think my family . . . can accomplish it . . . My funeral shall . . . be a quiet affair . . . .'

'Yes,' said Sir Francis, feeling a small shiver at his spine and not knowing why Simon should be so merry. 'Quite so. Well. If ever you have need of me, Mr Ames, know that I am your friend.'

Thus it was that every sheet of paper pertaining to the Accession Day Tilts and the firedrake found its way into the bread oven at Seething Lane where it was burned and raked and burned again. For here is the great weakness of the *Mundus Papyri*, which is the wide creation of so many minds. Within the real world a city may be destroyed only with great hardship and labour and expenditure of gold, but within the Paper World a little fire suffices.

Hearing of my deeds from Becket, Sir Francis also paid for my funeral, which was most respectable, with eight paid mourners and two black horses to pull the hearse, and Becket and Anthony Fant leading the procession. So there was no need for my little gold plate with fishes on it, that was once wrought to bear Christ's Body upon it. Simple Neddy found that where he had marked me burying it and sold it for a quarter its worth to a Cheapside goldsmith to buy new plants for his wrecked garden. The goldsmith liked not the old-fashioned style of it and so prised out the stones and melted it down.

Adam had him a pauper's grave, which was more than he deserved, and should have been left on a midden for the dogs and the pigs as he left my boy Ralph. But little Ralph will not have it so, and Agnes neither, and I will not quarrel with them now I have no more need for lunacy. And it is true, as she said, there is joy shining through all the world like the rising of the Sun.

> With a heart of furious fancies,
>   Whereof I am commander,
> With a burning spear and a horse of air,
>   To the wilderness I wander.
> By a knight of ghosts and shadows
>   I summoned am to tourney
> Ten leagues beyond the wide world's end
>   — Methinks it is no journey.

THE END

Historical Note

This book is set in late October and early November of the year 1583, five years before the Spanish Armada of 1588.

Elizabeth I had reigned since 1558 and was at the height of her popularity in England. Her mother Anne Boleyn had been the catalyst for the English Reformation. In order to divorce his first wife, Catherine of Aragon, and marry Anne, Henry VIII broke from the Roman Catholic Church and made himself Head of the Church in England. Henry wanted a son and Elizabeth's birth on 7th September 1533 was a terrible disappointment. When he tired of Anne because she could not give him the son and heir he needed, Henry had Anne executed on a trumped up charge of adultery.

By the time Henry's marital odyssey had finished he had three children. The first, Mary Tudor, was by Catherine of Aragon and a Catholic. The other two, Elizabeth and Edward, were both brought up as Protestants.

To ignore religion in the 16th century would be as foolish as to ignore politics in the 20th century. Catholics and Protestants hated and killed each other with as much virulence as Fascists, Communists and democrats in this century. Elizabeth came to the throne after the death of her sister Mary who had tried to bring England back into the Catholic Church, partly by burning more than 300 heretics. She had also married Philip II of Spain, the greatest power in Europe at the time. Through this marriage Philip had a claim to the throne of England.

Elizabeth threaded her way through the vicious politics of the time with consummate artistry. She often promised to marry but she never did, mainly because she had no intention of handing over any of her power to the husband who was expected by the mores of the time to be her lord and master. As a result the choice of her successor was a source of constant anxiety to her Councillors, most of whom like the Earl of Leicester and Sir Francis Walsingham were convinced Protestants.

First in line of succession to her, by right of descent, was her cousin, Mary Queen of Scots. A Catholic, she had got herself kicked out of Scotland through a series of blunders and had been Elizabeth's prisoner since May 1568. The small son she abandoned when she fled became James VI of Scotland and was brought up a Protestant. Eventually he would succeed Elizabeth and become James I of England and Scotland. However this was by no means certain in 1583, especially as Elizabeth refused to make a decision about it.

A kind of cold war had been going on between the premier Catholic power, Spain, and the third-ranking, small, unpredictable, half-barbaric backwater of a power, England. Elizabeth had used every trick in the book and invented a few of her own to avoid coming to hot war with Spain, while France degenerated into civil war and the Netherlands revolted against their Spanish masters. Spain, rich with gold and silver from her possessions in the New World, maintained internal orthodoxy with the ferocious and efficient Inquisition, and had in the tercios the finest troops in Europe. The English Protestants saw themselves as Godly Davids against the Goliath of Spain, but were more interested in the thieving activities of Jack and the Beanstalk. The South American treasure was at its most vulnerable en route to Spain across the Atlantic where many English pirates tried to make their fortunes by capturing it. Sir Francis Drake had pulled off a notable coup during his famous circumnavigation of the globe in 1577–80. He captured so much booty that he brought back a 4,500% return on his investors' money – a group that included the Queen and most of her Councillors. This naturally enraged Philip despite all Elizabeth's bland assurances that Drake had acted against her orders. While the two sides jockeyed for position, Mary Queen of Scots became involved in a variety of plots paid for by Philip designed to assassinate Elizabeth and use Spanish troops to put her on the throne.

Elizabeth was in daily danger of her life and knew it. Only a year after the story in this book, William of Orange, the leader of the Dutch rebels, was shot to death by a Catholic assassin.

*   *   *

I read history for pleasure and adventure and it would be pretentious to try and supply a bibliography for a work of fiction. There are books I would recommend to anyone interested in the 16th century: Paul Johnson's biography of Elizabeth I; Muriel St Clare Byrne's *Elizabethan Life in Town and Country*; *Spain and the Netherlands 1559 to 1659* by Geoffrey Parker; *Sir Walter Ralegh* by Robert Lacey; William Starkey's *The Reign of Henry VIII*; *The Weaker Vessel* by Antonia Fraser; *Elinor Fettiplace's Receipt Book* by Hilary Spurling; *Mr Secretary Walsingham* by Conyers Road . . . . The list could go on for pages.

Anyone wishing to know more about the remarkable Ames family in 16th-century London should read L. Wolf's article 'Jews in Elizabethan England' in *Transactions of the Jewish Historical Society of England, Vol XI*.

Tom O'Bedlam's Song is a genuine Elizabethan ballad, printed around this time but with a different chorus from the one I invented for the book. Nobody knows who wrote it.

The central story of this book, an assassination attempt on Elizabeth during the 1583 Accession Day Tilts is entirely invented. There are, as far as I can make out, no records describing those Tilts, though there is plenty of information on the Tilts of 1582. However Francis Throckmorton's plot did happen and was one of Walsingham's first great counter-espionage successes. Reading accounts of it gave me the feeling that there was more to it than the records held and hence helped to inspire my story.

The accounts of Englishmen sailing over to the Netherlands in 1572/3 are based on Walter Morgan's report to Burghley 'The Expedition in Holland' of a particularly inglorious episode in our military history. The siege of Haarlem took place much as was described. The revolt of the Netherlands was Imperial Spain's Vietnam, and the savagery displayed there by both sides bears comparison even with 20th-century nastiness.

Walsingham and Philip Sidney were in Paris during the Saint Bartholomew's Eve massacre and there is a story that during it Sir Francis was forced to hide from the mob.

The Topographical Society's *A to Z of Elizabethan London*, compiled by Adrian Prockter and Robert Taylor has been my major source for guiding my characters around their city, along with *Stowe's Survey of London*.

Cast of Characters

Duc D'alencon*: a French princeling
Goodwife Alys (Flick): an alewife
Dunstan Ames*: Purveyor and Merchant to Her Majesty of Grocery, a Marrano gentleman
Francisco Ames*: his brother, a soldier
Benjamin, Jacob and William Ames*: his sons
Simon Ames: another son, clerk and cryptographer to Sir Francis Walsingham
Rebecca Anriques: a Jewish girl

Balfour*: a Scottish soldier
Mr Barnet: an English pawnbroker
Count Batenburg*: one of William of Orange's generals
Baynes: a soldier
David Becket: a soldier of fortune, and Provost of Defence
Goodwife Bickley: a cook
Rocco Bonnetti*: an Italian swordmaster
Richard Broom: a carpenter
Jemmy Burford: a neighbour of Mr Becket's

Mr Carbury: a tutor
Mrs Carfax: David Becket's landlady
Corday: Francis Throgmorton's friend
Mr Custance: a lesser merchant, suitor to Mrs Fumey
Mr Dawkins: keeper of the Records at Gray's Inn
Dorcas: a wet nurse

Mr Dowl: clerk to Sir Francis Walsingham
Edmund Dun*: a ballad seller

Queen Elizabeth I*
Mr Ellerton: one of Sir Francis Walsingham's men
Henri Estienne*: a Huguenot printer, friend to Sir Philip Sidney

Anthony Fant*: a gentleman, once a soldier
Agnes Fant (née Strangways): his wife
Edward, Elizabeth and Mary Fant: his children
Sir William Fant: his father, now dead
Don Fadrique/Federico*: Duke of Alva's son
Eliza Fumey: a widow

Gabriel: a wild young rogue
Humphrey Gilbert*: a leader of the expedition in Holland
Snr Phillippe Gomes*: a pawnbroker
Fulke Greville*: gentleman, friend to Sir Philip Sidney
Duke of Guise*: a powerful French nobleman

Mr Hardy: a pimp
Sir Christopher Hatton*: Privy Councillor, the Queen's 'Bel-wether' and
  old favourite
William Henderson: one of Sir Francis Walsingham's men
Henri of Navarre*: the future Henry IV of France
Father Hepburn: a Catholic priest
John Holder: a mercenary
Pericles Howard: gentleman
John Hunnicutt: Sir Francis Walsingham's dispatcher

Ilse: a Dutchwoman

Jardin: a bearwarden
Jerome: Rocco Bonnetti's catamite
Joan: a wet nurse

Thomas Kinsley: one of Sir Francis Walsingham's men-at-arms

Henry Mall: one of Sir Francis Walsingham's men-at-arms
Marguerite de Valois*: wife of Henri of Navarre
Maud: a serving woman

256

CATHERINE DE MEDICI*: the Dowager Queen of France
CAPTAIN MORGAN*: a leader of the expedition in Holland

SIMPLE NEDDY: a simpleton
CATHERINE NESBIT: Mrs Fant's aunt
THOMAS 'RACKMASTER' NORTON: a priestfinder and interrogator
DR HECTOR NUÑEZ*: a Marrano physician and trader
LEONORA NUÑEZ*: his wife

WILLIAM PAGE*: a Puritan printer, offensive to the Queen
CHARLES PAGET*: the Queen of Scots' man in Paris
ISAAC PARDO: Mr Ames' cousin
FATHER PARSONS*: leader of the English Jesuits on the Continent
PELLEW: a courier
THOMAS PHELIPPES*: Sir Francis Walsingham's most senior crypto-
grapher
LAURENCE PICKERING*: the King of the London Rogues

WALTER RALEGH*: the Queen's new favourite
JAMES RAMME: one of Sir Francis Walsingham's men
MICK REYNOLDS: Clapperdudgeon to the beggars on London Bridge
M. RICARD: Sir Francis Walsingham's majordomo in Paris

SIR PHILIP SIDNEY*: the premier knight in Christendom, Walsingham's
son-in-law
FRANCES SIDNEY (née WALSINGHAM)*: his new wife
SIMIER*: a French envoy
BONECRACK SMITH: a footpad
PETER SNAGGE: a pedlar
ADAM STRANGWAYS: a Catholic traitor
AGNES STRANGWAYS: his sister, married to Mr Fant
RALPH STRANGWAYS: his brother, a madman (see TOM O'BEDLAM)
NICHOLAS SUNNINGDALE: a gentleman

FRANCIS THROGMORTON: a Catholic traitor
TOM O'BEDLAM: a madman and poet, friend to Mr Becket
TOPCLIFFE: priesthunter and torturer
TYRREL: another King of London's Rogues

SIR FRANCIS WALSINGHAM*: Privy Councillor, the Queen's Secretary and
head of her secret service

257

FRANCES WALSINGHAM*: his daughter (see SIDNEY)
URSULA WALSINGHAM*: his wife

* – denotes an actual historical character

Glossary

(TC – denotes Thieves' Cant)

abram – (TC) mad
Agnus Dei – wax disc imprinted with the Lamb of God and the crossed keys
 of the Papacy and blessed by the Pope
ague - malaria
aqua fortis – nitric acid
aqua vitae – brandy
arquebus – primitive musket fired with a lighted slowmatch

backsword – heavy one-edged short sword
bale of dice – (TC) 2–3 matched dice
falling band – Puritan-type plain linen collar worn instead of a ruff
bastard sword – could be used one or two-handed
biggin – close-fitting cap worn by babies
bombast – stuffing for clothes
booze – (TC) traditional English slangword meaning alcoholic drink (originally sp. bouse)
boozing ken – (TC) worst kind of pub
bread sippets – slices of toast laid under meat to soak up the juices
buck – large wooden tub with a lid
buckler – small leather shield

calenture – a stroke
Canary – fortified wine
canions – loose breeches

carrel – cubbyhole office in library or cloister
caudle – hot spiced wine drink made with gruel
charger – serving dish
citron – pale yellow colour
clapperdudgeon – (TC) chief beggar
the Clink – debtor's prison
close stool – chamber pot hidden inside a seat with a lid
clyster thread – inserted in the skin to cause localised irritation believed to
    draw infection out of another part of the body
cockle – corncockle – a weed of cultivation
cog – cargo ship
collops – chops of meat
comfits – sweets
complected – the balance of one's humours
coneycatch – (TC) to con or cheat
costiveness – constipation
courser – large horse specially bred for tilting
cramoisie – dark blackcurrant red colour
cruse – clay jar
cuirass – piece of armour covering chest and back

dag – early pistol
dish-of-coals – like a frying pan containing hot coals of charcoal with a griddle
    on top, a sort of mini-barbecue
duds – (TC) clothes
Duke of Exeter's daughter – nickname for the rack which was imported by
    the Duke of Exeter in Henry VIII's reign

Feast of Esther – a minor Jewish feast of great importance to the Marranos
filch – (TC) a thief
flense – to skin
flux – dysentery
to foin – to stab with a spear, also to fuck
footpad – mugger
French pox – syphilis

goodman/goodwife – term of respect for a common person, one down from
    Mr or Mrs
gossip – (lit. God-sibling) old friend, especially female
groat – four pence piece

halberd – spearhaft with a blade like a cross between an axe and an old-fashioned tin-opener – still carried by Yeomen of the Guard

highmen/lowmen – (TC) false dice altered to throw high/low

hookman – (TC) thief who uses a long hook to steal things from open windows

horse-coper – farrier

humour – basic to Elizabethan medicine: four humours combined to make a man – blood (sanguine h.); phlegm (phlegmatic h.); yellow bile (choleric h.) and black bile (melancholic h.)

Iconoclasts – Protestant religious hooligans who broke up images on the grounds that they were idolatrous

jakes – toilet

leman – (arch.) male or female lover

lour – (TC) money

marchpane – marzipan

Marrano – Portuguese Sephardic Jew

melancholia – depression

mint – (TC) gold

murrey – dull purple brown colour

nightrail – nightgown

nithing – (arch.) wimp

orangado – a Seville orange, partly hollowed and stuffed with sugar

the ordinary – set meal at an inn, normally stew thickened with vegetables and bread

palliard (TC) beggar

pannam – (TC) bread

passado – early version of fencing lunge

patten – high wooden overshoe worn to keep expensive leather out of the mud

penner – leather pouch worn on the belt and used by clerks to carry pens, penknife and ink

petard – explosive charge used in sieges

piccardils – stiffened strips of cloth to support a ruff on a collar

pike – very long, thick spear used against cavalry by men standing in serried
  ranks
pillicock – origin of pillock or penis
points – laces for tying clothes shut or together
pottage – stew
posset – warming or medicinal drink
prig – (TC) steal
primero – a complicated card game similar to poker
punk – (TC) whore

recusant – someone who broke the law by refusing to go to church on a
  Sunday, usually Catholic
roaring boys – (TC) thugs, hooligans
rushlight – cheap candle made by dipping a dried rush stem in tallow (aka a
  tallow dip)

sack – sherry
samite – heavy satin
San Lorenzo – now known as the Escorial, Philip II's part-built palace
Secretary hand – old style of handwriting similar to German Gothic
stays – corsets
stews – brothel
stockfish – dried salted herring
stomacher – boned triangular piece of cloth, often embroidered, pinned to
  the front of the bodice

tawny – orange gold colour
tertian fever – three day malaria
tercio – Spanish equivalent of a brigade, including pikemen and arquebusiers,
  of approximately 3000 men in triangular formation
tester – roof of a four-poster bed
tobacco – introduced into England from America by Hawkins (contrary to
  popular belief) and rapidly becoming very fashionable, it was often cut
  with incense or other herbs such as the seeds and leaves of the hemp plant
trencher – dinner plate, earlier of coarse bread or wood, now usually of pewter
  or silver
trucklebed – small bed on wheels normally pushed under another bed when
  not in use
trull – whore
Tunnage and Poundage men – Customs officers

upright man – (TC) sturdy beggar or vagrant

veney stick – heavy stick like a sledgehammer handle used for sword practice
playing a veney – friendly practice fight with sticks, occasionally ending in
  broken bones

winding up a jack – winding the clockwork mechanism for turning a spit,
  latest kitchen technology

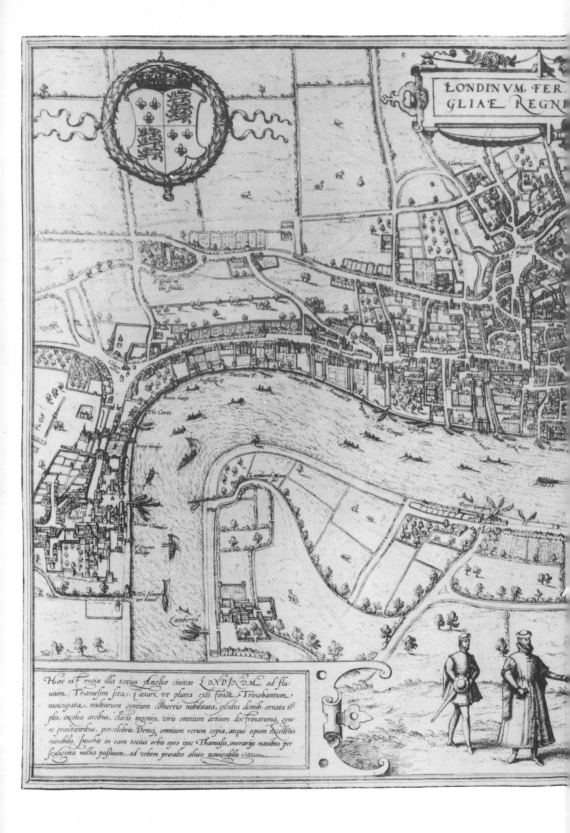